# attack of the unsinkable rubber ducks

## christopher brookmyre

LITTLE, BROWN

LITTLE, BROWN

First published in Great Britain in 2007 by Little, Brown

Copyright © 2007 Christopher Brookmyre

The moral right of the author has been asserted.

A CIP catalogue record for this book
is available from the British Library.

HB ISBN: 978-0-316-73012-9
CF ISBN: 978-0-316-73013-6

Typeset in Palatino by Palimpsest Book Production Limited,
Grangemouth, Stirlingshire
Printed and bound in Great Britain by
Clays Ltd, St Ives plc

Little, Brown
An imprint of
Little, Brown Book Group
Brettenham House
Lancaster Place
London WC2E 7EN

A Member of the Hachette Livre Group of Companies

www.littlebrown.co.uk

For James Randi and Richard Dawkins

# I

No testimony is sufficient to establish a miracle, unless the testimony be of such a kind, that its falsehood would be more miraculous than the fact which it endeavours to establish.

David Hume, *An Enquiry Concerning Human Understanding*

# The Voice of the Dead

(Extract from *Encounters in the Borderland*, Jillian Noble's biography of Gabriel Lafayette, as amended and serialised in *The Mail* ahead of publication.)

Do you believe in ghosts?

That's what this all ultimately comes down to, doesn't it? It's going to colour your impressions of everything you're about to encounter, perhaps even determine – very quickly – whether you're going to read on or just put this down and move on to something else. The fact that you've begun at all is no guarantee to me that you're going to give me a fair hearing; I know how delicious a prospect it would be to see someone of my profile and reputation make a fool of themselves.

I don't believe and frankly don't much care whether I'm likely to change anybody's mind, because short of the abortion issue, I can think of no other area that so rigidly divides people into irreconcilable opposition. It is said of the believers that they remain credulous despite a lack of evidence, but it is equally true – more so, in my experience – of the so-called sceptics that they will remain unconvinced no matter how much evidence they are presented with.

Sceptics, we are told, are open-minded and intend not to debunk or automatically disbelieve, but merely seek proof of what is being claimed. And the band played, believe it if you like! In practice, I have found, they are as slavish and inflexible in their fidelity as the most dedicated religious fundamentalist. Nothing will sway them from their beliefs, and they exhibit a staggering level of closed-mindedness that stems from an unshakeable faith in their own intellectual superiority.

I am therefore not wasting my time here in any good-hearted but naïve attempt to convince the inconvincible. The Jehovah's Witnesses have been doing that for years, and all it's ever got

3

them was a close-up view of a rapidly closing front door. Nor am I comfortable with the likelihood that my work will be embraced by the army of crackpots and fantasists who make it so easy to discredit genuine study of the paranormal. I have more in common with the hardest-bitten sceptics than with any of the New Agers, conspiracy theorists, spook-hunters and assorted peddlers of superstition and mumbo-jumbo. However, that won't stop the first constituency from lumping me in with the others as a lazy way of discrediting my inconvenient testimony.

It probably goes without saying that I have little to gain and a great deal to lose by publishing this. If you are a regular reader of mine in the press, you may well be reading this with a hand clasped over your mouth in concern, asking yourself, 'What is she doing?' And not just on my behalf. When your husband is Holyrood's education minister, you don't need reminding of the potential fall-out amidst a political culture that rewards insincerity, posturing and outright cynicism but rushes to ridicule genuine faith.

So why am I doing this, laying myself wide open and my husband vulnerable by association? Well, for one, I feel humbled by and duty-bound towards those who are risking more and exposing themselves to far worse, simply because they appreciate that there are more important things at stake here than egos and reputations. The advent of every major juncture in man's understanding of himself and his environment, every staging post on the journey of knowledge that we *all* have the right to call science, was heralded by the sound of scoffs and guffaws. In the words of the German philosopher Arthur Schopenhauer, 'All truth passes through three stages. First, it is ridiculed. Second, it is violently opposed. Third, it is accepted as self-evident.'

Ridicule will merely represent the trumpet-blasts of the approaching foe. There is a battle looming, one that was prematurely dismissed by many as a storm in a teacup, but which has already seen storm clouds gather over one of our country's most esteemed seats of learning. Before the end, it is likely to have been joined in all our schools and surely our parliament. And once its dust has settled, man's greater understanding will be the victor over small men and closed minds.

For another, I feel duty-bound towards my vocation and my profession. There has been rumour, exaggeration and innuendo, from both sides of the credulity divide, over what is believed – or not believed – to have happened almost three years ago on the night of 7 October 2003 at Glassford Hall. I am hereby presenting an honest and accurate account of remarkable events. The sceptics will no doubt say that of itself it does not constitute any evidence, despite its being corroborated several times over. I am content to present it, no matter the consequences, because I know for a fact that it *does* constitute the truth, and that is the only thing that any journalist ought to care about.

Before my account begins, in an admittedly perhaps futile bid to pre-empt some of the hysterical nonsense that will inevitably be precipitated by this piece, I would like to state as plainly as possible that I did not see a ghost. Got that? I'll spell it out again. I have never seen a ghost and nor did I see anything that I would describe as a ghost at Glassford Hall.

Do I believe in ghosts? Three years ago I might have said a flat-out no. After Glassford Hall, I would amend my response to say I don't know, because, quite simply, I don't know what a ghost is. I'll state it one more time for the guys on the red-tops: I did not see a ghost. So with that cleared up, I can freely relate what I *did* see, what I *did* feel and, most importantly, what I and several corroborating witnesses most definitely did hear.

Bryant Lemuel is no stranger to controversy, and certainly not one to retreat from a battle he considers worth the fighting. There are not many shrinking violets on the *Sunday Times* Rich List, and you get the sense that the fifty-eight-year-old furniture tycoon enjoys every moment of the cut and thrust that has seen him bloody no end of noses in business and, more latterly, politics.

'They'd see me walk in, hear me talking, clock my accent, and reckon they had the beating of me right then,' he explained to me the first time we met, speaking in his unapologetically broad Lancashire register. With a warm but shrewd twinkle in his eyes, he went on to inform me: 'That were always the moment I knew I had the beating of *them*.'

This tendency of his opponents to underestimate him has

frequently proven costly, and is something those currently mustering against him around the academic quadrangles of Gilmorehill would do well to consider. The Scottish Executive all but laughed him off as a crank when he began fomenting opposition to the Developing Sexual Health bill, before Lemuel took them to a messy and thoroughly damaging fifteen rounds. The Executive claimed a Pyrrhic victory when the DSH bill finally passed, but let's not kid ourselves: the legislation that finally made it on to the statute books was a very different creature to the draft initially proposed. He wasn't happy with the outcome, but Lemuel knows he won on points, and it was only the devastating death of his wife later that same year that granted the politicos some ill-deserved respite.

'People tell me I don't belong,' he said to me a few days ago, after Professor Niall Blake made his widely reported intemperate remarks regarding Lemuel's intended largesse towards the university. 'It's not my place. It's not my right. I've been hearing it all my life. I heard it in boardrooms: "What does that upstart think he's about?" – usually just before I took 'em over. Then when I moved to Scotland, any time I got involved in public issues: "What does he think he's doing? Who does he think he is? He's not even *from* here." Now it's: "What does a furniture salesman know about science? Or about education? Stay out of it, keep that shut," they say. Well, I've never stayed out of it and I'm bloody well not keeping it shut.'

That is why he has given me his permission to publicly reveal something that is, for him, deeply personal in the most delicately fragile way, making it no mere act of candour, but one of immense bravery. These may be matters that the rest of us can argue and debate, the cynical scoff at, or worse, the patronising pity, but for Bryant Lemuel, each reference, each revisitation must be a source of great pain. I remain aware, even as I write this, that doing so will inflict another pang should he read it, but he has asked me not to flinch. In the face of that, my own trepidation about revisiting that night fades to nothing.

I was invited to Glassford Hall a number of times during Lemuel's campaign against the DSH bill, this newspaper being a proud supporter of his opposition. It is a magnificent, even daunting eighteenth-century pile nestling amidst endless acres

6

of Perthshire beauty, and standing within its wood-panelled walls, it is difficult not to unconsciously project its stature and grandeur upon the individual who owns it. One finds it difficult to imagine many people disagreeing with Bryant Lemuel under his centuries-old roof. However, what was truly impressive about the gatherings he convened at that time was his enthusiastic deference to anyone with something to contribute. Undoubtedly it is this ability to bring forth such disinhibited energies that has been instrumental to his business successes, and it made for a formidable crucible of thought and conviction as we sought ways to help a cowed majority of concerned Scottish parents find their voice. A man of impermeable religious belief, Lemuel forged a powerful alliance of faiths – Christian, Islamic, Jewish, Hindu and Sikh – by demonstrating how the same fears and concerns were felt across each of their communities. Nobody invited to Glassford Hall would have left feeling their own community was merely a bit player in another largely Christian game. It was everybody's battle, and only with everybody aboard could they fight it. At a time when the Executive were publicly and expensively espousing their 'One Scotland, Many Cultures' philosophy on every billboard in the land, there must have been a few in Holyrood thinking they ought to be more careful what they wished for in future.

Lemuel is not merely a religious man, but one who is interested in spirituality whatever its stripe. He talks expansively of witnessing faith healers achieve what conventional medicine could not, from Kansas to Kirkcaldy, and presents fascinating accounts of his trips to the Philippines to watch the work of their remarkable 'psychic surgeons'. He has seen, with his own eyes, these men remove shrapnel, diseased tissue, and even tumours, by reaching their hands inside patients, without the aid of a scalpel and, other than a little blood, without leaving any trace of an incision.

'Science has no explanation for what these men achieve,' he told me in impassioned tones. 'They see their gifts as belonging to God, belonging to everyone, so they don't even take any money for it. These are remarkable people. Why is their work not being researched?'

Lemuel's interest in the spiritual extends to what is often termed the paranormal, though he eschews that word with open anger. 'It's a word they use to scrunch it all up into a ball and chuck it in the corner.' To him, the existence of unexplained forces and the question of what lies beyond this world are not issues to be swept to the fringes and dismissed.

'Physicists now say there are unseen dimensions and parallel universes only a molecule's width away. But to me, they're just catching up with what some of us have always known. Man has been talking about "the Other Side" forever, hasn't he? About an unseen realm just beyond our own. It's long past time for the scientific and the spiritual to be reconciled.'

Lemuel's interest in the world of spiritualism was both established and documented before the death of his wife, Hilda, but inescapably, his devastating loss added a tremendous poignancy to his search for what lies beyond this state of consciousness.

He still finds it very difficult to talk about. Childhood sweethearts, he and Hilda had been married for more than thirty years and were inseparably close. 'I always said I could never live without her,' he told me, his normally sharp eyes clouding with tears. 'And I often think I were right. It feels like I'm existing, aye, half living, that's all. Anything that ever happened to me, she was the first person I wanted to talk to about it. It almost felt like it didn't count *until* I'd talked to her about it. Without her, I sometimes feel like I'm just a machine: I'm still functioning, but I'm not feeling. Then other times, it's as though she's nearby, so close I could almost reach out.'

You no doubt already know what happened, so I won't dwell on the details. One bright, crisp April morning, Hilda went out to walk her dogs by the river that was at that time running in spate through the sprawling Glassford estate. A few hours later, after she had failed to arrive home, the dogs were found wandering, off their leashes. Hilda's body was discovered downstream two days after that, having lost her footing and been dragged beneath the water by the early spring undercurrent.

'I can only think of her a tiny little bit at a time,' Lemuel said to me. 'Half a moment, a few remembered words, then something inside stops me. It's as though if I let too much of a memory into my head . . .' With which he broke down again. And that was last week, three and a half years on.

I'm aware of my own procrastination in couching this serialised version. All this preamble, you must be thinking: get to the goods. But believe me when I tell you that there is literally cold sweat on my brow and the hairs on my spine are standing on end, merely at the prospect of revisiting that night. All this time in the news business, I've never been accused of being backwards about coming forwards. But nor have I ever been recounting an event such as this. Even just thinking about it can be dizzying. It's as though, due to the details of it contradicting so much of what my experience and expectations have led me to believe is normal or even possible, my brain is reluctant to reprocess this information. But reprocess it I dutifully must, so here goes.

The seventh of October 2003 was, perhaps coincidentally (and, according to some, perhaps not), six months to the day after Hilda's death. It was also the first time Lemuel had been prepared to speak to a journalist since the tragedy, and it must have taken tremendous strength and courage for him to step back, even tentatively, into the public eye. We hadn't arranged it to be a formal interview, but there was a tacit understanding that I'd be free to write a retrospective piece partly coloured by my quotes and impressions from this visit. I spent a couple of hours talking to Bryant Lemuel that afternoon, and was pleasantly surprised to learn that I was not the only guest. He was convening a small, very informal gathering that evening, and invited me to stay. With my husband due to remain overnight in Shetland, and (for once) no deadline looming, I accepted.

It turned out to be something of a reduced, gentle version of the gatherings I'd attended previously, and as such a good sign that Lemuel was determined to once again find his feet – and his voice. In attendance were the Reverend Harry Garden, Lemuel's long-term friend and minister of the church he attends in Perth; Jonathan Galt, Lemuel's lawyer; Hilda's close friend Martha Nugent, head of Scottish Aid to Africa, for which Hilda worked tirelessly to raise funds; and two men I had not seen before. These were introduced to me simply as Gabriel Lafayette and Easy Mather, and had been Lemuel's house guests for a couple of days. There were no fanfares and no descriptions. In common with the vast majority of people in this country at that time, I had never heard of Gabriel Lafayette, nor did he – or Lemuel – give the impression that he expected me to know who he was or why in particular he was there.

Let me underline that he was not there to perform any kind of demonstration. Almost the opposite, as it turned out.

We ate early in the evening in Glassford's magnificent dining room, eating off eighteenth-century china, seated around a table worth more than most people's houses. The only incongruous twenty-first-century note was struck, I must confess, by my Dictaphone, which I was graciously permitted to place on the table. I mention this to underline that this account is not mere recollection, but verifiable, recorded fact.

At the risk of being accused of further procrastination, I can state with absolute authority that all those snide remarks in other newspapers about 'the furniture tycoon with no taste' are founded on nothing but spite, envy and not a little class snobbery. Lemuel built a business on cheap modern furniture, but he is a man who loves and appreciates objects with a history, and enjoys having the wherewithal to acquire them. It was, in fact, a remark of mine about the provenance of my chair that first led me to learn why Lemuel and Lafayette had struck up a relationship. Having been informed of its age and origin, I speculated as to what stories it could tell of those who had sat upon it, if only it could talk. The Reverend Garden then rather pointedly speculated about allowing 'one of those ghastly TV mediums to lay hands upon it', looking specifically at Lafayette.

I very quickly got the impression that I was the only one missing the joke. That was when I first learned – in rather a roundabout way – that Lafayette was reputed to have psychic gifts. Lemuel explained that he had corresponded with Lafayette since meeting him at a 'psi' conference (psi is the term preferred over 'paranormal') in Las Vegas a few months ago, and in the wake of Hilda's death, Lafayette had provided invaluable advice.

'Fake mediums fall upon the bereaved like vultures,' Lemuel told me. 'Gabriel explained that, being known to have an interest in these matters, I'd be even more vulnerable. He were right, too. I'd already had approaches from people with what appeared to be amazing information, things it seemed they couldn't have known about myself and Hilda. Gabriel blew the gaff on all of them, taught me how they worked.'

Lafayette then gave us an eye-opening account of the tricks and deceits engaged by such charlatans, augmented by contributions or reminders from Mather, whom it emerged had debunked more than a few in academic studies back in California. It was easy to imagine their stories being uproariously funny under other circumstances. As it was, the tragedy was never far from anyone's thoughts, and the mercilessness of those who would prey upon human pain just too close. The other factor militating against such levity was that Lafayette did not appear to be feeling his best, something he put down to the lingering effects of jet-lag.

'Every time one of these parasites pulls a cheap stunt, it makes it all the harder for those of us who are interested in doing proper work in this field to be taken seriously,' was how Mather put it. His scientific background emerged piece by piece throughout this discussion, and it was my assumption by this point that both he *and* Lafayette were simply interested in researching psi phenomena. It was when the conversation turned back to 'those ghastly TV mediums' that I realised matters were a little more complex than that.

'Some of these TV programmes are just as damaging,' Mather said, 'because they're turning it all into a sideshow. There are men and women on television back in the States who have exhibited genuinely intriguing phenomena, which ought to be properly studied, but instead they end up whoring themselves, doing hammy parlour tricks, because the money's too good to resist.'

'The haunted house stuff is the worst,' Lafayette added. 'I don't believe *anybody* involved in that junk has genuine psi, for the simple reason that if you have, you don't put yourself in harm's way – no matter how good the money. They act like it's a talent, like it's something *they* do. It's not. It's something that happens *to* you, and when it does, it's something you ain't in a hurry to have happen to you again. It's not a talent and it's not a gift. It's a burden, and mostly it feels like a curse.'

11

Lafayette's words were given added weight by his pallor. These days we are familiar with images of him as a flamboyant and charismatic individual, and in all of my subsequent experiences of him, he has been, but there is a genuine sadness and a strange sense of regret kept hidden beneath his upbeat public persona.

He has made not a few enemies among the 'showbiz psychics' for reiterating the sentiments expressed above, but latterly he has intimated a more conciliatory attitude, in a manner that is not quite the *volte-face* some would have you believe. Responding to my polite mention that there were those who accused him of hypocrisy once he had become a regular on the airwaves himself, he said he now understood that it wasn't just about financial reward. 'When you're dealt a hand like this, it isn't easy. I've always said it was a burden. But my TV work has let me see there is another side to it, that it can reach out to people. It makes me feel less like it's something I have to cope with alone, and I guess that's true of some of the people I was a little too swift to judge.'

You'll note the word 'some', which was his shorthand way of still excluding those involved in 'the haunted house stuff'. Once you know what happened at Glassford Hall, you will vividly understand why.

Lafayette ate very little, which, in combination with his pallid complexion, drew concern from Lemuel, who asked him if the food was okay and made the typically solicitous offer to have something else prepared.

'It was delicious,' Lafayette assured him. 'Believe me, if I was feeling tip-top, I'd have had an elephant's sufficiency.'

Lafayette's words attempted to make light of the moment, but his visible discomfort and facial grimace were at odds with his intentions. When I glanced across the table, it appeared to be contagious. Lemuel suddenly looked noticeably paler and a little shaken. Meanwhile, Mather insisted Lafayette get some air, and perhaps a lie-down, and escorted him from the dining room.

I was to learn from Lemuel that the expression 'an elephant's sufficiency' had been a favourite of Hilda's, and one that Lemuel would most often have heard her use when seated in that very room. It isn't a unique coinage, but neither is it a very common turn of phrase, particularly in New Orleans, and Lafayette was to state later that though he couldn't guarantee he'd never heard it before, he certainly didn't remember *using* it before.

We adjourned to one of Glassford Hall's smaller public rooms to take coffee and digestifs. It was Lemuel's favourite drawing room, and the one that had at times begun to resemble a battle headquarters when he was on a war footing against the Scottish Executive. Mather joined us after a while, passing on Lafayette's apologies but adding that he might return to the gathering if he felt a little better.

Mather on that occasion did seem a little protective of Lafayette, but this is not always or indeed often the case. Adversarial would at times be a more accurate description, though Mather admits he feels a certain responsibility towards him, as does any scientist towards the welfare of his subject. Their relationship is a complex and at times strained affair. On the surface there seems a genuine cordiality between them, but it can only go so far due to their roles as observer and observed. Mather talks of the need for a certain distance and objectivity, which is a polite way of alluding to the tension that must permanently exist over the possibility that Lafayette could turn out to be a fake.

Ezekiel 'Easy' Mather is twelve years Lafayette's junior. The Desert Storm veteran met Lafayette in Glendale, California, where Mather, who has a science degree, was working on post-graduate research at Reed University. Describing himself as a 'hard-bitten sceptic', he had got himself involved in a para-psychology project run under the auspices of Reed's psychology department.

'I wanted to be the guy who shot it all down,' he says wryly, 'and frequently I was.'

But then along came Lafayette.

Mather would argue that nothing really changed; he still approaches psychic claims with a methodical, sceptical, scientific bent. As he puts it: 'Unlike some, I don't "believe" in Gabriel. I'll say this much: I have witnessed things around him that I cannot explain, and I'm in the business of seeking explanations. I'm only interested in hard evidence, not superstition.'

Mather claims to be thick-skinned when it comes to the inevitable barbs about him being merely another scientific dupe, but I suspect he is more wounded than he lets on. There are those who have suggested his reputation will be in tatters if it ultimately emerges that Lafayette has been deceiving him, and still others who have claimed he will simply proceed into denial should this be so, but Mather rejects both as unscientific notions. 'If I discover that Gabriel is merely a fraud, then I admit I'll be disappointed, because one of the world's more exciting possibilities will have been closed off. But I'll accept it because I'll have done my job as a scientist. That's what's first and foremost.'

Mather looked concerned rather than relieved when Lafayette reappeared in the drawing room that night, though he did seem to have a little more colour in his cheeks. I remember Mather asking him if he was warm enough. Lafayette said he was and told him to stop fussing. A few polite jokes were made about the Scottish climate compared to New Orleans. I took it as an indication of Lemuel's returning strength that he was able to mention how Hilda, despite her love for her adopted country, had always hated the weather. 'She could never stand to be cold.' The room was, in fact, perfectly cosy, with an open coal fire supplementing the heat from the pre-war iron radiators.

I've seen plenty of scornful explanations – most certainly correct, in most cases – for alleged supernatural incidents, that point to surroundings, ambience and atmosphere being conducive to a certain suggestibility. Creepy environments lead to creepy thoughts; cold and poorly lit places lend themselves to a sense of insecurity that can lead people to project their fears and thus glimpse ghosts where there are merely shapes and shadows. The reason I mention this is that Lemuel's drawing room that night was about as far as it is possible to be from the conditions described above. The only spirits suggested by the convivial surroundings were already sloshing around the finest crystal.

In common with everybody else, I discounted what in retrospect was the first indicator of something strange. The lights flickered for a few moments, after which they dimmed a little.

14

At the time, I thought they must have been deliberately altered by one of the house staff, as seemed appropriate for the hour. What I did not know at that time was that none of the rooms in Glassford Hall is equipped with a dimmer switch.

Lafayette had more colour in his cheeks, as I have said, but there was a palpable fragility about him, a gingerness in his gait. It reminded me of myself with a migraine: someone who wishes they could block out all incoming signals, because every last vibration – even a truck going past your house – seems to add to the pain.

Nonetheless, he did his best to participate in the gathering. He refused the offer of a seat, choosing to remain standing like everyone else, but didn't stray from the fireplace, where he had somewhere to place a supporting hand or elbow.

Lafayette apologised to Lemuel for his lack of appetite. 'It's the worst form back home to partake less than wholeheartedly when someone extends their hospitality,' he said.

'Oh, don't mention it, truly,' Lemuel replied.

'No, no, I must. I mean, normally I could eat a buttered frog.'

It seemed a jocular remark, but Lafayette looked like he just *had* eaten such an item as he was saying it. His face was strained, confused, and once again, Lemuel's matched it. They stared at each other in a kind of mutually bewildered silence for a few seconds, as though something was passing between them and neither of them could quite come to terms with what it was.

Mather attempted to intervene.

'I really think you should have a seat,' he said.

'I'll be fine,' Lafayette insisted. 'Just feel a little woozy.'

'Let me get you your tablets, then,' Mather suggested. Lafayette relented at a second pass on this offer and Mather withdrew.

I recall the conversation flowing fairly well at this point, but that both Lemuel and Lafayette – the latter in particular – were conspicuously reticent. Lemuel looked a little preoccupied, with what I know now was a longer contemplation of what had given him pause in the dining room. Again Lafayette had used an expression that belonged more in Lancashire than Louisiana. Lafayette was not so much preoccupied as increasingly detached, like an individual silently fighting dizziness or nausea. I remember moving closer to the fireplace because I feared he might faint, but after a while he seemed to rally. I may also, less altruistically, have been motivated by the fact that I did at that point begin to feel that the room had become colder.

Mather returned with the medication, prompting Martha Nugent to remark that he was a useful man to have around.

'My husband *has* been known to run and fetch something for me, but it's not exactly a regular occurrence,' she added.

'Once every Preston Guild,' Lafayette suggested. Again he looked pained as he said it, but this time it wasn't only Lemuel who shared his pallor. Nugent also seemed shaken by what she'd heard.

I wasn't the only one to notice on that occasion, either.

'Is something wrong?' the Reverend Garden asked them both.

'Just a strange coincidence,' Nugent responded. 'That was exactly what . . . Hilda would have said.'

Now, I appreciate that the strangeness of this coincidence could have had a psychosomatic effect, but I distinctly recall feeling colder at that moment, and I mean considerably so.

The reference to Hilda all but snuffed out the harmonious thrum of conversation. The atmosphere became instantly awkward. I remember, in dutifully British fashion, trying desperately to think of something to say to fill the gap. I think I mumbled the beginnings of something before being silenced by the unnerving distraction of another flickering and a further subsequent dimming of the lights.

Someone laughed politely, I think it was Galt, inviting everyone to dispel the tension of the moment. The Reverend Garden did his bit, asking Lemuel whether even his millions were perhaps not enough to pay Glassford Hall's electric bill. Lemuel just about managed a smile, but his attention was drawn to Lafayette, who looked dreadful: weakened, breathing heavily and visibly tremulous.

'Okay, time for us to say good night,' Mather said insistently, and put an arm around Lafayette to lead him away from the mantel.

That was when more than our conversation was snuffed. As soon as Mather attempted to lead Lafayette from the room, the fire in the hearth went out, suddenly and spontaneously. It was as though some freak gust of wind had, against all under-standing of meteorology, channelled itself fully down the chimney. The coals were blown out like candles on a cake.

It may seem redundant to state that the temperature got much colder right then, but the sudden absence of the flames could not account for just *how* much colder. Standing where I was, mere feet from the hearth, it felt as though the fire had never been lit.

Nobody spoke, and for a few seconds nobody moved either. Then Lafayette shrugged off Mather's arm and sat heavily upon the edge of a chair.

'We need to get you out of here,' Mather stated, trying to sound calm, but clearly very agitated.

Then Lafayette, tearful and shaking, spoke the words that froze the whole room.

'I can't leave her. She needs me.'

This seemed to engender a horrified, impotent acceptance in Mather. He took a step away from Lafayette and urged the rest of us to give him space.

'Who needs you?'

It was Lemuel who asked. His voice was a mixture of awe, fear and, he later admitted, hope.

The answer was no less dreadful for it being the one we all expected.

'Hilda,' Lafayette stated in the driest of whispers.

As he breathed the word, the lights flickered again and then went out altogether. Only the embers in the hearth and one table lamp in a remote corner continued to illuminate the room.

I will freely admit that I had never felt so scared before in my life. Shortly afterwards, however, I was to develop an entirely new understanding of what scared was.

Nobody moved. I'm not sure anyone even breathed. We all remained in what was close to a circle around Lafayette. Mather was the furthest back, almost outside the circle, which further unnerved me, as he was the one who was supposed to have witnessed things like this before and he was keeping a greater distance than any of us.

'Don't be afraid,' Lafayette said, very softly. He still sounded pained and breathless, but there was a note of calm in his voice.

17

Despite that, I estimated he'd be struggling to reassure any of us, until I realised with his next remark that it wasn't us he was talking to. 'We're all friends here.'

Lafayette sat with his eyes closed, his hands gripping the arm of the chair he was leaning against as though if he let go he'd be sucked out of the window.

His eyes opened again. Even in the dim light, I could still see the fear in them, the confusion, but there was a determination too.

'Join hands,' he said. 'All her friends.' Mather reluctantly stepped closer, but was rebuffed. '*Just* her friends.' I wasn't sure whether this ought to exclude me, as I'd barely known her, but I felt Lemuel's hand reach out to mine and grip it tight, and I was so grateful for the sensation that I wasn't about to give it up. Martha was slow to join, clearly disorientated.

'Come on,' Lafayette encouraged her. 'Don't be standing there like cheese at thruppence.'

At this Martha broke into a sob and looked again at Lemuel. He also was in tears.

It is often said that man turns to religion in his times of greatest fear and uncertainty, and that there is no such thing as an atheist in a foxhole. How ironic, then, that I, a lifelong Christian, in my moment of terror sought my refuge in rationalism. It must be some kind of trick, I told myself, though weighing against this was the question of why Lafayette would do such a thing after enlightening us about the ways of the predatory phoney mediums. He had told us of their spirit cabinets – usually a curtained-off area behind which they hid props and sometimes an unseen accomplice – and how they carefully chose the location so that they could control the environment. However, this location was not Lafayette's choice, there was no spirit cabinet and this was an environment so unfamiliar that guests got lost just fetching something from upstairs. Unless, I considered, it was intended as a bad-taste – but for that, unforgettable – means of driving home his point.

Yes, that was it, I convinced myself, my rationalism rather selectively ignoring the fact that lights and fires were extinguishing themselves and that the temperature was plummeting of its own accord. It was a stunt, and the next part would involve

Lafayette giving evasively ambiguous answers on Hilda's behalf to queries nervously volunteered by Lemuel.

But rationalism, unlike faith, came up wanting, because unlike faith, rationalism no longer does its job when you run out of answers. And I have absolute faith that I will be waiting for a 'rational' explanation of what happened next until the day I die.

The room gradually filled with a sound. It must have been building a while before anyone noticed it, the kind of constant background noise you normally only become aware of if it is suddenly switched off. In our case, it grew in volume until we couldn't fail to be aware of it, and then further until we could barely hear anything else. It was a mixture of white noise and wind, and by wind I mean a whooshing, violent gale, and yet it was coming from *inside* the room. It got so loud that Lemuel's housekeeper, Mrs Glebe, came to investigate, and in short order found herself the next terrified soul invited to join hands in the circle around Lafayette.

Then, within that wind, distant, like from within the centre of a tornado, we heard a voice. At first, lost amid the violence of that engulfing noise, it sounded like the mewling of a cat, but then it grew and repeated until it became unquestionably human, articulating a single unmistakable word.

'Bryant.'

I felt every pore close, every part of me attempt to contract as surely as had I been dropped into the Arctic Ocean.

The hands clasping my own threatened to crush my bones, and no doubt mine theirs. I wanted to close my eyes. A few others had. The circle closed; arms that had been extended were pulled near, drawing us all closer to Lafayette in the centre. His eyes were shut tight like he was in a sandstorm. His whole body was shaking; not trembling or shivering, for they come from within, but *being* shaken. He struggled in vain to speak, then somehow managed to find a voice.

'Answer. Someone. Please.'

The word 'Bryant' got louder, though it was still buffeted within the storm of sound, always far away.

Lemuel's voice was choked and broken, difficult to hear above the chaos.

'Hilda. Hilda.'

The voice in the storm spoke again. 'I am here,' I thought she said, but upon repetition, I realised it was: 'I can't hear.'

Registering this, Lemuel reacted with a desperation that cut through his fearful paralysis, and shouted her name with all he had.

No words came from amid the storm for a few seconds, causing him to shout again. He was cut off as the voice returned.

'I can feel you. I can't see, can't hear. I feel you.'

'My God,' Lemuel said, almost collapsing. Galt and Garden had hold of his hands, keeping him upright as his legs threatened to buckle.

No further words emerged for a spell, despite more futile shouts from Lemuel, and although the sound continued, I remember thinking – perhaps hoping – that it was over. It might have been this notion that made me think – too late, I believed – of my Dictaphone, now sitting in my breast pocket. The kind of regret that must haunt a photographer who has just missed the snap of his life was dawning on me even in my state of terror.

And then the voice resumed, at greater length, irregular pauses between the communiqués.

'I'm not cold.'

'I'm not lost.'

'I'm home.'

'I'm here.'

The emotion in her voice was difficult to gauge, as one can hardly detect the finer nuances in the midst of such tumult, but to me she sounded like someone trying to mask her own fears in order to spare the fears of those she loved.

Lemuel looked like he barely dared believe it. There were tears streaming down his cheeks; tears of unfathomable loss, but there was a joy in there too. I knew he didn't want it to end.

'I'm always here.'

'Always in St Anne's.'

'Always in La Castillo.'

From the corner of my eye I noticed that Mather had got out a notepad and was frantically scribbling down what was said. He didn't know I had gone one better, at the expense of momentarily breaking the circle with my right hand.

The messages continued.

'I miss you.'

'I love you.'

And finally:

'We'll be together again . . . in time.'

After that, just the wind and white noise. We listened to it for an age: on the tape, it's fully four minutes, all of us silent, rapt, entranced. Nobody dared believe it was all over until the noise finally began to die and then, just as inexplicably as they'd gone out, the lights suddenly came back on.

Like when the house lights come back on in a darkened cinema, one felt the sense of waking from a dream, instantly more distant from what had just happened than the few seconds that had elapsed.

Shaking us all from our daze was the sight of Lafayette, who fell forward from his seat and slumped to the carpet. Mather was upon him instantly, warding the rest of us back as he squatted down nearby.

I turned to look at Lemuel. He stood trembling, eyes unfocused, tears still streaming.

'I don't think he's breathing,' Mather announced, panicked and distraught.

'Turn him on to his side,' I told him, and knelt down to help roll Lafayette into what is known as the recovery position. Almost immediately, he began to splutter and gasp. He made to sit up. We both attempted to keep him where he was, but were thrown off with unexpected strength. Lafayette got up into a squat and looked around himself frantically, like he'd just surfaced from a long time underwater.

'Are you okay?' Mather asked. 'Are you okay? Gabriel?'

Lafayette seemed to look through him at first, and even when he did focus on Mather, he seemed to disregard him and his question like they were both irrelevant.

'La Castillo,' was the first thing he said. 'I felt this surge, this amazing surge, when she said La Castillo. It felt like it might rip me in two, it was so strong, but at the same time it was warm, it was good, like . . . like the touch of God.'

'What's La Castillo?' Mather asked, turning to look at Lemuel.

Lemuel, all eyes now upon him, appeared fit to collapse, and delicately took his ease on a sofa as a precaution. He seemed unable to speak; confused, disorientated, his mouth opening and closing like a landed fish. Someone offered him a glass of water and he drank it like he'd just crawled through the desert.

Mather asked him again, but Reverend Garden warned him off. It was hardly the time to be putting pressure on anyone.

We all needed some time and space. Lafayette announced that he was going outside for some air. Mrs Glebe insisted on going to the kitchen to make tea, despite looking like she wouldn't be able to hold a kettle in her trembling hands. I suppose it was a coping mechanism: seeking the reassurance of familiarity in her normal routine. The rest of us remained in silence. What could anyone say, after that? There was an element of ignoring the elephant in the room, but it was as much a state of recoil.

In the end, it was Lemuel who chose to speak first, and I can't decide whether, under the circumstances, he was the most or least likely person to do so.

'St Anne's,' he said quietly, a note of almost incredulous reverie in his voice. 'We first met in St Anne's, in 1974. We got married in Southport in 1975. Went to Spain for our honeymoon, a place called Mijas. We stayed in a hotel called . . . blimey, would you credit that?'

'La Castillo,' Martha said.

'No. That's the thing: I can't remember the name. But our room, our little honeymoon suite, though it were hardly that, were up in this little turret. La Castillo were what Hilda called it: our soft little honeymoon joke. Something that were just between *us*.'

Lemuel then broke down into heaving sobs again. Martha put an arm around him.

'I'm sorry,' he said, recomposing himself. 'It's just that I hadn't heard Hilda say it since. It weren't just like I were listening to her voice tonight – it were like she were actually back there, back then – and I could still hear her through space *and time*.'

Mrs Glebe did manage to make her pot of tea, and brought it through shortly after. Lemuel had some, but withdrew as soon as he had drunk it, without saying another word. The rest of us sat there a while, but no-one could find anything to say. It was as though there was so much to discuss, it was too daunting for anyone to know where to begin. One by one we bade our good nights and retired to bed, though I don't imagine anyone slept. I know I certainly didn't.

We had all witnessed something utterly extraordinary, something inexplicable by conventional knowledge and comprehension. But just because conventional knowledge cannot comprehend it does not mean it should be given up as merely an inconvenient anomaly and shunted out of science's way. New knowledge and new means of comprehension are necessary, not only to seek answers for what happened at Glassford Hall, but because this could prove to be the most important frontier of human exploration bar none.

Those opposing Bryant Lemuel's efforts to establish a Spiritual Science Chair at Kelvin University ought to remember that men like them, so utterly sure of their own knowledge, once showed Galileo the instruments of torture.

They didn't stop us learning that the Earth went round the Sun.

## Voice of the Dead II: This time it's Parlabane

Do *you* believe in ghosts?

Away and give us peace. Are we not past this? You'd think we ought to be, wouldn't you? You'd think an abject lack of any kind of reliable evidence *whatsoever* would have this one filed away and forgotten, gathering dust between the folders marked 'Fairies at the Bottom of the Garden' and 'Iraq's Weapons of Mass Destruction'. But no, it's still clinging on to the hairy ring of human comprehension, and the lavvy paper of reason just can't quite wipe it off. And what's worse is that we're not just talking about some fringe minority comprising folk who wear cagoules indoors and smell of cat-pish. They're not the problem. The problem is that even among otherwise intelligent and perfectly rational company, there's always some fanny who starts telling you about the time he saw his deid granny in the upstairs hall of her house; or the weird thing that happened to so-and-so and her mate on a camping trip; or the time the phone rang in the middle of the night and they knew before they answered it that Auntie Jeanie had copped her whack. Then instead of rightly and justly engaging in a merciless point-and-laugh fest, highlighting how so-and-so and her mate were no doubt ganjed out of their boxes at the time, or that Auntie Jeanie *did* happen to be their oldest living relative and had spent the last six weeks on the fucking oncology ward, everybody goes: 'Oooooh. That's so weird. See, you just never know. There's things we can't explain. You shouldn't close your mind.'

And I bet you're fucking doing it right now, aren't you? Admit it: your last thought was to wonder: 'Yes, but what about granny in the upstairs hall? You didn't offer an explanation for *that*. See, you just never know. There's things we can't explain. You shouldn't close your . . .'

Fuck off.

Can I ask a question? Take any spooky old house that's said

to be haunted: people will have been living and dying on that spot for thousands of years. How come the ghosts people claim to see are always in period costume? How come nobody ever describes one that looks like a caveman, or wearing a mullet and a 'Frankie Say' T-shirt, having snuffed it in 1984?

And here's one I've been asking for a while, even asked it in print (and you should see the feats of logic-mangling that got flung back at me in response): how come astronomers never see UFOs and physicists never see ghosts? Think about it: astronomers, professional and amateur, the people who spend as much time as they can staring up at the sky, never see a flying object they can't identify. Physicists, professional and amateur, the people who spend as much time as they can studying forces and energy, never encounter any evidence of psychic forces, never detect any trace of the energy that would be generated by the most anorexic of spooks. Are they just really, really unlucky? Oh no, wait, don't tell me: 'They're not seeing because they don't believe.'

Okay, true story: I do recall witnessing a spectral apparition myself. It was in a park in Paisley around 2002: it looked like a man, dressed in black and white stripes. Whenever someone kicked a football into his vicinity, it seemed to go right through him like he wasn't there, and sometimes it was as though he had completely disappeared. Legend says his name was Andy Dow. Used to send chills down everybody's spine whenever it was read out over the PA at Love Street.

*That's* a ghost. Get the picture? Good. Because I want my credentials – and in particular my position with regard to this sort of thing – very thoroughly established before I make what is for me an extremely awkward and, frankly, embarrassing revelation.

Fucking bastards, you're going to love this. You're going to lap this up for all it's worth, a veritable gloat-glut. Fill your boots – I don't grudge you it. Well, actually, under the circumstances, truth is I *sincerely* fucking grudge you it, but what I'm saying is I'd be exactly the same. I'd point and laugh with unrestrained glee, because there are few things more hilarious in this world than someone who is smugly convinced he is right about something (and let's face it, I can be abominably smug when I *am* right about something) suddenly being in the un-dignified position of *himself* constituting the living proof that he's wrong.

Or *not*-living proof, as the case may be.

Oh, yeah. You read that right. Uh-huh.

You really are going to love this – serious dancing-on-the-spot, tongue-out-and-flicking-the-vicky, gerritrightupye love it – and therefore I'd like to say once more just how much I really, really grudge you that. Oh, and to mention also that, as my grand-father used to say, the clock goes around. Not a threat, just a warning.

Shite. Okay, here goes.

My name is Jack Parlabane and I'm pan-breid. Aye, that's right, don't kid on you can't understand the rhyming slang. And let me finish before you laugh – you'll get more out of it once you hear the details. Killed in a typically foolhardy endeavour (let's avoid the word 'undertaking', shall we?), death by defenestration, gravity finally delivering the ultimate skelp in the arse in revenge for my years of insolent defiance. A four-storey fall out my own living-room window. Ironic? Inevitable? Hilarious? Take your pick. Surprising? Not my call. I guess you could call it the ultimate humiliation. Certainly looked pretty fucking ultimate from my perspective. Actually, truth be told, the fall itself isn't so bad, no matter the height. It's that last inch that's a cunt.

And yet here I am, still observing and reporting. Still self-indulgently ranting and editorialising. Like I said, awkward, especially given my uncompromising pronouncements above. I'll say this much in my defence, though: I was right to believe what I did, on the strength of the available evidence. However, the same would no doubt be claimed by certain people I've been rather scornful of throughout this messy and unedifying wee episode; and that should serve as a warning to you, before you get too smug. Yes, it's amusing just how wrong a person can be, and just as funny how gullible. But as you will learn, *anybody* can be fooled, especially if they place too much trust in a single human source rather than objectively evaluating the data. No need the tangled web to weave, when mugs are desperate to believe.

Remarkable claims require remarkable evidence, and yet very often, the more remarkable the claim, the more people are prepared to take on trust. I know you're aware I *would* say that just to make my own situation seem less embarrassing. It's like I'm saying I should get credit for the working I did on a separate sheet of paper even though my answer was wrong, whereas the ones who got it right just made a lucky guess. But look at the Glassford Hall stuff, for instance. I take it you've read Jillian Noble's book, or at least the bits they serialised in that shitey newspaper she writes for. What did you make of it? Apart from her melodramatic prose, pompous self-importance and *The Mail*'s house-style sycophancy towards the rich, I mean? Did you believe her? Think carefully, and pay close attention to what you're being asked. Take it from me, who really is in the position to know: nothing here is what it seems.

'Why ever would she lie?' That is a question I have heard asked a great many times. The advance she got, not even including serialisation rights, would provide two hundred and fifty thousand reasons. Would you like to change your answer? Runaround . . . *now*!

But here's the thing: I now know for a fact that she was telling the truth. Jillian Noble lied about nothing in that account. Okay, she's a bit deluded in thinking that being another dreary why-oh-why columnist means she has a public profile, and comparing herself to 'the hardest-bitten sceptic' is pretty tough to swallow for anybody who knows she's a fully fledged God-botherer and is on record extolling the virtues of homeopathy. Yeah, and while I'm at it, I should mention she's laying it on *extremely* thick about Lemuel's all-colours-of-the-nutter-rainbow alliance winning any more than a fig-leaf of a concession from the Executive over the DSH bill. But about the events of that night? Nope. Sorry. I'd dearly love to be able to say otherwise, and I have no end of reasons to question her integrity – anyone who writes for *The Daily Hate-and-Fear* has, in my book, forfeited the right to call herself a journalist – but the bottom line is that she wasn't fibbing.

So were you right to believe her? Were you wrong if you didn't? Tricky, isn't it? But there is a correct answer. See if you can work it out. Do you want that separate sheet of paper?

Or . . . would you like a little more information?

Congratulations. *That*, folks, was the correct answer.

And I might as well oblige you: it's not like I've anything I can be getting on with. Not right now, anyway, though I do have some unfinished business (to put it bloody mildly), which I will be tending to in due course. See, there are some handy fringe benefits to finding yourself in my unearthly position, but timing and discretion are of the essence. When the appropriate moment arrives, a-haunting I will go, but in the mean time, I'm free to talk.

Now, where should I begin? Let me see. How about this:

Once upon a time, there were two little girls who told a very big fib.

No, too far back. Maybe I should start with a little about me. Ha! Don't be ridiculous, why would I need to bother with that? You know everything about me already, don't you? Everybody fucking well thinks they do, anyway, and the saddest part is, they're probably right. So let's skim briefly through the greatest hits, shall we? Unless you'd rather just wait for the obits.

Okay. John Lapsley Parlabane. Journalist. Ex-con. Married, to Sarah. No kids.

Cut my teeth in Glasgow at first, then get the big move to London. Garner a reputation as an incurable pain in the arse – sorry, tenacious investigative journalist – my fact-finding dubiously enhanced by a facility for and disposition towards . . . oh fuck it, there's no point in sugar-coating this any more: burglary. Lock-picking, scaling buildings, breaking and entering; plain old criminal behaviour necessitated (and thus, in my driven and simplistic mind, excused) by it being frequently the only way to get to the evidence.

A few mildly uncomfortable police interviews aside, this is all working out swimmingly for myself and my newspaper until my investigations become contrary to the interests of its propri-etor, Roland Voss. My discovery of a statutory-minimum-sized package of Class A drugs in my flat, with the police imminently due to be paying a visit, convinces me to seek a change of climate. I move to Los Angeles, where I work as a crime reporter until my investigations become contrary to the interests of, well, pick any name from a dozen. Once again, I become convinced

28

that the time has come to seek fresh challenges, this time by the attendance of a professional hitman at my house and the prospect of considerably less comfortable police interviews focused largely on the subject of how said hitman ended up on my hall carpet full of bullet-holes.

Back in Scotland, let's see: uncover some rather robustly direct ward-clearance methods at the George Romanes Hospital. Crooked chief exec tries to have me killed. Uncover senior-government-level conspiracy behind murder of the now late Roland Voss. Crooked cabinet minister tries to have me killed. Uncover murderous truth behind 'Moundgate' scandal, though not without going to jail in the process, during which crooked PR guru tries to have me killed. Are you starting to recognise a pattern here? Right, where are we up to? Oh yes. Get invited to corporate junket in highlands with biggest collection of wankers it's ever been my misfortune to congregate amongst, outside of Parkhead or Ibrox. Crooked and utterly bonkers Intelligence types try to have me and entire aforementioned collection of wankers killed, but not before, as the tabloids keep fucking reminding everybody, we had 'dined on human flesh'.

And no, it doesn't taste like chicken. (Ironically, it *does* actually taste like ostrich, but that could simply have been down to the way it was prepared.)

Get elected rector of Kelvin University.

Yes, indeed: get *that* up you. And don't be bloody pedantic: was I rector or not? Thank you. Uncover . . . well, can't really say that yet, unfortunately. *Dis*covered plenty, but the 'crook tries to have me killed' part got bumped up the running order, and before I could finish the uncovering bit . . . Christ, three wee dots. Is that my current status? Guess so. I exist now in the realm of the ellipsis.

So, does that just about cover it? Have I missed anything? Oh yeah. Of course. You were never going to let me away with that, were you? No, it's not particularly relevant, but yes, it is on your list, so, if you fucking insist, here goes: wife shagged some surgeon at a Christmas party a few years back and it made the papers. Satisfied? Well, don't get too excited. It's thoroughly behind us now. Yes, yes, obviously *everything* is behind me now, but prior to my demise, our relationship was fine. We've had tougher and more important things to cope with than drunken infidelity. I've been to jail and she's worked for the NHS. You think a stray hump registers when your scale's been calibrated by that shit? What do you mean, 'a river in Egypt'? Yeah, okay. Maybe. Look, do you want me to tell you this story or not?

Right. So, where were we? Bollocks. Hadn't decided where to begin, had I? And me a journalist, too. Let's think. Should I start with the first time I met the villain of the piece? Yeah, that would work, wouldn't it? Very James Bond. Late night, low lights, opulent surroundings, champagne and chandeliers, the women in tight dresses, the men in their sharpest evening suits. You're waiting for the punchline, but no kidding, that *is* how it happened. The early face-off, the looking into each other's eyes and mutually identifying an adversary, weighing up the threat, a flirting, near-sexual chemistry developing between goody and baddy, subtly sparring with words, mouth-watering prelude to inexorable deeds.

But no, on second thoughts, I'll save that bit. Far too early yet. This sort of mystery story usually starts with the discovery of a body. Who am I to mess with the convention? Let's go with that, and I don't mean my own. Hell, let's start with the discovery of two, as that's how it was. Not a murder scene as such, but there's plenty of that to come, don't worry.

It was one of my first, albeit unofficial, tasks as rector of Kelvin University. Yeah, we'll get to that as well. Let me tell you about the bodies first.

The post of rector is like that of executive producer: almost entirely undefined, from a role with the potential to make an invaluable contribution, to an honorary title merely acknowledging the clout your name carries elsewhere. Nobody gives you a job description, merely a list of formal engagements asterisked with humble caveats acknowledging that earning your daily crust might restrict your availability to attend. Above and beyond that, you can make of it what you will. It's reassuring to know that some of the previous incumbents were political prisoners throughout their tenures and therefore you can't do worse than their records for event attendance or hands-on involvement (though I'm told one or two celeb predecessors did give it their best shot). Granted the nature of my appointment to the post, I decided early on that lording it in the role of figure-head really ought to take a back seat to finding ways in which I could muck in and quietly make myself useful. Acquainting myself with the issues most pertinent to the modern student seemed an early prerequisite, and there are fewer more perti-nent student issues than somebody turning up two dead ones.

It was towards the end of Week Nothing, the student satur-nalia before term proper began. I was tipped off about it by a police contact of mine: Ursula Lomas, one-time colleague of my friend Jenny back in Edinburgh, but now moved to the Strathclyde force and working out of Partick. She'd read about my improbable elevation to the heights of academe and guessed correctly that I'd be more comfortable looking into the harsher realities of campus life than doling out prizes in a cape.

They were taking the bodies away just as I got there, the ambulance headed for the Western Infirmary where the post-mortem would take place in order to formally confirm what was already obvious: two young men in their prime had been killed, as they slept, by carbon monoxide poisoning.

The flat was just off Dumbarton Road. I belled Ursula when I reached the address and she came down to give me the escorted tour. We didn't exchange much in the way of pleasantries, as I don't know Ursula that well. I can only assume I've had a decent write-up from Jenny, as Ursula's been nothing but cooperative since I moved through to Glasgow, despite me not having the occasion to return any favours. Maybe I'd just been living in Edinburgh too long and forgot that folk in Glasgow don't expect a receipt for being civil to you.

I've seen some pretty squalid student gaffs in my time, often from the close-up perspective of crashing out on the sticky carpet, so feel qualified to say that this one was in pretty decent nick. I know this sounds harsh, but part of me was disappointed as Ursula showed me around the place. There was no big story, no campaign waiting to be waged on student living conditions and negligent landlords. The whole tenement floor had been subdivided and subdivided again; the plumbing work probably looked like the inside of Terry Gilliam's head, but it was hardly the Black Hole of Calcutta.

'Looks like it was a dodgy heater,' Ursula told me. 'We'll

know for sure once the gas board engineers have had time to examine everything.'

'And if that's the case, will the landlord be in deep shit?' I asked, almost optimistically.

'Landlord was here earlier, weeping up a storm. A Mr Patel, older guy, in his sixties I'd say. He says he's got all his gas safety certificates up to date. We'll be checking that, naturally, especially as it turned out the battery in the CO detector was dead.'

'What does he say to that?'

'Swears blind he changes them regularly. Gut reaction: he's telling the truth. I deal with a lot of students on this turf. It's hardly unknown for them to nick the battery from the smoke alarm and swap it for the dud in their MP3 player.'

'Christ.'

'Yeah. Such a tiny thing, seems so stupid. But that's the problem when they're that age: you cannae tell them anything because they're convinced they're gaunny live forever.'

I looked at the names on the door on my way out. Keith Baker and Michael Loftus. This latter rang a bell. Don't get over-excited: there's no crashing minor chords on the soundtrack, I just recalled hearing the name.

No, no crashing chords, no big story. Just a very sad one. Nineteen and twenty, they were. There was nothing for me to write about; leave that to the local press.

The landlord's story later checked out. He was up to date with his safety inspections, gets all the appliances serviced as part of a maintenance contract. The heater malfunctioned, but it would take the engineer a while to work out how. The other tenants' CO detectors turned out to have healthy batteries, so it was either a duffer or Ursula was right about one of the flatmates swapping it. A deadly confluence of shitty luck, but as Ursula said, try using it as a cautionary tale and you'll only get a chorus of 'yeah, yeah's. Another campus poster campaign for the would-be immortals to ignore.

That was the very thought, those the very words in my head when I remembered where I had heard – or rather seen – that slightly familiar name: a campus flyposter. There were three or four on every lamp-post between Hillhead underground station and University Avenue, advertising gigs or pimping candidates for student elections. There had been more than usual around then because of Week Nothing, when everyone is vying for the attention, signatures and money of the freshers. This one had briefly caught my eye because of the name in large-font block capitals, rather than the one more modestly incorporated below:

## THE AMAZING MAGIC OF

# GABRIEL LAFAYETTE

## A TRIBUTE BY MICHAEL LOFTUS

Gabriel Lafayette. Aye. Him again.

The advertised date had been the night before. I hoped this Loftus guy had put on a memorable performance, as it had turned out to be his last.

I remember thinking: Christ, has our popular culture not bottomed out yet, we're actually having tribute acts to tacky psychics? I mean, I reckoned we had left the coopers with some serious maintenance work on the barrel when I saw ads for Oasis tribute bands, considering that I had previously thought Oasis *were* a fucking tribute band. However, my debilitative grumpy-old-fartism was obscuring the discordant note: tribute it might be billed, but I couldn't imagine Gabriel Lafayette would consider himself honoured by being described as a magician, even an amazing one.

I had barely heard of Lafayette until about a year before this. Sure, I knew the name, in a hearing people say 'How much of a prick is that Gabriel Lafayette fudknocker?' kind of way, but like Beckhams and Big Brother contestants, I was determinedly zoning him out. In a media-saturated age, you can really start to resent the amount of information you absorb, despite your steadfast disinterest, about certain utterly unworthy subjects. It's like the data equivalent of secondary smoke inhalation.

He only registered any sort of signal on my radar when he was elected rector of Kelvin University. Aye, those wacky students: just shows the esteem with which they regard this

33

position when you look at the state of the folk who end up holding it. Once upon a time it might have been a vital and honoured post, or the occasion of deeply felt political gesturing. Nowadays, if it was run as a party system, then the Monster Raving Loonies would represent the mainstream consensus: an election where novelty candidates were usually favourites over anyone perceived to be remotely serious. Thus despite never having been to university, and in all likelihood never having been to Glasgow, Gabriel Lafayette was a shoo-in because of his appeal to a key constituency: stoned students vegging out on sofas watching afternoon telly.

Consequently I wasn't surprised at him getting the gig; more so that he did apparently show up from time to time and make a pretty committed go of it. (This, of course, was before I knew he had been a frequent visitor north of the border due to his relationship with Bryant Lemuel.) But as far as I could see, he was just another dumbed-down student cult figure, the latest tacky personality being patronised by campus trendies due to his po-mo ironic value. Yeah, I know. I've already admitted I hadn't really been paying attention. Let me be the millionth person to say it: Gabriel Lafayette is not who or what I thought he was.

In the 1970s, *Deep Throat* was credited with making hardcore porn palatable to respectable middle-class sensibilities, reaching an audience that would previously have taken demonstrable pride in having nothing to do with it. Thus in the noughties, Gabriel Lafayette was lauded as having managed the same trick with the paranormal: taking it 'from the end of the pier to the doors of the laboratory', as the cover quote on all his DVDs has it. I choose my Linda Lovelace comparison advisedly, as it could be said that she and Lafayette have both instigated unfeasible feats of swallowing. However, that would just be more sour grapes from grumpy old me. Why not, in the interests of the scientific method, balance my impression with one from a different source?

# Unbelievable truths

(A further extract from *Encounters in the Borderland*, Jillian Noble's biography of Gabriel Lafayette, as amended and serialised in *The Mail* ahead of publication.)

'I don't claim to be psychic. I don't even know what psychic is.'

That was Gabriel Lafayette's response when I first formally interviewed him, shortly after the premiere edition of *Borders of the Known* aired on Channel Five. I say 'formally', as we had by this time met several times under various auspices, and had we not, it is doubtful whether this or any other interview with the man would have taken place. Lafayette is naturally rather shy off stage and screen, once he has shed the persona he regards as much of a construct as any theatrical costume. His shyness extends to publicity, despite the impression his sometimes ubiquitous public visibility can convey. He accepts it as a necessary burden of his work, but does not consider himself well suited to it. Thus, this was the first newspaper interview he had granted, and even at that, it never seemed a firm arrangement until we were actually sitting face to face with my tape recorder switched on.

'If it's a passive thing, a sensitivity to something, a means of perception, then I can relate to that. But if it means a power, something you can consciously effect, then no, that ain't me. Things happen around me, some of them very, very strange. And not just around me, but sometimes around people I've had close contact with. I am not conscious of doing anything, of trying to bring about anything. I tend towards the bitter, as a matter of fact, when I hear anyone talk about me having "powers", because power is the last thing I have. Mostly I feel helpless.'

Lafayette's attitude to the phenomena that have surrounded him is a far cry from the stridency and posturing of his predecessors as celebrities of the paranormal, most notably Uri Geller, with whom he is inevitably but inaccurately compared. A former male model, Geller burst on to the world stage as an attractive, young and virile figure, as much bedroom pin-up as man of mystery. It was a time when Bruce Lee movies were generating unprecedented mystique for the martial arts, and Geller's demonstrations suggested hidden abilities of the human mind to match these mysterious oriental disciplines of the body.

Lafayette, by contrast, is adamant that he is not the one exerting any conscious influence when strange phenomena occur around him. 'Just because something happens which conventional wisdom can't explain, it doesn't follow that I did it. It feels like something, I don't know . . . neutral, yeah, neutral like the water or the air. It's not a presence and it's not a force. But it gets a push from somewhere, and there's a ripple. It doesn't feel like I made the ripple, but sometimes it feels like I'm uncomfortably close to whatever did.'

So are we talking about dead people here?

'That's what I'm determined to find out, why I'm kinda letting myself be Easy Mather's lab rat. People talk about me hearing voices, but that simply doesn't happen. It's like I feel something within me and the words come from there, though what comes out is sorta like my translation, my interpretation. That's why it don't always make a lot of sense sometimes,' he adds, laughing. 'It's like I don't know what's coming until the words are out, kinda like I'm just the radio, not the broadcaster. But the broadcaster feels human.'

Lafayette was born in New Orleans in 1955. Plastic surgery has cancelled out the effects of a tough paper round to leave him looking probably about right for his age. He is up front about the cosmetic work: 'The things I've seen, if it wasn't for the surgeons, I'd look about ninety,' he quips.

His mother, Marie, was of Cajun stock, and it is her name that he has chosen to carry. 'The superstition goes that you'll have psychic gifts if you're the seventh son of a seventh son. I don't know what they say about being the sixth son of a son-of-a-bitch.'

The line sounds well rehearsed, and is delivered with a knowing weariness, but it is revealing enough. Lafayette's father,

Arthur Davenport, was a violent alcoholic and inveterate gambler who often left the family penniless for days or weeks at a time before returning either penitent or broke. Davenport was, however, the youngest of seven boys, something Lafayette smiles wryly about. 'One more big brother and I'd at least have something to hang all this weird stuff on.'

The earliest instance of this 'weird stuff' came, he says, when he was seven years old.

'There was this old black woman on our street, lived in this real run-down-looking shack, even more run down than ours. Ma Lawsey was her name. Lot of ju-ju round the place. Lot of folks came for readings: she read the Tarot cards, but that was vanilla, for the tourists. Not real tourists, you understand, but you got folks from other neighbourhoods. She did darker stuff, though, far darker: chicken blood, augury. Kids from other streets were real scared of her, like she was the boogeyman, but we all knew her, used to play in her garden. She used to make cous-cous in this big old pan out back, always had plenty to go round. Sometimes it was the only meal we got.

'And man, she always made a fuss of me, like she was my grandma. Guessed it was because I was the youngest. But she used to look at me sometimes like, I don't know, like she was scared. Not scared of me, but . . . scared for me. And one day, when I was seven, she took my chin in her hand – real big hand, felt tough and calloused like a man's hand – and she said to me: "They's drawn to you, boy. Like they's moths and you the flame. You gonna need strength for the journey."

'Only time in my childhood I thought we were goin' on vacation!'

Lafayette laughs, but is clearly concealing the pain of a long-borne burden.

'I didn't know what she meant back then. I sure as hell know now.'

After what I witnessed at Glassford Hall, I know too.

However, it would be misleading to give the impression that Lafayette has been an entirely reluctant pilgrim on this journey.

'It's like when you're in school and you first learn about space. I've learned about still another distant realm, and though it can be scary, it's undeniably exciting too. Plus – and this cannot be overstated – there's a true joy in what it can give to people. You only have to look in their faces when they recognise the presence of a lost loved one for all the frightening stuff to feel worth it.'

The Glassford Hall incident provided as vivid an illustration of this duality as it is possible to imagine: the horror and fear on one hand, against Bryant Lemuel's tears of loving joy on the other. However, the happier side of Lafayette's world is better exemplified by his more public work, both on television and, for those of us who have had the privilege, up close and in the raw in front of a live audience.

I witnessed him appearing before a crowd of students at the Kelvin University Union Debating Chamber, shortly after being elected rector. The appearance was meant to be merely a thank-you to the students who had elected him, and in particular those who had campaigned on his behalf. Lafayette was billed as giving only a talk, with no suggestion that he would attempt any paranormal demonstration. Nonetheless, tickets had been like gold-dust, so much so that the entertainment convenor informed me he had been forced into keeping a waiting list of names in case any were returned. 'Sometimes there's a band or a comedian who sells out immediately, but folk normally accept that once the briefs are gone, they're gone. I had folk demanding I start a waiting list the minute the event sold out, and that was a week ago.'

And did any of them get lucky?

'Not many. We had six or seven returns, but without being too cynical about my fellow students, I'd imagine a lot of the tickets have been sold on for a profit. Someone said there were two on eBay the other day.'

Lafayette did intend merely to give a talk: part thank-you speech and part Q&A session. He even had a laptop and a data projector with him to illustrate some of what he intended to discuss, with his one concession to showmanship being the hardware necessary for a practical illustration of an important point.

'I don't do "demonstrations",' I've heard him say, somewhat irritably. 'You can't just turn up and expect things to happen. That's what makes me laugh about the attitudes of the cynics who say it's all tricks. If it was just tricks, I could do them three shows a day, seven nights a week.'

That night, however, as he later told me, he had a change of heart only moments before the doors were due to open.

'There was an energy that evening, something really incredible, just everywhere, everywhere. It was one of those occasions as happens now and again when I find it hard to believe the people around me don't feel it too. Sometimes I think maybe they do, but they just don't understand what they're feeling, so they kinda edit it out or put it down to something else. That night, I kept expecting to see sparks leaping to my fingertips like I was touching one of those plasma balls. Just this amazing energy, and I think it was because the occasion was kind of a conductor for positivity. There was so much positivity coming in because it was a wave of positivity that had put me in this honoured position, and I felt like I was radiating pretty good myself. I wanted to say thank you, that was all, but I felt like I was going to burst from it.

'I'm from beginnings about as humble as you're gonna get, and I never had the chance to go to college. You've no idea what it means to a guy like me to be given a position like that in one of the world's oldest seats of learning. So that night I thought: hell, yeah, let's see what happens.'

What did happen, I witnessed from among the crowd. Though it was perhaps the only time I have been at any kind of event where I had 'access all areas', I wanted to gauge the reaction from amid the throng, and I can confirm that Lafayette spoke the truth. There really was an electric sense of excitement and anticipation in the air, and a notable absence of cynicism and scorn, which was truly remarkable given that we're talking about an audience of students. It was an undeniable tribute to the impact Lafayette has had in changing people's perceptions of this field. They weren't there to poke fun or shout the odds. They were there because Lafayette was offering a peek through the door into a different realm, and had made that realm seem a fit subject for mature and intelligent study, rather than a seedy and desperate sideshow.

'I want to explore that other realm,' he says, 'and I'm lucky enough to have had glimpses through the telescope, as have many others before me. The difference between those others and myself, though, and the reason I'm working with Easy Mather, is that we're not just content to gaze through the lens in awe. We're like the natural philosophers of old: we want to measure it, document it, understand it. We want to know the *physics* of it.'

The science of the spiritual, he calls it, and it's the reason why *Borders of the Known* has captured the imagination. The programme has attempted to reconcile science with the para-normal by looking for the ways in which work being done at the frontiers of the former can offer glimpses that may help us understand the latter. *Borders of the Known* not only took the paranormal into the mainstream, it brought cutting-edge science out of the graveyard intellectual slots and on to primetime. Audiences reared on reality TV discovered a fabric-of-reality TV. Before Lafayette, could anyone have imagined White Van Man tuning into a show featuring advanced physics? Who could have predicted that the phrase 'electron bubble' would be over-heard around thousands of office water-coolers? And yet thanks to Lafayette, millions of ordinary Britons have come to learn that what they previously believed to be science fiction is irrefutable science fact. For instance, physicists now accept that there are parallel universes and hidden dimensions. Lafayette's programme illustrated this lucidly, and fascinatingly recreated the photon experiments that had led physicists to their mind-bending discoveries. Who can forget also, thanks to those aforementioned electron bubbles, the revelation that electrons – and hence matter – can in fact be in two places at once?

But the real secret of the series' success has been Lafayette's speculations about how these scientific phenomena might also provide insight into other areas of the unexplained. It's an ingenious trick: he hooks an audience with the promise of the supernatural, then ambushes them with science, before making both factors seem even more amazing by bringing them together – the science seems more amazing because it represents what we may have thought impossible; while the supernatural becomes more amazing because the science suggests it *is* possible.

Just as exciting – but undoubtedly more controversial – has been the series' parallel contention that conventional science's failure to detect evidence of certain paranormal phenomena proves only the limitations of conventional science. With typical audacity, one of Lafayette's most memorable arguments is made by an analogy borrowed from Sir Arthur Stanley Eddington, one of the most eminent astrophysicists of the last century.

'Imagine an ichthyologist casting a net into the sea, then analysing what he's caught. He's a disciplined man of science, so he's categorising and systematising until he comes up with two logical deductions: one, that no sea creature is less than two inches long; and two, that all sea creatures have gills. We try and tell him we believe otherwise, that some of us have seen things that don't bend to his rules, but he says we're talking nonsense and we've got no evidence. As Eddington put it: "Anything uncatchable in my net is *ipso facto* outside the scope of ichthyological knowledge and is not part of the kingdom of fishes. In short, what my net can't catch isn't a fish."

'Or, to put it another way, if his instruments can't detect it, it ain't there; it doesn't exist. Science needs to find new ways of observing and detecting. The lack of evidence *acceptable to scientists* is not down to a lack of data, but down to flaws in how they gather it. When it comes to the paranormal, scientists need to find a new kind of net.'

Thus several hundred of us filed into the Kelvin University Union that night not so much looking for answers as in search of new ways to pose the questions.

As the audience came through the main entrance, we were each handed a card and an envelope by one of several union helpers and asked to comply with a small request before proceeding into the debating chamber to take our seats. The polite but nervous young girl in an official union polo shirt asked me to write on the card a question about a loved one no longer with us, then to seal the card inside the envelope and put my initials on it. I did this, then deposited the envelope in a glass bowl held by another helper as I entered the auditorium.

Lafayette took the stage around three quarters of an hour after this; ten or perhaps fifteen minutes later than billed. The delay only served to maximise the crescendo when finally he appeared, dressed simply, wearing jeans, a white T-shirt and a white linen jacket. He seemed a little self-conscious, bashful even, in the face of such effusive adulation. He looked small and a little isolated on the stage, which was bare but for a table holding a jug of water and a glass, and a black curtain off to the right. Lafayette will confess privately that he doesn't consider himself much of a showman, and he certainly didn't seem naturally equipped to greet a crowd who were whooping it up like that. He seemed more comfortable once the initial euphoria had died down, though the energy in the atmosphere was tangible throughout. I can't lay claim to feeling the things he does, but I do know there was something special passing from the floor to the stage. Before too long, that energy was travelling in both directions, an alternating current.

He began with his thank-yous and his thoughts and plans regarding his tenure as rector. He regretted that he would not be able to base himself in Glasgow, but would endeavour to visit regularly, and would be keeping a close eye on matters through whatever channels were available; 'And there are more channels of communication available to me than to most people,' he joked.

He then went on to discuss some of the themes explored in *Borders of the Known*, in particular the ways in which scientists and advocates of the paranormal misunderstand each other. 'So much of what was once believed to be paranormal came down to ignorance of science on the part of its adherents,' he said. 'And it's still the case today. People talk about the sixth sense, but really they're just underestimating how much we detect with the five we have.

'Man has faculties that have fallen into disuse – when we lived in the great forests we had to have a heightened awareness: of our prey, of our environment, danger. We had to draw more information from the senses we have. Our lives have gotten easier, so those faculties have become dormant – but not extinct.

'I had an uncle who used to tell us he could sense change in the weather because he could feel it in his legs, where he suffered from rheumatoid arthritis. He was usually right; handy man to have around given the kind of storms that can hit New Orleans. We now know that his legs – never entirely free from pain – were sensitive to changes in atmospheric pressure. We know what they were detecting. The problem in my case is that science can't say what I'm detecting, but I *am* detecting it. I'm detecting a lot of it tonight. Sometimes the weather is calm, sometimes there's a lightning storm. As you may have heard me say before, it's like a body of water or air, something that waves can pass through. Many forces of energy exist in wave form. Ask any physicist. But ask *some* physicists and they'll say that *matter* exists in wave form too. Something in me feels those ripples, something in me reads them, like they're grooves on an old vinyl disc and I'm the stylus. The part I really don't understand is the process whereby those tiny, tiny peaks and troughs, once they've vibrated the stylus, are transformed into signals our ears can decode. I'm sure an engineer could explain it to me, though I'm less sure I'd understand it. But what I'm still waiting for is the engineer who can tell me how those waves and ripples, once detected by me, are transformed into thoughts, images and words. But they are. And I'm going to prove that to you right now.'

At this point an assistant appeared on the stage, bearing the glass bowl with the envelopes in it. She was a student on the union's entertainments and events committee, named Helena. She placed the bowl on a table next to Lafayette, then proceeded to exit by the stage-side stairs and waited there, holding a radio mike.

'Now, on your way in here tonight, you were asked to write down a question about a loved one who has passed, and to initial the envelope. The reason I asked for your initials only is because sometimes having a full name in front of me causes confusion – it's like a form of suggestion that interferes with . . . whatever the hell it is inside me that transforms those waves into words. Same reason the question must be sealed. I mustn't see it. I say sometimes, because it ain't always so: sometimes the signal is so strong that nothing can interfere with it, and others it don't matter how few distractions are in my path, there's nothing to see here, folks, move along.'

The audience laughed, though rather nervously, it must be said.

Lafayette then took an envelope from the bowl and held it in his left hand. He closed his eyes and a calm seemed to come upon him. In a room full of hundreds of people, sparking with

43

anticipation, he was all of a sudden as relaxed as had he been reclining on a tropical beach.

'William,' he said. 'That's who the question is about; and at such times, I think we mean that's who the question is for. William, though in this case I think William is known to those who love him as Billy.'

I heard a gasp from somewhere to my left. There was a girl covering her mouth, her face suddenly ashen.

'Billy is proud. Proud of you. He sees you. He sees . . . Katherine.'

Helena moved towards the girl. 'Are you Katherine?' the assistant asked, speaking into the radio mike. The girl nodded, to gasps all around, and was handed the mike.

'Katherine . . . Gates?' Lafayette suggested.

A further nod, more gasps, mine among them.

'KG,' Lafayette said, glancing at the envelope. 'What did you put on the card, Katherine?' he asked.

'I . . . just asked if Billy could see me,' she said nervously.

Lafayette opened the envelope and looked at the card, then nodded before placing it back into the bowl.

'Billy felt real close, family close.'

'He was my uncle,' she revealed, filling up with tears. 'He was a teacher. He used to help me with my homework.'

'That's why it was pride, it was all about pride. He's proud you're here at this fine university.'

The girl looked up at him with gaping, tearful eyes and said, simply: 'Thank you.'

Everything Lafayette said about his burden being worth it was there in that moment. But there were more remarkable moments to come.

Lafayette did this with five more cards, eliciting amazed and grateful responses as he answered these unseen questions. When he closed his eyes to concentrate upon the seventh card, however, the serenity that had come upon him before was contrasted by a look of genuine strain. It was as nothing compared to what I had witnessed at Glassford Hall, but it was reminiscent enough to unnerve me and set me, in my discomfiture, at dramatic odds from the excited faces around me. I'll admit I even felt disdain for them, like I considered them callous and selfish for being here in search of mere distraction when I knew what this could be asking of the man on that stage.

To my relief, this remained merely a dilute version of the ravages Lafayette has been known to suffer, but the reason behind it was no less powerful.

'This is not the question,' Lafayette said, his eyes remaining closed. 'Not the question Laura wants to ask, not the answer her mom needs to give.'

He opened his eyes. 'I'm sorry,' he said, a little hoarsely. 'This is . . . there's confusion. It doesn't seem . . . no, no, that's why. *That's* why. The question is about the pain. Laura needs to know about the pain. Anna is her mom's name. Anna Beth.'

A few rows behind me a girl suddenly let out a soft cry, like she was gulping down air after holding her breath.

'Laura?' Helena asked. The girl nodded, trembling, her face frozen in an expression of confusion and what I could only call a fearful hope.

'Anna Beth,' Lafayette repeated, closing his eyes again. 'Her daughter needs to know about the pain. But that's not the question. But it is the question. Laura asks if she's at peace. She means is the pain over. There was so much pain.'

The girl, Laura, was already filling up, nodding confirmation of Lafayette's every word. Helena offered her the mike, but I don't think she could even see it: her eyes were fixed upon Lafayette.

'She was taken too young. The pain was here,' he said, and beat his left hand against his chest, clutching the card. 'The pain that broke her was here.'

Laura, eyes now streaming, mumbled something. Helena held the mike for her, Laura seemingly too tremulous to do it herself.

'My mum . . . she died of breast cancer.'

Lafayette, eyes still closed, shook his head vehemently and clutched the card so tightly that it bent.

'No. That's not the pain. The pain that broke her was Gordon.'

At this, the girl let out an involuntary sob that was almost a scream, but not one of distress.

'Gordon. That's the confusion. The second signal. Gordon, Anna Beth's son. She lost him. A car . . . oh sweet Jesus, he's only four, he's only four.'

45

There are not the words to describe the atmosphere in that chamber right then. There is an unnerving stillness about a large number of people frozen in utter silence, as anyone who has witnessed such minutes of respect in a sports stadium can testify, but this was something else.

Laura was shuddering with sobs, her eyes closed, her face flushed. Lafayette climbed down the stairs to the chamber floor and made his way towards her.

'No, don't cry, don't cry,' he said, his voice lowered, soft and gentle. 'The pain is gone. All the pain is gone. Anna Beth is whole again. Anna Beth and Gordon are one again. There is peace. There is peace.'

The girl made her way past the two people sitting between her and the aisle and embraced Lafayette like he *was* her mother. 'There is peace,' he said again. The mike was grasped away from his face as he held the girl in his arms, but the silence throughout the room meant we could have heard his softest whisper. 'There is peace.'

I should pause at this juncture to confess that later, once the euphoria had died a little, my journalistic instincts did lead me to ponder whether this might have been some kind of set-up. It wasn't that I was naturally suspicious of Lafayette (that's Mather's job), but I had to ask myself how I could be sure it wasn't; how could I know the girl, or anyone else, wasn't a plant? I did my homework, asked the right questions of the right people. Part of me would have been relieved to discover that it *was* a fraud, as that would have neatly tied up a burgeoning new universe of difficult questions; it would also surely have earned me a finder's fee from a theatrical agent, as the girl would need to have been a magnificent actress. But no, there were no confederates and no lies. Laura Bailey was indeed a student at the university, known to several people I spoke to. Some of them knew she had lost her mother to breast cancer when she was sixteen. None of them had known anything about her brother, but discreet checks revealed that he had been knocked down and killed outside their house when she was six.

(I did some more in-depth background checking in order to verify another story, but I'll blow your socks off with that later.)

Laura was no plant, and neither was engineering student

Grant Neilson, who provided the occasion of a second breath-taking moment of revelation. Lafayette conveyed details of the break-up of Grant's parents' marriage, in particular his late father's regret at how it cost him time with his son; time he had not known to be so limited. It was truly painful to see this burly six-foot prop forward break down in tears of sorrow; equally uplifting to see the gratitude and release in his expression as he gazed up at Lafayette.

It was an emotionally exhausting evening, to say the least. But Lafayette, for all he disdains his own showmanship abilities, was still able to lift the place in order to end on a high. One could even say that he pulled it out of the fire.

The stage lights dimmed as Lafayette talked some more, this time about how 'science is merely a system of measuring our world and our universe, but lacks the instruments to measure some of the ways human consciousness interacts with it'. As he talked, another student assistant, a male this time, drew back the curtain that was obscuring an area on the right of the stage. He revealed a metal tray on the floor, about two metres long and one metre across, upon which sat a layer of glowing coals.

'Physics purports to tell us about the nature of the universe, but it is largely based on predictive equations that describe the universe in terms of mathematics: they create models to represent phenomena that we do not have the telescopes to physically look at. Just like chemistry creates models, formulae, of protons, neutrons and electrons to represent what we do not have microscopes to physically see. But the models are not the reality: only an attempt to understand that reality. And sometimes reality does not conform to what the models, the formulae and the equations say it should be.'

With this, he lifted a poker that was lying with its tip among the coals. Held aloft, the audience could see that the tip was red hot.

'Science, in as much as it is a system of measurement, tells us that the temperature of these coals is four hundred degrees Fahrenheit.'

Helena then emerged from backstage carrying a plate upon which sat a piece of steak.

'This is what science tells us should happen when organic

flesh comes into contact with a solid at that temperature,' Lafayette announced, then placed the tip of the poker against the steak. We could all hear it sizzle, saw the smoke it gave off, and within moments could smell the cooked meat. The union's snack bar probably did a roaring trade in burgers shortly afterwards. Lafayette then dunked the tip of the poker into the water jug on the table. It emitted a high shriek as it was submerged, giving off a cloud of steam.

'On this occasion, the predictive equations have accurately described the outcome. But the equations don't always add up when human consciousness is thrown in as a variable.'

With this, he took off his shoes and socks and walked upon the glowing coals from one end of the tray to the other.

'Science does not have all the answers,' he said. 'And anyone who tells you it does is not practising good science. There is much to discover if we open our minds enough to take the journey . . . into the borders of the known.'

And with that, the stage lights faded to black. When they came up again, Lafayette was gone, leaving a room rocking with cheers and thunderous applause.

As I've said above, in many ways it would actually be comforting to believe that there was a simple explanation for the things that happen around Gabriel Lafayette (I'll reluctantly accede to his wish that people refrain from describing them as things *he* does). Otherwise, the ramifications about our world – and the way we observe and understand that world – are extremely daunting. Perhaps that is why sceptics cling to the belief that it must all be down to tricks: because science can't possibly be wrong, or at least can't be, as Lafayette claims, unequipped. They cling to this like an article of faith because the alternative is too frightening: precisely the behaviour and motivations the sceptics disdain in the religious.

I've frequently heard Lafayette declaimed by sceptics as a charlatan who is only in it for the fame and fortune. Sceptics, we are told, only go by the evidence – except when it suits them. Lafayette does not lay claim to being much of a showman, but for someone allegedly only interested in fame and fortune, he's not much of a self-publicist either. He could have made a mint, could have built a *career* upon what happened at Glassford Hall, especially given that there exists documentary proof. Just imagine the book deals, TV interviews, publicity tours that might have ensued. However, he was just as reluctant as Bryant Lemuel to let the story go public, which is why it was only recently, amidst the scorn and sniping surrounding the proposed Spiritual Science Chair, that Lemuel agreed to allow me to break the silence.

'What happened was principally a private thing between Bryant and his wife,' Lafayette said to me a year ago, when I asked him if he had ever been tempted to go public. 'I wouldn't want it turning into Bigfoot or the Loch Ness Monster, or there being some lame "based on a true story" movie making his grief someone else's entertainment. Bryant shouldn't have to go through that. Nobody should.'

Nonetheless, I have discovered that there is one way in which Lafayette has knowingly misrepresented himself; a way that further illustrates where self-promotion lies among his list of priorities.

Shortly after my first interview with Lafayette was published, I received an email. In fact, I received quite a few in response to the piece, the majority of them positively gushing with praise and goodwill. This one, however, stood out not merely for being in the negative minority, but for its seething bile and disgusting language, most of which I cannot sully myself to reproduce. I would have deleted it and thought nothing further were it not for my own journalistic integrity, grudgingly brought to bear on this occasion, in relation to an allegation against myself.

*You bought all that down-home bull\*\*\*\* about Gabriel Laughable being from this po' white-trash background. Did you think to check any of that \*\*\*\*? The dogs in the street know he's a good little middle-class boy who's taking everybody for a ride.*

The email contained a catalogue of vitriol from someone who, I think it safe to assume, had a long-standing grudge against Lafayette, and I would have dismissed it entirely were it not for the one kernel of truth that stood out among the screeds of swear words and insults: I had not checked up on Lafayette's family background. In my defence, the piece was an interview, and only carried his words with regard to this matter, which I had no reason to doubt. Now, however, I did have a reason to doubt; albeit one that ought not to carry too much weight, given the clearly disturbed state of its source. Nonetheless, I had to investigate, if only so that I could satisfy myself that this and therefore the rest of the abuse in the email was founded on nothing more than spite.

As it was a delicate matter to directly question the veracity of a subject's account, and in particular when that account was of the subject's family background, I approached Mather about it first. He laughed it off, though rather bitterly, saying it came as no surprise, and was one of the reasons Lafayette was reluctant to be the subject of newspaper pieces such as mine.

'There are a lot of cranks out there,' he said, 'and a particularly high concentration around the area of the paranormal – on both sides of the argument. You should hear some of the stuff that gets thrown towards *me* by some of Gabriel's more enthusiastic fans, who don't understand why I'm not just giving him a wholehearted scientific endorsement. It's important you put this to bed, though. Gabriel's family is a sensitive area, and it's something he would *not* want any smears or innuendo around.'

Mather informed me that Lafayette had two surviving brothers: 'Louis and Remi were killed in Vietnam within weeks of each other, and Jean-Jacques died four years ago of a heart attack. He was sixty-three. Philippe is the eldest brother. He still lives in New Orleans, but he and Gabriel don't speak. Philippe was the closest to his old man. The guy's been dead decades but he still divides his sons. It's a damn shame. Which leaves Tobin, the youngest after Gabriel. Tobin and Gabriel get on pretty good, but Gabriel wouldn't want him drawn into anything like this. It's Gabriel's world, he chose it. Tobin didn't.'

'It would just be a phone call,' I assured him.

Mather said he'd see what he could do.

I had to wait a couple of days, then he got back to me with Tobin's number and told me he had agreed to take my call. Lafayette had been reluctant, but felt that I had been honest and fair in my dealings with him, and so spoke to his brother and vouched for me.

Tobin Davenport (it is only Gabriel who has chosen his mother's name) spoke to me from where he now lives in Los

Angeles. He is softly spoken, but despite moving west more than a decade back, he retains a pronounced Cajun accent.

He laughed heartily when I asked him what he thought of the suggestion that he and Gabriel had enjoyed a cosy middle-class childhood, before going on to talk a little about what his family life had really been like. He, like Gabriel, shied away from the subject of his father, but was happy to discuss other aspects of his upbringing, such as the neighbourhood they lived in, with its characters such as Ma Lawsey.

'Ma Lawsey was probably the closest thing Gabe had to a grandma,' Tobin told me. 'She loved *all* them kids in the neighbourhood, but she made an extra fuss of Gabe. But then, Gabe was used to being the favourite. Our mama treasured him like you would not believe, *cher*. Didn't like to let him far from her sight.'

'This was because he was the youngest,' I suggested.

'Oh, yeah. They's seven years between me and him, and I'm the second youngest, so he was always gonna be his mama's little pet, but what happened to Mama *between* Gabe and me made him a whole lot more precious.'

Delicately, I encouraged him to elaborate.

'Mama lost a child, died right in her arms after bein' born. Strangled by the cord, doctor said. Course, there was no doctor *there* – I'm talking later. This was in our house, where we was all born. Ebbe, Mama called him, though she never spoke about him. You'd think all those boys be enough, but no. Meant a lot, meant so much when Gabe was born. Gabe could trade on that, lot of folks in his position would, but he don't. Won't do it – out of respect for the memory of our mama, and out of respect for a brother he never knew.'

So captivated was I by Tobin's story – to say nothing of being entranced by his mellifluous voice – that I did not at first understand what he meant his brother could have traded on. Then the astonishing implication sank in:

Gabriel Lafayette is the seventh son of a seventh son.

# View from on high

I will endeavour to be magnanimous, as befits one who has discovered himself confounded.

Who? You, Jack? Say it ain't so!

I know. Not exactly my style, but in my current circumstances, I feel I can afford it. Gabriel Lafayette is not a man about whom one should make assumptions before gathering evidence. You only end up being made a fool of.

Once again, I must assure you, Jillian with a J is telling the truth: amazing as it sounds, everything she writes is just the way it happened. Mind you, it can't be said that she's telling the *whole* truth: there is a sin of omission, a minor detail regarding some hi-jinks that immediately followed Lafayette's departure from the stage at the KUU. It's possible she had swiftly left the debating chamber herself by this time and missed it, though it was bound to have been reported among the students she later spoke to. Perhaps it may have been a judicious and understandable editorial decision on her part not to grant publicity to what was little more than an attention-seeking student prank. I don't know, but unfortunately it may be a little late to ask her.

The only reason I mention it is that . . . well, as you'll discover, when reporting on this kind of thing, any and all editing is by its nature *in*judicious. You can't afford to leave anything out, no matter how apparently tedious, mundane or insignificant. It doesn't sound like it will make for good copy, but ask any sub-editor how often he or she has found the real story buried in the seemingly extraneous detail padding out what has been filed.

To be fair, I'm speaking with the benefit of hindsight, but that only further serves to emphasise what I'm saying: the significance of a point may take time to reveal itself. A student prank, perhaps predictable, certainly juvenile. If you were Jillian Noble, would you sully your amazing story about a remarkable man by making mention of some ne'er-do-well taking the piss? So let's not be judgemental. Yet.

But here's a couple of details that might alter your perspective.

One: Gabriel Lafayette was not the only person to walk on hot coals that night.

Two: the second person to do so was named Michael Loftus.

These things I know, and more, because I'm not the only dead guy with a story still to tell.

**II**

There are truths appropriate for children; truths that are appropriate for students; truths that are appropriate for adults; and truths that are appropriate for highly educated adults, and the notion that there should be one set of truths available to everyone is a modern democratic fallacy. It doesn't work.

Irving Kristol, godfather of neoconservatism

# The eyes of Laura Bailey

As the good book says, I was lost, but now I'm found. That's what it feels like, anyway. Or if not found, then at least in possession of a half-decent map and no longer holding the bloody thing upside down in typical ditzy-Laura mode.

I can't overstate the impact of what happened to me that evening in the KUU debating chamber. I have never felt like that before, not since childhood, and maybe not even then. I could talk all night and not come close to describing it. You could only understand if you'd been looking for something your whole life and somebody, some complete stranger, just plucked it out of the air and handed it to you as a gift. And I *had* been looking for something my whole life; most of my life anyway, though it was only when Gabriel Lafayette spoke to me that I even realised what it was. My wee brother Gordon died when I was six, when I was too young to make sense of what it meant to me, and definitely too young to understand what it was going to do to my mum.

I suppose I wasn't really equipped to understand what it did to me at that age, not even conscious of some of it. The thing I most remember is how I cried, or how I felt when I cried. It was so desolate. Every other time I'd cried, my mum or dad was able to tell me that it would be all right, that it would get better. This was something so dreadfully different: this was something that could never get better, and I'd never had to come to terms with anything like that. Gordon was gone, and would never come back. The closest thing I'd dealt with before was when my friend Rhona next door moved to Dingwall. I cried because she left, but she came to see us again, and so thereafter I always knew she might be back some day when I least expected it. What I couldn't deal with, because of its insurmountable enormity, was the notion that Gordon wouldn't be back, no matter how long I waited: that he wouldn't get better; that I wouldn't wake up the next morning or any morning and he'd be there in his bed. I was six, for God's sake!

But at that age, you adapt, don't you, no matter what is thrown at you: you're at an age when you're constantly having to accept the world around you and just get on with it. It's the adults that have it hardest. My mum never recovered. Even as a child, I was aware that she had changed. She had a sadness about her that never left. I don't mean she sat there weeping all day, though you would often find her weeping when she thought she was alone. I mean that even during happy times – Christmas, holidays, days out, even just playing out the back garden – she'd be smiling, but if you caught a glimpse of her when she didn't know you were looking, you could always see the sadness she was trying to conceal behind her smile. It was like during every happy moment, the first thing she thought of was her wee boy who should have been there. And that, as I say, was the happy times.

She and my dad . . . that was never the same either. I think what wore my dad down was that he couldn't help her. He couldn't take away the sadness. And I think she was so messed up by her own grief that she forgot about his. Unsurprisingly, I've read up a bit on this stuff, and it's common for mothers to feel like they're the only one to have lost something, because they're the one who carried the child. Unfortunately, something else that's common is for it to end the marriage. They divorced when I was thirteen.

I stayed with my mum after that. Never much question of anything else: she'd barely let me out of her sight since Gordon died. I loved my mum *so* much, so much. I'm sorry, I need a moment. I'll be okay.

We were almost inseparable, really close . . . but somehow never close enough. Not as close as part of me wanted – needed – to be. She loved me but I never felt like my love for her was enough. Like my dad, I couldn't take away the sadness either. When you're with someone you love, you want to feel like you're making them complete, like at that moment, as you hug them, there's nothing more that person wants. I never got to feel that way with my mum. I couldn't make her feel complete. I was always just a part – a loved and treasured part – of something greater that she once had but would never have again.

Most of the time when somebody close to you dies, what you're grieving for mainly is your own loss, isn't it? What you'll never have again, the love you can no longer give or receive. But when somebody dies young, you're grieving for what they've lost too, especially if they've died in pain or fear. When my mum died, I had all of that going through me, but there was something more: I was grieving for the fact that she had never got better after Gordon and now never could. Part of me always hoped that she would find peace again; that I'd one day see her looking at the world the way she did before she lost Gordon. So when she died, it hurt all the more to know that day would never come.

I was a mess after that, though not in ways that immediately showed. My dad had set up home with another woman, Josephine, so I moved in with them. She had been married before too, and had two sons, but one had already left home and the other was about to. Josephine was really good to me – we'd always got on okay – though being with Dad was weird, as much pain as comfort. Just being around him, so many little things you'd never anticipate would invoke memories and emotions. I sometimes felt like I'd be best on my own, or living with people who didn't know me. And, I suppose, that became what I aimed for. I got through my last year of school due to seeing it as some kind of finish line, as well as the comfort of routine: head down, concentrate on the lessons, the books, the studying, the exams. It meant there were fewer gaps through which all those pain triggers could slip. I got the grades I needed and headed here to Kelvin Uni.

I was seventeen. Dad thought I was too young, but he knew I needed this. I came here looking to lose myself and hoping to find . . . I don't know what, but definitely something. But I was wrong about it being better among people I didn't know. There were ways in which it was easier, or rather simpler, but it was only once I was on my own that I realised the extent to which I had been suppressing how much I missed my mum. I had numbed myself to cross that finish line, but now I was on the other side, I just felt lost and alone. I needed affection, which isn't so easy to get. Not as easy as sex.

Gabriel Lafayette saved me, no question. Saved me from

myself. It's no wonder the world of the psychics and the world of religion end up intertwined. Any Bible-bashing preacher would have been proud of what he did. It was a life-changing moment. Stopped a wayward young girl's downward spiral of promiscuity and self-loathing stone dead in its tracks. Tell me *that's* not a miracle.

Okay, first of all, like I told that journalist, I had never met the man before and there was no way he could have known who I was, never mind what had happened to me in my past. What he was able to tell me was therefore truly, astoundingly, breathtakingly, mind-blowingly amazing. However, and I cannot stress this enough, it was not the words he said or the things he knew that changed everything for me, but how I felt. Or more accurately, *what* I felt.

It was like an avalanche, a sudden overwhelming onslaught of all these emotions I had suppressed for years, unleashed and now unstoppable: emotions about my mum and about Gordon, some of them buried so long but still raw, undiluted, like they'd been in suspended animation. And I mean good emotions, things that it was *good* to feel.

I remembered Gordon more vividly than ever. Most of my life I just had these snapshots, mostly corresponding to actual photographs of him that I used to look at; I'm sure my mum looked at them too, though we never looked at them together. But when Lafayette said what he did, I was suddenly deluged with memories of him, images, things he said, games we'd played. I felt the way I had done when we were together. It was the same with the thoughts and memories of my mum, along with this euphoric relief, this joy of remembering her, knowing her as she once seemed to me: happy.

But it was more than that: I didn't just experience memories and emotions, I felt both of them, felt their presence, what it was like to be with them, as vividly as had they been standing there beside me once again. I knew, I *knew* they were present, that they were somehow with me in that room, and I realised that was how Lafayette knew what he did. He was interpreting them, but we were both feeling them. I was sure of that.

What he gave me was a gift, an amazing gift. He gave me back my mother, my brother, and gave me knowledge of my mother's peace – not just in that moment, but for a long time afterwards.

I swear, if I'd had a chequebook on me right then, I'd have signed away all my savings in gratitude. If he'd asked me to sleep with him, I'd have been there in a heartbeat. I'd have done anything for him. Later I spoke to that big guy, Grant Neilson, and he said much the same – apart from the sex part, obviously. He said Lafayette had given him something invaluable, and he'd do anything in return. He was in tears, big burly macho guy like that, normally hanging out in the KUU bar having burping contests with his mates. He confessed he had only gone along in the hope of taking the piss. He left a changed man.

I was in tears too, this engulfing mix of sadness and joy: a good sadness, a healthy, cathartic sadness, in the midst of which I felt more happy than I had done in years. Years.

I sat there, transfixed, throughout the rest of the event. I barely remember any of it, in fact. I was just transported, cocooned in this state of grace. I do remember Lafayette walking on the hot coals, and thinking that he could probably walk on water too right at that moment.

And then, as you know, there was the one sour note of the evening. I was still a bit glazed over. My friend Gail, who I was with, was nudging me to get up because everybody was leaving, but I was still in a bit of a dream. I was staring at the stage when it happened. Most folk turned around when they heard people shouting, but it was over so fast, I'm sure the majority of them missed it. That's why there were so many conflicting accounts: people claiming it didn't happen, that he was huckled away before he could do anything, or that he only walked over the very end of the coals. But what I saw was this figure in a long brown coat run up the steps at the side and bound on to the stage, holding his hands in the air. He whipped the coat off and dropped it, then, as you know, went over to the tray of hot coals and proceeded to walk the length of it *on his hands*. He moved quicker than Lafayette – it only took maybe a second and a half – so he had almost made it to the end when the bouncers moved in. I remember seeing him being grabbed around the elbows and marched out of the hall, during which he was looking straight at me. The look on his face as he stared

61

at me, it was . . . you might expect me to say scorn, but no. It was almost apologetic. It reminded me of the way the nurses on the oncology ward used to look at me when I was leaving after visiting my mum. It was pity, wasn't it? Yes. Pity.

It jarred because pity was, right then, something I considered inapplicable: at long last. I was going to be all right. And yet his expression haunted me. I was going to say like the ghost at the feast, but this feast already had its ghosts, didn't it?

I didn't expect to sleep that night, but I was wrong. I had never enjoyed such a sense of release or of calm, so I felt both utterly drained and completely relaxed, and I was out like a light before sleeping thirteen hours solid. Thirteen hours! That was about half as much sleep as I usually averaged over a week. The next day, I woke up to a new world, one in which I had a lot of thinking to do, as all of the old one's rules seemed to have been rewritten overnight.

I felt wonderfully reassured, truly warm inside, that I had received this contact from my mum and from Gordon, and the thought of them being together again: if I could bottle it . . . But trying to reconcile all of that with the way I'd been taught the world works was a vertiginous thing to contemplate. I borrowed some of Gail's *Borders of the Known* DVDs and was utterly exhilarated by the possibilities Lafayette was exploring. The idea of universes or dimensions a molecule's width away really helped me to find a way of at least thinking about how these things could be.

The only downer was that once the euphoria and release had worn off, I wanted more. My mum and Gordon had been with me in the debating chamber, and it thrilled me to think that they could be almost by my side at any time: but why couldn't I feel them again, the way I'd felt them that night? Lafayette was the answer. He must be some kind of lightning rod or catalyst, I decided. I made enquiries about how and where I could speak to him again. You can imagine how that went. There were hundreds, maybe thousands of people wanting the same thing. I was, however, sent an information pack and a donation slip for his research foundation, and told that members would be given priority access at any future events or public appearances. I felt a bit stingy ticking the minimum box, after what he'd given to me, but I'm a student. And even being the minimum, a hundred pounds was still more than I could afford. Not a lot of nights out ahead of me *that* term. Though, as it turned out, I wasn't going to need quite the same socialising budget as before anyway.

I had started going to church again for the first time in years. I didn't really have much of a view on God either way: an indifferent as opposed to an agnostic. But after Lafayette, believing in the Almighty seemed a no-brainer. With the theory of an afterlife – or at least some form of tangible consciousness – beyond death having been unquestionably proven to me, it actually seemed quite frightening to think I might be in deficit with the Man Upstairs.

That wasn't the only impetus towards me cleaning up my act, though. Truth was, after that night, I didn't feel like the same person. Classic cycle: I'd end up in bed with people because it made me feel wanted, then I'd feel disgusted with myself, then I'd end up looking for sex again because I needed affirmation that I wasn't as loathsome as I sometimes felt. But now the cycle was broken, and I was looking for something else: looking for explanations, and looking for more contact with my mum and Gordon.

I didn't find those things in church, though. Not the C of S one I was going to, anyway. I thought if I had faith, if I prayed, if I believed, then that would bring me closer to them, or bring them closer to me. There was the odd time when I thought it might be happening, but it was only my imagination. Sitting in a pew, I'd find myself thinking about them in a quite pleasantly meditative way, but mainly this was because I was so disengaged from the tedium that was coming from the pulpit that my thoughts had drifted.

I needed the lightning rod, a conduit. A medium.

I found out that there was a spiritualist church in Partick and started attending the services there. When I say church, it was more like a church hall; I think it hosted Scouts and Girl Guides either side of the meetings. A pretty down-at-heel wee place, and thus not the most inspiring upon first impression, but looks can be very deceiving. It was nonetheless the site of some amazing things, not least the eclectic mix that comprised the congregation. You might assume it would be full of lonely old ladies with message-bags full of cream cake and cat food, but you'd be miles out. They rolled up in BMWs as well as Shanks's pony. All drawn to hear the lady herself: Mabel Wragg; or the Reverend Mabel Wragg, to give her her formal spiritualist title. And no wonder: the things that woman could tell were, well, inexplicable. Sometimes she answered specific queries from members of the congregation, and sometimes she had spontaneous, unsolicited messages for them. And I'm not talking about vague, one-size-fits-all platitudes here; often this was very specific stuff. A lady in front of me once asked if Mabel could help her find her engagement ring, which she was sure she had misplaced somewhere in the house. Mabel closed her eyes for a few seconds, then told her she would find it 'frozen in ice'. At the next service, the lady returned, almost tearful with gratitude, to report that she had found the ring indeed frozen, in the ice-cube tray of her fridge.

Another time, she successfully directed a very serious-looking businessman to the very floor, very section and very shelf of Waterstone's in Sauchiehall Street where he would find the important document he had accidentally misplaced there while browsing.

And if you think that's unbelievable, I haven't even mentioned the 'apports'. On a number of occasions, objects appeared in the hall out of thin air; but not just random objects – objects that had been missing, and even objects that their owners didn't *know* had gone missing. Car keys, bracelets, photographs: they just dropped out of nowhere to land on the floor in front of Mabel's feet. On my second visit there, something seemed to flutter down in front of her, and I utterly froze when she asked if there was a Laura Bailey in the hall. I didn't know anybody there, and nobody I *did* know knew I was going to these services. But then she held up this tiny white rectangle and said, 'I believe this must be yours.' It was my bloody university library card! I checked my purse and sure enough, it wasn't there. I'd have been in real bother without it, too.

Mabel always came out to the foyer to greet everybody before and after the services. She was such a warm and also very humble, unassuming woman. There was no charge to attend the services, which struck me as crazy, given what people would surely pay to see her do what she did. All she asked was for donations towards the fund she had for building a proper church. A lot of large-denomination notes went into that bucket, but you only had to look at the surroundings to see how much it was needed. This woman was trying to run a church out of a scout hall, for God's sake!

The only thing she charged directly for was individual sittings. It was a minimum charge of a hundred pounds, though you were encouraged to add what you could afford to the New Church Fund. She didn't do them very often, as she said they were very exhausting, so there was a waiting list: usually about a fortnight, but quicker if you were lucky, and quicker still if you were a regular, I was told. She had a lot of regulars, because she was reputedly as amazing one-on-one as she was when serving to the congregation.

I spoke to a woman who had come up from Liverpool to stay with a friend; she got a sitting after only four days because she was just visiting Glasgow for a week. Her actual sitting was therefore only her second ever visit to the church, and yet Mabel was able to tell her her late husband's name, when he had died and even what hospital he'd died in, as well as an important message asking for her forgiveness for his infidelity with her sister back in the sixties. I have to stress: this woman's friend had only moved to Glasgow the previous year, and this was her first ever visit to Scotland. There was no way Mabel could have known anything about her before she walked into the hall for that sitting.

When I heard about that, I knew I had to give it a shot. It had been six months since the event at the Union, and the feelings I had had that night were fading further and further into memory. I needed that lightning rod. I was skint, but I managed to cadge the money from my dad. I didn't tell him what it was for – he wouldn't have understood. I paid my deposit (fifty per cent) and got my name on the waiting list.

It was in the mean time that I happened to be back in the Union, having a coffee in the comparative quiet of the music-free Word Bar while I looked over some lecture notes, when I overheard a discussion at an adjacent table.

'There is definitely a kind of sixth sense, whether you want to call it that, or ESP or whatever,' a male voice was arguing. 'Something that lets us know things we could not by any other means know.' I glanced up and saw that it was Grant Neilson, the other major recipient of Lafayette's spiritual largesse that night.

'Bollocks,' declared a second male, whose face I couldn't see.

'Of course there is,' rejoined Neilson. 'Just the other day, I was about to call my brother in Dundee, and as I reached for the phone it rang, and guess what? It was him. And that happens all the time. Something inside you knows things before they happen, and you can't explain it.'

'I *can* explain it,' the other came back with a laugh. 'How many times have you gone to call your brother in Dundee, or your mum, or anybody else for that matter, and the phone *hasn't* immediately rung with them on the other end of it? Factor in also how many times your brother calls you when you *aren't* just about to call him, and you'll see it's merely a statistical probability that a certain percentage of those times he's going to call just when you're thinking about doing the same thing.'

'Naw, naw. It's got to be more than a random percentage. It happens a lot.'

'No, that's just because you remember the times it happens and forget the times it doesn't. The "hits" stick in your mind because they're memorable; while the "misses" are instantly discarded. The punter remembers the horse that wins. It's like how they used to say Scottish goalkeepers were all dodgy. Every time a Scottish keeper had a howler, it got cast up by the English pundits as further proof, ignoring all the times Scottish keepers had blameless games and ignoring the fact that goalkeepers of all nations have just as many howlers. Statistical probability. Bell-curve distribution.'

'Naw. It just proves that your sixth sense must come and go: sometimes it's stronger than others.'

'So it's strong when you guess right but weak when you guess wrong? Are you hearing yourself, mate?'

'I don't care about what the statistics say. Gabriel Lafayette has shown that statistics and data are unreliable when it comes to this kind of thing, because the way they gather them is flawed

66

so as to skew against the evidence of psychic phenomena. And reality doesn't always conform to the models and the equations the scientists lay down.'

'Yes it does. Gabriel Lafayette just uses science to put a shiny new ribbon around a stinky old jobbie. He talks about science and then grossly distorts it or completely ignores it. Take his fire-walking stunt, for example. He whacked a red-hot poker against a steak and said this was what happened to flesh at four hundred degrees, then claimed that human consciousness could somehow throw out all the equations. Utter rubbish.'

'So how do you explain the fact that he then walked across the hot coals? Are you saying it was a trick?'

'*I* walked across the bloody hot coals, and I did it on my hands.'

At this, as I'm sure you'll appreciate, I looked up again. I still couldn't see the face of the person speaking, as he had his back to me, but I knew who it must be. I don't know why, but I felt a chill, an unease run right through me.

'I never saw you do that, I've just got your word and a few conflicting accounts—'

'Listen, I did it. *You* could do it, that's the bloody point.'

'Are you saying the coals weren't hot? Because that poker was heated up by lying among them.'

'The poker was four hundred degrees. The tray was four hundred degrees. The coals were four hundred degrees. But coals are light and porous: they have a poor capacity to contain heat and a very low conductivity. The air in an oven is the same temperature as the metal ashet inside it and the pie inside the ashet: you can put your hand in the oven and even briefly touch the pastry without getting burned, because neither the air nor the pastry conducts enough heat. It's science, respectfully obeying those equations that describe reality. You want Lafayette to demonstrate that the human consciousness can skew thermodynamics? Ask him to walk barefoot over just the metal tray: I'll be first in the queue to come and see that.'

I remember Neilson pausing to chew over that one, as I was doing too. I hadn't thought about the fire-walk, to be honest: at the time, it really just washed over me.

'Yeah, okay, but even if that was just a stunt, it doesn't prove anything else. The guy was there to say thanks: it's expected of him to put on a bit of a show. Maybe you can explain that, but you can't explain the other stuff.'

'I could reproduce half the things he did right here.'

'Just because you can reproduce what he did using tricks doesn't mean *he* used tricks to do them. And anyway, you're talking shite. You couldn't possibly explain how he knew the things he did that night. He didn't know me from Adam.'

'Listen, I could tell you how he did just about everything he did that night. I'll start with the envelopes . . .'

Which is as much as I heard, because at that point I gathered up my folders and got out of there. I can't easily explain why, but I knew I didn't want to hear what he was about to say. Weird, isn't it? I simply felt compelled to leave, as quickly as had I been escorted out backwards by a couple of burly bouncers. I remember feeling pretty huffy and self-righteous about it, too: like I was walking out because I wasn't going to be insulted. He didn't know I was there, but there was the implication, wasn't there, that I was some kind of gormless dupe. Utter nonsense. As Neilson said, this guy might know how a few things could be accomplished by tricks, but that didn't mean Lafayette accomplished them that way, and there was no trick in the world that could explain what I had felt that night.

Unfortunately, nothing could recreate it, either. I had my sitting with Mabel Wragg, and must confess to coming away very disappointed. Don't get me wrong, she was pretty amazing in terms of what she was able to tell me: she knew about my mum and about Gordon, without me saying much at all. First thing she said, in fact, was: 'You're here because you miss your mother's love. And your mother misses loving you. She sees you, but she's got her boy to love now too.'

She told me my mum was proud that I was at Kelvin Uni, but 'mothers being mothers . . . she says you have to pull up your socks and work harder in your Politics classes'. I had just failed a Politics essay a couple of weeks before. I got a hell of a fright when she said that, because I could just imagine my mum getting on my case if she knew I wasn't doing well in something – especially if, as I'd admit in this case, it was down to not putting enough elbow grease into it.

However, that was the only time I felt anything like a connection to her, despite Mabel knowing so many things. There was information, but no such sense of presence. I came away feeling really deflated. Disproportionately so: I felt so low, so disappointed. I had just heard some amazing things, many of which confirmed what I had learned from Lafayette, so I should have been happy, or at least reassured, contented. Instead I felt like I had lost something: maybe my hope that those feelings of contact could be repeated; maybe something worse.

Perhaps Lafayette had something Mabel didn't. It stood to reason, didn't it? That was why he was increasingly famous while she was soliciting donations so that she didn't have to operate out of a glorified Nissen hut. I thought about his TV shows, the astonishing possibilities he was exploring in the very borderlands of theoretical physics, compared to dowdy little homespun Mabel. And I thought – though part of me tried hard not to – of Lafayette's fire-walking: how some scrawny student in a brown coat had not only replicated it, but arguably trumped it.

Thoughts came into my head that were escorted out again by those imaginary bouncers. Increasingly I found myself asking why I had left the union cafeteria in such a hurry, asking myself what it was that I was running from.

*I could reproduce half the things he did right here.*

That was the remark I most remembered, the one the bouncers couldn't expel. It dogged me most of the summer. Then, when I returned for the new term, I saw a poster advertising 'The Amazing Magic of Gabriel Lafayette', and when I saw your name underneath, I knew that this time I had to hear you out.

# Jack screws up and makes everything worse

As everybody else has been at it, I suppose I should come clean and describe my own first encounter with the amazing Gabriel Lafayette.

In all seriousness, it was one of the proudest and most memorable moments of my life.

I was standing beneath the ornate oaken arches of the university's unapologetically opulent Maxwell Hall, a glass of Taittinger in my hand, looking unaccustomedly *un*like a doorman in my bow-tie and black DJ. There were waiters in waistcoats and waitresses in kilts smilingly ferrying the fizz upon gleaming salvers, the pale bubbling fluid in the glasses reflecting soft gel-tinted hues from subtly concealed spotlights, while high above upon glacial chandeliers, dimmed bulbs glowed so faintly as to illuminate little more than themselves. The faces of sharp-eyed luminaries sternly scrutinised from their vantage points upon the walls: giants of science and academe preserved in oil, spanning the six centuries that Kelvin University had been a renowned seat of learning. A string quartet played Bach upon a dais, while all around, tables glinted with silver, glass and china. All of which will naturally have you wondering: how did I get past security?

To which I reply: get it up ye.

No subterfuge, fraud, deception or acrobatics required. I wasn't merely a legit guest; this none-too-shabby wee soirée was, I'll fucking well have you know, being held in my honour. Or in honour of the office I was holding, anyway. So go on, take refuge in pedantry if you must, cast any aspersions you like, the tickets all had my name on them. It was Friday night on the first week of term. I had been elected rector towards the end of the previous term, but the business of assuming the mantle (whatever form that might take) didn't begin until the commencement of the new academic year.

To reiterate, get it *right* up ye.

I was surrounded by beauty, elegance and finery, but none of it could match what was to my eyes the most beautiful, elegant and fine adornment the room could have. She was standing in a light but exquisitely clingy peach dress, her Titian locks hanging between her exposed shoulder blades, where it almost but not quite succeeded in concealing the straps of a matching silk camisole. But the most dazzling thing she wore was a smile, a special one just for me that said: 'I love you and it's going to be all right.'

A bit purple for me, I know, but that's how I felt right then, and my current circumstances do tend to accentuate the emotional. Sarah had been through something very rough – we both had – and come out the other side, and it was just one of those times when you look at each other and are mutually conscious of all the good and bad that has brought you to be standing right there, right then.

By 'right there' I don't just mean the Maxwell Hall, though it felt curiously appropriate, a private acknowledgment of a new chapter in our lives that had seen us both, after so long in Edinburgh, find ourselves with roles at Kelvin University. Sarah got there ahead of me, by way of the research job she had taken with a pharmaceutical company after leaving medicine. Or didn't you know? Hard to believe you could have missed it, but then I'm forgetting, that story didn't get quite so much coverage as the one a few years back about her and the surgeon. You'd have needed to look a bit further through the paper to find it, but it was there, even in the red-tops. That, after all, turned out to be largely the point of the whole squalid exercise. Allow me to explain.

Doing what Sarah's been doing for over a decade, there's a price to pay, a cumulative psychological bill, with compound interest. You can't clock off at the end of the day and leave the job behind, not when the job involves dealing with people on what is frequently the worst – and sometimes last – day of their lives. Ask yourself: have you ever encountered someone whose world had, merely a moment ago, truly fallen apart? Even if you weren't close to them, it still shook you, didn't it? Stuck with you, so that you can vividly relive their pain, even years later. Now imagine having an encounter like that several times a week. It's like a kind of emotional direct debit: taking a little bit all the time, which you feel you can afford at first, but gradually it eats into your reserves. And then, just when you feel you've nothing left to give, that's when you get hit with something far worse than you've ever had to face before.

Sarah quotes the Samuel Shem axiom about practising hospital medicine: 'They can always hurt you more.'

They hurt her pretty badly one Friday night about two years ago, when she was on call at the Royal Victoria in Edinburgh. If you're wondering how I can describe these events in such detail, it's because I've been over them a lot, for reasons that will become apparent soon enough.

Ten thirty, she gets called to the Resuscitation Room. RTA, Ford Ka versus oak tree. Seventeen-year-old driver dead at the scene, his fifteen-year-old sister brought in by the paramedics with head and chest injuries. Sarah and the surgeons are in theatre with this girl for two and three-quarter hours. She doesn't make it. It's the chest injuries that do it. Parents are outside. Sarah has to tell them, but worse, the kid's carrying a donor card, so she has to ask consent for that too.

Two forty in the morning, she's on her way to the Intensive Therapy Unit to check up on a twenty-two-year-old she anaesthetised for a below-knee amputation earlier in the day. Industrial accident. The guy's got a part-time contract with Raith Rovers, an open secret he's going full-time and signing for Hibs in the transfer window. Sounds like I'm laying this on, doesn't it? Welcome to Sarah's world: this is what it's like. Savage, bleak irony comes as standard.

And they can always hurt you more.

Her bleep goes off: Resus again. This time it's an eighteen-month-old with meningitis. He's septic, deteriorating fast. Sarah leads the effort to stabilise him enough for transfer to Paediatric ITU. After almost four hours, it's obvious that this isn't going to happen. Sarah hands the child to his mother, so that she can hold him, so that he can die in her arms. That's what they do in situations like that.

There's some internal source – some combination of adrenalin, psychological displacement, intense focus on the job in hand – that keeps Sarah together until morning and through-out the drive home, where she collapses into a sobbing heap on the end of the bed. I've seen it a hundred times. That night, however, it fails her.

The breakdown comes at around eight thirty a.m. Nothing dramatic, just a quiet, private descent into beaten, shattered, snottery weeping in a ladies'-room cubicle. At that point, it would be fair to say, she feels like she has nothing left to give. Fortunately, she's free and clear in half an hour. However, when you're on call, that last half an hour is a long time. And they can always hurt you more.

It's a little after nine. She is writing up some paperwork and already dreaming about her bed when her bleep goes off once more. A&E again.

Sarah makes her way into the resus room past two anxious-looking parents. She finds a boy in his early teens dressed in a mud-spattered rugby strip, attended by a surgeon, a nurse and one of the paramedics who brought him in.

'His name is Kerr Whelan,' the paramedic informs Sarah while the surgeon, Robbie Stewart, examines the boy's abdomen. 'Took a sore one and collapsed at early-morning training on The Meadows.'

'I think he's ruptured his spleen,' Robbie says. 'He's haemo-dynamically unstable. We need to get him to theatre immediately.'

The parents are called through and given the latest. As the kid is only fourteen, they need to consent before he is taken to surgery. Robbie explains that an ultrasound has shown that the kid is bleeding into his abdomen, so they're going to have to perform a laparotomy and probably a splenectomy.

And here's where it starts to get all kinds of interesting.

'He can't have blood,' the father says.

Sarah feels a tightening in her own abdomen at this point as she shares a very quick glance with Robbie. They both know what's coming next, and they also both know their jobs have just got massively – and utterly unnecessarily – more difficult.

'We're Jehovah's Witnesses,' the mother adds, confirming the worst. 'He can't have anyone else's blood, or any kind of blood product.'

Ooooookay.

You may be wondering why not. Don't even begin to go there. Trust me: you could read the Bible back to front and you'd still be wondering why not. That's unless you've got an edition with an extra verse about Jesus throwing the money-changers and the Palestinian Blood Transfusion Service out of His Father's holy temple. Like every other insanity that claims sanctification from the Good Book – racism and homophobia, for instance – it takes a very singular and extremely elastic feat of interpretation to get from the source material to the doctrine. But don't take my word for it, read it yourself. It's in Acts of the Apostles, Chapter 15, Verse 29. 'You are to abstain from food sacrificed to idols, from blood, from the meat of strangled animals and from sexual immorality. You will do well to avoid these things.' That's it! I've read over that verse very carefully a great number of times and I'm fucked if I can find mention of platelets, plasma, red cells, white cells or haemoglobin anywhere.

But if the Bible isn't reason enough, there's always the dangers to consider. The Flatnoses' literature on the subject includes stories about people who have had transfusions suddenly experiencing criminal urges, such as the desire to steal, rape or murder, because the poisons that produce these impulses are in the blood. Suspiciously, neither the *BMJ* nor any other reputable medical journal has ever printed a paper on this amazing discovery. Conspiracy? I'm saying nothing.

It's just ignorant, primitive Bronze Age thinking: a combination of squeamishness and superstition, and for my money the quintessential exemplar of religion's main practical impact on the human race: irrational beliefs making life harder than it needs to be. But there I go, ranting again. You don't want to read me editorialising, you want me to get on with the story. Unfortunately – very unfortunately, as you'll learn – the above ranting *is* part of the story. My part. Also known as 'the bit where Jack screws up and makes everything worse'.

Robbie decides he needs to raise the stakes.

'There is a very real danger that Kerr may die if we don't give him blood. He's lost some already and he's going to lose more in surgery.'

'You don't understand,' the father replies. 'If you give him blood, it will be like he is dead to us anyway. He won't be admitted to Heaven. He will be expelled, no longer able to call himself Witness. If you are given blood, you are shunned by the church.'

See? It's all about love, community, togetherness.

The mother's face is the thing that haunts Sarah ever after. She's being told her son may die if she doesn't consent to a transfusion, and her pain and fear are writ pitiably large. But there's no doubt there. She doesn't look torn, just wounded, grieving. If her son is going to die without a transfusion, then . . . her son is going to die.

Sarah pulls Robbie a step back.

'He's fourteen,' she says.

Robbie nods. He turns to the parents. 'Mr and Mrs Whelan, your son is under sixteen, which means that legally we don't require your consent. We're taking him to theatre.'

At this point, both parents all but throw themselves between Robbie and the trolley their son is lying on, almost knocking over the nurse.

'This isn't just a matter of our beliefs, Doctor,' Mr Whelan says. He is pleading, almost supplicant. 'These are Kerr's beliefs too.'

Sarah has a look at Kerr. He's lying clutching his stomach, paler by the minute. The nurse, Fiona Caldwell, is leaning over him, talking to him, her back to Sarah. Sarah can't hear what she's saying and can't think what she could possibly be asking a patient in his current state, when to her horror she realises.

'I don't want blood,' the kid says, his voice a dizzy croak, eyes rolling, unfocused. 'I'm not allowed it.'

'There, you see?' Mr Whelan implores, his eyes almost popping with his vehemence. 'It's against Kerr's wishes. You can't do it if he doesn't want it.'

By now, a couple of orderlies have arrived to take the kid to theatre.

Sarah and Robbie try to lead the parents away from the trolley, but they aren't for moving. The kid's eyes have closed now.

'Kerr's fourteen,' Sarah counters. 'Legally he's a child, and we have to—'

'He's Gillick Competent,' the father interrupts, indicating that, like many Flatnoses, he's read up on all the current literature. Gillick Competence is the measure by which it is decided whether a minor has sufficient grasp of matters to give informed consent on his own medical treatment. It came about due to the efforts of Catholic anti-abortion activist and mother of ten (I'm saying nothing) Victoria Gillick in attempting to prevent doctors prescribing contraception to under-sixteens without parental consent. 'There are a large number of doctors happily encouraging children to be promiscuous,' Gillick said, and she was spot on. Child Promiscuity Encouragement had up until then been a required course in GP training, though many believed this was purely because the compulsory CPE clinics helped fill up the schedules, GPs being well known for having way too much spare time on their hands. (Well, if the Flatnoses are allowed to go making shit up to bolster their point, so can I.) Gillick failed, and in a highly entertaining irony, her name is now invoked every time a GP prescribes contraception to a girl under sixteen.

Her name being invoked by Mr Whelan was less amusing.

'Kerr understands the issues,' he assures them. 'We've discussed these things many times.'

'He did understand,' Fiona chips in helpfully, with a blank, gormless, what-can-you-do? expression. 'I explained to him that he might need a transfusion, and, well, you heard him. He said—'

'Shut up,' Sarah snaps, provoking a look of supreme, incredulous outrage from the nurse. It also does the trick: she shuts up, the better to shrink into her huff and start composing her grievance letter in her head.

'You can operate without giving him blood, can't you?' asks Mr Whelan. His wife looks a little more torn now, like this unforeseen glimmer of light has inflamed instincts that are likely only to cause her more pain. It's as though she can barely dare to hope. The poor woman has to be suppressing so much in the service of her faith that she'd almost rather just be resigned to despair. At least her religion has coping mechanisms for that.

'We can operate,' Robbie says. 'But realistically—'

Mr Whelan cuts him off. 'There are documented cases in America of patients surviving with haemoglobin levels as low as two grams per decilitre. Hyperbaric oxygen given post-operatively has been proven to . . .'

Oh yeah, he's really done Jehovah's Homework. Truth is, there *are* documented cases like he said, but it's kind of the same as there are documented cases of people getting shot through the head and surviving that. Chances are, you won't be so jammy.

'Do we have your consent to operate then, at least?' Sarah cuts in, rather sneakily you might say, her disingenuous under-hand tactics deceitfully attempting to shunt attention back to the endangered fourteen-year-old.

'Yes, yes please,' Mr Whelan says imploringly. 'Do all you can. But no blood.'

While the orderlies are wheeling Master Whelan to the anaes-thetic room and Robbie is scrubbing up, can we all just take a step back for a second to think about what is really going on here and how absurd it truly is? This particularly goes for those in the 'we must respect people's beliefs' corner. People believe some remarkably stupid things, and most of the time we regard it as our responsibility to protect those people from themselves. Most of the time we call those people 'mentally ill', and treat them accordingly. If a person believes he can fly, and is heading purposefully towards the balcony of your high-rise apartment, do you intercede on the grounds that his irrational delusion will kill him, or do you leave him to it on the grounds that 'we must respect people's beliefs'?

Or to put it another way, imagine I pitch up in Casualty requiring emergency surgery and tell the sawbones I have a non-negotiable constraint due to being a member of a literalist Christian sect, much like the Flatnoses. Matthew, Chapter Six, Verse Three, I quote: 'But when you do merciful deeds, don't let your left hand know what your right hand is doing.' Surgery is, I explain, by any definition, a merciful deed. It is unaccept-able for me, as a Christian, to be the occasion of sin or of wrong for the surgeon. Therefore, in order that the surgeon should respect my beliefs and comply with Matthew 6:3, I require him to operate with one hand tied behind his back.

Somebody, anybody, tell me the fucking difference between that and the no-blood nonsense, please. Perhaps you could start the ball rolling by pointing out that respecting *my* absurd belief would give the patient a better shout of survival.

Up in theatre, Sarah is trying her best with acceptable fluids – saline and artificial starch solutions – while Robbie does his part, fortunately with the use of both hands. He performs a laparotomy, revealing that there is a lot of blood in the abdomen. With only clear fluids on board, there are not enough coagulation factors, so the kid is only going to lose more.

'We can't stabilise him without blood,' Sarah declares, merely vocalising what everybody knows because she needs to bring it to a head.

'The parents mentioned something about hyperbaric oxygen,' says Lesley Robertson, one of the theatre nurses. Sarah sighs pretty loudly at this point. Lesley's pal Fiona Caldwell must have passed on this wee nugget to her fellow nurse before Kerr was wheeled into theatre, which indubitably means she has also communicated how she 'consulted' the child, as well as the truly vital information that Sarah is currently in her bad books.

'The nearest hyperbaric unit is in Dundee,' Robbie says. 'This patient isn't fit for transfer out of this theatre, never mind out of the city.'

Sarah is looking at the kid and at the machines around him. The coagulation issue is critical. The kid is oozing blood from all manner of places because it's running too thin to clot. There's only one direction his haemoglobin is going to go from here, which means that without blood he's going to go into either the record books and all the subsequently updated Flatnose literature, or more likely the morgue.

'Get me six units of O neg,' Sarah tells Lesley. Sarah looks to Robbie, who, as she expected, is already looking back. He nods: he's with her.

The same cannot be said for everybody, though.

'You can't do that,' Lesley replies.

Which is when Sarah kind of loses it.

'Can't do it? Let me tell you about "can't do". I watched two kids die last night because neither I nor anybody else could do anything to save them. I *can* save this one. Get me six units of O neg.'

Lesley stands her ground. If there's one thing nurses can do brilliantly, under any circumstances, it's adhere strictly to protocol.

'There's no parental consent,' she says. 'And it's expressly against the patient's wishes.'

'The patient is fourteen and *dying*.'

'He was consulted and made a Gillick Competent decision.'

'Consulted? He was fading in and out of consciousness. He wasn't in a condition to even be assessed for Gillick Competence, never mind make an informed choice to die.'

'Fiona Caldwell asked him and he said he said he didn't want blood.'

'He said "I'm not allowed it". And we can vividly imagine who by. I'm not prepared to watch a child with his whole life in front of him become a human sacrifice to his parents' idiotic religion. Now get me six units of O neg or get your fat arse out of this theatre and send in someone who understands what the hell we're doing here.'

Oooh, fightin' words. Lesley, visibly simmering, nonetheless goes and gets the blood. This shouldn't be interpreted as her professionalism objectively rising above personal feelings, but rather the path of least resistance. Sarah has threatened her with repercussions if she doesn't toe the line, so she now knows her aforementioned fat arse is covered for the inevitably ensuing shitstorm. She was only obeying orders.

And then, a miracle happens. The kid's haemoglobin levels improve, his coagulation factors increase, he ceases to ooze blood from every minor crack, oxygen is restored to his ailing organs and he is haemodynamically stabilised enough to transfer to ITU. An utterly amazing recovery, I'm sure anyone would agree. True, all of the above happens because Sarah has pumped some new blood into him, but that doesn't make it any less amazing or miraculous, does it? Or is it only a miracle if something physically impossible takes place? I don't know, some people are awful hard pleased.

Happy day: the kid lives. The mother collapses in tears of relief on his ITU bed. Nobody says nothing. The parents, too overcome with emotion, ask no questions. It's around this point that they're most probably appreciating what truly matters in this world. Sarah and Robbie both make a sharp exit. They figure that what the Whelans don't know won't harm them; as the whole issue has been of sustaining beliefs regardless of evidence, then the belief that Kerr got through without a transfusion ought to be a piece of piss compared to some of the other things they have faith in. It's looking like a result all round.

Except . . .

Well, see if you can guess. It's the same answer you're looking for when you hear about those cases where the physician has assented to a suffering terminal patient's pleading wish to end her agony. Doctor ups the diamorph, patient dies peacefully and, for the first time in perhaps years, feeling no pain. Then the doc ends up in the dock. How, you ask yourself, did the authorities find out?

A big cuddly gonk wrapped in a red ribbon if you answered: 'Some fucking nurse with an axe to grind grassed him up.'

Lesley Robertson told the parents, and they demanded, as was their right, to see the case documentation. It's impossible to say for sure whether they'd have stuck with the ignorance-is-bliss position, but she made their minds up for them. They sued the health trust, and specifically Sarah.

Some relatives send chocolates when you save their loved one's life. To each his own. The Whelans sent a writ.

Most times, on its merits as described above, the case would never have made it to court. Kerr Whelan might have been Gillick Competent – and he was certainly well coached to give that impression on the witness stand – but he was not, nor could have been, assessed properly to determine this prior to going to theatre. Most times, however, the plaintiffs could not have afforded a lawyer as big-hitting (or low-reaching) as Jonathan Galt. In fact, the Whelans *couldn't* afford Jonathan Galt, but he worked the case no win no fee because: one, it was high profile; and two, he's a bonkers-again Christian with an agenda.

You know the guy, Bryant Lemuel's lawyer: gangly, super-cilious, utterly creepy, pops up as the legal spokesman every time a religious pressure group wants something banned. Kind of bloke you can picture enthusiastically operating the rack or strappado for the Holy Inquisition had he been born a few centuries back.

His tactic was smart, simple and effective. He claimed that

Sarah would have given the transfusion even if Kerr *had* been fully assessed for Gillick Competence because she had no respect for the Whelans' beliefs or the beliefs of any Jehovah's Witnesses.

But before getting to depicting her as a bigot, he had to trash her credibility. He threw that awful night's previous tragedies at her like they indicted her competence, as well as claiming that these 'disasters' had left her 'desperate to redeem herself professionally'. And that was before he even got to the medical arguments about Kerr Whelan's treatment.

As happens with just about every medical lawsuit, the plaintiffs' side produced a doctor of their own as an expert witness, his job being to testify that he'd have done absolutely everything differently and that there is a precedent for better outcome under the procedures he would personally advocate. In this case, it was a physician flown in all the way from the US to make out Kerr Whelan could have all but played the second half of his Saturday-morning rugger match with a haemoglobin of two. He just happened to be a Jehovah's Witness, but it would be beneath me to impugn his integrity by insinuating that his beliefs were infringing upon the objectivity of his professional judgement. Bryant Lemuel paid his ticket. Don't ask me how I know that, because even here on the other side I won't name my sources, but trust me: it's a fact. Lemuel isn't a Flatnose, but he's a great believer that 'my enemy's enemy is my friend'.

When he got Sarah on the stand, Galt asked her about her marriage, whether she was under stress because her relationship with her husband was in difficulties. It was just a sneaky pretext to bring up her well-publicised infidelity of a few years back, thus undermining her credibility and subjecting her to a wee spot of gratuitous humiliation before the court. So now she's no longer merely an incompetent doctor, she's a deceitful, incompetent slut of a doctor who was hanging on by her fingernails when she turned up to work on Kerr Whelan. Give her her due, though, Sarah kept her cool and destroyed his suggestion. She assured the court that Galt was miles out: we were very close, having come through a lot, and far from a source of stress, her marriage was a source of stability that helped her cope with the real stresses of trying to do a very difficult job.

Get that up you, we all thought. But that was because we didn't realise Galt was thinking several moves ahead.

He was building a case that sought to depict Sarah as prejudiced against Jehovah's Witnesses and against religious people in general. And Yours Truly was Exhibit A. The bastard dredged up just about anything in print featuring me being less than respectful towards religion (yeah, imagine how deep he had to sift), and must have been punching the air when he came across a piece I'd written about this very subject.

*It's just ignorant, primitive Bronze Age thinking* . . . Yeah, that one. Told you it was part of the story. . . . *the quintessential exemplar of religion's main practical impact on the human race: irrational beliefs making life harder than it needs to be.*

And he really kicked the arse out of my coining the term 'Flatnose', with regard to the cumulative effect of Jehovah's Witnesses having doors shut in their faces.

The court did hear the minor technicality that these were not Sarah's words, but he was claiming more than guilt by association. 'It is not hard to imagine the conversations that must go on in the Parlabane–Slaughter household,' he told the court. 'Dr Slaughter has already, on the witness stand, depicted her close companionship with her husband. Is she expecting us to believe that Mr Parlabane's choice of subject, and highly offensive take upon it, was not largely influenced by his wife's accounts and attitudes? After all, you have already heard Nurse Lesley Robertson testify that Dr Slaughter called Mr and Mrs Whelan's religion "idiotic", and how she talked about them making their son – their only and utterly beloved son – "a human sacrifice".'

That, I'm happy to say, was where Galt got tripped up: the human sacrifice bit. See, Sarah had a good lawyer too, in the shape of Nicole Carrow. We can't afford her these days any more than the Whelans could afford Galt, but I saved her life once and she takes a different view from the Flatnoses of how to respond to such favours.

Galt trashed Sarah and parachuted in his expert witness to talk about hyperbaric medicine, but his case was built largely on respect for beliefs and in particular the right to live your life by a strict interpretation of the Bible, no matter whether that clashed with the values of non-believers. Nicole seriously bollocksed that up for him.

She threw in Genesis, Chapter 22, where God demands that Abraham sacrifice his son to him during a rather revealingly insecure episode of divine brinkmanship.

'"And he said, Lay not thine hand upon the lad, neither do thou any thing unto him: for now I know that thou fearest God",' Nicole quoted. 'God stopped Abraham before he could sacrifice Isaac. God would not permit even his most faithful believer to kill his only son purely as a demonstration of religious faith.'

This was when she was able to wheel in Robbie: co-signatory to the decision to give blood, the surgeon responsible for Kerr Whelan's care, and son of a Church of Scotland minister. As a lifelong Christian, raised in the manse, et cetera, et cetera (and skimming over his failure to darken a church's door in two decades), he could not countenance allowing . . . you get the picture.

Nicole then switched the arbitration of our twenty-first-century medical decision-making processes from Bronze Age Hebrews to Bronze Age Greeks by invoking a chap by the name of Hippocrates, whose oath both Sarah and Robbie had sworn. She quoted that in court too. It starts like this: 'I swear by Apollo the physician, by Æsculapius, Hygeia, and Panacea, and I take to witness all the gods, all the goddesses, to keep according to my ability and my judgement, the following Oath.' The hope was that Galt might question anyone's professed belief in Apollo, et al, but he was too smart: he saw where Nicole was leading him and didn't rise to the bait.

Nonetheless, he still lost. To this day, I'm not convinced he ever really expected to win. My guess is that he really just wanted the fight. Getting the case to court and consequently all over the news was a win in itself. Like I said before, Galt thinks several moves ahead. He plays the long game.

Technically, you could say Sarah won, but sticking with the classical references, it was the epitome of a Pyrrhic victory.

It takes a considerable vocational commitment to get yourself through medical school, the slave labour of junior doctor rotas, the postgraduate exam marathon and on to the mere day-to-day soul destruction of working in the NHS. Nobody, therefore, could question the dedication of anyone who had reached Sarah's position. She had put up with a hell of a lot, but being sued for saving a child's life was the ultimate proof that they can always hurt you more. There was only one way to prevent that eventuality. She quit.

That covers the bad part of us getting here; though while Sarah's was the harder ride, at least she got the more dignified passage. Mine, while ultimately constituting 'the good part', was not exactly a garlanded procession upon a path strewn with rose petals flung from the joyous hands of well-wishers. Aye, I know, a real change from the way things usually go for me.

Given the dealings I've had with politicians and the other forms of human detritus associated with their profession, I had long ago sworn that nobody would ever see my name on a ballot paper. However, when I was nominated as a rectorial candidate, I was prevailed upon to accept by a sense of duty towards the greater good; or Sarah, as she is less formally known. She had been working in the Pharmacology department for a few months, enough to start getting a feel for the issues that were prompting discussion among staff and students, and one of those was the rectorship.

Contrary to the impression you might have got from Jillian Noble, not everybody at Kelvin University was cheering to the echo at the election of Gabriel Lafayette. Some of the more politicised students (apparently they still exist) – perhaps having had their ears bent by a few older and wiser campus heads – felt there was a need to re-invest a little more gravitas into the rectorship, as it was a role that ought to provide an aspirational figurehead for the students and a respectable public face for the university itself. Thus when Lafayette's tenure was coming to an end, there was a drive in certain quarters to propose a candidate whose name would carry sufficient weight as to enhance the post and firmly draw a line under the less academically desirable implications of his predecessor.

This isn't where I come in, by the way, so you can relax and lay off the guffaws.

The candidate approached – and who accepted with typical gratitude and enthusiasm – was Charles Alderton: esteemed zoologist, ecologist, writer, broadcaster, anti-poverty campaigner, Kelvin University graduate and, perhaps his most bankable electoral asset in this constituency, one-time children's TV nature-show presenter. He was the perfect nominee: serious but not dour, of unquestionable academic pedigree, a visible and un-selfish public campaigner on issues from debt relief to gay rights, the face and voice of countless acclaimed, challenging and frequently controversial science documentaries, and, of course, fondly remembered by adolescent students as the wild-eyed bloke in jungle fatigues who presented *Zoo Tube* when they were kids. He was a respected and popular figure, unlikely to mobilise much antipathy except among militant God-botherers who auto-matically had him on their shit-list for his outspoken atheism.

His election would not only augment the post of rector, but would also (as far as the Science faculty was concerned, though nobody spelled it out) function as a solid rebuke towards the attitudes that had prevailed in electing many of his recent prede-cessors. However, this was still a student election we were talking about, so the attitudes in question were hardly on the wane; and those who held them far less likely to even notice that they were being rebuked. Thus, the second nominee, and very quickly installed as favourite, was reality-TV star turned wild-boy rapper turned druggie wash-out turned has-been turned rehabilitated celeb on reality TV, Markus 'Mucous Mem' Brane.

So if the beard-stroking-inclined on campus intended their nominee as a rebuke towards the flagrantly lightweight tendency, then the flagrant lightweights were clearly lobbing back as big a fuck-you as they could muster towards the beard-strokers. Mucous could not have been a more appalling affront to their values if he had been genetically manipulated for the purpose. He had been third runner-up on *Big Brother*, on which his compar-ative longevity was widely attributed to his fellow housemates never nominating him for eviction because while he was still around they all looked relatively intelligent, clean, witty, inter-esting, considerate, mature, emotionally balanced and indeed fully toilet-trained.

It wasn't just his unique charm that the intellectuals were guaranteed to be baited by, but what he represented in terms of fast-forward disposable culture. He had, in the space of only two years, gone from nowhere, to *Big Brother*, straight into a chart career, followed rapidly by a nose-dive (and I really mean nose) into being merely a tabloid sideshow geek and latter-day cautionary tale, before his chemical rehabilitation was matched by the PR equivalent and he was flown off to Australia to take part in – and win – *I'm A Celebrity Get Me Out Of Here*. Following that, he was back in the charts and back not just on the covers of the supermarket glossies, but this time all over the supplement pages of the broadsheets as well, where the pseuds debated his consecration as the latest epitome of ironic po-mo cool: thick is the new smart. Or as some baffled wannabe-trendy Oxbridge fud in the *Telegraph* put it, 'acting like Mucous: it *is* big and it *is* clever'.

Battle lines had been drawn, and to some, the stakes were very high. Amid such white heat and unbearable tension – work with me here – there had to be contingencies. Stratagems were devised, tactics debated, hush-hush meetings convened. Some brilliant students were involved, not to mention several highly esteemed and internationally published academics, and together they proved precisely why they were (for the most part) forging careers in the sciences, as they clearly knew fuck-all about politics. In short, and I'm sure you'll agree this says it all, *I* was the beard-strokers' back-up plan.

Why me? Well, obviously, they were trying to strategically raise the bar, marginalising the celebrity/popularity element by making it seem a contest – and thus a post – for serious, committed and capable individuals. I was a respected journalist, bound to find recognition among students for my fierce integrity and tirelessness in holding both individuals and institutions accountable to the public, and . . . No, you're not buying this at all, are you?

I'd like to say it was considered that my part in bringing down certain vastly unpopular figures would strike a chord with the righteousness and idealism of the modern young student, but that would be even more of a reach than the first suggestion. Truth is, I don't even know why I was nominated in the very beginning: I never even met the guy who asked me, just corresponded with him via email. Malcolm Reynolds, his name was: science student, that's all I knew.

The reason I accepted – or rather, the reason Sarah told me to, and therefore the reason the beard-strokers were encouraging me to run – was, I will freely admit, an act of unashamed and calculated gerrymandering. I was in there to split the novelty vote.

Yeah. Told you they weren't flinging rose petals. Rent-a-gonzo, that was me.

It was true that certain individuals really *did* reckon it wouldn't hurt to have more than one serious candidate on the ballot, in order to make the students think that bit harder about whether they really wanted to put their X next to someone who made Paris Hilton seem a net contributor to human society. However, my true value in swinging the contest lay in a less distinguished capacity. It was a science student who had proposed me, and a few official campaign leaflets were produced and distributed on my behalf, but my most active and visible support came from the recently formed Kelvin University Cannibal Society. Suspiciously recently formed, in fact, but nobody seemed to notice. Whether I liked it or not – and I don't suppose many people expected I *would* like it – I became their adopted candidate, and they stuck posters all over the place advertising the fact.

My other credentials, whatever they might be perceived to be, were very quickly swamped amid this truly jubilant seizing upon the fact that I had, as everybody on the fucking island must know by now, eaten long pig for dinner at McKinley Hall.

And, of course, I was in on the whole thing. The crucial factor was that my candidacy had to look hijacked. Thus, by becoming the adopted candidate of some oh-so-wacky bunch of student pranksters, I became the novelty candidate to rival Mucous. Sure, the spoiled white-boy rapper might have punched Andrew Marr, shagged a couple of *FHM* cover girls, opened for Goldie Lookin Chain and snorted up a pyroclastic cloud of coke, but Jack Parlabane had eaten somebody! A cannibal for rector: that's much funnier than Mucous.

That was the plan, anyway.

In the end, they needn't have bothered. Perhaps the physicists ought to have calculated that in this fast-forward culture they so bemoaned, the highly unstable 'celebrity' isotope had a very short half-life. In the brief interval between his nomination and the election taking place, Mucous had already started to look sooo three weeks ago, according to the chatrooms and gossip mags. The kudos value of involuntary cannibalism was not calibrated.

Come the election, Alderton romped it, taking seventy-two per cent of the vote, a worthy and deserved triumph soured only a little by his dropping dead of a heart attack somewhere along the Amazon on the day of the count. This left the university with a bit of a problem. It was argued that plenty of rectorial posts had been held by prisoners, such as Nelson Mandela and Aung San Suu Kyi, who could never attend the universities concerned or even, in some cases, send so much as a letter to them: thus it was at those times merely a figurehead role, and therefore the ability to attend (or indeed the ability to breathe) was preferred but not essential. However, aside from the precedent it could set for future elections if death was ruled no impediment to candidature (vote Caligula for rector!), it turned out to be down in black and white in the university's constitution: no pulse, no post. The election must therefore go to the second-placed candidate, even though he polled only eighteen per cent of the vote, and even though his academic prowess was such that he'd need three guesses to work out which way a lift was going.

It was the beard-strokers' nightmare scenario writ large: stand up Rector Mucous!

'I'm right juiced abaht vis, for real,' he told reporters in response to the good news. 'An' I wanna give a big shout to all my bruvs at Kevlin University what bigged me up for vis award.'

Meanwhile, all of Mucous's non-bruvs at 'Kevlin' University were bracing themselves for a year of tabloid siege and mortifying embarrassment. Happily, though, before Mucous could set foot on campus to accept his 'award', he had first to set foot in the dock before a high court judge in London, charged with Class A possession, driving under the influence of drugs and alcohol, two counts of assaulting photographers, four counts of criminal damage to property at his now former record company's offices, and, of course, resisting arrest, which the polis throw in automatically like prawn crackers whether asked for or not. He got six months, and there was much rejoicing.

As mentioned above, many universities had accepted rectors

who were imprisoned for their beliefs, but as the only belief Mucous could be arguably being persecuted for was the belief that he ought to be allowed to do whatever the fuck he liked, a line was swiftly and gratefully drawn through his ridiculous name, and his candidature disqualified.

All of which left, with eight per cent of the ballot (I don't know whether that sounds better than 104, which is how many votes I actually got), the Cannibal's Choice, the novelty spoiler candidate: John Lapsley Parlabane. Thank you, thank you. You're too kind. No, I never lost faith. The people have spoken, who am I to argue?

Like I said, not the more dignified route. Though give me my due: my detractors might say it was nothing to shout about, but I managed to outdo George W Bush's achievement in getting comprehensively humped in an election yet ending up with the job anyway. *That* loser only came second. Hail to the thief? He's a fucking amateur compared to me.

I had bagged a post I didn't want, didn't deserve and definitely didn't merit. No lap of honour, then, but an honour it most certainly was, and I wasn't going to lose sight of that. It meant a lot to Sarah, too. Her change of direction had been quite a wrench, not something undertaken lightly nor something about which she had the greatest of confidence. Christ, you try changing horses after all those laps. She didn't know whether she was doing the right thing by moving into research; only that she couldn't carry on doing the job she was in. Me landing a role – and a prestigious one at that – at the same university, she interpreted as a major indicator that things were working out for the best.

Okay, so it turned out she's in the middle of the bell-curve for her future-reading abilities, but that's how it looked right then. She was feeling positive, looking amazing and we were standing in this magnificent hall, listening to Bach and drinking champagne as we prepared to celebrate my new-found and ill-gotten respectability. As I said, it was one of the proudest and most memorable moments of my life.

Oh yeah, that's right: and that's also when I first met Gabriel Lafayette.

## Jack's wife screws up and makes everything worse

In retrospect, lovey-dovey thoughts of Sarah notwithstanding, my first meeting with Lafayette *was* a pretty momentous occasion, but then so was abseiling down a dead mercenary's intestines at McKinley Hall mere hours after heedlessly eating part of the chef. And though Lafayette was perfectly charming on the night, given how things were to work out, the memories of those two gory incidents make me feel considerably less icky than that of pressing the flesh with the New Orleans necromancer.

Lafayette was invited in his capacity as outgoing rector, though his making the effort to show up was nothing to do with observing any decorous formalities attending his departure. Rather, he was serving an agenda aimed at ensuring he'd have a role at the university for a long time to come.

A university dignitary with a distinct whiff of the mid nineteenth century about him was swooshing around the place like some caped protocol crusader, quietly but convincingly urging us to gather around our allocated tables. Unaccustomed as I was to this kind of shindig, I had neglected to check the seating plan, so I swear it wasn't some posture of aggrandisement-seeking fake humility when I asked Sarah which table we were at, only to be told 'the top one'. Grand, I thought: like getting married again, except this time without having to put up with any relatives.

Thus it was only as I approached the table that I discovered Lafayette hovering behind the chair next to mine, accompanied by Easy Mather, as well as their new best friend and Lafayette's personal fluffer, Jillian Noble. Her book about him was due to hit the shelves very soon, and the serialisation had started in *The Mail*, in conspicuous support of his aforementioned academic aspirations. Noticing my approach, she smiled at me with all the warmth of a penguin's fart before demonstrably resuming her discussion with the university Chancellor, Sir William Kentigern, and the Principal, Dr Judith Rowe.

As soon as we reached the table, Sarah was intercepted by the Dean of Science, the ageing and skeletal but sinisterly predatory-looking Professor Niall Blake, who was allocated the seat to her right. He completely blanked me, going straight into shop-talk with Sarah about protocols for a study he was designing. I was surprised, but only slightly: it wasn't the first, second or even hundredth time a colleague of Sarah's had come up and talked to her without acknowledging that I was even there. Non-doctors are largely invisible to a certain (and sadly prevalent) strain of medic, triaged out of their vision on the grounds of irrelevance, and since she had moved into research, I found the same visual defect to be common among scientific academics. The reason I was surprised at all was that I did think he might make a special exception given the occasion, what with me being the reason we were actually having this dinner. Then it dawned on me that it wasn't really me he was ignoring: he had buttonholed Sarah as a convenient barrier against having to acknowledge the presence of Lafayette. I simply happened to be in the vicinity: collateral blanking. Whoever put the seating plan together must have been seriously taking the piss sticking the pair of them on the same table. Hats off to him, too: I'd have done the same thing – had I been safe in the knowledge that I wouldn't be sitting there.

Lafayette had a hand outstretched even as I watched Sarah turn towards the sepulchral dean. He had a bittersweet smile on his face as he cast a wry glance in the deliberately heedless professor's direction.

'You must be Mr Parlabane,' he said, gripping my hand.

I glanced openly at the place card on the table in front of me.

'They *said* you were psychic,' I replied, wanting to see if he'd take the huff. He didn't.

'My powers amaze even myself sometimes.'

'Just so long as you don't bend all the cutlery before we've had a chance to eat.'

'No, I don't do psychokinesis. Even if I did, I'd lay off the knives and forks. Wouldn't want a man of your appetites getting too hungry, now, would we?'

'Touché. I'd say you'd done your homework, but there can't be many people in this room who *don't* know that about me.'

'Oh, I've done my homework. That's how I do all my tricks – leastways according to the likes of your wife's boss over there.'

'So what did your homework uncover? What else do you know about me?'

'About the same as everybody else in this room. At this stage, leastways.'

'At this stage?'

'Yeah. You never know what the spirits may tell me over dessert.'

'You're assuming I'm a teensy bit sceptical about this kind of thing, then?'

'I find it sensible – not to mention polite – to regard it as the default position in people until indicated otherwise. Plus, I read your mind.'

See? Told you: charming, funny, self-deprecating, personable. You'd like him if you met him. I liked him. Until he started trying to kill me, obviously, but so many people get around to that sooner or later, latterly I have endeavoured not to let it bias my overall impressions.

'Are you out to convince me, then?' I asked him.

'I'm not out to convince anybody. Not many people change their minds about this area, whichever side they take. If Easy there ultimately falls on my side, it will be one hell of a first. So no, I'm not evangelising. I've experienced some very weird things, and I'm in the business of looking for explanations. Not so different from yourself, from what I gather.'

'In my experience, the explanations usually come down to some chancer having his eyes on the prize.'

'Which is where we cross over again, believe me.'

'So you acknowledge that a lot of so-called mediums are faking it?'

Lafayette laughed. 'Acknowledge it? Mr Parlabane, in my experience, the term "fake medium" is practically a tautology. The only real distinction to be drawn is between the ones who know they're fakes and the ones who are also deceiving *themselves*. What I'm still trying to work out is whether the latter also describes me.'

I noticed that everybody was beginning to take their seats, in response to the gesticulations of the etiquette enforcer. The chairs were in a tight circle around the table. I stepped aside to let Lafayette squeeze in first.

'I appreciate your lack of presumption,' I said, sitting down, 'but I think you're kicking the arse out of it a wee bit with that. I've read an advance proof of Ms Noble's book, and there's some pretty remarkable incidents described. Glassford Hall, for one. Are you saying you could have been party to some form of group delusion?'

'I'm saying I don't make any claims for myself. Weird things happen around me, like knowing things I shouldn't know, hearing things – but that doesn't mean I'm the one doing anything. Maybe it will turn out everybody can hear these things, but right now I'm the only one listening. Maybe there are explanations, *within* science. That's what I'm determined to find out.'

'Explanations within science?' said a voice to my right. It was Professor Blake. His expression was so scornfully sneering that it seemed to exaggerate his already aquiline features until he resembled some grey-headed species of carrion fowl. I could picture him with talons, unhurriedly picking at Lafayette's disembowelled corpse. 'You mean like the explanation within science for how you can walk across hot coals?'

Lafayette's eyes widened a little, his only detectable reaction to the tone of Blake's interjection. He took a sip of mineral water – buying a moment, I thought – and was nodding before he swallowed it.

'Precisely,' he agreed, now addressing the whole table, Blake having deliberately grabbed everyone's attention to put him on the spot. 'The science behind it is exactly what I'm talking about here. It's a great way of illustrating the ways in which we restrict ourselves because of our ignorance, and because of our wrong assumptions, when scientific enquiry can open up what we thought was impossible. People are afraid to walk on the coals because instinct and experience tell them not to. We are afraid until science renders us an explanation, gives us a way of understanding it. *I'm* afraid: I keep getting the crap scared out of me by strange events. That's why I'm looking for explanations. What are *you* afraid of, Professor?'

'I'm afraid of charlatans being given the platform to con unwary scientists into ratifying crackpot mumbo-jumbo for which there is no reliable evidence. You see, Mr Parlabane,' he added, verifying that he *did* know who I was, 'what your rectorial predecessor' – and why I was here! – 'is angling towards, as irresistibly as gravity and twice as predictable, is the proposed establishment of a university chair dedicated to what he likes to call Spiritual Science. Also known, by any truly scientific definition, as Not Science; or plain old Bunkum.'

'I have to say, that is an incredibly arrogant attitude, Professor Blake, and one that surely flies in the face of true scientific enquiry.'

The interjection was from Jillian Noble, her face rather flushed with indignation and no doubt the effort of getting up the nerve to have a go at the grey-feathered raptor. He eyed her with a look of utter disdain, like this sort of indignity was the reason formal university occasions were a test of his endurance. Beneath the table I felt Sarah give my leg a squeeze. It was a gesture of affection, but it was a warning too: sit tight and stay out of this. Blake said nothing, so Noble felt sufficiently encouraged to press on. My impression was not that he was hearing her out, but that he considered it beneath himself to respond.

'That very absence of what *you* term reliable evidence – in the face of so much human experience – is one of the things the Spiritual Science chair would address. In the words of Werner Heisenberg, the German pioneer of quantum mechanics: "What we observe is not nature itself, but nature exposed to our method of questioning."'

I could hear Blake sigh with a degree of almost amused incredulity that she was telling him who Werner Heisenberg was. Noble failed to clock this, or perhaps ignored it, her eyes sweeping around the table. She knew she had the floor and was no doubt less concerned with convincing the impermeable Blake than with having her case heard by Kentigern and Rowe.

'Surely you see that this is a question of whether science itself is handicapped by the limitations of its own methodology.

Mr Lafayette made this point brilliantly on his TV series when he quoted the astrophysicist Sir Arthur Stanley Eddington. Imagine an ichthyologist casting a net . . . actually, it's best if you explain it, Gabriel.'

This finally did spur Blake into a response. 'I am sure we are all familiar with Mr Lafayette's preferred Eddington quote,' he interrupted before Lafayette could take the conch. Then, glancing dismissively at Noble, he added: 'Though Sir Arthur is more popularly renowned for another remark: one concerning monkeys with typewriters.'

Three waiting staff appeared with consummate good timing, laying down plates of smoked haddock mousse and crudités, their emergence camouflaging what might otherwise have grown into an uncomfortable silence. Noble gave Blake a vicious look that betrayed her own frustration at having her arse kicked more than it threatened reprisals. He also received an admonitory glower from Judith Rowe, the Principal. Play nice, it said. She glanced towards me, either reminding Blake of the occasion or saying 'not in front of the children', which came to the same thing.

Lafayette clocked this too, but he was not remotely interested in the subject being laid to rest, and Rowe had inadvertently fed him a new route back in.

'What do you think, Mr Parlabane?' he asked, while I had a mouthful of my starter. 'You're noted for having an enquiring mind, I reckon it's fair to say. If it turned out that the evidence-gathering procedures in an investigation might – and I stress might – be designed in such a way that certain details would always slip through the net—'

'The scientific method is not the "net" of Eddington's analogy,' Blake interrupted.

'Please, I was asking a question of our guest of honour, Professor,' Lafayette countered, smiling and polite in contrast to Blake's haughty abruptness.

I didn't much fancy being the ball in this wee game, and thought up a diplomatic cop-out about not being equipped to debate matters of science. However, that wasn't the response I gave, for two reasons. First, I could see this being interpreted as meaning 'ask the wife' and didn't relish the prospect of getting my hawmaws booted by Sarah later for dropping her into the middle of that one. Second, and more typically, I had by this point decided Blake was a self-satisfied wank and wanted to see him forced into fighting his corner a little. Lafayette, I reckoned, was at least prepared to argue his case, whereas Blake seemed to regard even debating the matter as beneath him. If that was the attitude he brought to science, then maybe Lafayette had a point.

So I weighed in, just a little. Aye. They're playing my song again: Jack screws up and makes everything worse.

I was subtle about it, I believed, ever mindful of the Sarah-hawmaws-docking scenario.

'I'm afraid I'm a wee bit out of the picture,' I said. 'I understand what it is you're disputing, I think, but I'm missing the here and now regarding the university. This is the chair Bryant Lemuel wants to fund, right? So what is Professor Blake's objection to it?'

Blake sighed, quiet enough for it not to be audible around the table, loud enough to convey his displeasure directly to me. He'd now have to descend bodily from on high and sully himself in discourse with the mortals. His eyes briefly locked upon mine, narrowed and steely to convey the message 'your card's marked'. Yeah, right. I should worry.

'You are indeed out of the picture, Mr Parlabane, and thus to be forgiven for getting it quite wrong,' he said, smiling thinly for the benefit of the table. I don't know whether any of them were buying it, but I didn't believe forgiving me for anything was high on his agenda. 'I am in no position to object to the establishment of a university chair, by Bryant Lemuel or anyone else.' Noble opened her mouth to contest this, but he silenced her with the kind of look with which a perching hawk regards a rodent. 'This university,' he resumed, 'like every other on these shores, needs all the investment it can get, particularly when it comes to research. So if someone such as Mr Lemuel has a spare two million pounds – that's the minimum – for an endowment, then he can establish a research chair whose work will be funded by the interest. In Mr Lemuel's case, I believe it is four and a half million he wishes to invest.'

Noble and Mather both nodded, but Blake's eyes were on

Rowe and Kentigern, who looked uncomfortable to the point of irritation, and I was about to learn why.

'When you're waving around a cheque that size, it is very difficult for someone in the Chancellor's or Principal's position to say no, regardless of how . . . controversial the intended subject of research happens to be. The only potential spanner in the works is that the proposed chair has to come under the auspices of a particular faculty, and that faculty must therefore be in approval. If the Psychology department, or the Theology department, or the Philosophy department wishes to take Mr Lemuel's chair under their umbrella, then, as I said already, I am in no position to object. However, Mr Lemuel, and his champions, such as Mr Lafayette and Ms Noble, are all adamant that this chair should come under the banner of the sciences. As it is *not* science, but rather bunkum, then that is why I cannot in good conscience allow that to happen.'

'But who are you to say what is not science?' Noble demanded. 'Surely that is one of the crucial aspects of what the chair would be seeking to undertake? That there *are* scientific explanations for certain hitherto unexplained phenomena, and therefore one of the big questions is why science hasn't yet found them.'

She had to wait for her reply, as the waiting staff returned to replace the starter plates with main courses and replenish our glasses. Blake took a large mouthful of wine, then milked the pause a little by following it up with a long gulp of mineral water too. Reluctant as he'd been, he now had the floor, plus the obligation of providing an answer, and he was making the most of it.

'Ms Noble,' he eventually replied, 'I will do you the courtesy of referring to what you describe by the term "meta-science", which is the study of how we carry out the practice of science. If that were at the root of this proposed chair, then I would be *delighted* to see it established under the auspices of my faculty. It is an area of vigilance and self-examination from which science can only benefit. However, the field of meta-science only interests Messrs Lemuel and Lafayette in that it serves their agenda of claiming that current practices are to blame for a lack of evidence, as opposed to it being the case that current practices simply filter out flawed or downright fraudulent evidence. If

97

they wish to carry out research that does not conform to those practices, and Mr Lemuel wishes to fund this, then by all means go ahead: but what they will be doing will not be science.'

I glanced at Lafayette. He was still putting on a diplomatically patient smile, perhaps biding his time to make his case. Mather, who had barely said a word since I arrived, looked subdued and disengaged, indicating that he agreed with Blake, albeit for different reasons, that there was little point in having this discussion again.

'So there is only one way of doing things?' Noble asked. 'And if it doesn't conform to your model, you can't call it science? Isn't that exactly what Eddington accused his hypothetical ichthyologist of? "What my net can't catch isn't a fish"?'

'There are a million ways of doing things,' Blake said, sounding a little exasperated, like he was fed up having to explain something over and over to a child. 'But there are certain principles that must govern any method calling itself science. The scientific method most basically involves gathering data to test natural explanations for natural phenomena. It is primarily a practice of observation and recording, then secondarily a process of hypothesis and verification, the latter again through observation and recording. How you observe can vary from looking with the naked eye to analysing the results of a sub-atomic event lasting a millionth of a second inside a supercollider. Just what is it that you think we're missing?'

Noble had no answer to this, but Lafayette decided this was the time to play his next card.

'The Heisenberg Principle, for one thing,' he said. 'That the act of observation interferes with the phenomenon being observed. The physicist John Wheeler put it best when he said that "even to observe so minuscule an object as an electron, you must shatter the glass and reach in. The measurement changes the state of the electron. The universe will never afterward be the same." The methods and protocols necessary to conform to conventional definitions may be precisely what is inhibiting the observation of the phenomena this chair wishes to research. Therefore we have to employ observation conditions that do *not* inhibit the phenomena, so that we can record them; then move towards, plank by plank, isolating precisely which of the conventional conditions were having an inhibitive effect. That in itself would lead us into exciting new territory.'

Kentigern was nodding, looking genuinely engaged by this rationale. Rowe by contrast seemed a little sour, eyeing Blake like there was no point in getting excited because she was looking at the reason why this – and the donation of a four-and-a-half-million-pound greenback – was never going to happen.

Blake was, for the first time this evening, grinning broadly as Lafayette spoke. Towards the end, he even began to quietly applaud. This did nothing to soften Rowe's scowl, so I suspected he was not on the road to Damascus.

'Bravo,' he said, laughing insufferably smugly to himself. 'Mr Lafayette, congratulations. I don't believe I've ever heard a pseudo-scientist state their aims so honestly. If we employ observation conditions that do *not* inhibit the phenomena, we will be able to record evidence of these amazing things. You see, Mr Parlabane, this is why Heisenberg is a particular favourite of the paranormalists. Wheeler too, though as he was still alive when they began invoking his name, he was able to state that they were wilfully misinterpreting him, and that the Heisenberg Principle only applied on an atomic or sub-atomic level; beyond that it is merely a metaphor, often of dubious propriety. But they insist on using the argument that observation affects what is observed, in order to explain why psychics can't perform their tricks under properly controlled test conditions. To that, Mr Lafayette is adding Eddington as a new twist on an old argument: that they'd find more evidence of amazing things if only the stuffy old scientists would stop insisting on controls. And you're damn right they would, which is why this chair will be part of the science faculty over my dead body.'

Lafayette finally lost his air of affable calm and glanced, with a mixture of hurt and exasperation, towards Rowe and Kentigern, before turning back to Blake.

'That is just . . . I can't believe after all this time we're still . . . What Professor Blake is describing is just a gross misrepresentation of what this chair seeks to undertake. I mean, to the point of libellous,' he added stiffly, barely suppressing what had evidently been a long-growing anger.

Perhaps in an effort to mollify Lafayette, Mather chose this moment to weigh in calmly himself.

'I can assure Professor Blake we are not for one second talking about carrying out experiments without proper scientific observation. I worked under Karl Creedy at Reed University, and he wrote the book on protocols for this sort of research. We have members of the science faculty on board and willing to act as strict observers and supervisors. Dr Kline from the Physics department and Professor Ganea from Organic Chemistry would be involved at every level and every juncture, with unfettered access. I mean, with respect, do you think the three of us would be prepared to put so much effort in – not to mention spending valuable research funds – only for our work to be instantly discountable by the scientific community due to our methods?'

'Damn straight,' Lafayette agreed. 'What would be the goddamn point? It's true I've proposed experiments to determine what conditions do or do not inhibit psi phenomena, but make no mistake, the scientists would be recording everything, *particularly* what controls were present or absent. How the hell would we learn anything otherwise?'

Lafayette shook his head and looked appellantly around the group. He made to go on but his words dried in his throat. He took a drink of water and sat back in his chair, fuming.

Kentigern was gazing sympathetically towards him, grimacing a little at the atmosphere around the table.

'Forgive me,' Kentigern said softly. 'I'm aware there is an intractable conflict here, so compromise is ultimately going to have to be found somewhere. I therefore have to ask, wouldn't you be able to carry out this same work under the auspices of another department? Surely it would be peer-reviewed by the scientists and live and die on its merits just the same?'

Lafayette sighed, rolling his eyes. Blake didn't even attempt to hide a degree of satisfaction at this, the nub of his opponent's discomfiture.

'But it *wouldn't* live or die on its merits, any more than it would be peer-reviewed. You only have to listen to Professor Blake here to get an idea of what kind of resistance we would be up against. We need to win this battle once so that we're not fighting it over and over again. If science is what we are doing, then science is what it deserves to be called.'

'And if science *was* what you were doing—' countered Blake, but the now indignant Lafayette steamrollered his dispassionate glibness.

'My God, man, can't you overcome your prejudices for one moment and see that what we are about here is serious? I'm the last one who needs to be told about the charlatanry this field has long been notorious for, but that is why I have endeavoured to immerse myself in science: to cut through the bullshit and find out what is truly worth knowing. The history of science is also riven with paradigm shifts. Who are you to say that the next one won't come from a field you refuse to even contemplate examining? Tread carefully, Professor. I would remind you that the president of the Royal Society said, as recently as 1895, that "heavier-than-air flying machines are impossible". That president was Lord Kelvin, after whom this very university is named.'

There ensued an uncomfortable silence, and not merely in response to Lafayette's temper. I saw Rowe wince on Lafayette's behalf as he spoke. His point had been a good one, but he'd tripped up at the end. She decided it would be better coming from her than letting Blake skewer him with it.

'The university is actually named after a river,' she said quietly, 'and was standing here for centuries before Lord Kelvin was born. But that should not detract from the validity of Mr Lafayette's point.'

Blake shrugged. 'True,' he said. 'And Mr Lafayette's point is also true. However, the history of science is also riven with daft notions that were soon forgotten about when their proposers failed to produce any reliable evidence to back them up.'

'And if that is what we discover, then so be it,' Lafayette said, opening his arms. 'But it seems the difference between you and me is that I'm prepared to find out for myself.'

'And at what point would a lack of evidence bring you to the conclusion that what you were looking for doesn't exist? Or would you just keep plugging away indefinitely, looking for a tiny flake that you believe might herald the motherlode somewhere upstream?'

'I can't possibly answer that question, Professor Blake, as well you know. Nor should I, as it works on the prejudicial assumption that there is nothing to find even before we have begun looking. And yet you're the one calling *me* unscientific.'

Blake seemed to be enjoying Lafayette's indignation. He reminded me of a big kid winding up his wee brother because he liked watching him lose it and didn't reckon he carried any threat. It wasn't pretty, and Rowe evidently wasn't impressed either.

'I have to say, you're not covering yourself in glory here, Niall,' she told him. 'If Mr Lafayette is prepared to participate in tests under scientific conditions, with the supervision of Mr Mather, Dr Kline and Professor Ganea, then I'm sorry, but now I have heard the details, I can no longer see how you can justify your objection. You gave me the impression that you believed this work would be carried out with a lack of adequate controls, but what is being proposed *is* scientific if all of the conditions are accurately recorded. Surely you aren't meaning to impugn the integrity of not only Mr Mather, but Dr Kline and Professor Ganea also, are you?'

Blake suddenly looked very rattled, the implications of Rowe's words making him realise that all the time he was smugly dismissing Lafayette, he was actually being outflanked and talking himself into a position from where he could only lose the argument.

'I would not, for a second, question the integrity of the colleagues you mentioned, nor our visitor from Reed University,' he insisted, his face flushed with an adamant sincerity. 'In fact, it is all of their reputations I would fear for, were they to be delivered into Mr Lafayette's hands. The benefactor behind this chair strikes me as over-enamoured with Mr Lafayette, and consequently I detect a very real danger of the tail wagging the dog. I fear Mr Mather would end up less in control of the procedures than he would wish to be, and than indeed he would believe himself to be.'

Mather's expression betrayed that Blake had bull's-eyed a not-so-minor insecurity. After all, Bryant Lemuel wasn't standing by to fork out millions because he was dead impressed with Ezekiel Mather.

'Scientists are easily fooled because they are logically minded and methodologically predictable,' Blake went on. 'They would be highly manipulable in the hands of a skilled deceiver, which is what I believe Mr Lafayette to be.'

Lafayette shook his head. 'I have already acknowledged the deceit that has gone before me in this field, but I should not be judged and indeed condemned for the sins of others.'

'Quite right,' Rowe agreed. 'Niall, you are accusing this man of dishonesty in research work before he has even begun to participate in it. Are you the one claiming to be psychic now? Shouldn't you wait until you have some *evidence*, or is the scientific method not applicable to your decision-making process?'

'I don't *have* any evidence, and nor will there be any: that's the point. I don't know how he does his tricks, which is why I, like Heidi Ganea and Rudi Kline, would be powerless to detect his deceptions, just as Mr Mather has been powerless to detect them up until now.'

'So you're saying you find a *lack* of evidence to be the most compelling argument for your case?' weighed in Jillian Noble triumphantly. 'Is that not roughly the same rationale as you were ridiculing Gabriel for?'

'The inability to detect legerdemain is what keeps conjurors and pickpockets in work,' he snapped back. 'The inability to detect ghosties and ghoulies and other pseudo-psychic flim-flam is what indicates that one's instruments are calibrated properly and that one's brain is functioning rationally.'

Rowe, looking fairly disgusted at this last contribution, was waving a hand dismissively, unable to speak due to her mouth being full of wine. Her glass was draining pretty fast, in fact, and not in testament to the jollity of the occasion. Me, I was lapping it up, mainly because I was seated comfortably in the grandstand.

A long pause ensued, the intractability of the impasse making further comment superfluous. The chirp and hum from the other tables seemed all the louder against the silence, their laughter the sound of another evening somewhere else entirely. Only the clatter of our cutlery contributed to the wider hubbub. Mather looked disengaged, more than a hint of I-told-you-so about his expression. Clearly he knew the stubborn ways of his fellow scientists. I looked at Sarah, expecting to glimpse that hidden naughty-girl smirk she gave me when we passed a couple bickering in the street; the self-congratulation and vicarious pleasure of being apart from someone else's quarrel. Instead, she seemed deep in thought and genuinely concerned, the look she has when she's working out the best way she can help.

Go, girl, I thought. After all, she did have an investment in this in that she worked in the faculty. She had stayed out of the debate, which in Sarah's case usually meant she was listening to both sides and was thus better equipped to digest the arguments. If anybody had anything to contribute that wouldn't simply be taking us back around the same circle, it would be her.

That's what I thought before she started speaking inaudibly to Blake, anyway. They were whispering conspiratorially, though at first it didn't look like he wanted to hear any solutions, as the impasse suited his position just fine. However, I could tell he was curious, not least because he respected Sarah; or respected her more than he respected anyone else at the table, anyway. I watched as the ire in his face was slowly dissolved, replaced by a twinkle of devilish mischief. I didn't like it, and not just because the devilish co-conspirator role at Sarah's side was usually mine.

'I think there *is* a way around the problem,' she announced quietly to the table. 'Mr Lafayette is prepared to submit to the conditions imposed by the chair's appointed scientific observers, but the concern is that the scientific observers will be deceived, largely because they *are* scientific observers. That about right?'

Blake nodded with the satisfied anticipation of someone setting the catch on a bear trap. Lafayette, across the table, looked surprised and thus a little concerned that a new variable was about to be introduced. I was a little anxious myself, as I began to anticipate what – or rather who – that variable was most likely to be.

'So it sounds like the perfect control would be the inclusion of an observer who was an expert in deception. You know: in scamming, underhand methods, subterfuge, crookedness, corruption, dishonesty. Basically, all the things you would want someone to be on the lookout for.'

Rowe's eyes lit up, perhaps reflecting the imagined glow of that four-million-quid endowment, until moments ago locked forever out of reach by this Mexican stand-off.

'Can you think of anyone who might fit the bill?' she asked.

# The other dead guy with a story still to tell

It's the more mundane stuff that freaks me out when I recall that day. No big fights between my flatmate Keith and me, nor time-of-your-life moments; no words you can't take back; no great promise left forever unfulfilled. That's what's most unsettling about it: it's the last day of your life, but you don't have a fucking clue. Even if the superstitionists were right and there were signs, omens, portents everywhere, you'd still be none the wiser, because you wouldn't think for a moment that they were aimed at you. There could be a gorram billboard poster outside bearing the words 'MICHAEL LOFTUS: TODAY IS THE LAST DAY OF YOUR LIFE' and it'd barely get a second's thought.

I couldn't say it was just an ordinary day like any other, because it wasn't: it was one I'd been working towards and looking forward to, the day of my Gabriel Lafayette tribute show. Clearly, the aspects concerning that are going to remain vividly memorable, but it's the ordinary stuff that's the more affecting. Same old penny-ante shit, same round-in-a-circle arguments with Keith. No poignant ironies, no higher stakes to it, no bloody different from any other day we spent together, but for it being our last.

For instance: 'Oh, before I forget: your maw called again,' he said, just to annoy me. He knew this would annoy me on two levels: one, it was distracting us from the matter in hand, and two, he was aware that the mere mention of my mother annoyed me.

We were in the flat, having microwaved baked potatoes for tea as we went over his part in the show; or rather, crucially, his part *before* the show.

'I want you to explain it to me once more,' I had said to him. 'Just so I'm sure you know it.'

'I know it, Michael. For Christ's sake, how many times?'

'It's all in the preparation, Keith. You can never be over-prepared. Tell me it again.'

Which was when he decided to change the subject.

'Do you want to call her back?' Bastard knew the answer to that one.

'Not this second,' I said, fanning out the envelopes for admittedly the fourth or fifth time.

'But you are going to ring her back?'

'What do *you* think?'

'She said something about money. Asked if you'd received her latest cheque. Have you?'

'Yes. And I binned it, just like all the others,' I told him.

He promptly reached for the black refuse sack that lay in the corner. A farty smell emerged as he pulled at the twisted polythene neck.

'Don't be bloody stupid,' I told him. 'It's ripped up.'

'Don't be bloody stupid? You're the one ripping up cheques. Didn't I just spot you twenty quid the day before yesterday? No, maybe it is me that's stupid: I'm giving out loans to jokers who can afford to throw money away.'

'I can afford to throw *her* money away,' I said. 'What I can't afford is to accept it. Too much of a cost to the soul.'

'You don't believe in the soul, Michael. You've gone on about *that* often enough.'

'You know what I mean.'

'No, I really don't. You say you can't afford to accept her cheques, but what the hell's paying your way here?'

'My dad's money. He left me an endowment for going to uni.'

'He left your mum money too, though, didn't he? So couldn't you think of her cheques as just her passing on more of *his* money, and then you could maybe nudge those twenty beer tokens back my way?'

'No. She's a woman of independent means. It's her money and I'm not bloody touching it, any more than I'm bloody phoning her back.'

We left it at that. Keith knew it was a no-go area. Superficial probing, the odd wind-up and a polite modicum of genuine concern were as far as I tolerated his enquiries. He knew we didn't speak to each other, or at least that I wouldn't speak to her, but he didn't know much of anything else. He had probably spoken to my mother more than I had over the past year or so, but I don't think it went beyond telephone pleasantries and message-taking. I couldn't see her volunteering any sensitive details any more than I could imagine him asking, and if he had found anything out, Keith wasn't the type to keep it to himself. He'd have got maximum mileage out of intimating that he knew something, before exploiting the full headgames potential of the information itself.

Which is not to put the guy down (any more than he'd consider obligatory; he'd have been very disappointed to think either of us would let a little thing like death get in the way of our mutual slagging contests). He wasn't lacking in sensitivity. It always amused me, in fact, that he never made the kind of sexual jokes and insults about my mother that he – or I – would about anyone else's. This was because he had begun to suspect that my mother really *was* a prostitute. Admittedly, I did very little to disabuse him of this; indeed I actively began to culti- vate it once I realised it made him uncomfortable and that he feared I would be genuinely vulnerable on the subject. It prob- ably started due to my letting slip that our falling-out was down to my long-term and increasing disapproval of how she was supplementing her income. Keith's list of possibilities for what this could be was undoubtedly narrowed down by certain remarks disparaging her clientele, and after I realised his horri- fied mis-deduction I started referring to them as 'punters'. It amused me, but more importantly it also prevented him from digging any deeper into the subject.

As far as I was concerned, the truth was far more shameful.

We got back to the matter in hand. Keith, with exaggerated reluctance, demonstrated to my satisfaction that he did know the drill. In fact, he had demonstrated it to my satisfaction at least three times, but he wasn't the only one who enjoyed point- lessly annoying his flatmate. Not to mention the fact that it was also imperative he knew his role inside out. Like I said, you can't be over-prepared, though maybe you can be over-annoyed.

'There,' he said indignantly. 'For the umpteenth time, I've got it. We're shiny, okay? Look, I know the show's tonight and every- thing, but can you chill about it a little, Michael?'

'You're not the one who's going to be left looking a total twunt if it all goes tits-up.'

'So why bother, if you're so worried about it?'

'I'm not worried, I just want it to work, otherwise what's the point?'

'A question I'm asking myself more and more the closer we get to this. I agreed to help you out because I thought it would be a laugh. You're getting really heavy about it though, man. Way too serious. Obsessive, in fact.'

'If you want to make miracles happen, Keith, you have to practice and you have to pay extreme attention to detail. You want to call that obsession, that's your shout, but we're just quibbling over terms.'

'Okay, I'll use another term: zealotry. You're a man on a mission. Honestly, what does it matter if some people want to believe in ghosts, or that Gabriel Lafayette can hear voices of the dead?'

'What does it matter?' I spluttered, revving up. Keith knew what was coming and had heard it enough times to opt for a change of tack.

'Yeah, okay, it matters. But seriously, Michael: do you really think that any of the people who believe in woo will change their minds just because of what you show them tonight?'

'If just one of them does, it will have been worth it,' I replied.

To be fair to Keith's point, I didn't fancy the odds.

'Sure thing,' he said, sounding conciliatory: humouring me. 'But it's a long way from how you sold me this caper. Remember? "The crowd will gasp," you said. "Men will applaud. Women will throw underwear. And both will seek us out, as impressed as they are curious."'

I grinned. 'Well, there you go, I'm halfway towards making my point already. I've proved how easily one person can be fooled into believing the impossible.'

'Yeah, I'll give you that one. Realistically, the notion of you pulling a chick would be more of a miracle than any feat of Lafayette's you could duplicate.'

'True,' I conceded, though not without mitigation. 'Can't fight those odds. Chicks don't go for science students.'

'No, they don't go for science *geeks*. Minor but crucial distinction.'

'They don't rate brains, that's what it is.'

'They don't rate your hair, conversation or attire either, safe to say. Come on: if you were a girl, would you go for you? You're an obsessively committed astrophysics student with a chronic SF habit, whose idea of musical eclecticism is downloading a Jimmy Eat World album to complement your exhaustive collection of old-skool hair metal. You are a mass-production-model science-geek stereotype, Michael. Don't fight it: it's your destiny.'

'And what the hell are you? Mr *GQ*?'

'No, I'm a science-geek stereotype too, but I know my station and I don't go bitching about it.'

'I wouldn't call it bitching to expect *one* girl out there not to ignore me simply because I don't look like just another trendy clone. I know the score too. I'm not expecting an Inara to go for me, but shouldn't I be in with a chance of a second look from a Kaylee? There must be Kaylees out there. Kaylee liked brains: she was crazy for Simon, and he was a doctor.'

'I don't think it was his brains she was primarily interested in. He was handsome and dashing and sculpted, as opposed to a scrawny drink of water in a ghastly old brown coat.'

'Hey, now don't come it. You know why I wear that coat.'

'Yep, and the reason you wear it is even more sad and embarrassing than the coat itself. It's a badge of your geekdom.'

'I don't care. I feel right in that coat.'

'Good. But it's babe repellent, dude.'

I wished I could contest this, but the evidence was all on Keith's side.

Still, I loved the coat and I wasn't going to stop wearing it, babe repellent or not. I could happily admit it: the reason for me wearing the thing, the reason for me tracking it down, *was* geeky and embarrassing. But was it any more embarrassing than the dozen or so guys you'd find in any given lecture theatre trying to dress like Brandon Flowers or Alex Kapranos or whoever the fuck was cool this fortnight? Well, evidently, yes, but I didn't care. I embraced my geekdom, and Keith was right: I wore my coat proudly as its badge. I wore a brown coat because I *was* a 'browncoat': I was – Keith nailed that too – a science geek with a chronic SF habit, and my drug of choice was *Firefly*.

Scoff away. I dressed to look like the atheist renegade hero of my favourite TV show. I knew fine – though I didn't agree with it – that this was socially less acceptable than dressing like the singer in your favourite band, but it was not a fashion statement; more a statement of philosophy, or maybe even a statement of intent. I wasn't just a science geek, I was a *militant* science geek. And that night I was staging the first orchestrated offensive of a guerilla campaign.

Keith and I got to the Union for seven, with the doors scheduled for half past. I had booked the Gilmore Suite on the building's first floor, its entrance opposite the doors to the gallery level of the debating chamber. The proximity to the site of Lafayette's now legendary performance of a year back was both intentional and unavoidable, the Gilmore being the only other room in the building with a raised dais at one end. It was also, unfortunately, a good bit bigger than I seriously envisaged I'd require to accommodate the likely numbers. I reckoned I'd be struggling to make back the hire of the room – especially as I'd doled out a number of tickets for free – but I knew I couldn't do this without a physical platform. There were a few other meeting rooms I could have booked, but I just couldn't see this working if I was simply standing on the carpet in front of a few rows of chairs. I didn't require the full proscenium arch, but I knew I needed the distance, the detachment of being even a few feet removed. This was largely about stagecraft, so it was something of a given to actually have a bloody stage. I knew it would help me shed some self-consciousness, as well as helping the audience relax too. A foot or so's elevation – plus preferably a microphone – makes it showbiz. Without those, it's just a guy standing up and talking to a room; at best a party piece.

I was less worried about being out of pocket than about playing to a near-empty house. This simply wouldn't work without a minimum number, because it was all about the audience. Like comedy, the bigger the crowd, the better the odds that enough of them will find you funny for the material to take off: you only need to succeed with a few for it to cover the silence of those you failed. With what I was planning, the hit-to-miss ratio – as I intended to demonstrate – was actually even more forgiving, but if there was actually only five people there, I was fucked.

I gave out quite a few freebies, for this and other reasons. There was a price on the ticket, however, so that the recipients of the freebs thought they were getting something worth taking advantage of. Even at merely the price of a pint, it was enough to stop them just chucking the briefs straight in the bin; while for those who would be paying, the fact that you were charging at all was psychologically crucial. On campus, in my experience, the words 'Free Entry' translated to 'Don't Bother – This'll Be Rubbish And You'll Be The Only One There'.

I sound-checked the microphone while Keith shuffled a few seats into neater rows for a lack of anything much else to do. Then, at about quarter past, we went out into the corridor and were presented with the unexpected sight of a fast-building crowd. Ironically, given my intent and purpose, I had underestimated the popularity and fascination of Gabriel Lafayette. Best part was, from the chatter I was picking up, a lot of them were there because they didn't appreciate what was implied by the phrase 'a tribute to the amazing magic of'.

This could turn ugly, I thought, but only if I do it right.

Speaking of ugly, I could see the thick neck and watermelon head of Grant Neilson standing against the far wall, further down the corridor. He had been the first person I thought of when Keith asked me whether I believed I could change anyone's mind. Grant was an occasional drinking buddy of Keith's, the pair of them having been in the same Biochemistry class in first year. His experience with Lafayette had been a revelation to him in more ways than the obvious. The guy had a lot of pent-up issues concealed beneath a hypermasculine hide, and his encounter in the debating chamber had been the first time probably since early childhood that the guy had done anything but suppress his emotional side. Arguably, the credit for effecting that did have to go to Lafayette, but there was nothing supernatural involved. It all came from within. I'd tried to tell him that a few times, but no amount of evidence was ever enough: he always found a way of preserving his belief that Lafayette had received communication with his late father. In fact, it was my frustration at his ducking and weaving that had inspired me to demonstrate the truth rather than merely outlining it. I had once offered to tell him how the envelope trick was done, but he'd cut me off and changed the subject. Now there was no avoiding it.

I gave him credit that he had pitched up and was prepared to witness something that was bound to challenge his preconceptions. Most believers in this crap, for all their professed faith, would go to great lengths to avoid anything that might sow the first tiny seed of doubt. Of course, it was also possible that he was here in the hope of watching me fall flat on my arse, but either way, it was what this wee soirée was all about.

I was less comfited to notice Laura Bailey also among the growing queue. She had been the first major recipient of Lafayette's other-worldly beneficence in the debating chamber, and the bastard had really hit paydirt with her. Lafayette's fraternity mined for misery and pain like Klondikers mined for minerals, and with her I feared he had truly struck gold. I saw her face that night: fragile, bewildered, shaken, euphoric and sad, all at once, not to mention vastly, consumingly grateful. She was being used but had no idea, far more vulnerable than she could ever suspect. I didn't know what she was doing here tonight, what she was looking for, but the sight of her made me a little less sure of the responsibility of what I was about to do.

Grant was as thick-skinned as he was pig-headed, so I wasn't worried about the consequences for him if I did succeed in turning his new-found sense of wonder upside down. This girl, however, could be a butterfly on a wheel. She had lost a brother as a child and then her mother also at a cruelly vulnerable stage. It was, I realised, the one aspect of what I was undertaking that I had utterly failed to consider; all the less forgivable considering it was where much of my moral justification was founded. Still, it wasn't like I was a comic with a slew of paedophile gags, suddenly realising the audience might contain people who really were child-abuse victims. Laura Bailey had been abused, but she didn't know it yet. I wasn't going to be joking about it, but I wasn't so sanguine about being the one who broke the news to her either.

Anyway, there were at least forty people waiting outside the

Gilmore Suite, with ten minutes to go until the doors were even due to open, so I had no option of backing down. On top of that, Keith had already gone into action, handing out cards and envelopes.

'Before you go inside, please take one of these cards,' I heard him say. I breathed in, I confess, waiting to hear whether he got the next bit right as per our many rehearsals. 'Please write down some thoughts about a loved one who is no longer with us, with a few words about your relationship with that person: was it a friend, a relative, that kind of thing. Then put your name at the top, and seal the card inside the envelope. Seal it properly: don't just fold it over, and don't write anything on the outside. Lick it and stick it, so it's obvious if it's been tampered with, okay?'

Shiny, just like he'd said. Magic, even.

Thus assured, I was able to circulate, handing out cards also, but giving the recipients slightly different instructions. I told them not to write their names, but simply to put their initials on the envelope, which had to be sealed as per Keith's directions.

While they wrote their messages – leaning against walls, crouching to rest the cards on their laps – I was afforded the perfect opportunity to undertake some more preparatory work, in the form of acquiring a few items from bags and pockets. Glancing at faces, I noted who was present that I recognised, already compiling lists and crossing out names in my mind, as well as sorting and deselecting props ahead of my return backstage.

I had been very nervous about how much I could get away with during this part, but it was surprisingly easy. The only suggestion of suspicion came from Grant, and he was suspicious of the wrong thing. Grant was at an advantage over most in that he at least understood what I was about tonight. Plenty of the others seemed to assume I was some kind of franchise-psychic; still more hadn't even thought that far. I heard excited snippets – 'This is what we were asked to do the last time' – suggesting some were here accompanying friends who had missed the Lafayette show a year back, and had no doubt heard plenty about it since.

113

'Hey, don't let him peek,' Grant warned someone next to him. 'He's trying to see what you're writing.' This was a gift, something I really ought to have had Keith telling people, as nothing convinces the punters more than when they undertake an act of utterly misdirected vigilance to prevent you cheating. A big step towards making people believe you have special powers is having them convince themselves that they can't be fooled by mere trickery. I vehemently agreed with Grant, and further reminded both him and those who had heard him that the envelopes were to be sealed shut anyway.

We opened the doors at about seven thirty-five. Keith counted more than fifty people as I retired to the adjoining room to one side of the stage to prepare for my performance. It was a poky wee place, with little apparent purpose the rest of the time but to house a kettle and a few cupboards full of cups and saucers, teabags, jars of cheap instant coffee and a few packets of biscuits. It did, however, have a second door, out to the corridor, which helped maintain that sense of showbiz. It was one thing mingling out in the hallway, but there was just something a bit wrong about seeing any performer, not yet in character, walk through his audience to get to either the dressing room or the stage.

I shed my signature garment, slinging my beloved brown coat over the only chair. Underneath I had on a white shirt and jeans, same as Lafayette wore in the debating chamber. On top of that I added a white denim jacket, not an exact match for the linen one Lafayette wore, but its deceptively deep pockets were more important than precision of resemblance. I had opted to dress like him to underline the 'tribute' aspect, but as I pulled on the jacket and felt the growing tingle in my gut, I appreciated an unforeseen reason for having done so. It was a costume, a prop to help me play a part. I was no actor, but I was even less of a performer. I was as self-conscious and clumsy as any gawky male student, and it was hard to imagine any other circumstances under which I'd put myself centre-stage in front of a crowd (spontaneous acts of inverted fire-walking notwithstanding). I couldn't walk out there and be me, but I could walk out there and be A Psychic.

For that reason, I was glad I had ditched an early notion of playing the whole thing like Penn and Teller: showing how it was all done as I went along. To do that, I'd have to be me on stage, or rather, me with a winning and expansive personality, which, like the psychic phenomena everyone was here to see, quite simply didn't exist. Instead I was there to play it straight, encouraging the audience, if so inclined, to really believe it. Only later, once they were taken in, would I begin to break the fourth wall.

Keith played a CD over the suite's PA: some generic spooky music followed by an announcement I had recorded – complete with echo effects to enhance and disguise my voice – welcoming me to the stage. No way back now.

I walked on to the platform and looked out over what was indisputably a busy room. There was a liberal smattering of applause, I'm not sure what for: maybe a Pavlovian response, or maybe an appreciation of the man I was paying tribute to. I stepped up and took the microphone from its stand, next to a white-draped trestle table, my only visible prop.

'Good evening, ladies and gentlemen, and many thanks for coming here tonight.' I spoke slowly and more deeply than normal. I didn't sound like myself, nor did I much feel like myself, which was good, I decided. If I don't feel like myself, I won't feel self-conscious either. To that end, I avoided making eye contact with Keith, and for the early part with Grant or anyone else who knew me any closer than nodding terms. It was easy to keep my eyes off of Keith, as he was sitting alone at the back, by the door, the glass bowl full of envelopes beside him. (Keith's goldfish were in Tupperware for the evening. Every member of the household was making sacrifices for this show.)

'We are all here this evening because we are fascinated by the world of the psychic; me, I would bet, more than most. We have all been amazed by the exploits of Gabriel Lafayette, our university's outgoing rector, and perhaps by other practitioners in this mysterious field. We ask ourselves how they perform their impossible feats, most especially how they can know what they know: knowledge about people they have never met, information divined from unreachable sources, and, most unsettling of all, knowledge of those who have long since left this earth.'

There was much nodding, some very sincere looks. I glimpsed Grant, who had his arms folded and wore a stony, challenging expression with a certain smugness about it; and definitely a complacency.

'But the most amazing thing about Gabriel Lafayette, which lifts him high above his peers, is that he has shown us that if we open our minds to the amazing, then we can know these things too. *I* know this because I have opened my mind, and tonight I'm going to prove it. I'm just an ordinary guy, same as anyone here. I'm a fourth-year science student, and I don't have special powers. But as Lafayette has shown us, nor do I need them. In his words, it isn't something he does, it's something that happens to him. And it can happen to any of us. That's what's most amazing. You just need to open yourself up to the information, open your eyes and ears to what is being communicated from all around.'

I nodded to Keith, who was already on his feet waiting for my cue.

'Now, before coming into this room, you were all asked to write something concerning a loved one who has passed on, and to initial the envelope.' There were a few dismayed looks in response to this, roughly half the audience thinking they had screwed up by not initialling their envelope. I put them at ease by adding: 'This was so that I can't identify who submitted a particular envelope, and also so that their identity can be verified later.' So, maybe screwed up, but the same goals met in any case.

'Keith here is now bringing me the envelopes.'

Keith was walking around the side of the four rows of chairs, carrying the bowl in two hands. It had sat with him by the door all the time I was backstage, so there was no opportunity for me to have somehow examined or tampered with its contents. He climbed on to the dais and placed the bowl on the table.

I stirred the envelopes and selected one bearing no initials, then held it to my chest with both hands and closed my eyes. This resulted in a completely inadvertent piece of stagecraft, in that my right hand, bearing the mike, pressed it also against my chest, causing my heartbeat to be audible throughout the room. I intended to speak with my eyes closed, but I had this abiding fear that everyone would be making faces, or that when I opened them again, the room would have emptied. I opened them but looked to the ceiling.

'This is about Elaine,' I said. 'Elaine is no longer with us, but she is sorely missed by . . . not a daughter, no, it doesn't feel like a daughter, but close: a niece. Kate.'

A girl in the front row was holding her hands to both cheeks.

'You're Kate,' I said, to which she responded with wide-eyed nodding. 'Elaine was your aunt. She went before her time. I sense a pain.' I put my left hand to my forehead. She continued to stare expectantly at me. I moved my hand down to my chest, and she unconsciously moved her own hand there too. 'A pain here,' I went on. 'Cancer,' I suggested. 'Breast cancer.' She shook her head. I was already shaking mine before she had completed one oscillation. 'No, it's deeper. The lung.' Another shake. 'No, the pain is sudden.' Her eyes widened again. 'The heart. A heart attack.'

The girl was now not only nodding, but her eyes were filling up. Part of me felt like a cunt at this point for what I was doing, but I was on a mission. And, I have to confess, I was enjoying it.

'It took her too soon,' I added. 'Elaine misses her niece too. She's sorry she can't share in her life now she's all grown up. Kate's all grown up. Kate's unwed. No, it's her name: Unwin.'

I opened the envelope in my hand, examined it carefully and nodded, briefly holding it up, though it was too far for anyone to be able to read.

'Elaine, it says,' I confirmed.

The room went very quiet. This was the moment when it went from being they knew not what, to something, like Lafayette's performance, disquieting. I repeated the process with more and more envelopes, each time eliciting more gasps than the last as I divined the information within, and then – rather falteringly, but no less impressively, it seemed – embellished it, of which more later.

I felt emboldened by each success, more so by the gratification of the crowd's responses. For the first time I understood why, other than money, people practised this fraud. It was utterly exhilarating.

The astonished audience were in two tiers of amazement. The first tier comprised those who were amazed simply because I knew the names written inside sealed envelopes that had never been out of their sight as they sat in that bowl. The second, further amazed tier, comprised those who had been instructed merely to initial their envelopes and were thus unaware that the names of these audience members had been written down at all.

Lafayette had had at least four staff working the foyer. I guessed twenty-five per cent of the cards would have had full names on the inside, and those would be the ones he'd pick, easily identified because they had no initials on the outside. That ratio also allowed him to implement another discrepancy that my fifty–fifty would not forgive: most of his audience, as well as leaving off their names, were told to write a question, not a statement, and nor were they asked to supply any further details. Thus, three quarters of the audience were primed to be even more astonished. The remaining quarter would be unaware they had received different instructions until Lafayette reminded 'everyone' what they had been asked to do, at which point they would tend to assume that they had misheard or wrongly implemented the instructions. They would also assume themselves to be in a minority far smaller than twenty-five per cent. Silly me, I goofed it up, they'd each think.

But what would it matter what was written down – names or initials – if the envelopes were sealed shut anyway? Well, the answer is a technique that's been around as long as there have been gullible people to astound with it. It's called the One Ahead Method, and it works like this. While everyone was taking their seats, Keith surreptitiously removed one envelope – non-initialled, of course – and brought it to me backstage, where I opened it and examined the contents, committing the names and other details to memory. When Keith brought me the bowl, I selected another uninitialled envelope and held it to my chest while pretending to divine Kate Unwin's information. Then, right in front of everybody, I opened the envelope and read the details I would need for my next psychic feat.

I didn't lie to anybody, though, did I? Said it right up front: you just need to open your eyes and ears to the information that's all around.

There was no information about Auntie Elaine's cause of death. That was merely a clumsily executed but nonetheless successful example of what is known in the trade as 'cold reading', whereby you look for cues and offer the person prompts. One way or another, they end up telling you what you need to know, but you get the credit for divining it. When it comes to a subject such as cause of death, cancer, heart attacks and car crashes are always the best place to begin fishing. The head and chest are the two areas most likely to be associated with the fatal injury or affliction, so I put my hand over each in turn and looked for the cues. In Kate's case, it took me several guesses to reach the right one, but they always forget the misses as soon as you've scored a hit.

I winged it with some more extremely ropy cold readings for the first few cards. I was going down a storm, but privately cursing my luck at the names I was drawing. The audience were so impressed with me knowing what was inside the sealed envelopes that they failed to notice how shambling I was with the other information, but eventually I pulled out a plum and was able to really turn on the magic.

I hadn't given out free tickets merely in the hope of boosting the crowd, and I certainly hadn't given them out indiscriminately. Strictly speaking, I hadn't given them out at all: Keith had, so that the carefully specified recipients wouldn't recognise their donor as the same person who had, a few months back, got them to fill in a confidential survey ('for my Psychology coursework') on the subject of bereavement. I did this before the end of the previous term, guessing they'd have forgotten all about it – and me – over the summer. A lot of lead time, I know, but something like this takes careful planning and fastidious preparation. Besides, when I came up with the notion, largely in response to hearing about Bryant Lemuel's proposed Total Bollocks Chair, third term was almost over and everyone was about to bugger off for the summer.

The survey was confidential, so they weren't asked for their names, but it was easy enough to find out, sometimes even as I stood by waiting for them to fill in their answers. What they were asked included the following:

Which person's death hurt you most, and why?
What did he/she die of?
What was your relationship to them?

What do you remember most about that person?

What would you say to them if you could give them one last message?

What do you think they would say to you?

Sneaky, underhand and a bit creepy, I know, but that's psychics for you.

I had counted seven of my survey respondents outside in the corridor, and avoided them so that they would get their cards and instructions from Keith. Therefore, the only improbable feat I managed on that stage was randomly opening so many envelopes before I got to one of theirs.

Best not dwell on this part. The details aren't important. I admitted I got a buzz from doing the one-ahead billet reading, and a genuine adrenalin rush from the (albeit negligibly) more risky cold reading. This, however, was what is known as *hot* reading, and even though I undersold it, it just felt wrong. I felt like I was, at best, intruding on what should be private; at worst violating something sacred.

There were, as I said, seven of them I could have inflicted this upon. The luck of the draw dictated that the subjects were a girl called Jessica Nyman and a guy called Philip Begg. I made both of them cry; not weep a little, but seriously cry, full-on sobbing, even the bloke.

I caught the eyes of both Grant Neilson and Laura Bailey during these readings. Grant looked confused, the complacency gone, a lot of questions going through that outsize head of his. Laura Bailey's eyes had welled up as though she had been my subject. She didn't appear distraught, just deeply sad to the point of grieving. Perhaps the apparent impossibility and sheer poignancy of my divinations was bringing back how she had felt next door in the debating chamber. If so, I hoped she had brought plenty of hankies, as she was likely to be far more upset when I got to the evening's genuine revelations.

Before that, though, and to sweeten the pill, I took things into less emotional territory. Lafayette, like every good showman, knew that you had to go out on a high, hence the firewalking finale. In my case, as well as having some more tricks literally up my sleeve, I reckoned that putting everybody in lighter spirits would lessen the chances of one of the people

I had distressed kicking my head in when they found out the truth.

'Gabriel Lafayette talks about a field or a fabric through which certain vibrations travel,' I reminded them. 'And we can conduct those vibrations, in his case as a kind of sounding board, or even a stylus, in order to receive messages from another plane. However, some practitioners in this field have experienced phenomena that suggest this fabric can be the conduit for not merely energy, but actual physical material. Just like telephone lines used to be thought of as merely a conduit for spoken words, now we can use them to transmit the information that becomes pictures and videos.

'Objects have been known to travel across these planes, between what are known as points of bilocation: disappearing from one place and reappearing elsewhere. Gabriel Lafayette does not himself demonstrate this phenomenon, but he *has* demonstrated the principle that any one of us, if we truly open our minds, can make this happen. Though when I say we, I don't mean figuratively. I mean we can do it, right here, right now, as long as we work together.'

I put the microphone back on its stand and stood behind it with my arms held apart, hands open. I wanted it to look like a gesture of inclusion, but its real purpose was to free both of my hands and to subtly draw the audience's attention to the fact that I wasn't holding anything in either of them. I didn't go so far as to say 'Nothing up this sleeve,' but the principle was the same.

'I want everybody to think of an object, something small enough to travel through a bilocation portal, so we're not talking washing machines here.' I got a few laughs with that, and was relieved to see Jessica and Phil among them. Their emotionally overwrought states meant they'd probably have laughed at a door shutting right then, as it provided an outlet, but it lessened the immediate danger of the aforementioned kicking.

'I mean a personal object, something small that you have on you right now. Now, don't touch that object, or even the bag or pocket it's in, just think of what it is and then concentrate on it.'

I gave it a moment then added: 'Of course, we'll improve our powers if we are all thinking of the same object. What are you thinking of?' I asked someone – not just anyone – in the second row. Her name was Michelle, as I had divined from her card coming up during the billet reading.

'A mobile phone,' she said. Good girl. It was one of few possibilities, but I had skewed the odds through subtle suggestion with my remarks about telephone lines in the preamble.

'What about you?' I asked someone else, this time at random.

'House keys,' came the reply. Thank you. Banker possibility number two.

'Well, we'd better decide,' I said. I looked to a girl in the front row. 'Mobile or house keys?'

'Mobile,' she said.

'Okay, everyone think about a mobile. In fact, everybody think about *her* mobile,' I instructed, pointing to the first girl. 'Michelle, isn't it? Everybody think about Michelle's mobile. Leave it where it is, don't get it out, but tell us what to picture. Is it a Nokia? A Siemens? And where is it? Your pocket?'

'It's a Sharp,' she said. 'In my bag.'

'Everybody picture that mobile, and picture it inside Michelle's bag. Michelle, keep your hands on that bag, make sure it stays closed. Now, everybody picture Michelle's mobile dematerialising, turning into pure information, like binary files on the internet. Picture it moving through that invisible portal. Concentrate. Close your eyes if it helps.'

Most of them did, a few keeping their peepers on me, including Grant, confused but suspicious. Good, I thought. This'll mess you up all the more.

'Stop now. Open your eyes. I felt something there. Did anybody else feel something?'

Several people nodded.

'What about you, Michelle?'

'Don't know,' she replied bashfully.

'What about your mobile? Did it move at all, did you feel it shift?'

'Don't think so. Don't know.'

'Can I see it?'

She went into her bag, the practised reach of her left hand soon turning into a concerned rummage.

'It's not here,' she announced, more panicked at the possible loss than astounded at any psychic phenomenon. 'I had it. It's not bloody here.'

Every eye was on her, which was when I chose my moment to flick my fingers against the glass bowl, stepping away from it in the same movement so that it looked like I was turning around to respond to the sound behind me.

I stared intently at the bowl, then moved very slowly back towards it. I picked it up and pulled at a handful of envelopes, beneath which sat a Sharp clamshell mobile phone. I let the audience see it sitting there before picking it up and asking: 'Is this yours?'

Michelle clambered across the seat in front to reach for it as I walked towards her. I handed it over and watched her flip it open to verify it was hers. It was. I had swiped it from her handbag in the corridor earlier, and transferred it from my jacket pocket to the bowl towards the end of my billet-reading performance.

She stared at the tiny screen for a second, then looked up at me. 'How did you do that?' she asked.

'We all did it,' I replied. 'We all played our part. And if we can move an object from one part of the room to another, maybe we're ready for a stronger test of our bilocation abilities. Some psychics have been known to locate objects that people have lost: sometimes instinctively picturing where they are, but sometimes causing them to physically relocate to be reunited with their owners. Has anybody lost an object recently? Time is a factor: psychics have less success locating objects the longer they have been lost, so no Barbie accessories from when you were nine. A student union membership card, maybe, something like that.'

I scanned the audience for responses; or rather, pretended to be looking for them, avoiding eye contact with those my darting glances identified as being eager to talk. Instead I settled on Grant Neilson, who had actually put his hand in the air and was back to looking smug, as he now knew I had no choice but to ask him or else everyone would notice I hadn't. He had thought of something, not only that he had lost, but that was nothing like what he believed I was expecting.

'Have *you* lost something, Grant?' I asked reluctantly.

'Aye,' he said, folding his arms again with self-satisfaction.

'If it's a cheque for a million quid or Jessica Alba's phone

123

number, we can't help you: it has to be something you've genuinely misplaced.'

'It is,' he assured me and everyone else. 'My *Duke Nukem Forever* DVD-ROM. Cannae find it, and I cannae play the game without it.'

'A DVD?' I asked, sounding disheartened. 'From a computer game?'

'Yeah. A bit trivial, I know, but it's been bugging me, so worth a try, eh?'

'No,' I said. 'Not worth a try. We do or we do not. There is no try. Okay, everybody, I want you to concentrate on that DVD, concentrate on making it appear, however impossible that seems. Don't think about what is possible and what is not. Don't think about where it might be. Just concentrate on picturing it, like you did before. Close your eyes to blot out everything else.'

Again, a few of them still had their eyes open, Grant included, though he seemed a little fazed by the fact that I hadn't backed down or sought an out.

'Everybody close your eyes,' I repeated, as though they only needed encouragement. 'We want only positive energy. The negative energy from just one person can be enough to jam everyone else's positive forces.'

Even Grant, perhaps forgetting I had told him these would all be tricks, or perhaps in his desperation to get his computer game back, did acquiesce. He opened them again almost immediately, suggesting he was still trying to catch me out. If only he had applied such vigilance to Lafayette, he might not have been sitting there right then. But best not go there.

I picked up the bowl again, though this time there had been no chime. I rummaged around in it for a moment, then, shaking my head, held it out in front of me with one hand, for the audience to examine. With their eyes upon it, my free hand, behind my back, flipped Grant's disc into the air over my head. From the crowd's perspective, it must have looked like it had simply materialised somewhere above me and dropped down on to the floor in front of the stage.

Someone in the front row pounced to get it before I could put down the bowl, never mind step off the dais. It was Kate, the first subject of my one-ahead trick. Her gasp was audible throughout the room as she turned over the small silver disc to reveal its printed side. Grant was on his feet, hand out to demand the DVD as she read the name aloud: *'Duke Nukem Forever.'*

He gaped like Keith's goldfish, unable to respond verbally at all. Kate relinquished her hold on it and he took the DVD in his hands like it was some artefact of power, and not merely a computer disc that Keith had swiped, on my request, from Grant's flat when he was round there a week or so back. (Keith had done superbly well: he couldn't take anything valuable or indispensable, but it had to be something Grant would definitely notice the lack of and put it down to his own disorganisation.)

The audience seemed just as dumbstruck.

'You think that's amazing?' I asked them, taking the mike again. Most of them nodded, row upon row of car ornaments. 'I disagree,' I said. 'The truly amazing thing is that every last one of you is capable of doing what you saw tonight. Every last one of you. Gabriel Lafayette is right: it's not about special powers. It's about opening yourself up to the information. Do you want to learn how to do that? If you do, then remain seated. But it's only fair to warn you: what I am about to share with you may disturb you, and you might consider it a burden rather than a blessing. If you wish to leave, I'll hold off for a moment to allow you to do so.'

To my great surprise, one guy actually did bail, a wild-haired and whiskery older bloke in a manky old raincoat and taped-up NHS specs. He was sitting in the back row, nearest the door, and I suppose there was a strong possibility he had been in entirely the wrong room, or, from his appearance, that he was just a jakey who had snuck in out of the rain.

As for the remainder of the audience, nothing was going to move them from their seats, particularly the ones who truly believed I was about to teach them how to be psychic.

Which, in a way, was precisely what I did.

It went pretty well. I didn't get my head kicked in, though it was touch and go once or twice. Thus I was in perfect physical condition to be murdered later that same evening.

# A master at work

From his seat in the back row, heavily disguised, he watched the performance unfold with growing alarm. Deception upon fraud upon misdirection upon con, all executed by an informed amateur. Not good. Not good at all. A proliferation of people practising the same shtick was the last thing he needed on this campus right then. A tribute to Gabriel Lafayette indeed. If they only knew who was sitting right among them.

He had found out about this event only today, and was cursing himself for not having discovered it sooner, when there might have been time to avert the damage altogether. Now his options were down to merely limitation. His own fault, he knew. Too much time in the Ivory Tower, concerned with setting up the chair, removed from the chatter, thoughts and even thorough-fares of the students. A walk to the underground instead of taking the car to and from his rented flat would have been enough: the posters were on half the lamp-posts he'd passed on his way from the quadrangles to the student union. As it was, he'd only seen the advert in time at all because it had been anonymously slipped under the office door this morning, unquestionably intended as a taunt.

He didn't need to wait for the second part of the show. He'd seen more than enough to understand what this could lead to, and with battle lines already drawn over the chair, it wasn't difficult to envisage the long-term ramifications.

He had to act. Deep down, he had known this from the moment he saw the flyer. The surname couldn't possibly be a coincidence. In this game, there was no such thing. Nonetheless, he had told himself it could yet turn out to be benign, maybe even irrelevant, which was why he had to attend and see for himself. But inside he knew this was just a finite act of denial, a temporary suspension of an unavoidable course. Who wouldn't wish it otherwise? This kind of thing was never easy.

Simple, yes, and certainly necessary, given what was at stake, but never easy. However, like anything else, the more you did it . . .

He slipped quickly from the room, fortunately the only one to leave, so he was on his own out in the corridor. Having sat at the end of the backmost row, only a few people had looked his way during the performance, but they gave no indication of recognising him.

It had been a long while since he was in this building, but he remembered it well enough, and places like this seldom changed much. Change took money, which was always scarce, plus the agreement of a quorate number of students, which was rarer still. He made his way along the buffed linoleum and quietly opened the door to the little anteroom connecting the Gilmore Suite to the corridor. Stepping inside, he felt a brief lurch in his gut at the sight of the long brown coat draped over a chair. This was the same guy as had trumped the fire-walking stunt by doing it on his hands. He'd only caught a glimpse from backstage that night, and the coat was all he remembered, but there couldn't be two people going around in such a hideous garment. No question, the surname meant everything he'd feared.

He rifled through the garment's deep and many pockets, locating first a set of keys, then a wallet, a diary and a letter, still in its envelope, which between them confirmed Loftus's address. He checked his watch. It was quarter past eight.

After a quick stop at the office to pick up some tools, he walked to the underground station and took a train two stops to Partick. No car tonight, lest the plates get noted. No taxis either; no friendly driver to recall the address or a description of the fare he'd dropped outside, disguise or no. The accent would be plenty, and he was rotten at disguising that. He passed at least half a dozen posters advertising the event still in progress, tried not to think of the 'if onlys'. Look on the bright side: this way, he knew for a fact the guy wouldn't be home.

He walked past the place first, along Dumbarton Road, not even turning up the street, just stealing a glance as he crossed at the junction. It was student land, every tenement a sub-divided battery farm: you fed cheap beer and baked potatoes into the cramped cubicles and out came rent cheques once a month. He glanced at the rows of chimneys, lined up side by side like soldiers on parade. He knew what he had to do, had known it deep down from the moment he saw the leaflet.

He glanced up the next street, a wide avenue at a set of traffic lights. He could see trees on the left-hand side, maybe a couple of hundred yards along: a park or maybe just a square. He turned and headed north towards Hyndland. As he neared the trees, he could see that they delineated neither park nor square, but the borders of some unkempt playing fields. Ideal. He took a left then another right and found the entrance, a muddy gateway strewn with discarded strips of adhesive tape from shin guards, as well as the ubiquitous green broken glass of Buckfast bottles. It was the local equivalent of Mad Dog, and shattered empties either grew or were naturally precipitated in every site of urban greenery in this city.

He passed through the gateway and headed under the cover of some trees, shaded from the streetlamps but lit by the clear night sky. It was cold, the lack of cloud cover causing the temperature to drop fast. All to the good. The wind was picking up too, which would help in drawing all the right conclusions, or at least the conclusions that were right by him.

He had a selection to choose from. While it wouldn't be strictly accurate to say that they grew on trees, that was nonetheless where you found them. They never appeared on a Cluedo card, but in practised hands they were as effective as any object that did. He climbed a few feet and dislodged the largest one he could reach. It dropped to the grass beneath him almost silently. As he stepped back to earth, he felt something stiff under the sole of his foot and looked down. He was standing on the outstretched wing of a dead crow, its glazed eye glinting conspiratorially in the moonlight.

Less than ten minutes later, he was inside the flat. Michael Loftus's name was confirmed on a cardboard doorplate, along with his room-mate, or flatmate as they called them here: Keith Baker. Tough shit, Keith Baker. Nothing personal.

He had passed nobody in the close or on the stairs, nor was he likely to. It was the start of term: funds were high and exams distant. Everybody was out. From the street, it had been clear that most of the flats were empty, going by the unlit windows. There was evidence of life from the adjacent flat, the sound of a stereo belting out rock music from behind the door. No party, though, from the lack of voices, just somebody getting dressed and getting in the mood to go dancing. It was perfect: it covered the sound of his entry and of everything he did once inside.

He began by sliding open the windows looking out on the rear of the building, which would be unnoticed by anyone who happened to look up from the street. He opened the ones at the front too, but just a few inches, enough to create a through draught and bring the temperature in the flat right down to roughly the same as outside, which wasn't much, it being a clear night. Plus, it was wise to have plenty of air circulating when you were working with gas appliances in an enclosed space. Those things could be very dangerous if anything went wrong with their ventilation.

He disconnected the fire in the main room and carefully rocked it free of the hearth. It vented up an ancient but service-able chimney in the wall, the sound of the wind above audible as soon as he exposed it, brick dust and soot shaking free when he moved the appliance. He gathered a handful and poured it into a channel where it would block the flow of air to the burners. This would make them underfire, causing the heater to pump out carbon monoxide, making the efficient draw of the humble chimney a life-or-death matter. To that end – and for two people it really was the end – he placed at the bottom of the flue the bird's nest he had dislodged from the tree by the playing fields. Then, for good measure, he placed on top of that the dead crow, which one could say he had brought along as a bad-luck charm, not that a man like him was superstitious.

He reconnected the fire, then sought out a brush and shovel, sweeping up the spilled dust and grit and shaking it into the black polythene sack the tiny kitchen had by way of apology for a bin. Next, he closed all of the windows again as tightly as they would permit, remembering also to remove the battery from the flat's smoke and carbon monoxide detector, and replacing it with a depleted one. He placed Loftus's keys on the hall carpet beneath a coat hook, where they could have plausibly fallen from his pocket, before taking a tea-towel and wiping down everything he could remember touching.

His death trap set, he quietly let himself out, then went home to his bed, where he could sleep secure in the knowledge that Michael Loftus and Keith Baker would soon return to their freezing-cold flat, turn on the living-room fire, brew up some tea, watch some late-night TV, then nod off where they sat and die silently in their sleep.

# The condemned ate a hearty meal

Grant had sprung for a few of bags of crisps for us while he was up getting the next round, a very welcome bonus as my baked potato was starting to seem like a distant memory and the first pint felt like it had been administered intravenously. I felt light-headed, almost as though my feet weren't connected to earth. I could have been drinking Irn-Bru and I'd have probably felt the same: the high was entirely due to what I'd just done. I had my coat back on, the white jacket now rolled up in a poly bag at my feet, and was most definitely no longer 'in character', but I still didn't quite feel like I had reinhabited my own body. When I looked back, only minutes, really, I could remember being on stage but it didn't feel like it had been me who'd been up there. I couldn't have done that, surely, not me. Don't have the brass neck. No chance. And yet here we all were, a big gaggle of people huddled around Keith and me, like we were holding court.

We were gathered around one of the big horseshoe-shaped booths in the Word Bar, where we knew we could all talk without having to shout over the sound of a jukebox. It wasn't so much a post-show drink as an on-going continuation of the discussion that the latter, more revelatory part of my performance had precipitated. I'd still have been up on that dais fielding questions from the same folk if the janny hadn't come in and booted us all out, the booking only covering the place until nine.

Grant gently placed a tray bearing eight or nine pints of heavy on the table, crisp pokes stuffed in the spaces between as well as hanging out of his jacket pockets. He handed a pint each to Keith and me first, then placed another two on the table and nudged them in the direction of Michelle and her pal Susan, whose wrinkled-nose looks of annoyance were priceless. I think Michelle had asked for a gin and tonic and I definitely remembered Susan ordering a Diet Coke. There had also been, from

131

other quarters, shouts for Beck's, Smirnoff Ice, After Shock and two Red Bulls, one with and one without vodka. Grant, as he always did in such expansive company, had patiently listened to everyone's order, then gone up and ordered them each a pint of heavy. They always got consumed, though not necessarily by the people they were given to.

I'd continued to answer questions while he was at the bar, but now that he had returned – and not least because he was bearing this munificently large if not fastidiously selected round of drinks – he was quickly deferred to by the others and resumed the role of my chief interlocutor. The other reason they were happy to give him the floor, of course, was that he was playing their song.

Men will applaud, women will throw underwear: that was our joke about the projected aftermath of the performance. There was little question that I had impressed a great many of the audience – applause was forthcoming, though, as yet, no underwear – but that was not the portion of the audience who had continued downstairs to the bar. The majority had had their questions answered and their curiosity satisfied. This lot were looking for reasons to keep believing, and Grant had quickly identified himself as their champion. They were even reluctant to cease believing in *me*.

'You still haven't explained how you knew some of that stuff,' Michelle had said while Grant was at the bar. 'I don't mean from the cards or from that survey you were talking about. I mean knowing that Steve's uncle died in a car accident, or that Susan's grandmother died of a stroke; you got all that stuff right about everybody. Are you saying you found out all that information in advance, without knowing we'd even be here?'

'No,' I replied. 'Those details, the supplementary stuff, I didn't know any of it. I got it from cold reading. It's a guessing technique.'

'But you guessed right every time! See, that's impossible. There has to be something that communicates this information between people, whether they believe in it or not. Are you not surprised yourself that you got all these guesses right? Does that not tell you something?'

I laughed. 'I got all the guesses right?' I asked.

'Yes,' she insisted.

'Who else thinks I got all my guesses right? No, scratch that, it's too black and white: give me a rough percentage.'

'Eighty per cent, I'd say,' ventured Susan.

I looked around the table.

'More like ninety.'

'Seventy-five at the lowest.'

'Eighty-five.'

And so on.

'Keith?' I demanded finally.

Keith produced a sheet of paper from his pocket and placed it on the table.

'This is the cold-reading scorecard Michael made me keep. Total guesses: forty-nine. Misses: thirty-eight. Hits: eleven. Percentage right: twenty-two, and most of those came after other wrong options had been eliminated.'

'Not to mention the many non-verbal cues you were all giving me.'

'No. Those numbers can't be right,' Michelle responded. 'I don't remember you getting anything like that much wrong.'

'Which is exactly how it works,' I told her.

As some people shifted along to let Grant back into his seat, I spotted Laura Bailey sitting at the next table, on her own: listening in, but seemingly reluctant to join the group. She was still my ghost at the feast.

'Now, I'm not meaning to take anything away from you, Mikey,' Grant said. 'But all you've actually proved tonight is that you're a pretty nifty magician – not to mention a thieving bastard.'

'I'm not a nifty magician. I'm pish, in fact, but that's my point. I've proved that anybody can do what Gabriel Lafayette does.'

'But you haven't proved anything about him,' Grant countered. 'Just because you can recreate the *effect* of what he does by using tricks doesn't mean *he's* using tricks.'

There was much nodding around the table.

'In fact,' Michelle added, 'from what I've read, Lafayette couldn't even *do* the tricks you did tonight because he's got a memory like a sieve. I saw it in a newspaper article. He admits it himself: he's hopeless at remembering things, needs umpteen takes when he's doing his straight-to-camera stuff for his TV show. What you did tonight required you to remember tons of details about lots of different people. There's no way a guy with a dodgy short-term memory could do that.'

'And what's your source for this apparent affliction?' I asked.

'I told you: it was in the paper. It's been mentioned a few times, actually,' she added with a satisfied certainty.

'I'm sure it has,' I agreed. 'I'm also sure Gabriel Lafayette has a better short-term memory than anybody in this room. But wouldn't it put everybody off the scent of his trickery if he made out otherwise?'

'You've no proof of that, though,' Grant jumped in, seizing the moment. 'You're always on about evidence, but you've no proof Lafayette doesn't have a bad memory, and you've no evidence he used your tricks on stage. You can't disprove his powers, all you can prove is that you can replicate his feats, and that doesn't mean his were achieved the same way.'

'Yeah,' ventured Michelle. 'Hollywood special effects can recreate the wooden horse of Troy or the flight of the *Spruce Goose*. Does that mean there was no wooden horse, or that Howard Hughes never flew his plane?'

'Exactly,' Grant resumed. 'You've shown you can create the *illusion* of contacting the dead, but that doesn't prove Lafayette can't do it for real.'

I thought of Keith's grave doubts regarding my demonstration changing anybody's mind, and glanced at him. He was grinning at me over the rim of the pint he was quaffing, 'I told you so' written all over his face.

'Are you familiar with the scientific principle known as Occam's Razor?' I asked.

Grant laughed and pointed to his watch. 'Twenty-three minutes,' he announced. 'Susan wins. I said inside twenty, she said more than twenty but under half an hour.'

'For what?'

'Until you mentioned Occam's Razor.'

'Prick,' I said, less than graciously, though I couldn't help but laugh. 'Okay, so you understand that it states how the explanation that makes the fewest assumptions is usually the right one. I ask you: now that I've shown how anybody can create the illusion of reading minds or contacting the dead, doesn't my explanation for what Lafayette does make fewer assumptions than yours?'

'I don't know, Mikey. But you're assuming he's got a great memory. You're assuming he's practised in all these techniques. You're assuming that he had the time and wherewithal to go digging deep into the backgrounds of complete strangers – in a city he had barely visited up until then – just so that he could impress a crowd who already thought very highly of him. Occam's Razor states that the simplest explanation is usually the right one. Yours is a pretty convoluted affair.'

'While yours assumes, despite no evidence whatsoever, that human beings live on in some form after we die, not to mention its other less-than-insignificant assumption: that Gabriel Lafayette has super-powers. That he can do things beyond the ken of all known physics. I think that assumption on its own kind of outweighs the sum of mine.'

'I didn't say he had super-powers,' Grant protested, but I had him on his heels, so I pressed on.

'But that's what anybody who believes in woo – in psychics and mediums – *is* saying. That they have abilities to do things beyond the ken of all known science. If that's not super-powers, what is? Good job the comics don't hold their superheroes to the same low standards, though, wouldn't you say? Imagine it: Psychicman. He can read minds and contact the dead. However, his powers only work some of the time, and only when nobody is looking, and only when there's no-one in the vicinity giving off negative energy. Not going to fight much crime with that, are you?'

'You're just being facetious calling them super-powers. The fact that these phenomena – and Lafayette doesn't even call them abilities – are beyond the ken of known science is the point.'

'But they're *not* beyond the ken of science. They're tricks. He just gloms on about science to create a mystique around himself. Christ, the biggest irony is that conjurors and mentalists used to pretend that what they were doing was magic and sorcery to that very same end. His gimmick is that it's *not* magic but some unexplored realm of science, but it's a gimmick nonetheless.'

'Listen, Michael,' Grant said, his register and mode of address now more solemn. 'You put on a hell of a show tonight, but the difference between what you did and what Lafayette did is bigger than you could ever know, because it's in here.'

He put his hand on his heart. I knew what was coming, and I was about to lose. I couldn't convince him about the matters I had solid evidence for, so there was no chance of making any headway in this subjective and thus entirely immeasurable territory.

'I felt something that night when he was getting messages from my dad. I felt my dad's presence like I hadn't done since I'd been standing beside him. That's not something you can achieve with gimmicks and tricks. You can't fake what someone *else* is experiencing.'

'So why were some of the people here tonight in tears?'

'You were dealing with emotive issues, about people's lost loved ones. But I'm not talking about just coming over all emotional. I'm saying I felt my dad in that room, right beside me.'

'I don't doubt you did: Lafayette made you think about him more intensely than you had done for years, made you think about all the difficult and complicated things that still lay between the two of you.'

'No,' he said stiffly, shaking his head, his face stony. 'I know what I felt, and it was something else.' This was where Psychicman Lafayette and his fellow superheroes drew their greatest power: the need to believe.

It was futile, but I felt obliged and compelled to try and make him see sense. 'It was something else, all right, something incredibly powerful: your love for your father. Don't give away the credit for that to someone else.'

'And what about Bryant Lemuel's love?' asked Susan, politely but forcefully. 'Was that so strong that half a dozen witnesses have testified they heard his dead wife's voice up at Glassford Hall? Or are you going to show us how Gabriel Lafayette faked that?'

'They've got it on tape,' added Grant. 'Hard evidence. What do you say to that?'

'I don't know what they've got on tape, and neither do any of us, as it's never been released,' I replied. 'All you know is what's *claimed* to be on it, and I very much doubt, if anyone outside that suspiciously close wee circle ever gets to analyse it, that it will turn out to be a dead woman's voice.'

'So they're all lying?' Grant asked. 'Lawyers, journalists, a charity head, Lemuel, his housekeeper? They conspired to make it up, despite what it was likely to do to their credibility? Where's Occam's Razor now?'

'I'm not saying they're all lying, I'm sure they heard something. But I'm also sure it'll have been Lafayette's doing. I just don't know how.'

I knew it was feeble. Grant finished his pint with a look of triumph.

'See, if you can't explain something as huge as that, how does the fact that you can do a few tricks prove anything about Gabriel Lafayette?'

I shook my head, smiled across at Keith. 'You win,' I said. 'I didn't change anybody's mind.'

He shrugged and finished his pint. 'Come on, drink up. Let's hit somewhere more lively. You up for that?' he asked, turning to Grant.

'Fuck, yeah. The night is young. What about you, ladies?'

Michelle and Susan cast a glance at myself and Keith, at which point the coach turned back into a pumpkin and we turned back into social suicide.

They got to their feet, mumbling something about maybe seeing us in the union disco later, which I understood to mean they were going somewhere else entirely. The debate clearly concluded, the rest of the group around the table dispersed as well. I downed the last of my heavy and was about to get up when I saw Laura Bailey slide almost apologetically into the other side of the booth. She glanced at Grant and Keith, both standing holding their jackets, then back at me.

'Oh, sorry, if you're just leaving . . .'

'You want the booth? No problem,' I told her, though as I said it I realised the place was half empty, no shortage of seating.

'No, I meant, I don't want to hold you back.'

From what, I thought, looking at who was waiting for me.

'There's no rush,' I said, trying to sound accommodating, though in fact I felt distinctly uncomfortable. My ghost at the feast, the person I'd felt wary of somehow damaging, was now face to face and unavoidably about to force my hand.

'I realise it's getting late and you don't know me, but I'm kind of shy and I didn't want to, you know . . .'

She bit her lip, let the sentence hang unfinished. Her eyes flitted left and right, which I took to indicate the crowd just vacated, which she had sat apart from. She didn't realise the role she had played here tonight, nor that I so vividly remembered her from Lafayette's show a year back. I thought briefly of how I might use this advantage, but felt immediately wrong about even holding it.

'I do know who you are,' I confessed. 'You're Laura Bailey.'

Her brow furrowed momentarily in surprise. 'How did you know?'

'Psychic powers,' I said with a wry smile. 'No, I remember you from the debating chamber. Which is, I'm guessing, why you're here.'

'A mind reader too.'

'You know, a stage mentalist once said that he couldn't read minds, but he could read thoughts. For example, if somebody was running towards him with a meat-cleaver and a wrathful expression, he could read that guy's thoughts pretty clearly. As it gets incrementally subtler, obviously the reading difficulty level corresponds.'

I wasn't sure how interesting or even relevant she would find this, but I was feeling fidgety and nervous and it just kind of glommed out. By some accident I think it may have made me seem relaxed but sincere. Albeit in an incontinently garrulous way.

'I remember you from that night in the debating chamber too. Hard to miss. You must have been the only one in the hall not buying it.'

'I'd like to think otherwise, but I reckon that's probably depressingly true.'

She stared intently at me, almost accusingly.

'You must think I'm an idiot,' she said, sounding vulnerable, even embarrassed.

'I don't,' I told her, quickly. It wasn't the kind of question you could let the jury deliberate on or you were answering it without opening your mouth. 'Guys like Lafayette wouldn't be successful if they could only fool idiots.'

She nodded, immediately more relaxed, some unspoken doubt or worry dispelled. 'Thanks,' she added, after a moment's quiet.

Keith turned away from Grant and leaned into the booth at this point.

'Look, we're gonna head,' he said. 'Leave you guys to it. Gimme a buzz in a wee while and I'll let you know where we've ended up, okay?'

I looked from him to Laura and back. 'Eh, if, I mean, yeah. A buzz. Sure.'

Laura smiled a little at my state of fluster. 'Can I buy you a drink?' she asked.

'Eh, yeah, sure, pint of heavy would be . . . no, hang on, I should, let me . . .' But she was on her feet and heading to the bar. I watched her walk away, then was distracted by the sight of Keith and Grant on their way to the door. They were looking back at me, nodding towards Laura and making thumbs-up, get-in-there gestures. I felt myself blush and looked away, fixing upon the table. I'd be getting no end of ribbing about this later, and could already hear them laughing as they went out the door.

I looked up and watched her as she ordered drinks. To say she was out of my league didn't really narrow it down as far as campus female taxonomy went. In fact, I wasn't sure I could actually be said to *have* a league; I didn't even know how to play. But she was pretty by anybody's standards. Not a goddess, not an Inara, but definitely a Kaylee, which in a way gave an even harsher sense of perspective, as just looking at her made me confront the fact that here in the real world, even the Kaylees were way out of the reach of the geeks.

But tonight, however, tonight, tonight, I was at least talking to a girl for a change, and she was even buying me a drink. It was like being a normal student for a while.

She came back with the drinks and slid into the booth, alongside me this time. I put both hands around the cold glass of the pint, for want of knowing where else to put them. Crippling self-consciousness was preparing for attack, I knew. Laura leaned back in her seat after taking a long sip of red wine.

'You can tell me if I'm out of order, and you can leave if I'm boring you,' she said. 'In fact, *I'll* leave if I'm boring you, and I'll know I'm boring you, so don't be polite. It's just that . . . okay, I realise this is weird. We don't know each other, but I feel like you're the one person I can talk to about this.'

'Consider me now officially very intrigued. Fire away. I'm a good listener,' I assured her. 'An even better one with a pint in front of me.'

Laura smiled, though a little anxiously, looking slightly vulnerable again. Then she took a big gulp of wine and began to talk.

'As the good book says, I was lost, but now I'm found,' she began. 'That's what it feels like, anyway. Or if not found, then at least in possession of a half-decent map and no longer holding the bloody thing upside down in typical ditzy-Laura mode . . .'

She talked and I listened, that's how it went. I tried to intervene with reassurances or explanations where I thought they were being invited, but she waved them away. She wanted to tell her story, just how it looked from her point of view. I understood: when it comes to these matters, perspective is everything.

Besides, she could have the floor all night, as far as I was concerned. I'd so often heard it said that girls just wanted someone to listen to them, how that was the secret to making an impression. This had always struck me as a bit of a catch-22, as I'd never been able to make a sufficient impression as to get one to actually talk to me for any length of time. So just sitting there, being the one she was telling all this to, made me feel, well, something quite amazing. There were always guys on TV making shitty gags – and less than half joking – about how they couldn't get their wives or girlfriends to shut up. Spoiled, arrogant pricks, I always thought, *wishing* I had a girlfriend talking *my* ear off.

I knew that was all we were doing, and I shouldn't be daft enough to interpret it as anything else, but the point is, right then, it was *enough*. I loved the way she looked at me, with such imploring sincerity, or with that vulnerable self-consciousness. I felt so singled out, so trusted. I felt liked. And I understood the other reason why listening to a girl made such a good impression: as long as she was talking, there was less opportunity for me to open my dorky mouth and remind her what a female-repellent uber-geek I was.

Unfortunately, that state of grace inevitably had to end.

'I still have some questions,' she said. 'Some aspects of what Lafayette did that I still can't explain.'

I must have made a face. She thought I was taking the huff, but my discomfort was entirely down to anxiety at it being my turn to talk.

'No, please,' she implored. 'I heard your discussion with the others and I understand the psychology. The twisted logic goes that unless you can explain away *all* the feats and phenomena, what's left proves on its own that they were all real. I understand your frustration with it, but it *is* powerful psychology.'

'That's why it endures,' I ventured, trying to sound as unfrustrated as I could fake. 'It makes it really hard to let go, because there's always the seed of doubt taking root, feeding off the need to believe and making the whole thing grow again.'

'That's just it,' she replied. 'If I'm to exorcise this, fully and finally, there's something I need you to explain. If you can't, don't worry about it, I won't take it as proof that you were wrong about everything else. But I understand myself well enough to know it will never go away. It'll germinate like you said, some small part of me holding on to the belief that my mum and my brother were really back with me that night.'

'So, no pressure,' I said, thinking aloud. She laughed, an undeserved outcome from my involuntary brain-fart. 'Try me,' I invited.

'Your show tonight: by your own admission, you planned it months in advance. You were able to find out all that information using your questionnaire, then played the odds and managed – via free tickets – to get a certain percentage of the people who filled it in to come along tonight.'

I nodded.

'Lafayette's performance was spontaneous,' she said. 'It was just supposed to be a thank-you speech and maybe a talk. He wasn't planning to do anything else, but then he got caught up in the atmosphere – call it good vibes, whatever – and decided on the spot to put on a bit of a show. Now, I know from what you've shown me that he could do the billet-reading tricks at zero notice, but the things he knew about me, and about Grant . . .'

'He *was* planning to do a show,' I stated. 'Make no mistake about that. It's all part of his act to make out it was purely a spur-of-the-moment deal. I've read accounts of his performances elsewhere: he's never "intending" to do any woo-woo stuff, but then he gets such a great feeling of energy from the audience and decides on the spot to try a few things. More smart psychology: the audience thinks not only that there's something special in the air that night, but that it's down to them. Just like he claims he has a poor memory, he tells anyone credulous enough to buy it that he's a poor showman. He's a brilliant showman, got to give him that.'

'Okay. That all fits. But here's the part that doesn't, the part that's been haunting me for a year. Whether he was planning that show or not, unlike you and your questionnaire candidates, there was no way he could have known specifically that I was coming, or Grant, or anyone else. The things he knew, they would have taken some finding out. Not impossible, but not written on the back of my matric card either. He could, it's possible, have somehow found out about my mum and my brother. But what he couldn't have known was that I specifically would be at the show. I didn't even get a ticket until the last minute.'

She looked painfully perplexed, unsettlingly reminiscent of the bewildered face I had seen in the debating chamber. This doubt, this unknowing, and the hope of the unworldly that it kept rekindling, it was clearly still pulling her to pieces. Fuck you, Lafayette, I thought. This was the reason I did the show. She was no longer my ghost at the feast. She was someone with a pain I could not merely salve, but cure.

'You answered your own question,' I told her. 'You didn't get a ticket until the last minute, because it was sold out, but you were on the waiting list. I've asked Grant Neilson: he was on the waiting list too, as was everyone else Lafayette singled out for special treatment that night. Your name, your address, your phone number, all down in black and white, as well as your strong intention of attending the show. He knew you were coming, Laura, knew it for almost a fortnight. Was that long enough to go rooting through your past, you reckon?'

She nodded, her eyes rapidly filling with tears.

'Have you got a hanky?' she asked.

I reached into my pocket and produced a torn-off length of supermarket generic-brand bogroll. At least it was unsnottered. She took it from me regardless, dabbing at her nose and cheeks.

'Classy, eh?' I commented, covering the awkwardness of the moment.

She laughed, sniffing and swallowing. She looked somehow thoroughly open, laid bare, and yet no longer vulnerable. Despite the tears and the runny nose, she seemed lighter, more relaxed. I guess she'd bottomed out. Once you're reduced to sharing a booth with me of an evening, the only way is up.

'So that's why Mabel has a waiting list too,' she suggested.

'Quite. Needed to let you hang around for a couple of weeks so she had time to do a bit of background digging about your family, not to mention the opportunity to go through your bag while you attended one of her services. I'm betting that among your possessions on the day she managed it was a Politics essay bearing a sub-fifty score circled in red pen on the front.'

'I would have had that, yeah. I saw my Politics tutor on Wednesday afternoons that term, same day as Mabel held a service.'

'And if you'd missed her show, you might have found the waiting list got a week longer. On the other hand, she can bump you up the queue if the circumstances allow. Your lady up from Liverpool: she got in with a two- or three-day turnaround, didn't she?'

'That's right. But – forgive me another question, but this is something else that's been baffling me – how did Mabel find out about the woman's dead husband and his shenanigans back in the sixties? She'd never been to Glasgow before.'

'Never been to Glasgow, but doubtless a frequent flyer among mediums back down south. They trade information about regular "sitters", as they call them. Mabel is what's known as an open medium. That is, among her fellow practitioners, open about the fact that it's all a racket, open to scratching each other's backs. They keep files – which they call poems, so that they can refer to them discreetly in non-medium company – on every-body they read for. It's sometimes called the Blue Book. There's no actual book, but it refers to the collective body of work that's in circulation. As soon as this old dear asked for an appointment, Mabel would have been on the blower to her contacts down south to see if anybody had the goods on this particular sitter. Somebody comes up trumps and shazam, by a happy coincidence, Mabel can suddenly squeeze this lady in at short notice. The old dear is then blown away by the fact that this woman she's never met, in a city she's never visited, knows all kinds of stuff about her past. Your name will be on a "poem" now too. Wouldn't be surprised if somebody – maybe even Mabel herself – quietly noted it and a few others in the debating chamber.'

'Jesus, I didn't realise it was so organised. Mabel's set-up seemed so ramshackle.'

'All the more reason for her congregation to donate generously to her New Church Fund. Most mediums have got some kind of "project" on the go. You could donate a million quid but it wouldn't go towards buying one brick, unless you count the house Mabel's planning to retire to in some sunnier clime.'

Laura sighed, looking to the ceiling then back at me.

'All politeness aside, you really *must* think I'm an idiot.'

'Anybody can be fooled, especially when part of them wants to be. Lafayette did his homework on you and knew which buttons to push, knew where your hurt resided so that he could tap into it. When I looked at you in the debating chamber, you're right, it was pity, not scorn. Scorn I reserve for the unsinkable rubber ducks.'

She laughed, her eyes flashing with an intrigued delight. It was like having my ego electrified.

'The what? Unsinkable rubber ducks?'

'It was coined by James "The Amazing" Randi, a Canadian magician and world-renowned sceptic, to describe people who are determined to go on believing in woo, no matter how much evidence to the contrary you present them with.'

'You mean like Grant Neilson and the people who were sitting here tonight.'

'Yeah. With Grant, it's partly that he's pig-headed and loves an argument as much as he hates admitting he's wrong. Plus, he thinks it's all a laugh. The stuff with his dad touched him and surprised him, which is why he's so defensive of it, but other than that, he can't see why I take it so seriously, which is why he keeps coming back to wind me up. Keith doesn't understand it either. Everybody keeps telling me it's only a bit of fun, what does it matter if people want to believe this nonsense; if it gives them comfort, who am I to try taking that away? Keith says I'm becoming a zealot. Maybe he's right. Maybe it's a sign I'm going nuts that I seem to be the only one who thinks this stuff is dangerous.'

'You're not the only one who thinks that,' she said, and she placed a hand on my arm. Some part of me threatened to explode, as if my body could barely contain whatever energy had been released. 'Not any more. Christ, I got so messed up by it all, I feel like setting up a survivors' group. But at least I'm through it now, I *have* survived. No small thanks to you.'

She gave my arm a squeeze.

'I told Keith that if I changed just one person's mind, it would have been worth it.'

It was the first thing that leapt into my head, at a time when I desperately needed to say something, both to cover up the fact that I was melting inside and to prevent me from articulating that particular sensation. Even I thought it sounded cool, but it was sheer jamminess. On the down side, it kind of killed things for a while, like I'd brought the issue to a natural end. And she took her hand away, which served to underline that the moment was over.

We sat, not saying anything for a while, sipping from near-empty drinks. Once again, I got the feeling that a spell had been broken and a number of footmen's uniforms were now lying discarded at the front door, each one empty but for a bewildered-looking rodent. One of the barmen shouted for last orders. Until then, I had never understood why Cinderella ran. What would it matter what she was wearing: the Prince had seen the person underneath. But that's not something you're likely to feel very confident about when all of a sudden you become aware you're back in rags. Or a big geeky brown coat.

145

'So, how do you know so much about all this stuff?' Laura asked.

'Oh, that's a story for another day,' I said, offering a polite out from what I took to be merely a polite enquiry. She looked at her watch, which seemed to confirm as much.

'Well, in about half an hour, it'll *be* another day,' she said with a shrug.

I was still trying to decode what the shrug was intended to convey when my mobile rang.

'A text from Keith,' I reported. 'They're in Club Shub.'

'Och well, I'd better let you catch up with your pals,' she said. Which sounded to me a lot like '*Please* go and catch up with your pals.'

It was ending, but it wasn't ending in shame and acrimony, a major plus as far as I was concerned.

Maybe it was the drink, the residual feeling of her hand on my arm, I don't know; maybe a reckless death wish to precipitate the aforementioned shame and acrimony and get it over with. Whatever, it came out before I could believe I was saying it.

'Do you think I could see you tomorrow?' I asked her.

She smiled.

The last thing I remember is trying not to fall asleep, fighting it even as my eyes closed because I wanted to eke out every last moment. She said we'd have tomorrow. I should have surrendered willingly to hasten the dawn and all that it promised, but I didn't want the night to end.

**III**

I have allowed my mediumship to be subject to experiments in the hope that knowledge will grow from them. I have assisted the true seekers in tests, blind tests and double blind tests. It matters not to me whether people believe that what I do is genuine. All I can say is that I try my best.

Gordon Smith, the 'Psychic Barber'

# Cheating our children

*Can under-fire scientists continue to dictate the classroom agenda? Not after this*, says award-winning columnist Jillian Noble

So, this week's big question: which of the cynics – oh, I'm sorry, *sceptics* – is going to be man enough to stand up and apologise first? Perhaps they could form an orderly – and, of course, empiricistly rational – queue outside Kelvin University, where their prejudices and presumptions are currently in the process of being, to use a term they love themselves, debunked.

Then again, as a seasoned sceptic *of* the sceptics, I won't be holding my breath. They are infinitely resourceful at finding ways to wriggle and squirm their way out of ever admitting they are wrong, no matter how much evidence they are presented with. Since the publication of my book on Gabriel Lafayette, my in-tray here at *The Mail* has very quickly filled up with furious missives from these poor souls who seem outraged at me personally for reporting facts that they are very clearly discomfited to hear. Please don't blame me, chaps, I'm only the messenger. Surely you didn't believe your house of cards would remain standing forever, did you? Well, I didn't wreck it; I only wrote about who did.

I received several emails – possibly duplicate aliases, in this day and age – citing a demonstration they had witnessed, of 'tricks' similar to Lafayette's on-stage feats, performed by a student who claimed no psychic ability. (I would not be surprised to learn that said student was also the author of all the messages.) The simplistic logic applied was that as Lafayette's feats had been somehow replicated, the man was *de facto* a fake, his phenomena accomplished using the same methods. And the sceptics claim they're *not* the ones who'll believe anything!

If you're even tempted by such thinking, I would spare you

your later blushes by pointing you, politely, in the direction of none other than Sir Arthur Conan Doyle. As the creator of Sherlock Holmes, Sir Arthur, it would be safe to say, knew a thing or three about the ways of deceivers, not to mention examining the evidence and the art of drawing logical conclusions. His words on this are signal:

'I would warn the critic not to be led away by the sophistry that because some professional trickster, apt at the game of deception, can produce a somewhat similar effect, therefore the originals were produced in the same way. There are few realities which cannot be imitated, and the ancient argument that because conjurors can produce certain results, therefore similar results obtained by untrained people under natural conditions are also false, is surely discounted by the general public.'

As it surely must be discounted today, all the more so in light of my reports in this paper earlier in the week. Oh yes, the cynics' wriggling skills and squirming techniques are going to have to attain Olympic standard in order to evade the implications of what has been recorded over recent weeks in the austerely clinical laboratories of Kelvin University. 'Test conditions!' is the mantra they've constantly chanted to gainsay inconveniently inexplicable phenomena. 'Evidence is only admissible if it is observed under controlled test conditions!' (though they usually reserve the right to keep shtum as to what those conditions ought to be, so that they can always claim a crucial aspect was missing, after the fact).

Well, I'd like to see them wedge a needle through the protocols under which Gabriel Lafayette has been observed at Kelvin University. Three highly qualified scientists, all from different fields, worked to devise and enforce conditions that would prevent any form of 'cheating' by their subject, though for my taste the word is pejoratively presumptuous. It's hard to explain why Lafayette would wish to cheat when he has persistently maintained that the phenomena observed around him are not effected *by* him.

Plus, contrary to hysterical predictions and uninformed innuendo, Bryant Lemuel's influence did not fill this pilot project with compliant placemen, instead leaving all appointments to the university science faculty. Furthermore, the only moment of controversy was when an assistant was dismissed, not because she was making things difficult for Lafayette, but because her *laxity* had led to a possible breach in the protocol.

'Anything that can be used to poke a single hole in this project effectively punctures the whole thing,' one of the scientists told me. 'If we retain someone who left the gate open once, that would be enough to discredit the study.'

All of the scientists involved are ready to sign off on the chair's first formal report, a paper that will throw open the most exciting debate to face the scientific world in decades, arguably even centuries. Events took place – observed and recorded under the strictest security – that demonstrate incontrovertibly the influence of forces outwith the realm of modern physics.

'It's like the quantum theory parallel slit experiments,' says Dr Rudi Kline, who has been at Kelvin University for twenty-two years and confesses to seldom having been so excited by a project. 'People will be reluctant to accept the conclusions, because on the surface they will seem absurd, the stuff of fantasy. The same thing happened when it was suggested that the effects observed in parallel slit experiments were caused by the influence of "shadow photons" in parallel universes. Now that explanation is increasingly becoming an accepted orthodoxy. This could be the beginning of a paradigm shift.'

Ironically, however, given the accusatory predictions from certain quarters that this project would be unscientific, it is the involvement of a non-scientist that is likely to be cited by many as the most compelling evidence of the study's authenticity. Yes, forget all the protocols and safeguards, the real clincher is that no less an arch-cynic than Jack Parlabane – a man who sees conspiracy and deception in his cornflakes of a morning – has been casting a paranoid eye over all proceedings and, despite being a convicted criminal and thus eminently qualified to root out sleekit and dishonest practices, has admitted that he has detected none.

Parlabane's involvement was a deal-breaker, insisted upon by the late Dean of Science, Professor Niall Blake. Strange are the ways of scientific academia: Dr Kline, one of the university's leading physicists, and Professor Heidi Ganea, head of Organic Chemistry, plus of course Mather, formerly of Reed

University in California, were deemed insufficiently expert to conduct and observe the experiments. To get it done right, apparently, requires a journalist. I could have done it myself – I'd have gladly volunteered – but I doubt Professor Blake meant it as an endorsement of our profession. I don't like to speak ill of the recently deceased, but personally I think it was a form of smear. He insisted on a journalist synonymous with sleaze and deception, implying that there must be something underhand and corrupt about the whole thing. Blake previously suggested a conjuror be brought in, which Lafayette admits would have been even worse. 'We may as well have carried out the research in a big top, for all the signals that would have sent out.'

The current rector of Kelvin University is typically dragging his heels and has not finally signed off on the report, but he will, and soon. Those of us who know Mr Parlabane to be a time-served attention-seeker appreciate that this is no more than grandstanding. If I were to be more generous, I would say also that as a journalist, he knows his deadline and isn't going to file too early in case the story changes. The paper has been designed to include a submission by him, specifically listing his suspicions (even if that is all they are; not everyone is required to provide evidence, it seems) that trickery was involved. That section is currently blank. Parlabane fully understands how this will be interpreted and has privately admitted that he is as astonished as the scientists by what they have all witnessed.

He won't be the last person to have his expectations challenged by the soon-to-be-launched Spiritual Science Chair's work. When it was first proposed, Bryant Lemuel faced rancorous objections on the grounds that it would embarrass the university, but events already suggest that it could, in the long term, bring the science faculty its greatest renown. This paper is not going to change the world overnight, but it could constitute the first crucial step towards what Dr Kline referred to as a 'paradigm shift'.

'The paradigm is the accepted scientific understanding of the majority at any given time,' he explained to me. 'The pre-Copernican acceptance that the planets revolved around the Earth, for instance. But when enough scientists adhere to an idea that challenges the paradigm, a shift can occur, establishing a new paradigm, which itself becomes the accepted wisdom.'

I won't go into the details he gave as he attempted to explain the parallel slit laser experiments he mentioned, but the main thing I took from it was that science is replete with these paradigm shifts. The unthinkable becomes the self-evident. Tell a child that people used to believe the Earth was flat, and their expression should illustrate the point adequately.

And it is to children that we must unavoidably turn our attention whenever the kaleidoscope of human knowledge receives such a hefty shake. The findings to be imminently published in this paper clearly have massive long-term ramifications for education; not just for how we teach science, but for the demarcation of the boundaries of what *constitutes* science in our schools. Science cannot go on being used as a blunt instrument to muscle out the spiritual; nor can the two be automatically defined as mutually exclusive. They may indeed be on the way towards a momentous reconciliation. If scientists can observe proof of hitherto unquantified forces, forces that have staggering implications for the existence of life after death, then what other miracles and impossibilities, long ridiculed by the empiricists, may yet be ratified by the empiricists' own criteria?

Lemuel, whose generous endowment made the Spiritual Science Chair possible, is monitoring these developments with less a giddy sense of excitement than a wry nod that says 'I told you so'.

'It's exciting news, but in truth it's no more than the latest example of how the scientists' assumptions can be wrong,' he told me yesterday. 'So I have to ask, how can we then let those same scientists and those same assumptions govern what is taught in our schools? When they're not being caught out like this, they're busy changing their minds about what was written in stone the week before. They tell us that this is how science evolves. Sounds like they want to have their cake and eat it, to me. My question is, if they've been wrong about so many things before, what else are they wrong about right now? The Big Bang? Evolution? And yet they won't consider letting the kids in science classes learn about anything that might cast doubt upon either of those theories.'

Lemuel doesn't mention these matters idly in passing. He is gearing up to take this issue to the Executive, to 'start a debate that's half past overdue', as he puts it. And if he has a published paper from a leading university science department in his hand as he does so, he'll be even harder than usual to argue against.

'There is more to this world, this universe than these entrenched scientists are prepared to admit,' Lemuel said to me, thoroughly impassioned. 'If we don't explore it with open minds and open eyes, and we don't teach it in our schools, then we are cheating our children.'

Now, as I keep having to remind people, I may be married to the Minister for Education, but that doesn't mean I hold any sway over what my husband gets up to at work. However, I do know him well enough to assure my readers – and Mr Lemuel – that he is aware this will be a debate the politicians cannot afford to avoid.

Lemuel paints it as tantamount to cheating our children, and to cheat our children is to cheat our own future. In a society riddled with moral equivalencies, surely that's a crime none of us should stand for.

# Not knowing Jack

Strap yourself in, you're about to be surprised, even amazed. No, really. Ask Sarah, she'll verify the first bit.

Okay, here goes:

It's been one of my abiding principles that when you wake up each morning, you should welcome the possibility that later that same day, your most deeply held belief might be proven utterly wrong: from political convictions to the laws of physics.

Told you you'd be surprised. The amazing part we'll get to later. For now, let's just deal with your expectations of me. Everybody calls me a cynic, without thinking very hard about what a cynic is. I've heard or read it about myself so many times, I sometimes feel like checking it's not printed on a laminated badge and pinned to my breast. Jack Parlabane: Certified Cynic.

I'm not a cynic, or at least I *aspire* not to be. I aim for sceptic, but I'd confess (and if I didn't my wife would grass me) that sometimes I come up short. Admittedly, the distinction between cynic and sceptic can sometimes be difficult to detect, because the practice of both may on the surface appear identical. The cynic will do a very effective job of demolishing spurious arguments and debunking flimsy assertions, employing the same logic and positing the same analysis as the sceptic. The difference is, the sceptic does not set out to 'debunk' anything, but to objectively evaluate the evidence. His mind is not already made up, and is open to the possibility that, even if he has preconceptions, they may yet be disproven. The sceptic also, crucially, will turn the same cold, evaluative logic upon anything; whereas the cynic, if you scratch hard enough, usually has some cherished sentiment or belief upon which he will never bring his fangs to bear.

The cynic is an attack dog, but there's a precious cuddly toy in his kennel. That's what all the aggression is there to protect.

155

If he's mercilessly slagging something off, it's to make the thing he loves look better by comparison. He's usually a disappointed idealist, someone who has had his heart broken and decided everything's been shite since. That's his war-cry, in fact: 'Everything's shite since . . .'; or 'Everything's shite except . . .'

I have always been afraid of turning into that guy. That's why I try to live by the maxim above. Plus, as a journalist, I like to think it makes me that bit harder to fool. It's when you think you already know the story that you risk letting the *real* story pass right under your nose.

A few days before Project Lamda began, I received an email from a science student warning me of the responsibility that was on my head to *protect the reputation of the university as a respected scientific institution*. By which he meant it was expected of me to catch Gabriel Lafayette 'at it' and expose him as a fraud. *If you need help catching this guy cheating or want a word to the wise on how he does some of his tricks, just drop me a line.*

This from an aspiring scientist. I confess I was a little insecure and not at all comfortable with my prospective involvement in the project, so instead of deleting the message, I even emailed back. *Aren't we supposed to go into these things with an open mind?* I asked. *My instinct and experience has always told me this kind of thing is bollocks, but if I go in with my mind already made up and let my beliefs dictate my interpretations, I'd be behaving more like a religious person than a scientist, would I not?*

*No*, he replied. *It is scientific to assume cheating. For cheating, read 'rational explanation' if it makes you feel better, but assume it. At all times.*

Underlining the position of the science camp, Easy Mather was entirely in agreement with my email correspondent. I mentioned this exchange when we were discussing – not for the first time – my role in the tests; my role, as I said, being something I was as clear on as I was at ease with.

'Your job is to look for cheating, simple as that,' he spelled out. 'It is not biased or prejudiced to assume it: it is *scientific* to assume it. However, if you find none, then *that*'s when you have to be open-minded about your conclusions.'

I say all this by way of preface to the following account, which may read contrary to a few people's expectations. What I'm about to tell you is the truth, exactly as I witnessed it. There were many baffling events, about which you have no doubt heard rumours or read details elsewhere. But that's not the half of it, for there were incidents and phenomena surrounding Project Lamda that were far more jaw-dropping than anything you can convey in an academic paper. I had my preconceptions challenged and my eyes opened to things I did not believe possible. And to top it all, well . . .

You have heard about the voice of Hilda Lemuel at Glassford Hall, but believe me, that's nothing. Before these tests were complete, my involvement with Gabriel Lafayette was to precipitate a full, *multi*-sensory encounter – not just hearing, but seeing too – with a dead person.

# Project Lamda stage one:
# the pre-season friendlies

Before I begin, I really ought to mention the loss of Sarah's boss, Professor Niall Blake, as it would be appropriate to deal with such an issue sombrely before the tone changes to the farce that soon characterised the early part of the experiments.

Blake died only a few days after that dinner in the Maxwell Hall. He suffered a tragic accident in his Kelvinside home, where he had lived alone since his divorce from a long-suffering wife who had decided, a decade or so back, that she'd suffered enough. As often is the case with brilliant but single-minded dusty old academics, his brain was a cathedral but his house was a cowp, something Sarah could vouch for, having visited a couple of times. It was a tall and handsome enough old Victorian villa, but the last person to carry out much in the way of maintenance, never mind refurbishment, had been wearing a demob suit at the time, and so according to Sarah, it was the kind of place more likely to attract Kim and Aggie than Kirsty and Phil.

The poor old buffer put his hand on the banister one evening, only for the ageing wood to snap under his weight. He fell fifteen feet from the first-floor landing and broke his neck.

Sarah was pretty upset by it. He wasn't exactly everybody's favourite cuddly uncle, but I guess I shouldn't be complaining about her strange affection for spiky and unlovable males. We both went to the funeral, or 'Mid-Morning of the Living Dead' as I thought of it, seldom having seen so many bloodless stiffs in one place. It was on the way home from this that she reminded me I had an obligation, 'when this nonsense commences, to ensure that he's not spinning in his grave'.

I will start by relating something that wasn't part of the tests (because it did not take place under 'controlled' conditions), but which deserves mention in this context nonetheless. If nothing else, it will set the scene for the kind of thing I was about to find myself immersed in.

I walked into the Randall Building, where the experiments took place, at around four o'clock on the first day of Project Lamda proper. There had been two weeks of preliminaries on other subjects, and now we were ready to put Lafayette himself under the microscope. Much of the work commenced around this time of day, it being when our other commitments were largely out of the way and the facilities were not only available, but entirely ours to control. I had walked from the staff car park around the corner next to the Pharmacology department, and coincidentally reached the lobby at the same time as Lafayette, who had come in via the link corridor across Kelvin Avenue. I was concerned I might be skirting just the wrong side of late and was relieved to see the main man only just on his way in too. No show without Punch, after all. I had kind of assumed he'd be there well in advance, but was forgetting that, technically, he was the subject. Not only was he not required until the tests were set up, it was actually imperative that he not be permitted anywhere near the labs before everything was in place and secured.

The lobby was close to deserted, just a few stragglers making their way out from the last classes of the day. It was a hexagonal concourse that gave on to three large lecture theatres as well as the lifts and staircases that accessed six storeys of labs, conference rooms and other auditoria. I'd been in it before with Sarah, around eleven one morning, and it was like Central Station: hundreds of chattering students passing busily through. Places like that can seem eerily bereft when you see them empty; somehow smaller too. It seemed to emphasise the fact that Lafayette and I had found ourselves alone together.

We exchanged an uneasy greeting, though it had to be said all the unease was on my part. Lafayette looked entirely relaxed. He wore his trademark jeans and a crumpled white linen jacket that ought to have looked every mile from New Orleans out of place here in Glasgow but somehow worked on him. I'm not saying it blended right in; more that Lafayette himself always seemed so incongruous that what he wore could hardly trump the effect.

'Don't be so nervous, Mr Parlabane,' he said, smiling. 'I'm the one who's gonna be on the spot. Hey, do you want a soda?'

He nodded towards the monolithic soft-drink vending machine across the empty lobby, to the right of the elevators.

'No thanks,' I told him, already having a belly full of coffee from an interview that afternoon.

'Don't worry, it's not bribery. I'll log it as a legitimate expense and reimburse myself from the Spiritual Science Chair's funds.'

I smiled, acknowledging he was taking the piss out of the strict adherence to protocol we were imminently about to observe, but declined again.

'I'm not thirsty.'

'Well, if you gimme a sec, I'm gonna grab myself a Coke before we head upstairs.'

'Sure,' I said. I stayed where I was and watched him walk across the concourse, the footfalls of his snakeskin boots echoing around us. Before he'd made it halfway, I heard a thump from the vending machine: the thump of a can dropping from the fridge into the collection tray.

Lafayette turned on his heel and looked back at me, making a 'woo, spooky' gesture with his fingers.

'If you can do it again, I'll be impressed,' I told him.

'I didn't do nothin',' he insisted, laughing.

He turned and resumed walking. He had taken only two paces when it happened again.

'You sure you don't want a drink?' he asked. 'Machine seems to think you do.'

'I'm fine,' I said. 'Unless the machine does beer.'

Lafayette bent down and produced two cans of Coke from the collection tray. 'Spiritual Science Chair is two pounds to the good,' he said, indicating the price bars. He walked back towards me, whereupon the machine thumped out another can, then another, then another. Thump, thump, thump, thump, it went. Lafayette was smiling at first, then started to look a little less easy as the incontinent dispensing went on. Cans started spilling from the overloaded collection tray and rolling around on the floor. Thump, thump, thump, the machine persisted, the noise amplified as it bounced back at us around the towering concrete walls.

Lafayette looked uncomfortable, worried even. He dropped the cans he was holding and put his hands to his ears against the thump of the machine and the clanging of cans upon the tiled floor.

'Stop,' I saw him mouth. Maybe he said it, but the first time it was impossible to hear. 'Stop,' he stated more audibly, closing his eyes. He repeated it again, getting louder, then finally yelled it in a register that leaned just the right way between commanding and desperate. The machine ceased, the sound of Lafayette's last word still ringing around the lobby.

'Shit,' he said, breathing out, his tone suggesting thinning patience rather than surprise, and immediately began gathering spilled cans. I walked across to help. We retrieved them from where they had rolled – some of them from almost inquisitive distances – and stacked them next to the now pacified machine.

'This kind of thing happens around me all the . . . well, not *all* the time, obviously, but too goddamn often. Some people think it's funny, some people think it's scary. Depending on the circumstances, I can go with either, but mostly I'd describe it as a pain in the ass.'

I didn't know what to say. Machines do have spontaneous malfunctions. It ought to have seemed comic, were it not for his wearied response, a joke that wasn't funny any more, hadn't been for a long time.

'Do you think it's something you're doing that causes it?' I asked.

'I *know* it's not something I'm doing,' he insisted. 'If I was the one exerting influence, this kind of shit *wouldn't* happen. But it does, over and over. What's frustrating is it's impossible to investigate. It's not like this happens *every* time I pass a soda machine, or all the computers crash *every* time I visit a bank. I never know when it's gonna happen. Scientifically, there's no way to compare to a control sample: I don't know how often things like this happen around other folks. But I'm betting it's a lot less than around me.'

I said nothing, reflecting on the fact that, as he said, there was no control sample to compare with. That was then. Now I'd join him in his bet. This kind of thing cannot possibly happen anything like as frequently around normal people. We had so

161

many electrical surges and power outages during the project that it reached the stage where I was wincing every time I reached for a light switch or an on button; and as for getting in a lift with the guy, forget it. I've had elevators spontaneously stop on me between floors – who hasn't – but riding with Lafayette, it was more remarkable if it didn't happen. Suffice it to say I soon decided I'd always be quicker taking the stairs.

None of this kind of weirdness happened during the preliminaries, when we were testing a few other psychic contenders. In fact, it would be accurate to say that nothing out of the ordinary happened inside or outside the laboratories, unless you count the superhuman brass necks on some of the chancers we came up against.

'Useful idiots', Mather called them. He got most of them by placing an ad in *Destiny* magazine, though a few actually turned up on spec because word travels fast in those circles. Naturally, I suppose, what with them all being psychic. They were lured by the prospect of having their 'powers' officially ratified by scientific observers, though some merely wanted to see what we were made of, and others still simply wanted the attention.

These 'useful idiots' were a great success in as much as their dismal failures demonstrated the effectiveness of our protocols. Lafayette seemed a little deflated by this. I assumed this to be due to the ramifications for his own impending tests, but there was more to it than that.

'I was really hoping we'd see something special, something that would challenge our expectations,' he said one evening towards the end of the preliminary studies, when we were all gathered for a coffee in the mess room we used as the project's base. 'I know there's always going to be cranks, but I did have genuine hopes that we'd witness just a glimmer of something we couldn't conventionally explain. I guess what we've seen here doesn't augur well.'

'We're doing augury too?' asked Professor Ganea, trying to lighten things up. 'I haven't ratified the protocol.'

Personally, I thought Lafayette had disappointingly low expectations of himself if he thought he was on a par with what we had seen by that point, and I was bracing myself for the whole project becoming one long and laughable waste of my time. The preliminaries witnessed a cavalcade of crackpots, the most challenging aspect of which, for my part, had been keeping a straight face.

I won't catalogue them all – they will appear in an appendix to the finished paper – but will give you a few selected highlights, starting with my particular favourite, a woman who claimed to have a psychic relationship with her pet. Do I even need to say what species of animal we're talking about here? Hey, guess you're psychic too.

I'm not permitted to reveal her real name, so let's call her Carla. I mean the woman, not the moggie: it was called Felidae, though apparently its full name was Felidae Downpaws Golden Summer. Carla said that Felidae could read her thoughts, even if she was in the next room. She could demonstrate this by selecting a Zener card and concentrating on it, after which Felidae would prove receipt of this information by sitting on the corresponding Zener symbol drawn on a mat she had brought along. There are five Zener symbols – a plus sign, a circle, a square, wavy lines and a star – designed by the Swiss psychologist Karl Zener for studies by the parapsychologist Joseph Banks Rhine. Zener, it should be noted, was increasingly dischuffed with JBR's investigations to the extent that he later made efforts to disassociate himself from the spook-chaser altogether.

Felidae's first dry run was a confounding success. Heidi Ganea remained in the target room with Carla, who randomly selected a card from a standard deck of twenty-five. Heidi recorded the selection while Carla stared at the card, holding it in front of her face with her right hand. Her left, Heidi also recorded, was largely occupied with wiping her nose as she claimed to be suffering from a head cold. The target room was, in this case, a windowless lab offering no means of signalling to the cat, audibly or visibly, the receiving room being a second window-less lab two doors down the same corridor. Mather had suggested the rooms be more remote – at different sides of the building or even on different floors – but Carla said she and Felidae's psychic connection was strongest at short range. She also insisted on being the one who picked up Felidae from the target mat after each test, giving her a cuddle, to keep the connection 'warm' as she put it, before returning her to her transit box. We were warned that if anyone else handled the cat, or indeed the mat, it would interfere with the psychic wave-signals, or something; I heard so much such bollocks during the preliminaries, I can't precisely remember. We let her have her way, though I noticed Mather did run a hand over the mat each time she left the room.

I was in the receiving room with Mather and the feline telepath, the American charged with opening the door of the transit box whenever the green bulb lit up to tell us Carla had begun 'transmitting'. Rudi Kline was in the monitor room, watching closed-circuit feeds from both labs. I must confess I had visions of us staring at the cat for ages, waiting for the wretched thing to even approach the target, but each time we got the go signal from the other room, Felidae scurried swiftly to the mat, walked up and down it a bit, then curled up snugly on one of the symbols.

We did it a pre-agreed six times, and Felidae scored an emphatic, statistically inarguable one hundred per cent.

Carla seemed dizzily triumphant, less so when she was reminded that this was merely the dry run.

'How many times does Felidae have to accurately read my mind before you're convinced?' she demanded, as we sat watching playbacks in the monitor room. 'Or do you wait until she gets tired and starts to get it wrong, then call that the real run?'

'We did tell you, several times, that the first six tests were merely to allow us to establish the correct protocol,' Mather said. 'Technically, they were not controlled conditions.'

'But you had witnesses in both rooms,' she protested. Her cat's psychic powers were clearly a sight stronger than Carla's memory. All of this had been spelled out to her and she'd readily agreed.

'Go get Felidae a bowl of milk, and grab yourself a coffee,' Mather told her. 'We should be ready to recommence in about a half-hour. There's a cafeteria across the link corridor.'

Carla hesitated a moment, then said: 'I just need to get her mat.'

'The mat will be perfectly safe,' Heidi assured her. 'We'll be right here.'

'No, you don't understand. Felidae has to stay close to it so that she can remain familiar with the symbols. These are human symbols, so she's not only having to read my mind; she's having to interpret the meaning too. These would be like Chinese characters or hieroglyphs to you and me: not A, B, C.'

'You could take a deck of Zener cards,' Rudi suggested.

'No, no, just take the mat,' Mather said. 'We need to give Felidae every chance or the experiment wouldn't be fair.'

Carla nodded with relief and headed purposefully for the door. Once she'd closed it behind her, I noticed Mather was grinning.

'Doesn't want us touching that mat, does she?' he asked.

'Her cold seems better too,' I remarked. 'She was wiping her nose constantly on the playback.'

Mather cued up the target room video file and played it again. We watched Carla select a card, then concentrate on it. As she did so, her hand went to her trouser pocket to retrieve her hanky. Mather laughed to himself, nodding.

When Carla returned about twenty minutes later, Heidi informed her that we had one minor alteration to the protocol.

'After you select a card, place it down on the table in front of you, and put your hands flat either side of it as you concentrate.'

'I'm sorry,' she said, 'but I've got a terribly runny nose just now. I keep having to wipe it.'

'That's fine, but if you need to wipe it between selecting the card and completing the transmission, we'll have to call it void and ask you to select a new card.'

There followed some quality squirming. At first I didn't understand why nobody just outright told her we had sussed her method, but it was a salutary lesson in how stolidly the woo-peddlers are prepared to brazen it out, even in the face of certain defeat.

On the first run of tests under the new protocol, Felidae not only failed to score any valid hits, she failed to settle on any of the symbols at all, instead wandering up and down and occasionally looking towards the door for her beloved owner. (I say *valid* hits, because on two occasions Carla did reach for her pocket when she thought Heidi wasn't looking.)

At the conclusion of this run, she was asked to produce whatever was in her pocket. She refused, which was her right, but Mather told her he knew anyway. The mat had five embedded heating elements, one under each symbol, and she had trained the cat to settle on whichever one was warm, something any comfort-loving cat wouldn't need much convincing to do. She had a short-range transmitter in her pocket, controlling which element warmed up once she had selected a Zener card, hence her insistence that the two labs be close together and on the same floor.

Upon having this spelled out to her, Carla said she had no idea what Mather was talking about, and promptly left: mat under one arm and cat box under the other.

Within the month, she had turned up in *Destiny* magazine, claiming Felidae's abilities had been verified under laboratory conditions at Kelvin University, and quoting the dry-run results as proof. I wrote to the magazine giving a more detailed account, but they failed to print the letter. Right enough, I guess *Santa Claus* magazine wouldn't print any inconvenient testimonies from confessing parents either.

Carla was, at least, a motivated improvement upon some of the dismal efforts we were presented with. We saw two separate 'table-tippers', folk who claimed they could call the spirits forth for no nobler purpose than to shoogle a table. This was effected by paranormal forces, we were told, because those calling up the spirits would be seated with their hands flat on the table at all times. The fact that applying a reasonable amount of downward pressure to one side of a table will tip it had not, they assumed, occurred to us. One even claimed to be able to make the table levitate, which he achieved by getting the outside edges of his brogues under a leg each and pushing down with both hands. The levitator left rather huffily after we took him to the monitor room and showed him a close-up playback of his footwork, but he did at least seem prepared to admit the game was a bogey. The other tipper remained more resolutely self-deluded. Rudi drew a large square on the table in thick felt pen, about six inches in from the edge on all sides, then asked him to call up these ghostly furniture molesters while keeping his hands inside the lines. Further tipping failed to ensue; indeed, he wouldn't even try, because 'placing your hands inside an enclosed shape is a form of containment. It keeps the spirits out as surely as if it wasn't merely a two-dimensional shape but a lead-lined box.'

A second table was produced, minus the markings, and the tipper was instructed to keep his hands six inches in from the edge at all times. Nothing happened, despite the absence of the inescapably secure two-dimensional spirit-proof chamber, but this was apparently because we were giving off bad vibrations. 'The spirits don't like the idea that they're being tested, and they especially don't like the idea of proving themselves to non-believers.'

We also saw a bloke with 'X-ray vision', who could tell us what Zener cards he had drawn despite being blindfolded. We were allowed to examine the blindfold and even asked to try peeking through it in order to verify that the material was opaque. X-ray man then asked Mather to tie on the blindfold, the American being the burliest-looking and therefore most able to render it tight and secure. Then he began drawing Zener cards, placing his selections face up on the table in front of him, before accurately identifying each of his first five picks. The X-rays failed him when Mather held a sheet of thick paper immediately under his chin, thus blocking his line of sight through the gap that is naturally created in any blindfold by the material stretching across the nose. It was funny, if mildly embarrassing, to watch him jiggle his head around, ostensibly to better channel the psychic forces, but in reality to sneak a peek past the obstacle. Mather removed the paper only once he had made a (consistently wrong) guess. I almost felt guilty about the fact that the guy couldn't see what Mather was doing – like making faces at a blind person – but then reminded myself that he was the one effectively calling *us* idiots. In between his fifth wrong call and his sixth (and final) selection, Mather wrote the word 'caught' on the sheet of paper. He whipped off the blindfold and stormed out after that, so I took it that he'd been able to read it clearly enough.

Finally, I must confess, there was one subject who was there at my own, admittedly disingenuous, invitation. Her name was Miriam Gelaghtly, and I think it's fair to name her because she's

167

frequently elbowing her way into the media spotlight as the homeopathy racket's main rentagub north of the border. She was particularly conspicuous when a large number of senior doctors co-signed a public statement recommending that homeopathy receive no further NHS endorsement as a legitimate medical practice, largely on the grounds that it doesn't actually work and its advocates can produce no clinical evidence to support it.

The mere advent of the Spiritual Science Chair seemed to have been received as a beacon of opportunity for all manner of credophiles, so I guessed, rightly, that Miriam would come a-running if I dangled the prospect of an alternative analysis of the efficacy of homeopathic remedies. By 'alternative analysis', I accurately predicted she would optimistically assume I meant 'alternative *to* analysis'.

When she turned up at the lab, she gave us a sprawling prepared presentation relying heavily on anecdotal evidence, where it wasn't relying on skewed statistics, unfounded claims and outright porkies. Having finally shut up, she was presented with five numbered glass jars of clear fluid, and informed that one contained a homeopathic solution purchased in her very shop on Great Western Road, and the other four Corporation Haircream; or as it is more commonly known, Glasgow tap water. To secure a major academic stamp of approval, she only had to identify her own snake oil, and to do this she could use any testing method she required, with the entire chemistry department's hardware at her disposal.

We set her no time limit, and said she could bring in any equipment or experts she requested, with the one proviso that the samples remain in the building.

She declined the test, which was not surprising. Homeopathic remedies are so dilute – typically $10^{30}$ – that for one single molecule of the active ingredient to be present in a solution would require more water than currently exists on Planet Earth.

'There is no chemical analysis that would identify the solution,' she admitted to us. 'But that's because homeopathy doesn't work in a chemical sense. Honestly, I came here today because I thought you people had the vision to see beyond the hidebound notions of science. The water in homeopathic remedies

168

retains a "memory trace" of the active molecules. It won't register in chemical analysis because chemical analysis is too crude to detect it.'

'What *would* detect it?' Heidi asked.

'The physiological systems of countless grateful patients,' she answered.

In the corridor later, out of earshot of the others, she called me 'a deceitful little shit', which I believe may be a sentiment containing more than a memory trace of truth, but not even homeopathic-solution levels of self-awareness.

I'm guessing by this point you'll understand why I couldn't believe Lafayette was feeling disheartened, if this was all he had to measure up to. However, to be fair, the preceding shambles seemed to depress him largely because of how badly it reflected upon the nascent Spiritual Science Chair's entire field of study. The guy aspired, according to his DVD covers, to take the paranormal from 'the end of the pier to the door of the laboratory', but there was an inescapable whiff of mussels and candyfloss about the whole boiling. Not to mention raw sewage.

However, it was actually the least embarrassing of our preliminary subjects who really seemed to cause Lafayette the most unease. He was a short, balding, middle-aged bloke with an enquiring look and a restlessness about him. He gave the name 'Colin Playfair', which struck me as pseudonymous right away. He had quick movements and darting eyes, plus a controlled economy of movement that reminded me just enough of my friend Tim Vale to make me suspicious. Tim is/was a spy (you can never say the past tense for certain with these guys). Mr Playfair didn't strike me as a spook, but I had him down as a skilled deceiver, and the staginess of the made-up name suggested an amateur or possibly even professional magician. He said he was a teacher, which turned out to be true, after a fashion.

He was accompanied by his daughter, with a degree of apparent reluctance, it ought to be noted. Gina gave the impression of being there purely to keep a concerned eye on him, with particular regard to his heart medication which she scrupulously monitored and administered. He could be doing without engaging in this sort of nonsense, was her disapproving take on matters. We were often made to feel guilty of tacit negligence in merely permitting her father's participation. Her opinion on his psychic 'gifts' she kept to herself, though her permanent glower suggested she was just about tolerating this nonsense due to a daughter's love for an incorrigible father she could not help but indulge.

He attempted various psychic feats involving the transmission or 'remote reading' of Zener cards and of sketches drawn in isolated rooms. As with previous models, he was allowed a dry run before we imposed controls we felt were required to rule out possible means of cheating the initial run had suggested. The dry run was, as usual, a thorough success for the would-be psychic, but for once, the next round of tests shocked us by demonstrating only a minor fall-off in Playfair's success rate. Despite imposing strict controls to ensure he did not have access to the target materials, he continued to guess considerably above the rate of average probability. Lafayette was excited and encouraged at this point; Mather I would describe as intrigued, but demonstrating a more scientific countenance of restraint. Playfair was asked to stay another night – accommodation paid for by the chair – to which he delightedly assented. Gina assented too, though without, as you'd guess, the delight bit.

I can't take credit for being the one who tippled the scam; it was Sarah who did that. In describing the perplexing events – a heartening change from sniggering over the latest brazen deceit – I mentioned Playfair's medical condition and his daughter's near-aggressively defensive ministrations. Sarah instinctively homed in on the drug regimen I described, particularly noting the frequency of dosage and the absence of apparent side-effects upon this otherwise sprightly and mercurial individual.

'They're a double-act,' she diagnosed. 'The reluctance is her cover. She's his secret confederate.'

I thought back to the day's tests: Gina had been around the whole time, usually looking utterly disinterested, her head often buried in a magazine. She'd had ample opportunity to glimpse drawings or note which Zener cards had been selected. During the second, supposedly controlled run, Playfair had not made his guesses or drawn his corresponding sketches immediately, as had been the case first time around. There had been gaps while he 'concentrated', and sometimes he'd requested breaks, for medication or simply to go to the toilet. We had taken care to isolate him from the target materials during this time, but had not isolated him from his secret conduit: his apparently disinterested, even disapproving daughter.

And did I feel like all the mugs of the day.

I phoned Mather the next morning and we reviewed the tapes and observations. Gina had direct contact with Playfair during several of his 'concentration' periods, and left the room to go to the toilet or on a different pretext during others, most likely to secrete notes in some mutually agreed location, which he would visit during his own next bog break.

When Playfair and Gina returned that evening, we outlined the new protocol, which would require Gina to leave the building altogether during tests, with medication breaks only permitted *between* individual attempts.

Instead of the now familiar squirming and circumlocutions, the pair of them shared a brief look and then broke into giggly smirks.

'It's a fair cop,' Playfair said, before introducing himself properly as Len Philpott, physics lecturer, amateur conjuror and, on this occasion, undercover reporter.

'I write the odd piece for science magazines, mostly unmasking the woo-woo stuff,' he told us. 'That's why I answered the ad and came here. Understandably, there's been a lot of interest in this whole Spiritual Science Chair brouhaha in scientific – and conjuring – circles, and I wanted to see whether your controls were up to snuff. If they hadn't been, I would have maintained my pretence right up until you published the paper. Then I'd have blown it out of the water. I'm sorry to be so blunt, but you can't mess around with this nonsense, or it very quickly grows legs.'

'Tell us about it,' I said, *Density* magazine having already by that point run their fib-fest on Felidae the psychic fleabag.

'That was the plan, anyway,' he continued, 'but happily, it looks like it won't be necessary. I've seen some shoddy pseudo-experiments in my time, believe me. This is the real deal. You should be proud. On the down side, I fear it won't be much of a paper. Take it from a long-term scientist and just as long-term sceptic: nothing unexplained is going to happen here. You've got it wrapped up way too tight. Congratulations.'

# Project Lamda stage two: the real deal

A wee teaser for you, and a real stinker, I must caution:
   The words: 'Mr Watson, come here, I want you.'
   An image of a ventriloquist's dummy.
   A drawing of a castle.
   What do they have in common?
   Believe me, it's a bitch.
   The more astute might recognise the first two as, respectively, the first publicly demonstrated communication by telephone and the first publicly demonstrated transmission by television. The third, having been a necessarily closed-doors affair, I'll have to help you with. It was the first image drawn by Gabriel Lafayette under the strictest laboratory conditions imposed by Project Lamda, matching – within reasonable boundaries of interpretation – an image I had drawn in another room, only minutes before and two floors below.

Will it find its place in history? I've a funny feeling it just might. I'd be writing about it in the papers just now if it wasn't that I'm kind of indisposed, what with the whole being-dead thing. But the march of science is not without its wee jams and tailbacks. The story will be told and remembered in the end, and its significance will not be lost on the scientific community.

As with the preliminaries, we followed the format of allowing Lafayette a dry run, with the two-way benefit of letting him familiarise himself with what was expected and of letting us adjust our controls where appropriate. This was also the first place where results diverged, as initially Lafayette's dry-run attempts were a complete wash-out, compared with the all-out successes our hopefuls achieved before we sussed their methods.

Upon Mather's insistence, the target room and receiving room were now two storeys apart, rather than on the same floor. Ideally, he said, it ought to be more, but we only had access to – and thus control of – a limited area of the building. In fact, it took a bit of negotiation with various management and administration entities to extend our range over a third floor, and for a couple of days it looked like we weren't going to get that. However, after the chicaneries employed by Catwoman and Mr Playfair, Mather was adamant that the rooms have 'substantial barriers and distance across three dimensions, not two'. He negotiated the use of five rooms on the floor below the levels we were already controlling. The new zone occupied a stretch of corridor between a stairwell and two fire doors, which were locked shut during tests in order to cut off the area from the rest of the floor. In practice we only needed (and only used) one of those rooms, but required control of the others for purposes of what Mather called 'insulation'. The receiving room was an easy choice, there being only one candidate without windows (save for a pane in the door) and no walls abutting either a stairwell or a second corridor. After Playfair, Mather was paranoid about the idea of accomplices. 'A code of knocks or scratches to communicate Zener signs would be easy to establish,' he said by way of example.

'But how would the accomplice know what the target was if he didn't have access to the target room?' I asked him.

'I couldn't say, and that's the point. We can't anticipate every means of cheating, but what really damages the validity of experiments like these is failing to act upon the parts you *have* anticipated. If we set up the receiving room in a room abutting areas we can't secure, then we don't know for sure that an unseen confederate isn't helping. The critics can point to that and thus discredit the protocol. They don't need to answer the second issue of how the confederate could know what to communicate; they just need to show that we hadn't covered the first angle.'

'And *do* you suspect Lafayette could have a confederate?' I asked him. 'Someone whose relationship with him you're not aware of?'

I could sense Heidi tense a little at the awkward ramifications of this question, but awkward ramifications are how I make my living. Mather stared hard at me for a moment, definitely taking a beat. This was the sticky question Blake had bull's-eyed; and even Noble had alluded to it.

'I have to assume it, whether I believe it to be likely or not.'

A good answer, I reckoned. Scientifically ethical and yet deftly evasive. We both knew what my next question ought to be, but I left it unasked, acknowledging as our gazes locked that he'd only sidestep that one as well. I'd save it, I decided, taking in his wry smile. He thought he was parrying my thrust, but instead he was merely showing me the weak spot to aim for next time.

I had looked up the work of Karl Creedy on the web, the scientist Mather cited as his greatest mentor in this field. Creedy had indeed been a formidable architect of woo-test protocols, and it was clear Mather had been as impressed with him as he was intrigued by Lafayette. The trouble was, he was about to pit the former's practices against the latter, with the inevitable result that he'd cause one of the major figures in his life to be very disappointed in him.

Inside the appointed room, Mather had Rudi Kline oversee the installation of a Faraday cage, creating a small enclosure that would be shielded from electromagnetic signals. Outside the cage, Mather set up a number of sensors to detect transmission signals, such as radio, TV and microwaves, as well as other sensors calibrated to pick up signals 'outside the spectrum of standard human communications'. The former were intended, as Mather put it, 'to provide a hard trace if someone in another room is trying to send him a message. The latter are just rain buckets hoping to catch a splash if it turns out the messages are coming from someplace more than a little further beyond.'

It looked like a giant fridge, the kind of appliance you'd imagine in the kitchens of a Vegas-scale hotel; maybe even big enough to accommodate half of Oliver Reed's carry-out. However, even the biggest fridge doesn't easily accommodate more than a single human being, not fully assembled anyway, so the cage only had room for one person to sit comfortably at a short table. This meant that the receiving room observer would not be able to see Lafayette once he had been sealed off inside the cage, limiting his or her role to simply ensuring that the subject never left the cage during tests and that nor did anyone else approach it. Heidi expressed an objection to this, and not merely because it wouldn't make for a very exciting shift.

'We need to be able to observe the subject at all times,' she said. 'Simply recording that he was isolated in a signal-proof box would not satisfy me if I was making a critical reading of a report. My question, the big question everyone is going to ask, is: What did he do while we couldn't see him?'

'She's right,' Mather agreed. 'I'm uncomfortably reminded of Houdini. He never escaped before your eyes: a screen was always rolled in front of the milk can and he'd emerge at the side, *fait accompli*. We'd get ripped to shreds.'

Rudi shrugged and said it would be possible, if time-consuming, to install a window. This would not, he assured us, compromise the electromagnetic insulation, as the glass would be embedded with a mesh screen similar to the ones that prevent microwave ovens from cooking the person on the outside while he stares impatiently at his half-defrosted ready-meal.

I thought of the budgie-like head-bobbing actions familiar to anyone trying to see clearly into even the most state-of-the-art microwave oven. I reckoned that even with enough light inside to irradiate Lafayette, whoever was looking in would have no perception of any subtleties he happened to engage in, and as for a video record, it would be like one of those shots taken by photographers flashing their cameras at random against the windows of a prison van as it leaves the Old Bailey. Risking ridicule at my scientific ignorance, I asked why we couldn't simply put a camera inside the cage.

Mather turned deferentially to Rudi, acknowledging it as his privilege by rank to tell me why I was a complete diddy. To Mather's surprise, however, Rudi shrugged and said: 'Sure. The lens would have to be very wide to allow for the close-ness of the subject, but I can rig it, yes. Quicker than a window, too.'

'And it won't compromise the electromagnetic insulation?' Mather asked.

'No more than the cable that's already run into there to provide light.'

'Cool,' Mather said, looking hugely relieved.

Mather clocked that I had noticed this, knew it was some-thing he wasn't going to succeed in hiding. Once again I didn't pursue it, not there in front of the others. But later, while Rudi was working on the cage and Heidi had gone home, I hit him with it.

'You've caught him cheating before, haven't you?'

Mather sighed. He looked tired and tense, but when he answered, he seemed almost relieved to be talking about it.

'Yeah,' he said, coolly sanguine. 'I know he cheats sometimes. There are tricks, parlour tricks – stuff I could teach you in five minutes – that he does in front of an audience. It's bullshit. But it's showbiz, it pays the rent. And it kind of reassures me. The tricks are guaranteed successes. The other stuff that has happened around Gabriel, it doesn't happen on cue. If he could make those things happen every time, I'd be far more suspicious. That it's spasmodic is how I feel sure it's *not* tricks. Project Lamda means so much to me because it's my first proper chance, on a large scale, to control the environment, to call the shots and, crucially, to set the timetable.'

'So now that you have control of the test environment, do you think things *will* happen? And if they do, on demand, will that make you suspicious?'

'I have this fear,' he said. 'It's not like every minute of every day; it comes and goes, but when it comes . . . it literally wakes me up in the middle of the night and I lie there and ask myself, what if it is all cheating? What if he is tricking me and, despite my vigilance, what if I'm actually the biggest patsy in the world? That's why I have to know, why I have to cover every angle. I have to suspect him. And I guess, in answer to your inescapable question, a small part of me will always suspect him.'

'And what about Glassford Hall?' I asked. 'Does that part of you suspect he pulled something off there?'

'That's what makes it so goddamn complicated,' he said wearily. 'See, Glassford Hall, that's one thing I have no doubts about. None. Something definitely happened then, though admittedly it wasn't something that proves anything about Gabriel. But when I think about that night, it dispels the paranoid part of me that's afraid of being a fool who's wasting his career even looking into this stuff. I've analysed what happened there over and over, searched for possible explanations. Collective delusion, for instance. I looked into that, and there are some impressive instances, people reinforcing each other's

177

misperceptions until they are quite convinced they are genuine memories. But in this case, we know there was a voice because it was recorded on tape.'

'But can you say for sure what is on the tape?'

'No. Lemuel won't let anyone play it, let alone analyse it. He's understandably squeamish, and Jillian Noble refuses to release it without his consent, though God knows I've pleaded with her often enough. But regardless of what is on the tape, it's where the voice came from that still sends chills through me. It came from everywhere and nowhere. And what happened with the fire, and the way the room got so cold . . .' Mather shuddered, the recollection uncomfortable but strangely energising to him. 'Events like that are why I'm here. I've had a glimpse of something incredible and I want to explore it scientifically.'

'You want to know that it's true.'

'That's a fair way of putting it, yeah.'

'But part of you is afraid it's not.'

'Afraid of it, but not afraid to face up to it if that turns out to be so. You ain't cut out to be a scientist if you flinch when the facts slap you in the kisser.'

Lafayette's dry run took place while we were still making and tweaking the arrangements described above. It was only after the camera was installed and operational that we agreed we could call the tests controlled, though if there were any tricks Lafayette executed while nobody could see inside, they didn't help him pull off any paranormal feats. His dry run was an ugly shambles.

He didn't appear happy about the Faraday cage from the moment he laid eyes on it. He looked at Mather like some kind of betrayal had taken place, and I got the impression he hadn't been fully informed of the conditions. Perhaps Mather wanted to hit him with strictures he could not anticipate, but my greater fear was that he had simply been too reluctant to break it to him.

'I reckon there's a shitload of difference between a controlled environment and an environment designed to suppress any form of communication activity. What if this thing blocks out the very wavelengths that these messages normally reach me on?'

178

'We'll be monitoring outside to see whether any kind of signal, wave or force is directed towards you,' Mather assured. 'Plus we'll do some runs of tests outside the Faraday cage for comparison. If it turns out there's messages you can receive on the outside that you can't receive on the in, then that in itself will be a breakthrough. If they're coming in on a medium the cage can repel, then that could be the first step towards proof that they exist.'

This mollified Lafayette, though I feared that was its sole intention. The logic behind Mather's suggestion reminded me of something Sarah had said, quoting Blake on the 'reasoning' of pseudo-scientists working in this field: 'When they win, they win, and when they lose, they win.'

The danger was that, for all his previous sincerity, Mather might buckle in the face of Lafayette's displeasure. It certainly looked touch-and-go a little later, when Lafayette heard he'd be strip-searched before entering the controlled area of the building.

I watched the two men stare at each other wordlessly, so much going on between them in that moment. Was Lafayette discovering that Mather had always had his suspicions? Did Mather think Lafayette's indignation masked frustration that his true methods (ie cheating) would not be available to him? It lasted only a few seconds, but if you were there, it seemed quite a stand-off. You could have sought odds on who would speak first. I made Lafayette favourite, which showed why I was never a bookie.

'It's worthless without this, Gabriel,' Mather said, the inarguable truth nonetheless laced with an apologetic, imploring tone.

'He's right,' Heidi urged. 'You can't just walk into a controlled area for tests like these. Who is to say *what* you couldn't be hiding in that baggy white jacket of yours, for starters.'

'I know,' Lafayette grunted, gracelessly. 'I know. But I tell you this, Ezekiel, it won't be you who fucking does the frisk, okay? And if we're talking cavity searches here, I'm walking. If I wanted some guy's finger up my asshole, I could call myself Ahmed and try get on an airplane.'

Lafayette's humour did not improve much over the next couple of evenings, as he undertook his dry run of tests. He'd

179

been forced to strip to his underwear in front of Rudi, who examined his clothes and checked around the covered area with a metal detector, but even a stiff finger up the Celtic end couldn't have made him less comfortable than his abject lack of success.

He was started off with some Zener selections, randomised sequences of five chosen in the target room by Catherine, one of our two student volunteer research assistants. Her selections were noted by Melanie, the other student volunteer, and the sequence sealed in a lead-lined box, which was padlocked by Melanie and had to remain so, in sight of both of them, until Lafayette had made his attempts and submitted them. Catherine and Melanie were isolated from Lafayette at all times, or as near as possible, and instructed not to speak to him if for whatever reason they were not successfully kept apart.

Mather was in the target room also, ensuring that the assistants stuck to the protocol. Heidi was in the receiving room, observing that Lafayette remained in the cage. I had free rein to go where I wanted, but mainly I stayed with Rudi in the monitor room, watching both ends of the experiment.

The first sequence was void, Lafayette emerging from the cage without writing down any attempts.

'I am getting absolutely nothing,' he told Heidi. 'Absolutely nothing. If you could give me some white noise and a snow-storm to look at, I'd achieve total sensory deprivation.'

Heidi urged him to try again, even just make some guesses in order to complete the procedure. He very grumpily agreed, assuring her that guesses were all they'd be.

We called it a night after two hours and eighteen sequences. Lafayette scored well within the parameters of statistical prob-ability, tending towards the lower end of the bell-curve. The sensors around the Faraday cage picked up nothing.

Lafayette was dischuffed but unsurprised, and left the building in what I would describe as a quality huff. He shot Mather a look that suggested they wouldn't be meeting up later for a nightcap, then stormed off. I was almost expecting to hear the outside double doors slam from the lobby four floors below, but there was nothing. Well, not necessarily nothing. Read into it what you will, but we did experience one of the power surges that were to become common throughout the project, killing the lights on our floor until Rudi could get to the breaker-switch and start them up again.

The second evening, Lafayette fared no better, despite us ditching the Zener cards as target materials at his request.

'These symbols are meaningless,' he complained. 'They're emotionally sterile. I don't see the point in this. I've never professed to be clairvoyant or capable of remote reading. The messages I receive, decode, transmute, whatever you want to call it, they are personal, they're human.'

Mather explained that they still needed to do tests such as the Zener exercises for purposes of comparison. 'It's all data,' he said. 'If it turns out you can divine something more personal but strike out when it's just randomised patterns, then that helps us understand what we're dealing with. It may even give us hard proof of exactly what you're saying.'

Lafayette grudgingly conceded the point, but opined that we didn't need any more data 'to prove I can't do jack with Zener cards'.

On Lafayette's suggestion, we had Catherine draw a series of sketches – a man leading a horse over a bridge, a girl holding an umbrella, two disembodied arms locked in a wrestling grip and so on, all simple but slightly abstract – which were, again, locked in the lead-lined box until Lafayette made his corresponding efforts.

Again he said he was receiving nothing, and that his tries were random guesses. (His corresponding sample pictures were, respectively, an ice-hockey stick hitting a puck, a key entering a padlock and a house on fire.)

On evening three, with the Faraday cage partially disassembled for Rudi's camera installation, he was permitted another attempt at guessing drawings, this time sketched by Melanie. This was when it got truly ugly. Even sitting outside the hated cage, he failed on all ten images, getting more visibly heated as the procedure went on. He requested several times that we cease the whole thing for the night, as he still wasn't 'feeling' or 'receiving' anything. 'I'm getting no energy, no signals. Maybe it's not the goddamn cage . . . I don't just get these messages all the time. You can't simply switch this thing on and off.'

It was like watching our preliminary chancers after we'd applied appropriate safeguards. He looked like a man caught out.

Heidi made efforts to calm and comfort him as his frustration grew. On the monitor, I saw her put an arm around him at one point when he was threatening to walk, protesting to her that if he was feeling nothing, it was a waste of time. 'We'll record a shitload of failures,' he railed, going seriously off on one, 'and then even when I have hits, they'll be able to say these average the figures down to random chance. See, the scientists talk about repeatability, say if paranormal feats are sporadic or in any way inconsistent, then they can be explained away, even if the results are way above chance. But this is like a nascent medium of communication. Did all the old mediums of communication work *all* the time, *every* time when they were in their early stages? Radio? Nobody ever lost a signal, did they? TV? Jesus, the internet? Remember the dial-up days? Did that shit work all the time, every time?'

Mather looked like he needed some comfort too. He came into the monitor room several times that night, watching Lafayette sit at his table in the receiving room with the blank piece of paper in front of him. Mather was willing him to draw, willing him to get something right. With each dismal failure he grew more despondent and, as it turned out, even more combustible than Lafayette, because he utterly lost it with poor Melanie later on when we were taking a break. She had left open the door to the storeroom where we kept all of the project's transportable equipment, everything from spare video cameras to packs of Zener cards; and worse, she'd done it while Lafayette was out of the receiving room, his exact whereabouts therefore unknown. It turned out he wasn't even in the building – he'd gone outside for some fresh air in an attempt to 'calm down and find my centre' – but Mather was more concerned with might-have-beens than actualities, because might-haves and could-haves were what torpedoed the credibility of an exercise like this. He fired her on the spot.

She got an apology for his rage once he'd calmed down, but her arse was still out the window. We all took it as an appropriate juncture to adjourn for a few days, coming back for the official run of tests once the cage was finished and everybody had some time to cool off.

I couldn't see things taking much time to reach boiling point again when we resumed. What was going to change, unless Mather caved in to his subject's tantrums and relaxed part of the protocol?

But things did change, quite startlingly, and it was part of my remit to note every detail of how, in case it shed an unsensationally sobering light on why. Assume cheating, that's what that email had said, and Mather's obsessiveness had taught me that I didn't have to deduce precisely how a method of cheating might be achieved, only to highlight where it could be possible.

The first thing to note, therefore, was that we had appointed a new assistant, a girl named Juliet. I had my concerns that Lafayette could have taken advantage of this change of personnel to place a confederate in our midst, but Juliet, like Melanie and Catherine, was recruited through Rudi Kline, who selected from a pool of more than twenty. I knew nonetheless that if a conjuror can 'force' a particular card on a volunteer from the audience, then a volunteer could be 'forced' on a project (though, once again, I couldn't tell you how he'd do it), so I bore this in mind from the moment Juliet showed up.

The second change *was* to the protocol, though to give Mather his due, it was something everyone agreed to, not a concession he granted under pressure.

Lafayette suggested the change as soon as we reconvened.

'I've been thinking about this the past few days,' he said, 'trying to work out why I felt nothing. And I think it's inescapably because it's just not personal. It's sterile. Now, I understand why the protocol has to be airtight, but sterile is something else. The things that happen to me, the messages I've received, they've all been about connections with people. Sometimes I've felt the presence of something – I won't call it a spirit, because we don't rightly know what it is – but something that's close, real close to somebody in the room. Other times I just get these signals, these raw transmissions I can somehow decode, though I don't know quite how the hell I decode them. But even with those, I feel the message is coming *from* something *to* somebody, and I'm just the hardware that intercepts it and plays it back.

'See, what it is, I reckon I need to spend just a little time with whoever is sending the message, whoever is drawing the picture. I'm not saying she sits there and I'll just sit over here and I swear I won't peek. I just want time to make that connection, *then* you can slap me back in that goddamn toaster oven.'

With Lafayette absenting himself, we discussed the security implications. In terms of information leakage, things ought to be the same as long as the other arrangements remained in place. However, as Mather reminded us, stage mentalists were known for their suggestion techniques, thus it was theoretically possible that Lafayette could plant suggested images in the volunteer's head before she commenced drawing. We therefore agreed on two things. First, that all Lafayette's contact with the volunteer should be witnessed as well as recorded for analysis, so that we could discount any tries where we felt he had attempted to suggest an image; and second, that the target volunteer should be Catherine, not the recently arrived Juliet.

The rest of the protocol ran as before. Upon arrival, Lafayette had been strip-searched by Rudi, and allowed to go to the toilet before commencing any recorded testing. Another lesson from the Playfair tests, this prevented Lafayette having a pretext to go wandering around the building after any targets were set. He was allowed twenty minutes to sit with Catherine, the encounter taking place in the same meeting room as any discussions at which he had been present. This was because he was not permitted to enter the base, the monitor room or, especially, the target room at any time. Mather, Heidi and I were also present.

Lafayette had twenty minutes, but was in there for only twelve, and didn't say anything for most of the first five or six. It was pretty tough for Catherine at first, just sitting there with him seated across a short table while the rest of us watched from the other side of the room. They sat there in silence for a bit until Lafayette laughed out loud at the growing awkwardness and told us we should feel free to talk to the girl. We did, keeping it all to carefully unrevealing small-talk. Lafayette merely observed, his eyes usually on Catherine when they weren't closed in seemingly precipitous moments of contemplation. His mouth twitched involuntarily at these times, like somebody trying to fine-tune the settings on some highly sensitive device. Then he interrupted the conversation to say simply, 'Daniel.'

Catherine stopped and looked round at him, all of us halting in the beckoning expectation that he would elaborate.

'Dan,' he continued, nodding. 'Yes.' With which he stood up and told us he was ready to begin the test.

'Who's Daniel?' Heidi asked.

'Ask Catherine,' Lafayette replied. 'I don't want to say anything more in case it's interpreted as suggestion.'

Heidi did ask Catherine, while Rudi escorted Lafayette to the receiving room.

'I'm not sure,' she replied. 'There was a Daniel in my class at secondary school. He drowned in a swimming accident in a reservoir when we were fourteen.'

'Were you close?'

'Not especially. I liked him, he wasn't an arsehole. He sat next to me in Geography, I remember that, because we had Geography the day after he died. It was the empty seat that really . . . God, I can't believe I'm tearing up. I hadn't thought about Dan in years, but now it feels like . . . yesterday.'

'Are you okay to do this?' Mather asked.

She assured us she was. I accompanied her, Juliet and Mather to the target room, Heidi on monitor room duty.

With Lafayette securely isolated in the Faraday cage, Catherine drew a picture of a cable car going up a slope, with two skiers below. She was a more than competent figurative artist, so the image was no mere doodle, nor was there anything ambiguous about it. Nonetheless, before Juliet sealed it in the lead-lined box, Mather asked her to describe Catherine's image, and once Catherine had agreed the description was fair and accurate, to write down the description and place it also in the box.

'We can't allow any room for ambiguity,' he explained. 'If Gabriel draws an airplane, I don't want him to be able to claim it as a hit by saying Catherine was thinking about an object in the air. You'd be amazed at the wiggle-room some subjects try to negotiate around visual interpretation.'

Once the box was locked, Juliet hit the button to give a green light in the receiving room, whereupon Rudi would tell Lafayette the drawing was ready and he could commence.

A few minutes later, Lafayette emerged from the Faraday cage clutching a drawing, and not of an aeroplane or any other nondescript airborne object. It was cruder than Catherine's, but it was unmistakably a cable car ascending a slope above not one and not three, but precisely two skiers. Heidi retrieved the drawing and brought it to us, having been instructed by Mather not to let either of the pair in the receiving room know the outcome.

Catherine then drew two people having dinner, with a vase of flowers in the centre of the table between them. Once again, Lafayette rendered a less refined but unarguable representation of the same scene. He then also scored with a postman delivering a parcel and a lion attacking a gazelle, before passing in response to Catherine's drawing of a man fishing from a small rowing boat. He claimed he'd felt everything go fuzzy and suddenly very cold and said he needed a break.

Upon hearing this, Mather immediately looked concerned, and moved that we all convene in the meeting room.

Lafayette suggested Rudi escort him up to the roof for some air, rather than allow him to leave the building, which would have necessitated another strip-search upon return. Mather, however, suggested he call it a night. 'I've seen you like this before. Something happened in there, and it got heavy at the end, didn't it?'

'It was . . . exhilarating,' Lafayette countered. 'Then, yes, kind of uncomfortable. Cold, suddenly, very cold. But I'm good to keep going, just need a little air.'

Mather relented, following much enthusiastic assurance that Lafayette felt fine. Rudi and Lafayette departed for higher altitude, leaving much sighing and unease among the rest of us below. We were only talking about five scrawled drawings, but the ramifications were almost too intimidating to consider.

'The problem with using a hand-drawn image as a target is that there is no statistical average of probability to compare,' Mather said. 'I can't tell you the odds of correctly guessing someone else's drawing, other than that they would be high. The odds of guessing four in succession would be astronomical.'

'Four out of five,' Catherine reminded him.

'Though he *passed* the last one,' stated Heidi, 'which for statistical purposes is not the same as a fail.'

'I'd have thought, if anything, the boat would be the one he'd have most likely guessed right,' Juliet observed.

'Why?' Mather asked.

'Because this Daniel guy drowned. It would certainly be the one most likely to be ruled out on the grounds of suggestion.'

'Nobody told him Daniel drowned,' Catherine said. 'Oh God. He said he felt, what was it?' she asked Heidi.

'Suddenly very cold.'

'Jesus.'

Amidst this moment of melodrama, I looked to Mather and found him looking back at me. I silently eyed the door and he very subtly nodded. A couple of minutes later, we were alone together in the corridor.

'What's on your mind, Jack?' he asked.

'Same as, I'd wager, is nagging yours. That if you can "force" one volunteer on an experiment, you can force plenty more.'

He nodded. 'And that the "forced" one needn't necessarily be a new arrival,' he mused.

'You told me to assume cheating. Isn't it possible that Catherine could be drawing a pre-agreed sequence of images?'

He swallowed. There was a conflict, a reluctance to give up the wonder that had just presented itself, but he knew, like he'd told Lafayette, it was worthless unless you ruled these things out.

'Eminently,' he said regretfully. He sighed and took a moment to think, leaning back against the wall of the corridor. Then he gave a tiny nod, deciding something. 'Okay. Change of protocol.'

'How about *I* do the drawings?' I suggested.

He grinned. 'Assuming you're not a long-con plant.'

'Secret fraternity of rectors? That's just a risk you'll have to take.'

'Maybe. But only if my *first* change of protocol doesn't work.'

'And what's that?'

But he would only put his finger to his lips and walked back into the meeting room.

Got to hand it to him, it was simple but smart, a perfect

187

mechanism for scuppering the implied technique. When we resumed, Catherine drew a picture of a centaur taking aim with bow and arrow. A few minutes later, Lafayette aced it. I glanced at Mather, wondering when his new protocol was going to kick in, and he gave me a tiny wink.

Catherine then drew a picture of a woman and a dog sheltering beneath a tree in a rainstorm. Just as Juliet was about to write down the agreed description, Mather grabbed the drawing and pocketed it. He then instructed Catherine to draw the centaur again, exactly as before. Catherine didn't question, didn't bat an eyelid, just did as she was asked. If she was in on a scam, then I'd want her in on mine too. Juliet completed her description, closed and locked the box, and hit the green light button. Mather then asked me to follow him to the monitor room.

He stood with his arms folded, eyes fixed on the screen showing the Faraday cage. If Lafayette emerged with a sketch of a woman and a dog, I was guessing Project Lamda would end then and there.

It was definitely a hold-your-breath moment, but I was glad I didn't. Lafayette took an age to emerge from the cage, far, far longer than on any of the previous tests, including the one he'd blanked.

Eventually he clambered uncertainly from the big fridge, shaking his head. Mather turned up the volume on the sound feed.

'Sorry, took the longest time,' we heard Lafayette tell Rudi. 'I got all confused. I got this half-man, half-horse thing again. Same thing as last time. That can't be right, can it? But what really confused me was that just before it, I was getting this picture, I even started drawing it, see? A woman and a dog and a tree, and it's raining, and then it was like it just disappeared. I think I'm gonna have to call this a pass. It doesn't count if I submit multiple entries, right? I mean, maybe the half-horse guy just stuck in my head from before, but it came back so strong, even after the other image. Nah. Call it a pass.'

Which is why, on the records, it states that the subject declared a pass, even though his response was, in its unknowing complexity, more accurate than anything he'd submitted before.

It was also why, the next evening, in an attempt to remove all question of volunteer complicity from the experiment, I found myself in the target role, complete with the same agreed 'contact' or 'connection' period as Lafayette had been allotted with Catherine. On this occasion, he took an even smaller proportion of the permitted twenty minutes, declaring himself ready after just under six. This was something he had predicted too: 'The force is strong in this one,' he'd joked as we were about to enter the base.

He seemed less humorous once he'd been concentrating on me for a short while. I soon found him looking across the table at me with an expression of suspicion bordering on discomfort.

'What?' I asked.

'I don't want to say, Mr Parlabane, not here. And that ain't just to avoid the issue of suggestion. See, anything I say now has to be said in front of everybody, and this is something I think we'd both rather discuss in private.'

'I'm not shy, Mr Lafayette,' I told him. 'Spit it out.'

'Nonetheless, this had best keep. All I'll say is there's a lot of energy, lot of signals round you. Noticed it every time we've met.'

'Then this should be a piece of piss for you tonight,' I suggested irritably.

Lafayette shrugged, almost resignedly. 'Let's find out,' he said.

I felt the most absurdly disproportionate pressure as I sat in the target room and stared at the blank sheet of paper. Every notion that popped into my head was instantly over-analysed and second-guessed as I asked myself what manipulative mind-games the guy must be adept at. I tried to think of images that were far removed from my normal train of thought, then wondered if *that* was actually how his suggestion worked. I remembered an old primary-school game, somebody saying: think of a number, double it, add this, subtract that . . . now name a vegetable. Unless they've heard it before, everybody says carrot. Everybody. Was I about to draw the equivalent? Don't be daft, I told myself. You can only draw it once, and there will be several tests.

The other limiting factor was that, as my secondary-school art teacher observed, I couldnae draw the curtains, so I was having to consider images that were simple enough for even me to coherently render. Would Lafayette know that? I wondered. Had he seen me doodle? No, because I don't fucking doodle. Like I said, it was absurd. In the end, I thought of an image I no longer recall, then followed a chain of word association in my head until I came up with something both satisfactorily removed from the original idea and within the graphic capabilities of a cross-eyed chimpanzee: viz, a castle.

And it was most definitely a castle, not a chess rook, a turret or a wee section of rampart from a coat of arms. I gave it a moat and a drawbridge and, just to the south-east, a siege engine, though you'd have got points for saying 'lawnmower'.

There remained the absolutely faintest question mark over the issue of volunteer complicity. Mather's wee switcheroo had failed to expose Catherine as any kind of confederate, but nonetheless, that question mark and the possibility of 'forced' volunteers did still remain. Thus this castle of mine was, technically, the first image to be offered to Lafayette under Project Lamda's strictest protocol. He was shut inside the Faraday cage while I drew it, and the only people to see it – Mather and Juliet – never left the room.

Lafayette drew a castle, complete with moat and drawbridge, a siege engine in attendance to the south-east.

That was just for starters.

I drew a mushroom cloud; a man holding up a severed head next to a guillotine; an apple with an arrow through it; a rather Bunteresque schoolboy, braces emphasising his girth, reaching out towards a giant ice-cream cone; and a bus heading for a tunnel in a hillside.

Lafayette reproduced the lot.

To say I was spooked doesn't quite sell it.

The third test was the real lowlight; that was when the vertiginous sensation peaked and I actually thought I was going to be sick. After that, the rising balloon effect calmed a little as I became resigned to seeing another inexplicably reproduced image.

I confess, as the records will show, that it was me who called a halt that night. Everybody seemed slightly scared, but in an excited, vicarious, thrill-ride kind of way. I, having been the one doing these drawings and being the only one who truly knew for sure that I had no deal going with Lafayette, was just plain kacking it.

'This is freaking me out just a little too much to retain confidence in my own judgement,' I announced. I had an unprecedented perception that the world wasn't quite making sense, like some variable had been changed in all the equations; or perhaps it would be more accurate to say all of the equations were missing a constant. Something was missing. Something *had* to be.

I recalled Mather's words about my duty to look for cheating: *However, if you find none, then* that's *when you have to be open-minded about your conclusions.* Okay, I thought, I'm being open-minded here and I don't like it. Can I go back to closed-minded cynicism where the world still works according to all those rules I spent my whole life learning?

Feeling thus rattled, I was in a thoroughly vulnerable state to hear what Lafayette had been keeping back from our wee spiritual getting-to-know-you session prior to the tests. Having officially cried off, I tried to bail out of the building for the night without talking to him again, but the fucking lift stalled on me between floors.

As I've said already, I'd got into the habit of taking the stairs, but on this occasion, in my haste, I thought (these words really did go through my mind), 'The lift should be okay, as I'm not with Lafayette.' However, it seemed the lift phantom was still prepared to do his bidding.

After a long and thoroughly swearie-filled few minutes, the car resumed its descent and I all but bolted out across the lobby, at which point came my own wee ESP moment. When I heard the ding of the other lift as it arrived at my back, followed by the swish of the doors opening, I knew, without turning, who would be standing behind me.

'Not so sure about everything now, are you, Mr Parlabane?' he said. It wasn't smug or triumphant, more like he was offering solidarity: welcome to *my* world.

'Not entirely, no.'

'I'm guessing you're beginning to understand what I'm doing here. Why I'm looking for answers. Why I've come down hard on the folks who would trivialise these things, be they the cynics or the cheap-shit hocus-pocus peddlers. This ain't showbiz, it ain't entertainment, and I think you're learning that it sure ain't fun.'

I said nothing for a moment, just looked into his face: care-worn, etched with a tired sincerity.

'I'm learning you're a complex man, Mr Lafayette,' I said, trying still not to concede anything.

'I'm not the only one,' he responded pointedly. 'That's why I opted for discretion upstairs earlier. I sense energy around people, presences, something that doesn't have a name; maybe what we're working on here will one day help us *give* it a name. With some people it's faint, others strong. Sometimes there's almost nothing. But with you, Mr Parlabane, it's powerful, and I mean powerful like bad weather you don't want to go out in. There is a lot of death around you. Don't think I ever sensed so much death.'

'Yeah, I get that a lot,' I mugged, fooling nobody. I thrust my hands into my trouser pockets to conceal the fact that they were trembling.

'The line between this world and whatever else there is, I sense that too sometimes. It's like a membrane, like something one molecule thick, one electron thick, one *lepton* thick, that's all. And I feel it when people are close to that membrane. You feel as close, maybe closer than anybody I've ever met. In my experience there's only two types of folks who feel so close to that membrane: folks who are about to die, and folks who have pushed somebody else across the line.'

He paused a moment, looking me hard in the eye.

'See, that's why I thought you'd prefer this little talk wasn't happening in front of all those good folks upstairs. Because either you got cancer and you ain't tellin' nobody . . . or, Mr Parlabane, you're a *bona fide* killer. And I'm guessin' door number two.'

I reckon my poker face failed me at that point. Seemed he had seen my hand anyway. I wondered darkly what else he'd seen, this membrane he envisaged I was skirting. People who have killed, and people imminently about to die, he'd said.

Turned out I qualified on both counts.

It's the soul of a successful marriage and the essence of a spouse's true love that she can give you precisely what you require in your time of direst need, which was, in my case, short shrift.

'Don't be a bloody tube, Jack,' she told me. (I always loved it when she used Scottish terms of abuse in that English accent of hers.) 'The only psychic feat this joker has performed is that he seems to have softened your head by telekinesis.'

She did not look amused at my credulity in a 'silly you, come and have a hug' kind of way. Her disgust was such, in fact, that hugs looked well off the agenda for a calculated punitive period. I therefore felt compelled to justify my behaviour, despite years of marriage telling me this was always a self-compounding error.

'The guy knew I had killed somebody, Sarah. Does that not freak you out a little? It was a decade ago, and in all that time the number of people I've told I could count on the fingers of a yakuza's left hand.'

'The number of people you've told and the number of people who know are two different things. The LAPD know; some of them, anyway. Whoever sent the hitman knows, and by extension a truckload of other people in the Los Angeles dodgy-bastard community. But even without that, how many minutes' research would it take on the internet to find out some of the things you've been involved in? "There is a lot of death around you, Mr Parlabane",' she mimicked. 'Woooooo! Indeed, and it's largely documented in hundreds upon hundreds of newspaper articles. It's not a huge gamble to take a flyer on the possibility that among all that carnage, you've accounted for at least one of the bodies. Then he sees your response and confirms he's scored. This is how these people work, Jack. Informed guesses and reading the cues you don't even realise you're giving them.'

'Well, could you tell me what cues I was giving him that allowed him to draw all the same bloody pictures as me? How do you explain the fact that there's four intelligent people who have pitted their collective wits to construct an airtight – actually, airtight, sound-tight, vision-tight and electrical-signal-tight – protocol, and yet Lafayette can reproduce abstract images that *I* drew in a room two floors above?'

'I can't explain it, Jack, but I know this much. Any magician will tell you that clever people are easier to fool, scientists especially, because their great vulnerability is their certainty that

193

they're just too smart to be hoodwinked. Blake told me that, because this is exactly what he was afraid of.'

'Of course,' I said, my frustration lending me reckless bravery. 'Her master's voice. We can't entertain any notion that might suggest His Supreme Arrogance was wrong.'

Sarah halted herself, took a breath to let a moment of calm pass between us. It was long enough for me to feel the way Wile E Coyote must when he realises he's overshot the precipice and is now running on thin air.

'Jack, because I love you and because you're obviously a little off-kilter, I'm going to cut you some slack and *not* toe you in the peas for that last outburst. But I'm setting a clock on just how long I'm prepared to tolerate this wee fugue state you're enduring. I know you didn't like Niall Blake, mainly because he was almost as arrogant and cocksure as you. And in both your cases, what makes each of you all the more insufferable is that you're usually right. Clearly, this time, you can't both be, but you're on his turf, remember.'

'That doesn't mean he was infallible, Sarah. He was dismissive of this whole field without looking into it.'

'He'd spent his whole life studying fields that largely tell us how little rather than how much we know, but they at least illuminate the long path we've still to tread. Niall was dismissive of Lafayette because he'd seen this picture a dozen times. If he came across as arrogant, it was mainly because he was angry that there are still people who want to take all the rules, all the observations and understandings we have accumulated over thousands of years, and say they must be wrong because they don't tally with their infantile beliefs.'

'But this doesn't contradict any known science. We're using the established sciences to monitor and control the experiments. What this suggests is that there are maybe new fields science has yet to explore.'

'Occam's Razor, Jack. Parsimony. When there's more than one explanation, the least complicated is usually the right one. So either there's a whole new frontier that the greatest minds and cumulative technology of our species has hitherto failed to detect, or there's a guy from New Orleans pulling stunts that Mather, Kline, Ganea and *you* have failed to detect. He's cheating,

Jack. Right now, that ridiculous little creep is ripping the piss out of you. I would *not* expect the man I married to take that lying down.'

And with that, Sarah sloped off to watch property porn on the telly.

We had rented out our flat back in Edinburgh, and were temporarily living in a place near St George's Cross. We didn't know how long we were likely to be in Glasgow and therefore hadn't decided for sure whether to sell up and buy a place here in the west, but nonetheless Sarah devoured these shows like a horny teenager watching skinflicks, fantasising over what it will be like when the time finally comes to do the deed for oneself.

I heard her jack up the volume, letting me know Sarah Beeney would be getting her full attention and my presence was no longer welcome in the living room. The message was pretty clear. I'd be having a deep and meaningful relationship with my right hand for the foreseeable future if I didn't shake the scales from my eyes.

I went to the kitchen and booted up my laptop, then began sifting through my deleted emails folder until I came to the one from the science student offering me 'a word to the wise on how he does some of his tricks'.

Okay, I thought, you're so clever, let's see you solve this one, smartarse, and mailed him back with words to that effect, ie a humble and polite request that he get in touch.

He pinged an email back to me in less than a minute, offering to meet up whenever was convenient. I told him right now would be pretty helpful. He named a pub on Great Western Road and said he'd be there in quarter of an hour.

Twenty minutes later, I walked into the place and clocked him at the bar, easily distinguished by two characteristics. The first was that he was alone, his face eagerly scanning whoever walked through the door, and the second was the long brown coat he'd told me he'd be wearing.

'You must be Malcolm Reynolds,' I said. 'I'm Jack Parlabane. We meet at last.'

'Yeah, your mystery sponsor,' he replied, giggling a little nervously. 'Except it's not Malcolm. That's just an online alias I use, for emails and forums and such. My real name is Michael. Michael Loftus.'

# A story for another day

One of the barmen shouted for last orders. Until then, I had never understood why Cinderella ran. What would it matter what she was wearing: the Prince had seen the person underneath. But that's not something you're likely to feel very confident about when all of a sudden you become aware you're back in rags. Or a big geeky brown coat.

'So, how do you know so much about all this stuff?' Laura asked.

'Oh, that's a story for another day,' I said, offering a polite out from what I took to be merely a polite enquiry. She looked at her watch, which seemed to confirm as much.

'Well, in about half an hour, it'll *be* another day,' she said with a shrug.

I was still trying to decode what the shrug was intended to convey when my mobile rang.

'A text from Keith,' I reported. 'They're in Club Shub.'

'Och well, I'd better let you catch up with your pals,' she said. Which sounded to me a lot like '*Please* go and catch up with your pals.'

It was ending, but it wasn't ending in shame and acrimony, a major plus as far as I was concerned.

Maybe it was the drink, the residual feeling of her hand on my arm, I don't know; maybe a reckless death wish to precipitate the aforementioned shame and acrimony and get it over with. Whatever, it came out before I could believe I was saying it.

'Do you think I could see you tomorrow?' I asked her.

She smiled. 'In about half an hour . . .' she repeated.

I laughed. 'It'll *be* tomorrow.' Slow, but getting it. My expectations were clouding my analysis. Most unscientific. Lose five geek points. Examine the evidence without prejudice. She hadn't meant 'Please go and catch up with your pals.' She'd meant 'Go and catch up with your pals if you must.'

196

'Can I get you another drink?' I asked.

'I could use a really big latte.'

'Do they serve those in here?'

'No. But I know a great place that does, and they're open all night.'

I didn't tell her my 'story for another day'. Not right away. We just talked, like two normal people, or at least like two normal students. I had been in the café once before, when I got off an overnight train from Inverness and it was the only place open. It had been quieter then, which suited me. I had wanted some time alone, not wanting to go to the flat I was sharing in those days because it would have meant talking to people. I'd been returning from my dad's funeral. The café had been empty but for one other customer, a woman who had just sipped her coffee and let a cigarette burn down between her fingers without drawing on it, all the time staring blankly out of the window. It's funny, I can remember her sitting there now, can wonder what was going through her mind, whereas at the time I barely noticed her, just subconsciously filed her away as something I wouldn't have to negotiate. The music on the radio had been turned right down, the girl behind the bar untalkative, poring solemnly over a novel as a long night crept unhurriedly towards dawn. It had felt like everyone present, everything about my surroundings, somehow knew why I was there and how I was feeling: respectfully sombre, delicately keeping their distance. All of which was, of course, nonsense. The place could have filled up with loudly drunk girls wringing out the last drops of a hen-party pub crawl and I'd have muted them in my mind. Dad was gone, and I wasn't in the pain and shock phase any more, but something more numbing: the mundane, functionary business of getting on with life in a world suddenly duller and less full of promise.

Raising a glass of Irn-Bru to my lips, I glimpsed myself back then. I was facing the table I had sat at, but between it and myself now was Laura Bailey. She might merely have been picking my brains, but sharing a table with her late at night in that same little coffee shop, I was facing the enticing prospect

197

of getting on with life in a world suddenly brighter and more full of promise.

I declined to join her in the latte option. It looked like a *lot* of coffee, and I was jangling enough right then without taking caffeine on board.

We laughed a little about the intense nature of our introduction.

'Makes a change from "What are you studying?"' I suggested.

Laura was keen to correct any misapprehension I might have that she was some crazed attention-seeking serial confessor. I told her that in my experience, there hadn't been many of those to be found. I was merely glad that she wasn't seeking to correct any misapprehension I might have that something might be going on between us, but I kept that to myself.

'Are they common?' I asked.

'I don't know,' she answered. 'But I just want you to understand I'm not the kind of person who goes pouring out all of my personal tragedies to complete strangers. At least, I wasn't until I had my personal tragedies revealed to several hundred complete strangers for the aggrandisement of some phoney psychic. And now that I've poured all my subsequent woes out to you, I'm hoping I'm cured.'

'As long as that doesn't mean I've outlived my usefulness,' I ventured, hoping not to sound too leading or outright needy.

'We-ell,' she said coyly, rolling her eyes, 'you won't have until I've heard your story. After that, who knows.'

'What story?' I asked, knowing fine.

'The story you said was for another day.' She pointed to her watch, tapping the face with a fingernail. 'If you're not going to give up the goods about how you know all this psychic stuff, then you really are surplus to requirements. I'm a ruthlessly pragmatic kind of gal, dabblings in the paranormal aside. So cough: your story or I'll drop you like first-year Sociology.'

'Okay,' I said, 'okay.' Even as I agreed, I was still stalling. Maybe I should tell her to get together with Keith. They could compare notes on the things I was reluctant to talk about, and between them they could work out the uncomfortable truth.

'Let me tell you *a* story,' I distinguished, still allowing myself a bit of distance, like an emotional head start if I chose to run away. She gave me a sharp-eyed look, as if to warn me that this better be good; or at least relevant. 'Stay with me,' I requested. 'Even though it's one you may have heard before. It's kind of like an urban myth, except it's one hundred per cent true. It takes place in a small town.'

'Which one?'

'Any one. That's the point.'

'If it's so universal, you can name one, surely.'

'Okay. Inverness. Nairn. Fochabers. Huntly. Elgin. Keith. And all stops in between.'

'You're not speaking hypothetically, are you?' she asked rhetorically. I realised there had been an edge to my voice and hoped it hadn't sounded aggressive.

'No. But for talking's sake, let's say Nairn. It's an ordinary morning, midweek. There's some women in a shop on the main drag. It could be a greengrocer's or a newsagent or any local family-run business.'

'Hairdresser? Bakery?'

'Hairdresser, yeah. Bakery, that's perfect. The important thing is, it's a family-run store. Name above the door, loyal customer base, been there for years. So there's a couple of women in there getting their morning rolls and chatting to the staff like always, when in comes a woman in gypsy garb. She's chatty and flamboyant and she's pretty soon got everyone engaged in a bit of blether. She tells them she reads fortunes and deferentially offers first to read for the woman who owns the place. The owner declines initially, but the gypsy woman assures her she's not looking for her to "cross my palm with silver". She'll do her for free. What's there to lose?'

'You're asking the wrong person that one.'

'Quite. So the gypsy woman sits down with the shop owner and takes her hand, then starts telling her things about herself. She's married, but she can sense a worry about her husband. She loves him but fears for him. Turns out he's had heart surgery. She's got grown-up children. Older one is a son, but he's strangely distant. Distant but thinking of her. The signal is faint but the love feels strong. Perhaps he lives far away? Turns out he lives in Australia.'

'Wooo.'

'Then she moves on to the other child. It's a daughter, the gypsy says. She feels a lot of love there too, but it's not all for her mother. She's very attached to somebody right now, and somebody else who is not there yet. You're going to be a grand-mother, she announces, within the year.'

'Turns out the daughter is engaged, right?'

'Right. She then follows it up with a wee dabble on the dark side: dead relatives the woman was close to, including their exact relationship to her and even a few first names. Finally, she rounds it off with a few vague but positive predictions: busi-ness will dip but improve, you will worry about money but realise the money doesn't matter; stuff like that.'

'Because they're spending big on a wedding.'

'You *have* heard this story before.'

'Variations, yes.'

'So you'll know the rest. The others in the shop are impressed. Gypsy woman does some of them too, though by this point they're opening their purses without being asked. She hits them with some equally impressive feats of divination, and they go away amazed, all repeating the woo-woo catchphrase about the things she was able to tell them.'

'What's that?'

'See if you can work it out. You've used it yourself about the amazing Mabel.'

Laura smiled bashfully and rolled her eyes as she cast her mind back. It took her only a couple of seconds.

'There was no way she could have known that stuff.'

I laughed. 'That's the one. And they don't just go away amazed, they go away bearing the cards she has handed them, with her mobile number and an address for if they want to consult her again, or if maybe their friends want a reading. Cannae beat word of mouth, especially when the word of mouth is saying how she told them all these amazing things that – your turn . . .'

'There was no way she could have known.'

'No way at all. None. It doesn't cross anyone's mind that the proprietor's name is on the door. It's a small town. It doesn't take much research for the gypsy woman to find out all she needs to before she walks into the bakery and impresses the hell out of everyone present, all of whom do pass the number to their friends. In polls, more than a third of women in the UK admit to having consulted a psychic or medium.'

'Makes me feel less lonely in my gullibility.'

'And these same women, having heard such amazing things the first time, come back again and again, especially at times when they're worried and feeling unsure about the future.'

Laura nodded. She'd been there, seen it and, if not bought the T-shirt, then certainly had her pockets lightened all the same.

'Then presumably she moves on to the next small town,' she said, 'and does the same thing.'

'Developing a client base, yes. The jungle telegraph has probably got the news there before her, so when she presents herself further along the road, they're practically queuing up.'

'But to come back to my question from . . .' Laura held up her wrist, turned the watch dial towards us both. 'Yesterday. How do you know this? No, wait. Your accent. I'm taking it you're from . . .'

'Inverness,' I told her.

She looked at me rather solemnly, almost apologetic. 'The women in those shops . . . one of them was your mum, is that it?'

I laughed, tried not to make it sound too scornful or bitter. I didn't want to come across as disdainful of the gypsy's dupes, what with Laura placing herself as within their constituency. Nor did I want my anger to give the game away; not just yet, anyway. Laura's face, however, suggested that she was already processing by elimination. Her eyes widened, her mouth agape for a second before she could articulate the thought that had so opened it.

'You're telling me your mum is a gypsy?' she asked, incredulous but, I could tell, already fascinating over its ramifications.

I cut off her imaginings with a softer laugh and a shake of the head.

'No, no. Nothing so exotic. She's an academic. A psychologist. Retired now, or semi-retired I suppose. Still dabbles, it would be fair to say. She's always had a special interest in the psychology of the paranormal. In a way, it's kind of why I'm here, as it was a shared interest that brought her and my dad together, once upon a time.'

'Is your dad a psychologist too?'

'No, he was a physicist. Nuclear. Glenmore Reactor, hence Inversneck.'

Laura dropped whatever she was about to say. 'Was?' she asked delicately.

'He died two years ago. It was very sudden. Sub-arachnoid haemorrhage. He was only fifty-two,' I added, swallowing, feeling the tears form.

Laura put one of her hands on mine and squeezed it. 'I'm sorry,' she said, and I knew it wasn't a mere observance, coming from her. I felt a pulse run through me the second her skin touched mine, the warmth and softness of her fingers seeming to spread beyond the point of contact like a wave. The mention of my dad didn't usually bring back that pain of loss so intensely these days, but maybe being here in this café had already primed it. It hit in my gut and constricted my throat like an invisible fist, but on top of it came the thrill of Laura's tenderness. I could live with the trade.

'They met at Edinburgh University, when my mum was doing her PhD. It was on the Psychology of Deception. My dad came along to take part in an experiment she was running. He was a few years younger, an undergrad. The issue of psychics was big news at the time, with guys like Uri Geller and Stanislav Hoffman all over the media. As an aspiring physicist, my dad wasn't buying any of it, and he went along to the experiment because he was suspicious it might be some pseudo-scientific put-up job.'

'I trust it wasn't.'

'No. It was pretty mundane, in fact. It was a test involving deception, but nothing to do with the paranormal. Her PhD wasn't just about psychics and mediums. She studied things such as Operation Bodyguard, which the Allies carried out ahead of the Normandy landings.'

'Operation Bodyguard? What was that?'

'The Allies leaked a plan to land at Pas de Calais, preceded by a minor attack on Normandy as a diversionary tactic. The German high command had long believed Pas de Calais was the most plausible place for an Allied invasion and had fortified it accordingly. In practice, the Germans bought the ploy so thoroughly that they retained a huge troop presence at Pas de Calais for ten days after D-Day, waiting for this phantom invasion that was never going to show. The Allies' trick was to sell them a dummy that reinforced their expectations. '

'Kind of like telling someone their mother and wee brother have been happily reunited in the afterlife,' Laura said with a look of regret.

'People are more easily disposed towards swallowing a lie if it reinforces what they already believe. Or want to believe. My mum found that the principles of deception are the same, whether it be military stratagems, con artists or the likes of Hoffman.'

'I know about Uri Geller,' Laura said, 'but I must admit I've never heard of Hoffman.'

'No small thanks to my mum,' I told her, with an unexpected pride I hadn't allowed myself to feel for an achingly long time. Now, though, the pride carried with it a sour aftertaste, the initial sweetness making the ensuing acid burn seem all the more unpalatable.

'How so?'

'As a result of the work she had done and some of the papers she'd published, she was brought in by the BBC as a kind of technical consultant when Stanislav Hoffman went on the Parkinson show back in the seventies. He'd been all over the papers and had done *Nationwide* and a few small slots on TV, but this was to be his big break in front of a massive Saturday-night audience.'

'Who was he? I mean, what did he do?'

'Same shit as Geller, mainly. Spoon-bending, restarting timepieces, mind-reading feats. There were a lot of me-toos emerging in the Great Bouffant's wake. Some of them were actually better than Geller at what they did, my mum said, but Geller was the master at selling his own myth, and that was what really counted. Manipulating metals was less important than manipulating the media, so few of them got much of a look-in compared to him. Hoffman was the one most closely coming up on the rails, though.'

'Until *Parkinson*.'

'That's right. The studio crew followed all my mum's instructions, resulting in about ten minutes of the most uneventful but, from a certain perspective, utterly hilarious television you are ever likely to see.'

'What happened?'

'Nothing. That's the point. Hoffman died on his arse, having been prevented from tampering with the props and setting up all his usual wee stunts. Just sat there hamming up his German accent and muttering about the forces being weak tonight or some such babble. His career fell apart very swiftly after that, and the bastard turned out to be from Cleethorpes, not Leipzig, as he'd claimed. Only down side was it further cleared the field for Geller, who had set his sights on Blighty after having a similar embarrassment on the Johnny Carson show in the US. However, no amount of exposés would prevent certain people believing wholeheartedly in the veracity of these supposed psychic powers. You expose a hundred psychics as frauds and they'll tell you it's no proof that there's no such thing as psychic powers, nor that psychic number hundred and one won't turn out to be the genuine article.'

'But scientifically speaking, they're right, aren't they? It *is* no proof.'

'Correct, as my mum often reminded me: exposing a hundred frauds is no proof the next guy isn't genuine. That's science. That said, it's also science to take note of what patterns emerge from your research. It's how we predict what we can expect to see in an experiment. If we see what we predicted we would – such as the next guy along turning out to be a fraud also – then that tends to tell us something pretty compelling about the nature of a thing.'

Laura was looking at me with a fascination bordering on wonder, but I knew it wasn't me who was the subject.

'So your mum must have taught you all about this stuff from an early age. How amazing.'

'To be honest, I was always more interested in what my dad could teach me. Mum was telling me things about human nature that, once you've learned them, can seem self-evident. I understand how they fascinate other people, but when you grow up with them, like anything, they become mundane. Physics and astronomy seemed more alive with possibilities to explore a wider realm. Also, what my mum taught me seemed depressingly inescapable. It seemed that in physics, you could make progress, you could change things, and once something was learned, it was established. But in my mum's field, it seemed people were doomed to repeat the same mistakes, and no amount of evidence could change their susceptibility to all this nonsense.'

'It changed your susceptibility, though,' Laura argued, correctly. 'So it isn't inescapable.'

'Not inescapable, but a one-in-two-gradient uphill battle. My mum taught me that, too. She had a book published: a commercial one, aside from her academic publications. *Beautiful Deceivers: The True Talents of the Psychics*, it was called. Came out when I was nine or ten. When I was twelve, we were down in Edinburgh one time and we found ourselves in a bookshop, the biggest one I'd ever seen. She made a point of taking me to see her book sitting there on a shelf. We had copies round the house, of course, but this was the first time I'd seen it in a real bookshop, for sale to Joe Punter.'

'Must have been a big thrill.'

'I thought so. I was just at the age to appreciate it, but that wasn't the point of the exercise. It was in a section headed Religion and Spirituality. My mum's book was surrounded by dozens upon dozens of books about psychics and mediums, books *by* psychics and mediums, all unquestioningly credulous of the whole racket. Books telling you how to tap into your own psychic powers, books on ESP, books about clairvoyance, Spiritualism, Theosophy, horoscopes. My mum's book was this single little volume of facts and evidence, utterly engulfed by shelf upon shelf of nonsense, faithfully flogging the same old myths, scams and lies. That was nearly a decade ago, and the ratio hasn't improved since. *Beautiful Deceivers* is long out of print, but sales of this shit are booming. You walk into Borders right now and you'll find more books on astrology than you will on astronomy. I keep hearing that we're a secular society, but it doesn't look like we're any more rationalist. The sad thing about my little tribute tonight was how many people were there in the hope of seeing more psychic wonders, not because they wanted to see a racket exposed. Like I said, an uphill battle.'

I took a drink from my glass, relieved again that I'd stayed off the coffee. From the look on Laura's face, it appeared I'd come across as merely sincere, possibly just the right side of impassioned, as opposed to the ranting zealot often unleashed upon those who unwittingly strayed into this territory (and upon Keith, who trampled in there deliberately just to see the resulting pyrotechnics).

'Still, I think you won a small victory tonight,' she said. 'I'm sure your mum would be thoroughly proud. Did you tell her you were doing it? Did you give you any pointers?'

I thought about lying, and surprised myself with the speed with which I decided I couldn't. It wasn't just that Laura had been so open – even unnervingly so – towards me. It was that it just felt easy to talk to her. I thought briefly of Keith, which made me feel sort of guilty, but only sort of. All those times he'd tried to talk about my mum, only to be fobbed off with deflections and innuendo, and here I was, about to confide in someone I'd only just met. But that's guys for you, I suppose. I'm not saying Keith wasn't genuinely interested, but in his case, interested didn't mean the same as concerned. I guess I was always just afraid he'd take the piss, that he wouldn't understand.

'I didn't tell her, no,' I said softly, trying to convey as much as I could in advance with my tone and expression so as to lessen the task of saying this. I looked up at Laura, hoping to see that she'd read it. She looked back with eager eyes, still riding a wave of enthusiasm for my amazing sceptic-crusading mum and how chuffed she'd be at her wee boy's coup of a few hours back.

'Well, you must,' she insisted. She glanced at her watch. 'I mean, not right now, but in the morning. Would she not be just thrilled?'

Shit.

'Maybe. Probably. I don't know.'

'You don't know?' Laura looked confused. I'd been hoping she'd be further along the process.

'We don't talk,' I stated, as firmly as I could. 'Not very often,' I added, softening it, for whose benefit I wasn't sure.

Laura made to speak, halted herself, realised what kind of ground she was stumbling on to. Seems she decided the most delicate way to tread would be to say nothing and see what I offered. Thus I was spared hearing 'You don't talk?' or 'Why not?' Spared hearing them, but I still had to answer.

'We fell out a while back. Kind of an irreconcilable difference.'

Now she spoke. 'Nothing should be irreconcilable between a mother and her son. How long has this . . . impasse been going on?'

'Over a year.'

'A *year*? Without speaking?'

'Well, without saying much.'

'What's it about? Surely it's something you can work out. If you upset her, you should say sorry.'

'Sorry wouldn't sort it.'

'You've no idea how forgiving mothers can be. Especially of their boys.'

'Sorry wouldn't sort it because sorry implies the intention not to do it again.'

'So what is it you did? Or is it too delicate to talk about?'

'I don't particularly want to talk about it, but it's not something *I* did. It's something she did. And it is pretty delicate.'

'Whatever it is, Michael, it can't be worth cutting her off for so long, especially when you've both already suffered one huge loss.'

This all made sense at a logical level. It was hard to argue with her, especially with her eyes gazing so imploringly across the table. But there was something blocking out the logic, something impervious to logic because logic had had no part in creating it. She sensed it, too; or at least was tuned in enough to appreciate that a few words of reason weren't going to make it all better.

'I'm not going to nag you,' she said. 'I know nothing about this. But I know plenty about sorrow and loss, and I know better than most how you can have some weird reactions to the grieving process. Alienating the person who most shares your loss is not unheard of.'

'Believe me, she's the one who's had a weird reaction to the grieving process.'

'She's still your mother. Don't lose sight of that. Have you any idea what I would give to be able to talk to mine again, just for a day?'

'Yes,' I said, nodding slowly, because I didn't want this to sound like a comeback. 'About the same as I'd give to be able to talk to my dad.'

'So I'd advise you not to take it out on the one who *is* still here.'

'I'm not,' I insisted, though I was already asking myself just how close that was to the truth. I wasn't exactly ready to say she'd nailed it, but it did suggest a possibility worth considering: was my anger and disappointment in Mum all the greater because I now needed and expected so much more from her? Perhaps. Perhaps. But it was still a big disappointment, regardless of expectation, and I was, I still felt sure, damn right to be angry.

I took in Laura's face, something I could not get enough of. She looked like I could tell her anything. She wasn't offering coffee-shop counsel. She cared, and she cared because she had been there.

'Okay, maybe I am taking some of it out on her,' I admitted. 'But how about you try this one on for me: how would you feel if your dad did something that betrayed the memory of your mum?'

Laura said nothing for a while, nodding minutely, her eyes away from me, slightly glazed from fatigue. It felt suddenly very late to be discussing this kind of stuff, but then, in my experience, there was always a good reason not to talk about it. I could tell she was truly asking herself the question, not just looking for an answer that would satisfy me. Was this what having a real girlfriend was like? Or was this what being a real adult was like?

She sighed softly, heralding that she had a response, if not an answer.

'How would I feel?' she asked. 'As hurt as you, I don't doubt. How would I deal with it? That's the real question. I know it's easier to say this than do it, but here's what I'd like to think I'd do. I'd draw on all my love for him and all my faith that, whatever he had done, betraying my mum's memory was not his intention. And with that in mind, first and foremost, I'd *talk* to him.'

We said nothing for a few moments. I finished my Irn-Bru and she sipped the last of her latte, which must have been long-since cold. Things weren't awkward, which surprised me. It didn't seem like a silence. Nonetheless, I was still a geeky, anxious male, so I was compelled to break it.

At least I did it politely.

'Thanks,' I said. She smiled in response, didn't feel the need to respond. That didn't feel awkward either. However, things felt like they were coming to a natural end. I indicated her empty cup. 'Can I get you another?'

'Not tonight.' She looked at her watch. 'Jesus, it's almost two. Need to get some kip.'

'Well, let me pay for these,' I offered, the over-eager and underexperienced dweeb doomed never to play it cool.

'Okay,' she said, then followed it up with four of the sweetest-sounding words she could possibly have said. 'My treat next time.'

The bill was less than a fiver. I put my hand into my coat pocket, where I knew there were several pound coins jangling. That was when I noticed that my keys were missing. With increasing haste, I patted my coat's other pockets and then all the ones in my jeans. Christ, had I come out without them? No. Did I remember handling them when I was transferring stuff from my coat to the white jacket? I took the jacket out of the poly bag and rifled through it. Still no joy.

'You gonna stiff me for the bill now?' she joked, then it dawned on her that it wasn't an act. 'Have you lost your wallet?'

'My keys,' I told her.

'You know, I've heard some lines in my time. When I told you about my promiscuous period, you did get that it was in the past tense, didn't you?'

My look of horror must have been a picture.

Laura laughed. I felt relief course through me as I realised she'd been joking. However, it didn't change the fact that I was still minus my keys.

'I'll phone Keith,' I said, flipping open my mobile. It rang out for a while, relayed me to the flat. That rang half a dozen times, then the answering machine kicked in. I tried Keith's mobile again, then Grant's. Nothing.

'No response,' I reported. 'Shit. Union will be all locked up by now.'

Laura stood up and pulled on her coat.

'Don't sweat it. I've a pretty serviceable sofa.'

'You serious?' I asked, trying not to sound too incredulously delighted lest she think I was getting the wrong idea. 'I mean, I could go back to my place and wait, or try and wake Keith if he's already home.'

'If he's had a skinful, it'd be easier to try and waken the dead. Come on, I live just around the corner.'

'You're a life-saver.'

Her place wasn't exactly just around the corner, but the night was dry and clear and I felt like I could use the air. It sounded like she could too. She sighed and giggled a little as we walked away from the café, our pace unhurried.

'It all got a bit heavy in there, didn't it?' she said.

'Wee bit,' I agreed. 'But it's been . . . you know . . .' I could feel myself blushing, threatening to clam up. I had to get through this. '. . . really great to talk to you.'

'Might have been easier if we could have met through a shared love of music or art or movies or the usual stuff.'

'I know. I only met you properly tonight and I already feel like I've been through years with you.'

'Makes it sound pretty rough,' she said.

'Oh, no, no,' I corrected. 'Not rough at all. In fact, with measured consideration, I'd say it's absolutely shiny.'

She stopped and smiled, wondering, perhaps, about my turn of phrase, this private little joke with myself which might by sheer accident have made me seem comfortable being me in that moment. It was the point at which a guy who knew what he was doing would have kissed her. A guy who wasn't pinching himself and utterly amazed he hadn't blown it yet.

'We'll talk about all that other stuff later,' she said. 'There's plenty of time. We'll talk tomorrow. Today. *Later*.'

We both laughed.

\* \* \*

210

The last thing I remember is trying not to fall asleep, fighting it even as my eyes closed because I wanted to eke out every last moment. She said we'd have tomorrow. I should have surrendered willingly to hasten the dawn and all that it promised, but I didn't want the night to end.

# All just harmless fun

Okay, so it wasn't strictly accurate to say he was another dead guy with a story to tell, but it is true that I had a multi-sensory encounter with him. And come on: considering the scale of the deception afoot here, you can forgive an honest reporter the odd wee misleading figure of speech. In my defence, I truly believed he was dead, hence the ensuing moment of confused consternation as I stared at him in the pub.

'Michael Loftus?' I repeated. 'As in, *A Tribute to Gabriel Lafayette*, that Michael Loftus?'

He smiled nervously, suddenly apprehensive in reaction to my less-then-affable register. I wasn't meaning to come over aggressive, but in retrospect, there must have seemed a 'Didn't you shag my daughter?' tone to my disbelieving question.

'Eh, yeah,' he stumbled. 'I mean, it said "tribute", but it wasn't intended as a form of praise, if that's what you're worried about. Did you see it?'

'No,' I told him. 'And that's not what I'm worried about. Look, don't take this the wrong way, pal, but I was under the impression you were a wee bit closer to the spirit world than even Mr Lafayette professes to be.'

He looked back quizzically for a moment, then worked it out. Confirmation of this came in the form of a solemn nod. Clearly, all was not as it seemed, but I wasn't expecting a laugh-out-loud tale of crazy misunderstandings.

'You mean the flat,' he said, his voice lowering, throaty, like something in him had just been punctured. He swallowed, his previously bright young face sapped of its energy. 'Yeah. I wasn't there. I met someone. Kinda gave new meaning to the phrase "got lucky with a girl".' He grimaced as he spoke, and I could hear the break in his voice, the struggle to prevent tears.

'Can I get you a drink?' I offered, suddenly feeling like I needed one myself.

'Got one over there,' he said, and indicated a table further inside, where a girl was sitting. She was looking back towards us, gave an anxious-to-please wave. Christ. Young love. All of a sudden I felt about seventy.

'Let me line you both up another, then,' I said. He told me what they were drinking and I sent him back to his table. It gave all of us a wee moment to gather ourselves after such a rocky start.

I brought the drinks across and between us we almost dropped the lot as he overeagerly got up to assist me in putting them on the table at the same time as introducing the girl and me to each other. Laura, her name was. Michael sat down next to her, leaving me a seat opposite. She angled her chair slightly, bringing herself closer to his. Her body language could not have been more explicitly protective of him. Lucky with a girl, he'd said. I'd get the details in a sec, but the broad brush-strokes were already clear. He'd been with her that night and some other poor bastard had crashed at his place. What a torrid shit-storm of guilt and confusion *that* had to be. It was easy to imagine the mangled wreckage of a confluence like that driving both parties apart. Yet in their case it looked like it had fused them together. Some prurient but nonetheless halfway sensitive part of me hoped to fuck they hadn't lost their cherries that night. Imagine carrying that around in the same pouch as your libido for the rest of your days.

'Laura and I were out late that night and I crashed on her sofa.'

So he read minds almost as well as Lafayette.

'My flatmate Keith was out with a guy we knew called Grant.'

Michael's voice cracked and his eyes overflowed. Laura squeezed his thigh under the table. It was intimate and solicitous without being ostentatious, like an arm around the shoulder would have been. Yeah, these two were the real thing.

'Michael and I got up pretty late and had lunch together,' she said, taking over. 'It was well into the afternoon before he went back to his place. By that time, the police had called his mum and asked her to come to Glasgow to identify him. She was on the train down when Michael phoned her.'

'How did you know about it?' he asked me.

'Police friend of mine. She took me to see the flat. It was in case there was some student welfare issue to be addressed, but . . .'
I left it at that. Ursula had mentioned it only briefly the next time we spoke, telling me it had been ruled an accident, landlord exonerated, that sort of stuff. She never corrected the identity issue because she didn't realise I had picked up any names.

'It was a fucking crow,' Michael said bitterly. 'Fell down the chimney, dislodged all sorts of shit. Choked the vents.'

It had been less than two months ago, start of term. Hell of a way to kick off your year of study, and from his face I was guessing he must be close to the end of his degree.

'You in your final year?' I asked.

'Yeah. Laura too.'

'You doing okay? I mean, it must have been . . .'

'It was rough, but the most inescapable thing is that it could have been a lot worse. Makes it pretty hard to feel too sorry for yourself.'

'It's survivor's guilt,' Laura said. 'I keep telling him, but he's stubborn about anything emotional. Hyper-rationalist science geek that he is. Maybe he'd listen to you. You know about survivor's guilt, don't you, Mr Parlabane?'

'Just a little,' I said, trying not to sound testy about it. I'd had the same conversation a dozen times with Sarah. I knew Laura was right, but I knew pretty well how it looked from where Michael was sitting too. Feeling bad, then feeling worse because you don't feel you have the right to feel bad: try wrestling with that one on top of bereavement. At least the kid didn't also have to deal with having partially eaten one of the casualties.

'Where you living now?' I asked, offering him an out. He took it gratefully.

'Same place,' he said with a shrug. Laura scowled a little, betraying that this remained a matter of some contention.

'Is that not a bit . . . ?' I suggested.

'A bit what? I don't believe in ghosts, Mr Parlabane. I'd have thought that was understood.'

'Jack, please.'

'Plus it's about all I can afford.'

'He could afford more if he'd let his mum help out,' Laura interjected.

214

'Let's not go there again,' Michael replied.

'We never go there,' Laura informed me with a roll of her eyes.

'Why won't you let your mum help?'

'Long story.'

'Pride,' Laura volunteered.

'Are you worried she can't afford it?' I asked.

'Nah. He's in the huff with her.' Laura's wry tone told me this was something he took a lot more seriously than she did; as well as being an attrition he had a far more enduring patience for.

'Look, we're not here to talk about that,' Michael said, and like any fellow male I saluted this forthright sentiment. Anything that gets us off discussing our emotions can only be applauded; it drives us forward, away from petty distractions, in our never-ending quest to understand everything except ourselves. 'What can I do for you?' he asked me.

I summarised my predicament as best I could, leaving out the part about the prospect of self-dealt hand-shandies dominating my short- to medium-term sexual future.

'I need to know how he's doing it,' I concluded.

They both stared back at me for a moment, which I confess was as much a surprise as it was a disappointment. I had kind of expected him to barely skip a beat before rattling off an explanation, perhaps even with a weary chuckle at 'that old chestnut still reeling them in'. There was also a modicum of reassurance therein, in that it suggested I wasn't a complete numpty who was unable to see something staring him right in the face.

Michael started hitting me with questions about the protocol, and didn't seem to be expecting my answers. It became rapidly apparent that nothing obvious had been overlooked, and that nor had the four of us been lured into any less obvious pitfalls either.

'It's impossible trying to work from just a verbal account,' he said. 'If I could watch the tapes and see hard copies of the materials, then I'd maybe have something for you in a few days.'

'I don't have a few days,' I told him. 'I'm imminently going to be asked to draft my conclusions, including whatever suspicions I have. Unfortunately, "I just think he's at it" doesn't carry much scientific weight, especially as I've already submitted detailed accounts of what I've witnessed so far, minus any shred of evidence that he's cheating. But to be honest, trying to nail him in the report would be like trying to recover a hundred-point deficit on snookers. The others – the scientists on the project – are starting to seriously entertain the idea that something groundbreaking is taking place because that's what the data appears to be telling them. Whatever he's doing, I need to catch him in the act, and we've only got two more days of tests scheduled. I'm running out of time.'

Michael looked briefly at Laura as if for her sanction, then back at me. 'Well, there's only one thing for it,' he said. Her face brightened expectantly. 'You've got to get me in there for the next test.'

This was what I'd have been hoping for if I'd been clued-up enough to even know what to hope for. I'd need to run it past Mather and the others, but I couldn't see them raising any objection. Lafayette probably wouldn't be delighted if he'd gotten wind of Michael's wee tribute show at the start of term, but if I insisted on Michael's presence as a control, Lafayette would have to comply. If he didn't, then that would go down in the report, and would not look good: 'Subject cried off when new expert on psychic cheating methods was brought in.'

It was my best chance, perhaps my only one, and I was so relieved at having secured it that I failed to attribute much significance to the fact that Laura didn't share my enthusiasm. *She* hadn't heard what she'd been hoping to, and I didn't think to enquire what that had been.

I cleared it with Mather via a phone call. I thought about making up a cover story for Michael, but decided I had to be strictly open and honest about who he was and why he would be there. If you want your opinion to carry some academic weight, it's a bit of an own goal if your report concedes that lies and deceit were a big part of your methodology. I told Mather that Michael knew a fair bit about psychic chicanery and mentioned that he'd even put on a Lafayette tribute act. Mather paused for a while at the mention of this, which was not surprising.

'Sure,' he said eventually. 'I think it's a smart idea, but I'm worried about how Gabriel will take it. He could interpret it as an insult. I don't want him throwing a hissy fit and refusing to play ball. Might be best if we just don't tell him. We could keep the kid out of sight, then Gabe doesn't need to even know he's there, far less his story.'

'I thought we needed total disclosure. Wouldn't it give him an excuse later if there was something we didn't tell him?'

'It doesn't affect the protocol, so as long as it's logged in the reports, it shouldn't matter. But it's a good point. Psychic subjects often cite negative presences as having an inhibitory effect. What they usually mean is presences who might be wise to their moves. But you're right. If he flunks while this kid Loftus is present and we haven't been open about it, then he can point to this after the fact. Furthermore, he could point to having an inhibited performance while not knowing the kid was there as proof that negative presences can affect the outcome.'

'Michael's presence couldn't be much more negative than mine, and that hasn't inhibited him.'

Mather laughed. 'Well that's sure true. No, wait, I got it. Perfect compromise. We let him know about the kid, but we simply tell him he's a new volunteer, which would be accurate, and that way we wouldn't be telling him anything else beyond his first name.'

This made sense. Lafayette hadn't been told the other students' surnames in case he tried to research their backgrounds for 'hot reading' material.

'Works for me,' I said.

In retrospect, it's easy to see where I went wrong. Schoolboy error stuff, unforgivable both as a journalist and in light of the circumstances I've had to cope with down the years. Put simply, I didn't equip myself with all of the facts. I was sloppy in my research and consequently missed not only a salient detail, but the danger I was heedlessly walking into. In short, I should have pressed Michael harder about his mammy, and thus the significance of a surname that, had I realised was a red rag to a bull, I would not have trusted mere protocol to keep secret. But it's too late to change that now, and no two words make a more whiny sound than 'if only'.

Lafayette was introduced to our new volunteer the next evening.

We couldn't be sure whether he even knew there had *been* a tribute act, but as mentalists were adept at swiping wallets and the like, Michael had acted in accordance with my suggestion and turned up minus any means of identification, including that ridiculous coat. Unfortunately, such safeguards of his anonymity could not prevent the minor haemorrhage of information he must have passed on through simply his reaction to Lafayette when they were introduced. Michael so visibly stiffened, almost recoiling at the prospect of grasping the American's outstretched hand, that the question of Lafayette being able to detect a negative presence was rendered moot.

Lafayette bridled momentarily at this near-reflexive rudeness, then began to make light of it. 'Whoah!' he said, laughing uncomfortably. 'Now I've never claimed to be a psychic, but I'm reading some strong mental signals right now. Would I be right in suggesting there's a sceptic in the house?'

'There ought to be seven sceptics in the house right now, Gabriel,' Mather reminded him. 'Catherine, Juliet, Heidi, Jack, Rudi, Michael and myself. Otherwise we're all wasting our time.'

'No, no, sure thing,' he agreed. 'Just so long as we all understand the borderline between scepticism and open hostility.'

'Is there a problem?' Mather asked, causing me to stiffen in case he was about to acquiesce to any objection. He was as keen as me for Michael to observe, but was, as always, afraid Lafayette would take his ball and go home. After all, without a prize subject to work with, Mather was looking at a farcical future testing more psychic cats and table-tippers.

'No,' Lafayette decided, after a moment's thought. 'What's been happening here every night has been between me and the target. If Michael can affect that, then maybe you oughta start testing *him*.' He said this last with a smug little grin and began making for the door, indicating to Rudi that he was ready for the strip-search.

'And what if Michael *is* the target?' I asked.

'You got access all areas, Mr Parlabane,' Lafayette said. 'And if he's your man, then so has he. That's if being the target is okay with you, Michael.'

'Eh, sure,' Michael replied nervously. 'Why wouldn't it be?'

The answer to that question came during the subsequent 'contact' phase.

Michael looked like he'd have been more comfortable sitting down in an enclosed space with a hypoglycaemic tiger. When he did allow Lafayette to make eye contact, it was to glare any time the American looked like even thinking of laying a hand on any part of him.

'You know, I'm getting some really strong signals around you, Michael,' he said. 'And I don't just mean what you're projecting towards me. There's so much more anger than I could possibly be provoking, a real maelstrom of rage. So much pain there, too.'

'Why don't you drop the cold-reading shite,' Michael responded. 'I'm not going to throw you back any more pointers than the involuntary physical cues you're no doubt adept at reading.'

'I'm not picking up cues, son, I'm picking up emotions. There's presences around you, presences you won't let yourself feel because you're all churned up inside. Presences that want to help, that *need* to help.'

'Give them my email address.'

'They're people you're missing, people who can't rest because of your pain.'

I watched Michael swallow: a retort or his emotions, I'd never know. My money would have been on the latter or both, but not the former alone. He was holding on tight but he was crumbling.

'Your father.'

'Fucking shut up about my father. You know nothing about my father.'

'I know he hates seeing you like this.'

Michael was filling up. 'He must have some view from a buried box in Tomnahurich Cemetery,' he spat back.

'You know he's closer than that. You know but you won't let him in. You're too consumed with . . . it's not just rage, it's guilt. Guilt for the other ones.'

At this, Michael snapped his head around to face Lafayette.

'They died and you lived,' Lafayette said. 'You need someone to blame and you don't have anybody else.'

Michael stared at him with a disgust that was involuntarily giving way to incredulity. I was aware that my own mouth was agape at this point. The others looked tense simply from the developing situation, but I was the only one with such an informed perspective.

'It's raw, real raw, ain't it?' Lafayette asked softly. 'My God, this was . . . this was . . . feels like it could be last week. Jesus. They died. They died, but it was peaceful.'

Michael now lost his struggle and shed some sincerely begrudged tears.

'It was peaceful, painless. They don't have pain. They don't have anger. They don't have blame. They don't want you to blame yourself.'

Michael's mouth was trembling, his teeth gritted as he fought against any further loss of control. Lafayette closed his eyes, almost as though granting him privacy, but his brow furrowed in concentration.

'There was a bird,' Lafayette added, causing Michael to suddenly get to his feet. I thought for a second he was going to bolt. Perhaps Lafayette did, too. He grabbed Michael's wrists and this time Michael didn't recoil. Lafayette closed his eyes again. 'The bird . . . died, and then they died too. Somehow the bird's death and theirs are interlaced.' He opened his eyes, looked deep into Michael's. 'You're no more to blame than the bird.'

Michael's features stayed just about composed, but the tears continued to flow. He shook off Lafayette's grip and stepped away towards the wall, looking dazed.

Mather looked equally rattled, staring at me like the situation was my fault for introducing this unstable new element.

'I think we're all gonna need a little minute here,' Lafayette declared.

Michael was adamant that he was okay to proceed to the test phase, though he looked anything but. I urged him to take a while to compose himself, as he needed to be sharp and undistracted when we took him through the protocol at both the target and receiving ends. 'I'm fine,' he told me, rather defensively, like he was embarrassed by his tears.

'Fucker's good, I'll give him that,' he muttered with a sniff.

'But he's not *that* good,' he added, managing a wink. Even as Heidi led him from the base, I guessed it was bravado.

Lafayette nailed every one of Michael's 'drawings'. I use the quote marks because, in his growing frustration, Michael on the fifth pass 'drew' the words 'Fuck you'. At this point, Lafayette called a halt to the proceedings, saying that the hostility he was detecting, even from inside the Faraday cage, was having a disturbing effect on him. 'It's like being jacked right into some-body's centre of hate. Worse, it's like I'm not only feeling his pain, but I'm sensing this *echo* of his pain. My head hurts and I'm starting to feel nauseous.'

Michael didn't utter a word as I escorted him downstairs and out of the building. His expression was a facsimile of how I imagined mine must have looked on the same spot about twenty-four hours earlier. I hailed him a cab and handed him a few quid for the fare. 'Last day of the tests tomorrow,' I reminded him. 'Any changes you can suggest to the protocol, bell me right away. I don't care if it's four am or five minutes before we're due to start. You call me any time, okay?'

He nodded gravely. As I closed the door and watched the cab swing a one-eighty across University Avenue, I felt I was watching my last chance drive away. Somehow I knew he wouldn't be calling.

I resisted phoning Michael until about half five, when I was about to leave the flat for the Randall Building. The dialogues I had with myself in order to keep my finger from the touchpad that long were embarrassing, like a smitten teenager trying to play it cool by not phoning the girl who'd given him her number. Deep down I knew that if he really had something for me he'd call, though as the day wore on I tried to convince myself he was just taking all the time he had to iron out his theory and get his suggested protocol alterations just right.

When eventually I rang, it took him a reluctantly long time to answer, and he sounded sheepish to the point of apologetic.

'I just don't know how he's doing it,' he confessed. 'The protocol looks tight as a drum, so there's no way he can see those drawings. There's video cameras in the target room, and I gave those a lot of thought, but he's inside the Faraday cage, where there's no transmission possible, and no monitor for him to look at. I hate to say it, but scientifically speaking, I can offer no explanation for what he was able to do.'

'You're saying you'd concur with Mather, Kline and Ganea's conclusions?' I asked, rather taken aback.

'No,' he said. 'I'm not saying what he did was outwith the realms of scientific explanation. I'm saying he's smarter than us, Jack. I'm sorry.'

'Hey, don't sweat it,' I said half-heartedly. 'It's all just nonsense anyway. I've been had. I'll live with it.'

I was barely out the front door when Mather got me on my mobile to say Lafayette was ill and consequently the last day of the tests was cancelled. Project Lamda was over.

I felt a surprising sense of anticlimax. It wasn't like we were ever going to have a cheese-and-wine party in the labs, drinking out of beakers and posing for pictures with funnels on our heads, but the matter-of-factness with which he acknowledged that it was finished seemed in sharp contrast to some of the drama we'd all gone through together. It gave me a much-needed sense of perspective: for all I'd got caught up in the excitement, the mystery and the sheer bizarreness of it, it was, in the end, merely an academic exercise. Mather's sobriety about it reflected his professionalism, and reassured me that he wasn't about to go off the deep end about what the tests had apparently witnessed. Rudi and Heidi had, in fact, seemed more giddy about what they were seeing, though I suspected Mather's restraint betrayed the still lingering doubts he had over whether Lafayette was simply, as Michael put it, smarter than the rest of us.

Mather sounded a little more excited when he told me they had a window to get the Project Lamda report considered for the next quarterly edition of the highly respected *Journal of Nature*, but the deadline was tight. He needed to submit a preliminary version to the editors by the end of the following week, though there would be considerably more time to hone the finished paper before publication. Mather already had most of my blow-by-blow accounts, but this made it imperative that I submit the remainder – specifically yesterday's work with Michael – plus my conclusions as soon as possible. He wanted them ideally by close of play this Friday, with the following

Thursday the absolute cut-off. He was almost apologetic as he made it clear that if I failed to submit any conclusions, it would be interpreted that I was offering no opinion, and certainly not one dissenting from the other three, which were strongly inclined to contend that we had witnessed genuine paranormal phenomena.

I filed my final account, detailing Michael's uncomfortable target stint, later that same evening. The document entitled 'Conclusions? Suspicions?' remained accusingly blank on my laptop.

I was working on a couple of ongoing stories, as well as my weekly op-ed column. It was easy to put the whole Project Lamda issue on the back burner and ignore it. Mather's preferred submission date came and went. At that point, the sum of my efforts towards writing my conclusions amounted to having the document open in a minimised window now and again.

I read Jillian Noble's latest crap in *The Mail*, boasting about how Lafayette was proving the doubters wrong and accusing me of dragging my heels over my conclusions. It pissed me off that Lafayette had been feeding her stuff before even the preliminary paper on the project was finished, but it didn't change the facts. She was right: I *was* dragging my heels and holding on for the absolutely final deadline in the hope that the story would change.

Mather called a couple of times to hurry me up, told me that he had already sent off hard copies of all the other accounts, plus selected video files and photocopies of drawings. At five pm Thursday, he was emailing *Journal of Nature* with his overview and any last-minute clarifications from Rudi and Heidi. If I hadn't filed by then, I had missed the boat.

Five pm Thursday, I was in the flat alone. Sarah was in London at a three-day seminar, wouldn't be home until Sunday. I hadn't even told her that that night was the deadline; in denial I guess, hoping for the last-minute development that would change everything. She knew I had failed, though. I'd told her about my great white hope striking out. She wasn't impressed, but as I delicately pointed out, she hadn't been able to dream up any explanations either.

'I know,' she conceded. 'This is what Blake was afraid of.'

I thought back to that celebration dinner, to Blake's concerns about Mather, Kline and Ganea's reputations. 'He's smarter than us,' Michael Loftus had said. That was indeed what Blake had been afraid of: Lafayette being given a platform to dupe scientists who simply weren't sharp enough to catch him out.

I sat with a beer and watched the deadline pass on the little clock in the corner of my ageing laptop's screen. By the time I'd finished the bottle, the main thing I was starting to feel about it was relief. I revisited my sense of anticlimax when Mather had called to say the practical side of the project had wrapped up early. I couldn't believe I'd got so worked up about it, and couldn't understand why Sarah was taking it all so seriously either. In retrospect, I was actually quite embarrassed by how spooked I had been the night Lafayette and I had our little one-on-one.

Belatedly I reflected how, that little wobble aside, I had never found myself asking whether it really meant we'd witnessed paranormal phenomena. I knew I'd been mugged, that was all. The only thing that had been proven, as far as I was concerned, was that Lafayette was too cute for the rest of us. I could live with that. But as I clicked on the corner and closed the still blank window, I asked myself what reasons lay behind my private, now irretrievably undocumented conclusion. All I could offer was my prejudiced belief that Lafayette was a fraud, while all of the hard physical evidence appeared to prove otherwise. In scientific terms, I was now the one clinging to an unsupported faith while rational conclusion pointed to a reality I was stubbornly refusing to accept. I had assisted in setting up and refining a protocol that had been good enough to thwart Colin Playfair, aka Len Philpott, and for him to approvingly predict, as 'a long-term scientist and just as long-term sceptic: nothing unexplained is going to happen here'. And yet it had. I had watched in person and on monitors, examining every incident, entertaining every suspicion my paranoid mind could muster. Then, finally, I had brought in Michael Loftus, who had successfully duplicated all of Lafayette's stage tricks. Yet even he could neither prevent nor explain what the American pulled off again and again in those laboratories.

Again, I recalled Mather's words, way back at the start of

this bizarre undertaking: 'Your job is to look for cheating, simple as that . . . However, if you find none, then *that*'s when you have to be open-minded about your conclusions.'

So was my blank page a failure or a cop-out?

I like to think, scientifically, that it merely represented a call for more evidence. Nonetheless, my faith endured, so the blank page, with its tacit approval of the others' conclusions, constituted a failure *and* a cop-out. However, as I switched off the computer, there was one consoling thought.

Truth was, now that I could take a step back and look at the whole business again, it was all, quite inescapably, rather daft. In the end, it was just a group of grown adults playing guessing games, resulting in an academic write-up that might be chewed over by a few mouldy professors and seized upon by fruitcakes, but which would mean absolutely nothing to everybody else in the country due to their failure to even notice its existence. Besides, what the hell did it matter if a few half-wits wanted to believe this nonsense? The nutters would continue to believe what they wanted to anyway, regardless of whether we debunked Lafayette, so what difference was this obscure wee report going to make? Short of taking out a subscription to *Journal of Nature*, I doubted I'd ever hear about the whole silly project again.

I was wrong.

That gets a line to itself, but could be said to deserve a whole page, such was the exponentially vast, runaway, China Syndrome, chain-reaction, escalating scale of my wrongness. Perhaps the only way of truly conveying how wrong I was would be to describe . . . well, we'll get to that soon enough.

The earliest inkling of the approaching Dawn of Wrong was when I started getting phone calls from other reporters on Friday afternoon. The first was from *The Saltire*'s science correspondent, Nick Farrell, asking me about my involvement with Project Lamda and, with a degree of surprise and a larger degree of excitement, whether I believed it had witnessed genuine paranormal events. The Spiritual Science Chair had issued an all-media press release announcing that it had the world's first hard laboratory evidence of a psychic phenomenon, and that a paper detailing the project would soon be appearing in the peer-reviewed *Journal of Nature*. I was cited as having been brought on board at the university's insistence in the role of lay observer, and was said to have found no evidence contrary to the paper's claims. This was supplementary to the detailed findings of the paper's co-authors: Ezekiel Mather, Professor Heidi Ganea and Dr Rudi Klein.

I told Nick that I had submitted no conclusions because I was unconvinced that my failure to find evidence of subterfuge meant there had been none. He said the release had included a detailed description of the protocol, and confessed that he couldn't see any holes in it either. I muttered something about it all ultimately being just a silly exercise involving grown adults drawing wee pictures, but it was the big picture I was missing.

'It's the protocol that matters, Jack. Not the pictures or Zener cards or whatever. If the *JoN* are ratifying the set-up, this is going to be a big deal.'

A couple more calls came in from other reporters I personally knew, similarly surprised to see my name and the way my involvement was being spun. Then I started fielding enquiries from science correspondents on the London broadsheets. Tellingly, these were the only reporters calling me as a potential source of dissent. Correction: the broadsheet science correspondents were the only reporters calling me at all. For everybody else, the scientists, the subject and the chair's sponsor were far more enticing sources of copy, none of them likely to pour any cold water on a very hot story.

As I said, this was Friday afternoon that the reporters were working on their pieces. The insanity was therefore only truly unleashed on Saturday morning. It wasn't the biggest story of the day, but it was everywhere, and it was only just beginning.

The broadsheet coverage was typically restrained, if in some cases nonetheless tantalised by the possibilities. I was quoted as abstaining from endorsing the preliminary paper's conclusions, my position spun according to the individual journalists' degree of credulity towards the whole affair. In some, I was depicted as harbouring a muted dissent, while in others I came across like some kind of bad loser.

The closest anyone came to a spoiler story was one account carrying a quote from the *Journal of Nature* pointing out that the Project Lamda team had jumped the gun. 'We invited the authors to make a submission on the strength of the protocol and other preliminary materials, but we haven't reviewed the evidence in depth and therefore haven't made an absolutely final decision to publish.' It was hardly going to derail this particular runaway train. The statement came over as almost as straw-clinging and cautiously equivocal as my own quotes did. The word 'absolutely' in there before 'final decision' made it sound an all-but done deal, and even if it wasn't, nobody was going to let a small detail like that get in the way of all the fun.

And oh, what fun.

IS THERE ANYBODY THERE? YES, SAY SCIENTISTS!

THINGS THAT GO BUMP IN THE LAB!

SIXTH SENSATIONAL: BOFFINS FIND PROOF OF
PSYCHIC FORCES

TV PSYCHIC ROCKS WORLD OF SCIENCE

Reading between the lines, it looked like it was largely Lafayette and Bryant Lemuel who were behind the release. Mather was quoted, as were Kline and Ganea, but the three of them sounded like they were trying to cap the inevitable over-reaction.

'It's very early days,' Mather said. 'We can't say exactly *what* it is we've discovered, and I think we should be very clear on that. Gabriel Lafayette himself maintains he is not psychic, but that he is conducting some other force or signal. I guess the next step is to start looking at what that other force or signal might be. They say the longest journey starts with a single step. All we can be sure of at this stage is that we've taken a first step. There's a very long path ahead, but we're extremely excited to be on it.'

The sobriety of his remarks was at odds with the bombastic wording of the press release, which I'd got Nick to fax me, and even more so with the way the release's authors knew the story would be reported, especially in the tabloids.

 Plus, of course, if it turned out the *Journal of Nature* eventually rejected the paper, or that the scientific community were able to discover what I had not, then that would be a story for a later day: only it would be a much, much smaller story, if it was reported anywhere at all. Even then, it would make no difference to the intended impact of this news cycle: in the public mind, psychic powers had now been 'proven'. It was in all the papers, wasn't it? Didn't read the details myself, but I saw the gist of it. On telly too. So it only goes to show, doesn't it, these scientists don't have all the answers, and if they were wrong about psychics, then who's to say what else they might be wrong about. I've always known I had some psychic powers myself. I can always tell when somebody's looking at me, and sometimes when the phone rings . . .

 At first I thought they'd got their timing a little wrong: Saturday is the worst day of the week for newspaper sales. But in fact, they'd timed it perfectly. Saturday was just the splash day. It was in the Sundays that it would really play, not as a mere news piece, but as in-depth feature material and, most crucially, the subject of debate and opinion. On Saturday, it was a kicker, an unusual and colourful story that no news editor was likely to resist. By Sunday, however, it was setting its own agenda.

 For those who bothered to look that far, the science correspondents were, in general, cagily hanging fire on what the story did or did not prove. One even went as far as to say that 'the blank page where Jack Parlabane's conclusions were supposed to go may yet prove the most astute comment on the available evidence'. (Cheers, Nick, hope you cashed the cheque before you found out I'd snuffed it.) But the feature and op-ed writers were far less reluctant to contemplate the experiment's wider consequences. What did this mean for the future of science, if something scientists had previously been adamant was impossible had now been demonstrated in their own laboratories? What did it mean for the future of religion, if something previously dismissed as mere superstition was now a documented scientific phenomenon?

And naturally, nobody was pushing the agenda more explicitly than Jillian Noble. I'll spare you the full text. You've read her before, so there's very little that would be new. Selected highlights:

What scientific 'certainty' will be the next to crumble? And how quickly will we hear scientists revise their positions, disowning previously unquestionable truths as glibly as the Soviet propagandists? I choose the Soviet metaphor advisedly, because I predict that these events in Glasgow in 2006 will, for the science Stalinists, be their equivalent of Berlin 1989. The Wall has fallen, and from here on in, the domino effect will make quite a spectacle.

Billions of people around the world – the vast, vast majority of the planet's population, in fact – believe in a God and in an afterlife. Yet they are dictated to by a tiny minority who call their beliefs ridiculous, but who will stand there and tell you with a straight face that the entire universe was once a single object small enough to fit inside your handbag!

Here ends the tyranny of the science Nazis: in particular their stranglehold in deciding what areas we explore and, crucially, what theories we teach our children. It must be our sincere hope – nay, our Stentorian demand – that the amazing work of the Spiritual Science Chair leads to a fundamental rethink about what we can and can't teach in our schools and universities.

She didn't have to worry on that score: according to a sidebar on the same double-page spread, this would be imminently underway at Kelvin University at least. The Spiritual Science Chair was about to be seriously open for business. Postgraduate and undergraduate courses were mooted, but the Chair's altruistic mission could not be restricted to the matriculated minority. Anybody would be able to learn about this new field of 'science': there would be an array of night classes as well as postal subscription courses. The sidebar reported that the chair had

229

been fielding enquiries about such courses since its inception, and was being inundated with phone calls and emails now that the Project Lamda story had broken.

The sidebar mentioned the millions made each year on premium-rate psychic hotlines, adding that it was impossible to estimate what the psychic market was truly worth in the UK alone, 'with so much of it changing hands secretly as palms are crossed with silver under informal and often tawdry circum-stances'. It suggested that 'the Spiritual Science Chair will be able to bring respectability and even the first vestiges of regu-lation to the field'. Or, to put it another way, once the paper was published and the chair's scientific credentials established, it would be a licence to print money. Lafayette would be in the position to market a new, ratified brand of bollocks that would very quickly become a world leader. The Microsoft of Woo.

I had all the Sunday papers spread around the living-room carpet, the better to take in the full scope of the burgeoning insanity. I was kneeling on the floor as I pored over the Jillian Noble spread. I heard the door open and looked up to see Sarah walk in. It was the look on her face in that moment that truly brought home the scale of wrongness I was talking about. I'm not sure I can describe it; you really had to be there, though if you're married, you can probably just about begin to imagine it. This look was far, far, *far* beyond 'I told you so'. 'I told you so' doesn't even begin to approach it. This was 'I told you so' added to 'But would you listen?' multiplied by 'Now do you get it?' to the power of 'You useless prick.'

I gave what I hoped was my least pathetic apologetic smile and suggested: 'Hey, it's not all bad news. We'll save a fucking fortune on phone bills once the boy Lafayette's taught us all to communicate through the ether.'

Sarah laughed, to my colossal relief. It was wry and bitter, but she did laugh.

I poured her a coffee from the pot I'd recently made as she took a seat on the sofa. She was studying the Noblefest when I returned from the kitchen with her mug.

'This is why Lafayette and Lemuel were so adamantly holding out for the Chair to come under the auspices of the science faculty,' she said. 'It's just not the same sell if it's attached to the Psychology department. People think you're only talking about mind games when that's the tag, and the quotes don't sound as impressive coming after "Psychologists say". "Scientists say" carries a lot more weight, and when the full phrase is "Scientists at Kelvin University" . . .'

'All of a sudden they've got international academic credentials, and one hell of a brand endorsement. It won't just be pseudo-educational courses. The possibilities are endless. It'll be a gold mine.'

'Undoubtedly,' Sarah agreed. 'But Bryant Lemuel is already a very rich man. Lafayette's in it for the money and the fame. Lemuel is after something else.'

We didn't have to wait long to find out what. He was on the TV news later that same day. It was just *Reporting Scotland*, so it wasn't UK-wide – not yet – but it was the second story, a fire at a chemical plant coming first.

'The millionaire Bryant Lemuel is calling for Holyrood education chiefs to rethink how science is taught in Scottish schools,' the anchorwoman said. 'The controversial businessman was speaking at a press conference to officially launch Kelvin University's Spiritual Science Chair in the wake of the news that recent scientific experiments conducted at the Glasgow campus have recorded genuine psychic phenomena. Brian Deacon has this report.'

'Furniture magnate Bryant Lemuel is no stranger to locking horns with Holyrood,' the correspondent began, over footage of Lemuel addressing the aforementioned press conference. It was a close-up shot of him seated at a table in front of a cluster of microphones, the bottom of the Spiritual Science Chair's jazzy new logo printed on a screen behind him. There was a white-sleeved arm visible to Lemuel's left before Lafayette came briefly into shot as its owner. Deacon concisely rehearsed Lemuel's noisy but ultimately unsuccessful duel with the Executive over sex education, before moving on to his new crusade.

'Lemuel is calling for a meeting with education minister Dominic Reilly, at which the Spiritual Science Chair would make its case for what he called "open-minded new thinking" about what is taught under the science curriculum in Scottish primary and secondary classrooms.'

The report then faded up Lemuel reading his prepared statement at the press conference.

'Science is fluid, constantly evolving, not set in stone,' he said. I noticed he was softening the salt-of-the-earth accent, laying off the flat-cap-and-whippet act now that he was on the turf of the intellectuals. 'It is a never-ending journey, yet our children are often given the impression we are already at our final destination and there's nowhere left to go. Last week, if our children had asked, they would have been taught that telepathic transmission of images was impossible. What will we be teaching them next week?'

Deacon's voice resumed over archive footage of Lafayette addressing a meeting of students. 'Lemuel was referring to the Spiritual Science Chair's recent experiments, in which it is claimed that paranormal expert Gabriel Lafayette performed telepathic feats under strictly controlled laboratory conditions. Lemuel was joined on the platform by the flamboyant American, who was last year controversially elected rector of the university.'

The voiceover broke as the archive soundtrack was briefly faded up, allowing a few words of Lafayette's speech for context. It wasn't clear whether it was a hustings meeting or a post-election address. I caught a few words about 'this seat of learning that has stood here on the "bonnie banks" of the River Kelvin for centuries'. Something about it jarred, not just his naff wee Brigadoonism, but I had no time to consider what before the report cut back to Lemuel at the press conference.

'We should not be teaching a narrow version of science, having decided we have all the answers. We must not close our children's minds. Other possibilities must be considered. And if there are contending, rival possibilities, then our children should know about *all* of them, not just the ones we *currently* believe are correct.'

'Oh Christ,' Sarah said, dismayed. 'Teach the controversy.'

'ID,' I confirmed.

Intelligent Design: Creationism dressed up in scientific-sounding jargon in an attempt to get it out of Sunday school and into Monday-through-Friday science classrooms. Its proponents were trying to depict it not as a religious belief but a genuine scientific theory in opposition to evolution. Hence, 'teach the controversy'. This was their ostensibly reasonable-sounding strategy: to say that if there were two competing scientific explanations, children should learn about both. However, there were not two competing scientific explanations: there was one scientific explanation and one non-disprovable mythology with absolutely no science behind it whatsoever. Thus even to 'teach the controversy' would be damagingly misleading, as it would give children the impression there was some kind of comparable validity to ID merely because it had been placed in opposition to the true science of evolution. But the nutters didn't just want to teach the controversy, or equal science-class time for both 'theories', as they had been seeking in the US: ultimately, they wanted evolution off the curriculum.

We had all smugly sniggered as we read those news stories, hadn't we, laughing at the absurdity of those crazy Yanks. However, in the back of my mind was always the nagging awareness that whatever insanity went on in the US would soon enough attempt to gain a foothold over here. In the north of England, a number of independent faith schools funded by the used-car tycoon Reg Vardy were already teaching Creationism. In mainstream schools south of the border, the new GCSE Biology syllabus now included discussion of ID, and Sarah's journals were reporting that medical students were demanding parts of the Bible and the Koran be acknowledged as scientific texts.

But it was all just harmless fun.

Sarah remained intent on the screen, where we were back to Brian Deacon's voiceover.

'A spokesperson for the education minister said they had no plans for such a meeting at this stage, but would not rule it out in the future if they considered it appropriate.'

'The education minister's married to Jillian Noble, for God's sake,' Sarah said. 'They'll get their meeting. And if not now, then soon enough. This is what Lemuel's really about, the thing they've been looking for a way of wedging in for years.'

The camera pulled back to a wider shot of the platform as the voiceover concluded the report: 'This is Brian Deacon for *Reporting Scotland*, Glasgow.' It showed Lemuel flanked by Lafayette on his left and, to his right, Jonathan Galt.

Sarah froze.

'That . . . man,' she rumbled, like no swear-word could possibly do justice to her hatred. 'He's part of this.'

'Yeah, he's Lemuel's lawyer,' I admitted. 'He helped set up that multi-faith coalition bollocks over the Developing Sexual Health bill.'

'This is just the beginning.' Sarah's voice trembled a little as she tried to restrain her anger. Merely the mention of Galt's name was enough to ruin her mood on a good day. Seeing that he was involved in this squalid little scheme would have her close to homicidal. 'They'll be in this for the long haul, and that gold mine we were talking about will provide their war chest. That bastard Galt always thinks ahead. They'll fund pressure groups, nobble school boards. They'll commission polls. They'll mobilise religious opinion and manufacture a groundswell. And instead of fringe nutters, they'll be able to say their position is supported by a *bona fide* scientific body.'

She switched off the TV and turned to face me.

'You have to put a spoke in this, Jack, I mean it. You do whatever you have to. And in that I include all those things I made you promise never to do again.'

# The most important things in the universe

I was lying in bed with Laura. Afterwards.

Yeah.

It was Sunday morning, as in, two o'clock in the afternoon Sunday morning, and I was talking about the Copernican Principle. Silver-tongued devil, huh? You'd be surprised. For a while I was censoring myself when I was with her, putting the brakes on my train of thought before I started fully geeking out. That was before Laura convinced me that, well, she quite *liked* me geeking out. And on this occasion, to be fair, I was geeking out in a romantic kind of way.

We'd had sex for the first time just over a week ago, the night I had taken part in the Project Lamda experiment. We'd been taking things delicately and slowly. I was determined not to blow this, and was incredulously pleased to find that Laura felt the same way. (I was trying to rein in the incredulity, urging myself to grow up. If I kept telling myself that it didn't seem real, there was every chance that soon enough it *wouldn't* be any longer.) I wasn't a virgin – there was an unedifying drunken tryst at a party with a medical student who made it very clear she didn't want to hear from me again – but was a little intimidated by my comparative lack of experience, so despite my physical desires, I wasn't pressing that side of our relationship.

I think we both knew we were each holding back in our own little ways. We both deeply wanted to trust each other, but perhaps weren't quite ready to do so. Laura had opened up about her mum, had poured out so much about herself when we first met, and I think after that she feared she had gone too far, that I somehow thought less of her for it. My own failure to fully reciprocate was therefore hardly a balm, but I think that troubled her less than her ongoing suspicion that I thought she was damaged goods. We had joked about it that first night, how over-intense it had all been, but deep down she was scared she had opened up too far to someone who might not turn out to be everything she hoped.

But then I went along to help Parlabane and came home about as emotionally mangled as I've been in my adult life. Part of me didn't want anyone to see me like that, but a stronger part of me needed Laura. I got the taxi to take me to her place. Her flatmate was home, but at that point I didn't care about who else saw me looking spooked and tearful; I needed to be with her like I hadn't needed anybody since . . . yeah, okay, my mum after Dad died.

Lafayette had done horrible things to me in that meeting room, things that Laura alone could understand, and in telling her, she knew I truly understood what she'd been through too. I'd felt the love and loss of my dad like he was feet away, felt assaulted by all the churned-up, confused emotions I had about Keith and Grant, and while I was buffeted by all of that, I even found myself – briefly, but it happened – asking whether everything I'd come to believe was wrong, whether Lafayette really was in touch with the dead.

I cried, babbled incontinently about my dad, my mum, everything. Laura let me cry, let me talk, and when I had finally run dry, instead of saying anything herself, she took me to her bedroom.

We talked a lot afterwards. We always talked a lot afterwards. That was when I told her about my mum, what the big schism was all about. I was afraid she'd say I was being daft; that, in itself, was the problem: my mum always said I was being daft. Instead, Laura said she understood why I felt the way I did, and why it was important to me. However, what she *didn't* say had clear implications. I got the feeling I was on a clock.

Laura had always talked very matter-of-factly about meeting my mum, as though we already had a date for the trip and the train tickets booked. My own objection, while not ignored, was nonetheless not being regarded as a major obstacle in her mind. One of the things I was already learning about having a proper grown-up relationship with a woman was that there are battles you have already lost – you lost them ages ago, before you even geared up for conflict – so the sooner you realise and accept it, the better.

'The Copernican Principle says there's nothing special about our place in the universe,' I told her. 'Before Copernicus, people believed that the Earth was the centre of the universe, and we didn't have much grasp of what we meant by "the universe" anyway. We believed that the Sun, the planets and the stars revolved around us. Copernicus realised that all our astronomical observations made more sense if the Earth was just one of many planets in motion around the Sun. Nothing special. But then in the twentieth century, bigger telescopes allowed us to realise there was nothing special about our solar system, it being just one of millions in our galaxy, the Milky Way; and that there is nothing special about our galaxy, just one of millions in the constantly expanding universe.'

'That's dizzying,' she said. 'Doesn't it make you feel . . . insignificant?'

'It did when I first thought about it. But then I came to think of it meaning we were *massively* significant, because we're all that's here to notice. At least, all that's here across a head-meltingly large radius. Beyond that, who knows? But the point is, we're not the centre of anything. We're an accident, or arguably a statistical probability. Which makes it all the more imperative that we make the most of it. Me lying here with you right now is one of the most important events in the known universe.'

It wasn't exactly Byron, I know, but that's about as romantic as geeking out gets. It was a beautiful moment, one I cherished as it unfolded and knew I'd cherish for a very long time to come.

'So we've got a cosmic obligation to stay right here all day?' she suggested.

'Well, I've got an academic obligation to study at some point, but it's not urgent.'

'Good,' she said. She bent her left leg so that it lay across my thighs, and stretched a hand across my chest. I turned to kiss her, but she giggled as she continued to stretch over me and revealed herself to be in pursuit of the TV remote.

Which was when we saw the report about the Spiritual Science Chair seeking a meeting with the education minister.

Kind of ruined the mood.

We watched it in appalled silence, and when it was over,

Laura was staring fixedly at me with a look that I knew would brook no argument. The clock had just run out.

She didn't say there was now more at stake than my feelings. She didn't say that my pride was an indulgence I could no longer justify. She didn't say that the reasons I was angry with my mum were now the same reasons why I needed to get past this. She didn't have to. She just said: 'You know what you have to do.'

And I did.

# Dinner theatre

It is the mark of a genuinely loving and trusting relationship that you don't hold each other to any declarations, vows or bright ideas voiced after several drinks or prior to the imminent onset of orgasm. Thus I took Sarah's over-wrought condition into account and decided not to regard her impassioned plea as a green light for the kind of antics she had made me forswear in an even more impassioned plea that I avoid ending up in prison (again) or getting myself killed (no comment). Instead I filed it away as permission to break the glass in what would have to be a very major emergency.

For the moment I would stick with the most basic and dependable technique of my trade: talking to people.

A niggling thought had stuck in my head even amidst the *Sturm und Drang* of Sarah's ranting at the telly. It was the archive footage of Lafayette, smarming the students in front of a stand-up mike at a packed meeting. '. . . this seat of learning that has stood here on the "bonnie banks" of the River Kelvin for centuries,' he had said, and the words had jarred for reasons I couldn't place.

I pinged them around in my head for a while. It was annoying, tantalisingly close but just out of reach, like trying to remember a song from a snatch of lyrics in the days before Google. My trusted tactic back then was to think about something else as best I could for a few moments, then return to the puzzling phrase, trying to frame it in a random new context. It served me well now as then. I got it, suddenly hearing Lafayette speak corresponding words that did not, could not tally.

It had been at my big celebration dinner, in honour of the rectorship, while Lafayette was taking heavy bombardment from Niall Blake as the university chancellor, Sir William Kentigern, and the principal, Dr Judith Rowe, looked on with visible discomfort.

'I would remind you,' Lafayette had ventured, 'that the president of the Royal Society said, as recently as 1895, that "heavier-than-air flying machines are impossible". That president was Lord Kelvin, after whom this very university is named.'

I remembered Rowe wincing, the ensuing silence and the embarrassment around the table as she informed Lafayette that the university was in fact named after the river. I had felt for him in that moment; I was sure everyone but Blake had. Yet this earlier statement proved the fly bastard knew perfectly well where the university got its name.

He had taken a dive.

Lafayette was an expert at manipulating people's emotions. He had provoked Blake into slapping him around, making the dean look like a bully, then to really sell it, he'd humiliated himself with the Lord Kelvin remark so that Rowe and Kentigern would sympathise with him. It was only after his embarrassing 'mistake' that Rowe in particular started warning Blake off and taking Lafayette's side, putting the dean on the back foot so that he had to try to justify his objection to the chair rather than Lafayette make his case *for* it.

I recalled my musing from even before the arguments started: *whoever put the seating plan together must have been seriously taking the piss sticking Lafayette and Blake on the same table.* In truth, at the time I'd believed it more likely an oversight, an unthinking decision by someone who would have no idea they were bringing together a potentially combustible combination. Now I was no longer convinced it was happenstance.

I reached for my campus directory. The office I was looking for would normally be closed on a Sunday, but I was sure there was a formal reception scheduled that evening, so it was worth a try.

I was in luck. Once I'd remembered to introduce myself as the rector, I was put through to the man in charge of all such formal events in the university's Maxwell Hall: Gregory Elphinstone, the caped protocol crusader with a whiff of the nineteenth century about him. On the phone, he came across as considerably less starchy, though, once again, it probably helped if you were rector. I asked him who had drawn up the seating plan for the celebration dinner.

'That would be me,' he said, with a hint of laughter in his voice. I was missing the joke.

'It's just, I was wondering about how – and indeed whether – you consider issues of, shall we say, inter-personal delicacy when you're drawing up these affairs.'

'Oh, Mr Parlabane, I sometimes think a job at the UN would be a sinecure after some of the diplomatic intricacies I've had to negotiate. Though in the case of your evening at the start of term, my deliberations turned out to be moot.' Again the laughter. I guessed we were approaching the punchline.

'Moot?'

'Yes. I think I can own up to this now because it's all water under the bridge, but there was some inexplicable mix-up. I don't know what happened, but the seating plans posted for the girls to lay the tables and the guests to find their seats were completely different from the ones I drew up. By the time I actually noticed the discrepancies, it was too late to change. You were all due to take your places in a matter of minutes. So what does one do in these circumstances? You slap on a grin, pretend like nothing's wrong and hope for the best. Was there, em, a difficulty that evening?'

'Oh no,' I assured him. 'Everything went according to plan.'

According to Lafayette's plan. I remembered Mather's calm amid the sometimes acrid atmosphere at the table, like he was resigned to losing the debate, maybe resigned to working under the auspices of the Psychology department as had been offered. He didn't know Lafayette secretly had matters in hand. The only thing Lafayette hadn't scripted was that I would end up as part of the deal, but that had worked out pretty well for him too. He got himself a tame, high-profile sceptic, no more qualified to suss his methods than the three scientists he had run rings around. I was supposed to be an expert in the field of deception and sleekit behaviour, but I was putty in this guy's hands. Almost as if he could read my mind.

Ha fucking ha.

I felt a little helpless. I could dig some dirt on Lafayette and maybe expose some of the strings he'd pulled, but none of it was going to make much of an impact unless I could revoke his supernatural credentials before they were academically ratified.

I was left asking myself one key question: what *does* it take to catch a psychic?

# IV

Let a handful of sages, who know the truth and can live with it, keep it among themselves. Men are then divided into the wise and the foolish, the philosophers and the common men, and atheism becomes a guarded esoteric doctrine – for if the illusion of religion were discredited, there is no telling with what madness men would be seized.

Irving Kristol

# Grabbing the cheesecloth

'Empty your mind, Mr Parlabane, and concentrate on the cards,' she said softly.

The room was dim, a blind drawn down over its single small window. The blind was made of a heavy, dark fabric, a circle of astrological symbols woven into it in fine golden thread. The circle also appeared on a large chart on one of the walls, surrounded by more detailed depictions of the constellations and diagrams rendering the positions of the planets for each month in the calendar. Three of the walls were covered in a rich woven material, a luxuriant, almost decadent purple that seemed to swallow what little light there was like a sponge. The chart dominated one of these, the other two bearing several ornate and intricate gold-painted frames within which were inscriptions written in runes and thus indecipherable. A fourth wall was matt black, paint on plaster, but for a pentagram etched in blood red, further occult symbols and runic scrawlings at each of its points.

The sole source of light was a single low-wattage bulb housed in a velvet uplighter which hung a few feet above the room's focal item of furniture, a table draped to the floor on all sides with black cloth so that none of its legs were visible.

She sat behind it, directly across from me, her hands deftly fanning a Tarot deck around the cloth and then regathering it, before spreading it gracefully in a circle before me. She wore a simple black dress, tight but concealing, a jewelled choker around her neck. I don't know what I'd been expecting: a headscarf, hooped earrings, a shawl and two dozen bangles, perhaps. Instead there was a strange kind of formality about her appearance, something maybe just the austere side of decorous.

'Turn over the card nearest to you,' she instructed.

I looked at the table a moment, satisfied myself that she meant the card at six o'clock in the circle. I thought about picking one just to either side of it but decided this would be somehow impolite. I was here seeking her help, I reminded myself.

I turned over the card. The image was of a man in gaudily bright garb, carrying a stick over his shoulder from which was suspended a cloth bearing his belongings. He stood next to a precipice, a small dog at his heel. It looked like a potentially suicidal Dick Whittington.

'The Fool,' she said.

'Not the ideal start for a sceptic,' I remarked.

'Quite the contrary. It's the ideal card for someone beginning a new journey into unknown territory. The Fool is where knowledge begins. He's about to take a step over the precipice.'

'A leap of faith?'

'Knowledge always lies in the places we have not yet explored,' she said. 'Now, go to the card furthest from you.'

I turned that over too. It showed a man hanging from a tree by one foot, his other tucked behind him. For all his discomfiture, he looked fairly sanguine about it.

'The Hanged Man. The Hanged Man is an initiate, like you just now. He's maybe feeling a bit silly, a little undignified, but he's tolerating it because he thinks he'll get something worthwhile from it in the end. That's why he's smiling. Two very significant choices, I must say.'

'I didn't choose them,' I felt I had to point out.

'You may say that, but haven't they shown you a truth? Perhaps *they* chose *you*.'

'Mum, knock it off,' interjected Michael, who was sitting just behind me with his girlfriend, Laura. 'What are you playing at?'

Moira Loftus glanced briefly at me by subtle way of apologising for the interruption, before going on to answer. She was looking at Michael as she spoke but her words were, for that, all the more clearly intended for me.

'I merely wish to convey to Mr Parlabane that there is some value in myth and symbolism; that they tell us very important things about ourselves, truths that we would be foolish to overlook or to forget. A warning not to throw the baby out with the bathwater, by way of preface to whatever else I end up telling him.'

She looked back at me, but this time her message was aimed

at her son. 'Michael has something of a year-zero attitude to all matters of the occult,' she said. 'He's inclined to go smashing statues because he despairs that people will end up worshipping them again. I'm more of the philosophy that you need to educate people about the statue's *true* worth. You don't need to worship it to value it.'

'All of which would sound a lot more noble if you weren't actually encouraging this metaphorical statue-worship so that you can fleece the devout for every penny.'

'Michael, old ground,' Laura warned him.

Moira Loftus flashed me quite the least contrite naughty-little-girl expression, one unique to parents being told off by their children.

I'd heard all about it on the train to Inverness; or at least Michael's side of it, moderated slightly by Laura as advocate for a woman she'd never met but had clearly nonetheless already warmed to. Mrs Loftus was an expert on the methods of psychics and mediums, being published on the subject both academically and in the mainstream press. She was also fascinated by the occult and mythology, and had studied the evolution of superstitious beliefs as a parallel aspect of her explorations of the psychology of deception. She was the person I had really needed with me on Project Lamda, and the person, I now understood, whom Laura had thought Michael was going to propose that night I met them in the pub. Laura had worn a look of expectation followed by a disappointment I couldn't fathom at the time, but which was vividly apparent in retrospect.

The reason I was only belatedly meeting Moira now was that Michael had been in a prolonged cream puff with her. I ought to hesitate in using the past tense there, as at this point he was still fairly prickly over the subject, and had repeatedly made it clear that this concession to the greater good did not constitute his condoning of blah blah blah.

Christ, students were just in a whole different class when it came to self-righteousness, weren't they?

To be fair, Moira's crime was one I'd be hard pushed to defend under the circumstances. Nonetheless, I'd have to concede it was eminently understandable too, if that contradiction doesn't completely fry your logic circuits. Parent–kid stuff, I guess. Makes no sense from the outside. Makes precious little from within either; merely fails to make sense in comfortingly familiar ways. I don't know. I was just grateful I didn't have any of the little fuckers.

'Yeah, okay.' Michael backed down grumpily. 'But can you cut to the chase? You've looked at the stuff, tell us what you think.'

I had sent Moira all of the Project Lamda written materials by email, including scans of my photocopies of the test drawings, and uploaded some of the video files to a server, so she'd had a day to look them over. The remaining videos and the photocopies themselves we'd brought with us on the train.

'There is no cutting to the chase, Michael. That's why you haven't found any answers yet. Psychics, like all conjurors, work by subtly causing you to focus on the wrong thing while they get busy elsewhere. You need to see the whole picture, and Mr Parlabane here needs to hear the whole story.'

'I'm sitting comfortably,' I assured her.

'Then I'll begin,' she said, acknowledging my solicitation with the briefest smile and a twitch of her eyebrows.

'Once upon a time, there were two little girls who told a very big fib. Well, the fib started small, but very quickly grew bigger and bigger, until it was so big that it was out of their control. And now, more than a hundred and fifty years on, the fib is still growing, still being told.'

'By you, among others,' Michael muttered.

'Michael, darling, be a dear and bugger off to the kitchen. You've heard this story before, so if you're not going to sit nicely with the other children, you can make yourself useful and get some food together.'

Michael got up without hesitation. He looked to Laura. She glanced sheepishly towards her host, whom she didn't want to offend. Her host, however, knew her son pretty well.

'Told you this one himself, has he?'

Laura nodded.

'Off you pop, then,' she consented.

The pair of them exited, briefly flooding the room with light from the hall. I felt attracted to it, like a big moth. I wondered about asking if we could adjourn to another room, but I think

248

she wanted to do this here, perhaps to make me understand how it looked from the sitter's point of view.

'Now, where was I?' Moira asked, turning back to me. 'Ah yes. These two little girls were called Margaret and Kate, and they lived in a big wooden house in a place called Hydesville, in New York State. When they first told the fib, Margaret was twelve years old and Kate a mere ten.

'Their mummy and daddy were a Mr and Mrs Fox, and in 1848 their house began to witness strange, inexplicable rapping sounds. Perplexed but perhaps just a little excited, Mrs Fox even got the neighbours round for a listen of an evening. The sounds only happened when Margaret and Kate were present, which ought, you would think, to have led to some deductive reasoning about the source. However, these two little girls told their little fib and said that it wasn't them: it was a spiritual presence which they called "Mr Splitfoot". Give them their due, there was a big clue in the name. I like to think they were waiting to be caught out, maybe delighting themselves in a little-girl way that they could throw the answer down in front of all these adults and none of them pick it up. However, the sad truth is, nobody picked up on it because nobody was looking. These two innocent little girls couldn't possibly be up to mischief, could they? So they kept up the fib, perhaps with all the more reason, because suddenly these two ordinary little girls were the centre of so much attention.

'The raps would have been a nine-day wonder but that somebody suggested they might be able to form a code, by which this Mr Splitfoot could communicate. Thus was born "one rap for yes, two raps for no". When this system was publicly demonstrated, one of the visitors asked, rather dramatically, whether a murder had been committed in the house. There came, in response, a solitary rap. You can imagine the atmosphere at that point.'

'Vividly.'

'And thus the fib got that bit bigger. Now, Margaret and Kate had a much older sister, Leah, who recognised that more than just the neighbours would be interested in the possibility of communication with what lay beyond the grave. More importantly, she recognised that they'd be prepared to pay handsomely for it. Soon she had her younger sisters on stage in public halls, where audiences could ask their own questions of the spirits, as long as they were prepared to shell out further for the privilege. The fib got bigger again, sometimes by several hundred dollars a night, and soon it even had a name: Spiritualism. Its adherents – which were fast proliferating – called it a movement, but there is a more apposite term.'

She looked at me, inviting a response.

'Cult?' I suggested.

'True enough, but the word you're really looking for is "franchise". Remember this, Mr Parlabane: in the world of mediums and psychics, it's *always* about the money. So, very quickly, the fib spread as other fibbers decided to get in on the act. After all, it wasn't difficult to imitate these raps, and more accomplished fibbers were able to add their own, more dramatic special effects: tables that tipped or even levitated, slates upon which messages simply materialised. They took it out of the halls and into their houses, where private sittings could command bigger fees. These sittings, in darkened rooms just like this one, began to be referred to by their French name: *séances*.

'Better able to control the environment for these seances, the fibbers got more sophisticated, causing musical instruments to play by themselves, calling up voices and even apparitions. The sitters were required to always hold hands in a circle, usually with their eyes closed, ostensibly so that they could concentrate on calling the spirits, but really so that they didn't reach a hand out in the darkness and accidentally touch the fibber or an accomplice while they rendered their amazing materialisations. Cheesecloth daubed with luminous paint was used to create amorphous visual manifestations. They called it ectoplasm. The sitters were expressly forbidden to touch this ectoplasm, in case they or the spirit were harmed.'

'Not to mention the medium's credibility.'

'Quite. To this day, the practice of catching mediums in the act is known as "grabbing the cheesecloth". Unfortunately, in those days, not a lot of cheesecloth got grabbed, and it wasn't long before the fib franchise had gone global. The Catholic church was even worried enough to threaten its flock with excommunication if they dabbled.'

'Why?' I wondered. 'I'd have thought anything that strengthened people's belief in the afterlife would have been tacitly welcomed.'

'If you're McDonald's, you don't want another burger franchise opening up across the street, do you?'

'Good point.'

Moira continued.

'The fib became so big that there were an estimated eight million Spiritualists in the US alone by the twenty-first of October 1888. That was the night Margaret Fox was giving a lecture at the Academy of Music in New York. Earlier that day, she had published a magazine article in which she confessed the fib. It had started as a prank to scare their mother, who was very superstitious. They found that they could cause their toe-joints to crack against the floor, or sometimes the wall, resulting in the effect that made them the world's first rap stars.'

'Mr Splitfoot.'

'See? Laughable, wasn't it? So obvious, they must have been astonished that nobody saw through it. But they reckoned without the need to believe, as evidenced by what happened at the Academy of Music. That night, in front of two thousand Spiritualists – many of them jeering her, not for having deceived them, but for her "lies" in the magazine – Margaret demonstrated how the sounds were really made. It should be noted that physicians from the University of Buffalo had examined the girls back when they were children, and suggested that the noises were made by them cracking bones in their knees. However, nobody gave this "hard physical evidence" nonsense any heed, a tendency that persists to preserve the fib even to this day.

'In light of Margaret's confession, the Spiritualist movement adopted the line that she had been somehow forced into making up these lies about cracking her toes, a stance reinforced by her subsequently recanting her testimony.'

'I take it she found that nobody was prepared to pay much money for a private demonstration of mere bone-cracking.'

'It's always about the money,' Moira reiterated. 'And thus the fib went on and on, leaving the Fox sisters far behind, finding more and more practitioners, founding more and more fib franchises. One of the biggest was Madame Blavatsky, who called her version of the fib Theosophy. Despite having her cheese-cloth grabbed on numerous occasions, she attracted devout followers all over the world, notably a chap by the name of Heinrich Himmler. He was particularly taken by the racial theories of Theosophy, which taught that a race called the Aryans were humanity's masters. He told a few of his friends about it. They agreed.'

'All harmless fun,' I remarked.

'Yes. Genocidal racial superiority, and now Creationism. The fib is nothing if not versatile in feeding and supporting other insanities. And all because of two little girls.'

I sat in silence a moment, reeling as I took it all in. From tiny acorns, and just as tiny lies . . .

'I'm sure you can understand why Michael is so much on his high horse,' Moira added, rather apologetically. 'As you can imagine, I put a lot of effort into saddling him up.'

'I'd find it hard to defend you against the charge of playing your own part in perpetuating the fib,' I admitted, putting it as delicately as I could.

'I wouldn't be pleading Not Guilty,' she replied. 'But there's mitigation I'd like the court to consider.'

'I'm not the one who's judging, but feel free to take the stand.'

'I've been working to debunk and demystify the big fib for decades, only to find that no matter how much evidence I present that it's a fraud, people go ahead and believe in it regardless. The psychology of willing self-deception fascinates me, but the detachment of the academic perspective can only hold off the implications for so long. Eventually, what was fascinating becomes depressing. This desire to believe in things for which there is no evidence, or for which there is only evidence to the contrary, is nothing more than an act of intellectual self-indulgence.'

'I'm more inclined to call it self-destructive,' I told her, 'but any time I suggest that in print, I get inundated with letters from Christians telling me how Stalin was an atheist and informing me of the value of faith.'

'I tend to get *very* angry about this reverence for faith,' Moira replied darkly. 'I consider it insulting to be told that faith is of itself a virtue. The act of believing in things for no good reason is something we need to stop revering and start ridiculing. Kids believe daft stuff that makes the world seem simpler and more benign, but there comes a time, to quote the Bible, to put away childish things, because it holds back the child's development and true understanding. Why, if this is true of an individual child, is the same not accepted about humans as a species?'

She laughed sadly to herself at her growing indignation. 'Sorry. I've always been able to work myself up into a fair old rant on this particular hobby horse, but Donald – that was Michael's father – was good at talking me down.'

She smiled at the memory but I watched her swallow. Still very raw.

'I miss him terribly. We both do. And after he died, I had nobody to talk me down. Plus I was lonely. Maybe that's as much a reason as any for what I've got up to.'

'When did you first begin?' I asked. 'I mean, was it a conscious decision, or something that came about and you just acted on the spur . . . ?'

'No, it was very much a conscious decision. I guess it was building up, and the kernel of the idea must have long been in my head, but there was one morning . . .'

She laughed out loud and bent over, her hair draping down to conceal her face. Sarah had a habit of doing that too when something really tickled her. Drove me crazy, in the best possible way.

'I was listening to the radio, Radio Scotland, and there was a priest or minister on, talking about the importance of faith. He said that "belief in spite of cold rationality is a form of strength, and is itself a proof of God because it shows the power He exerts that He can make us believe in Him in the face of all contrary evidence". I felt the sane among us were fighting a losing battle if that was being broadcast by the BBC. Then, the next programme – purely coincidentally – was a phone-in discussion of "modern-day mysteries". They did Roswell, the Loch Ness Monster, the Bermuda Triangle. I remember thinking: I'm a mug trying to be a sheepdog when I could have far more fun being a wolf.'

'And make far more money,' I suggested.

253

She shot me a sharp look that made me fear I had just irreparably knackered the occasion's cordiality.

'That's a shocking notion,' she said. 'Psychics *never* seek payment. Though sometimes people feel they ought to show their gratitude with a donation.'

We both laughed, myself largely with relief. She'd got me. It's *always* about the money.

'It's a rush too, I have to admit. Doing my gypsy act and watching people's amazement as I tell them things—'

'Things there's *no way* you could know,' I contributed.

'Aye. There's an undeniable gratification about successfully deceiving somebody. Guys like Lafayette are addicted to that almost as much as they're chasing the bucks. That said, at the level I'm operating, it doesn't take much sophistication. Shooting fish in a barrel, mostly.'

'Would you say you're contemptuous, then; I mean, do you feel guilty taking their money?'

'I'm not targeting poor old ladies and consigning them to a cat-food diet. Though I do relieve quite a few *comfortable* old ladies of a few bob. But as they say, a fool and his money are soon parted. I like to think of it as a Credulity Tax. So, yes, I am contemptuous, but no, I don't feel guilty. Besides, I've got Jiminy Cricket through there being my conscience for me.'

'Did you anticipate that Michael would disapprove?'

'No,' she said, echoing a genuine surprise. 'I thought he'd see the funny side, see it as my despairing revenge on the disciples of woo. But there were all kinds of misfiring emotions complicating the picture. With his dad gone, Michael had to find ways he could still love him. One such was adopting the role of keeper of the flame, which provoked disproportionately outraged responses to any perceived slight on Donald's name or lapse in reverence for his memory. I think he sometimes forgets I married the guy.'

'He says you think he's being daft. But that sounds to me like another way of saying he doesn't think you care about how he feels.'

'Yeah, I know,' she sighed. 'That's how it always is with Michael, probably the same with all kids. Starts off you think he's being daft about something and you laugh it off, wait for him to come around. Then he realises you're waiting for him to come to you, so he digs his heels in, and from then on it's no longer about the thing that started it. And because you know it's not about that any more, you think he's being even more daft and you become even less prepared to concede and stop doing it.'

'Mexican stand-off in progress, then?'

'Not for much longer. When I thought I'd lost him . . .' She took a moment, looked suddenly off balance at the mere thought of it. 'Did he tell you I was already on a train down to Glasgow to identify his body?'

I nodded solemnly.

'Then the relief, Christ, when he phoned. I can still feel it. At a time like that, however, there's a parental discipline, a restraint you need to engage to stop you smothering them with your feelings and promising them the Earth. So I didn't come over all contrite about my little habit. It didn't even seem an issue right then. But it probably wouldn't surprise you to learn I had already told myself I'd stop if it would make him happy. I'm just not convinced it *will* make him happy.'

'Laura Bailey's probably doing as good a job as anyone on that score.'

Moira smiled and nodded in agreement. 'She seems a great girl, but *Michael* has to make Michael happy, otherwise neither of them will be. This is not about Michael and *me*. This is about Michael and his dad. My fear is that if I give this up for him, he'll find some other way of tormenting himself. He feels he needs to *do* something for his dad, strike some blow in Donald's name, and I don't think merely curbing my behaviour will cut it.'

'How about bringing down the Spiritual Science Chair?'

Moira grinned. 'Oh, I think that would probably help, yes. But it's rather a tall order.'

I felt a now depressingly familiar sense of deflation, much as I had done watching Michael drive away in that taxi.

'You're saying you're not sure you can tell us how Project Lamda was done?'

'Not at all. Of course I can tell you how it was done; I worked that out in a twinkling. But what I've been trying to make you understand is that knowing how it's done is not even half the battle. You're up against the unsinkable rubber ducks here, the people who simply *want* to believe. Bringing down the Spiritual Science Chair will take more than exposing Project Lamda as a fraud.'

'With respect,' I felt compelled to state, 'knowing how it was done would sure help.'

'Of course, of course,' she agreed. 'So let's adjourn to the kitchen and I'll tell you over whatever love's young dream have rustled up for us to eat.'

Moira held open the door and ushered me into the hall, lifting the lever-arch file containing the Project Lamda materials from a sideboard as we passed.

She stopped just outside the kitchen door.

'A word of warning before we do this,' she said, placing a hand lightly on my chest in a gesture of restraint. 'Are you married?'

'Yes.'

'Hmm. I just hope your wife's not the jealous sort.'

'Why?' I asked, wondering where this could possibly be leading.

'Because you're about to feel a bigger tit than you ever have in your life.'

Moira's was an expansively long open-plan kitchen with a dining area in front of two patio doors giving on to a view of the Moray Firth. A laptop sat upon a marble work surface, incongruous next to a microwave and an old-school Kenwood mixer. It was late afternoon, the light beginning to fade on a crisply cold December day. Michael and Laura had laid out a spread of antipasti and cold meats, alongside baguettes warm from the oven. Unfortunately, my appetite had been suddenly curbed by the anticipation of impending humiliation.

I took a seat with what must have seemed undue trepidation, while Michael was already impatiently tearing into some bread and Laura helped herself to cheese.

'Don't look so worried, Mr Parlabane,' Moira assured me. 'You already knew you'd been had. This is not your field, and you can console yourself with the knowledge that you were up against a skilled practitioner of deception delivering an extremely accomplished performance. Give him his due, he's very good at what he does.'

'I guess that's why he's the most famous charlatan in the country just now,' I conceded.

'I'm not talking about Lafayette,' Moira said.

Michael seemed to stop mid-chomp through his mouthful of baguette. Laura swallowed the water in her mouth and stared expectantly at Moira, who was happy as any showman to let the silence grow.

'Remember Mr Splitfoot?' she went on, a twinkle in her eyes betraying amusement concealed behind an otherwise neutral expression. 'Just like the Fox sisters did by using that name, the clue was laid down in front of you right at the start; a bit of a risk, but one it must have been considered worth taking for the pay-off.'

'Who, then?' I asked, though I suspected she wasn't going to simply tell me; nor that it was what she felt I most needed to know. This was science, after all: the answer itself is less important than understanding the process by which you arrive at it.

'All in good time,' she said, confirming as much. I saw Michael roll his eyes and resume loading his plate. Best dig in, he was thinking: we're here for the big picture. 'Let's see if you can work it out now you're far enough distant to see the wood for the trees. During the preliminary tests, you encountered a Mr Colin Playfair and his disapproving daughter, Gina. Mr Playfair was your Mr Splitfoot. He was brought in to endorse the credentials of the protocol. That was the pay-off.'

'He wasn't brought in,' I corrected. 'His real name was Len Philpott. He volunteered because he wanted a first-hand look at our protocol in case . . .'

As I spoke, I could see that same amused twinkle in Moira's eye, like she was trying politely not to laugh. I let the sentence hang unfinished, bidding her to fill the void.

'He *was* brought in, Mr Parlabane. And he suckered you with a classic double-bluff. Having been caught out – as he was always supposed to be – he put his hands up and confessed to who he really was and his true motives for being there. He told you he was a physics lecturer and amateur conjuror with a keen interest in psychic fraud, and his failure to beat your system was thus a reassuring endorsement to yourself and your colleagues that the protocol was solid. But in fact, it was *this* that was the real lie, and I'm afraid you bought it. I had a look at the footage and recognised him right away. The UK woo network is a small world. His real name isn't Len Philpott any more than it's Colin Playfair. His name is Ken Rylance, and the only thing he told you that was true was that the girl *is* his daughter, though her name is Charlotte. Sloppy journalism, Mr Parlabane. Did you check out his physics-lecturer credentials? Or seek out those magazine articles he claimed to have written?'

I shook my head and bit joylessly into a baguette. It was more a thumb-sucking oral comfort reflex than any indication that my appetite was returning. I suspected this was just the beginning: I was only feeling a B-cup model at the moment.

'He's been in the racket for decades in one way or another: private sittings, stage mediumship. He and Charlotte were a hire: paid to show up, get caught and thus enhance everybody's confidence in the protocol. Like I said, that was the pay-off. The risk was that their MO would give the whole game away, though maybe that was a double-bluff too: if you had successfully clocked this scam, you wouldn't suspect that the same trick was actually being pulled again right in front of you, on a far more audacious scale.'

'What trick?' asked Michael, who evidently hadn't given the preliminary tests much, if any attention. Instead he had been concentrating solely on Lafayette and failing, like me, to look at the whole picture. So even someone weaned on this mischief could be misdirected.

'Mr Parlabane,' Moira prompted. 'The Playfair MO please, in a nutshell.'

'The daughter was his secret accomplice,' I stated, wondering if I was stumbling into useful-idiot mode again, about to have another assumption debunked. 'We didn't suspect her because her disapproval was her cover.'

'Mr Playfair was the subject,' Moira said, 'but Gina was the one who really practised the deception, most impressively in her performance as someone who wanted nothing to do with the whole thing, thereby placing herself outside your suspicion.

It was a perfect misdirection. The speed of light dictates that the hand is never quicker than the eye. The trick is in making the eye look the wrong way. Gina rendered herself all but invisible, hiding in plain sight.'

I thought back to the tests, listed all personnel involved, but still failed to see a parallel. There was no-one who had been reluctant or disapproving; in fact, from an outsider's perspective, the person most beyond suspicion, going by those criteria, would have been me. And arguably, the only other person who could be said to . . .

Oh . . .

No.

No.

No.

I was aware of my head sinking. Only the fact that I'd have been dive-bombing a plateful of couscous halted its descent and prevented me from slamming it repeatedly off the table.

'How big?' Moira asked, talking tits.

'Very, very, very big indeed.'

'Well, as I said before, you have to credit him with a superb performance.'

'Stanislavsky would have applauded,' I admitted. 'Method acting at its best. He was quite brilliant. And I'd like to show my appreciation now by presenting him with a bouquet. Do you know any florists who do deadly nightshade?'

'Who are we talking about?' demanded Michael.

I sighed, not yet able to even mouth the name. Moira laughed a little at my deflation and picked up a large olive.

'Work it out for yourself. It's easy,' she said, popping the olive into her mouth with a grin.

'Christ, just tell me, Mum. If it was easy, we wouldn't . . .'

I watched him get it, saw the briefest flicker of pleasure at solving the puzzle descend with ear-popping rapidity into feeling, well, a bigger tit than ever before in his life. 'Fuck,' he concluded.

Laura laughed quietly.

Easy Mather. The man who had professed himself to be on a scientific mission to discover whether there was hard physical evidence behind paranormal phenomena. The man who had devised the strictest possible protocol for his experiment, telling me to assume cheating, firing an assistant merely for fear that her *potential* laxity could compromise the security of the tests. The man whose great fear, whose deepest insecurity, was that he was being fooled by Lafayette.

I remembered the vastly uncomfortable tension, their relationship under apparent strain as Mather held firm over the strip-search; recalled my own fears that he would buckle over that and other parts of the protocol. I remembered the blame in Lafayette's eyes as he looked at Mather during his unsuccessful dry run, the poisonous atmosphere as Mather insisted he persist with the tests, including the Zener cards, even though Lafayette was 'receiving nothing' and declaring the whole thing pointless. But most of all I remembered thinking how fucking cute I'd been, playing him on my line, sussing his weak spot, biding my time and choosing my moment in order to get him to confide. All that time, he'd been the one reeling *me* in.

'. . . it literally wakes me up in the middle of the night, and I lie there and ask myself, what if it's all cheating? What if he is tricking me and, despite my vigilance, what if I'm actually the biggest patsy in the world?'

He could sleep well tonight. That particular distinction was now firmly in my grasp.

'Give it to me straight,' I said to Moira. 'How early did you clock this?'

'It wouldn't be fair to say,' she replied, which I interpreted as 'about two seconds, tops'. 'It's easy to spot the twist when you've heard several variations of the story before. It goes back more than a hundred years, to when the Fox fib and Vaudeville were competing for the same audiences: the blurring of the mysterious, the scientific and good old showbiz. The magicians used to claim they had travelled to exotic foreign lands, such as India or Egypt, and learned of ancient and secret arts. They'd dress themselves and their sets accordingly, and it helped the audiences suspend disbelief and buy into the fantasy that they really were performing magic.

'Next night in the same theatre, or sometimes on the same bill, there might be a psychic or medium. Then, as now, the endorsement of a scientist helped give the impression that this was the real deal, and not just a new twist on tricks that were already becoming overfamiliar to audiences on both sides of the Atlantic. Psychics were often introduced on stage by the eminent doctor or professor who had "discovered" them. He would rhyme off his own credentials and the amazing story of how he came to be convinced of the gifted one's amazing powers, but would neglect to mention that he was now not only managing the psychic, but assisting him or her in performing their money-spinning feats.'

I recalled Sarah's words when she'd sussed Playfair and Gina. 'They're a double-act,' I said.

'Your attention is always on Lafayette, but it's Mather who works much of the magic. Such as elevators that suddenly stop, lights that go out, mysterious power surges, spontaneously malfunctioning vending machines. Mather rigged them all. I couldn't give you the technical details, but that's all they would be: technical details.'

I thought back to each of those events, dwelling with a bitter new perspective on the lift stopping the night I tried to bail out of the place at speed. Lafayette had been able to catch up and further spook me with his apparent insight into my dark past. Mather had made sure I wouldn't get away while I was at my most susceptible to such hocus-pocus.

It hadn't occurred to me before that Mather was the only one who'd never suffered the stalled-lift phenomenon. If it had, I'd probably have explained it to myself as being due to the fact that Mather and Lafayette never arrived or departed together. Mather was always in the building before Lafayette arrived and still there after Lafayette had gone. Of course he fucking was: Mather was always first in, last out, and I had abjectly failed to consider the implications of him having regular, ample, unwitnessed freedom to do whatever he wanted in the labs.

Blake had bought it too, worrying about Mather's professional vulnerability, and expressing disdainful concern that it would be Lafayette, and not Mather, who was running the show. But Mather was running it all right. He had complete control of the test environment, while we were distracted by fussing over the security arrangements for Lafayette.

'It was all for show,' I said aloud. 'Every detail of the protocol. Lafayette not being allowed into certain areas, always being accompanied, the strip-search, the ban on him knowing the assistants' surnames. Christ, the surnames! We were determined not to give Lafayette any leads for researching their backgrounds, and all the while Mather was filling him in on every detail. That girl Catherine and her high-school tragedy.'

'Me and what happened to Keith and Grant,' added Michael.

'Essentially the same shtick as he pulled on me,' Laura said.

Moira nodded, the levity in her expression suspended for now.

'Lafayette acting depressed about the preliminaries and his own early failures was textbook too,' she told us. 'Making out he really feared he wouldn't be able to achieve anything, then suffering repeated failures in the dry-run stage: all part of the psychology. Hoffman employed it to great effect: he'd notch up a few failures, start to seem frustrated and depressed, and it made the observers feel almost embarrassed for him, made them want a success to happen in order to break the tension, dispel the awkwardness. Often the observers subconsciously relax their vigilance because they are hoping for a result. The psychic makes the observers *want* him to succeed.'

I thought of Heidi trying to console Lafayette, urging him to persist. Same trick he'd pulled on Kentigern and Rowe.

'But in this case, the protocols weren't relaxed,' I said. 'Lafayette's depression and his arguments with Mather were all part of the scam to make the protocol look airtight. As was firing the assistant, Melanie: it was to make Mather seem uncompromising in his integrity.'

'Essentially, what he was doing was saying: "Nothing up this sleeve",' Moira explained. 'Magicians always suggest to you the ways you *think* they might perform a feat, and then make a big show of closing those options. But that was never how they were intending to do it. You were all uptight in your deliberations over letting Lafayette have his contact time with the target subjects. It had you wondering if it would give him some kind of advantage, hence the documenting of everything that was said in case he was using some form of subconscious suggestion. He wasn't. It also gave credence to his suggestion that he

262

was able to guess the drawings due to some kind of contact from spirits close to the target subjects.'

'And hence the Faraday cage,' Michael suggested. 'With all that signal monitoring crap set up outside it.'

'Well, yes and no,' his mother said. 'Yes, the principle of excluding radio waves or electrical transmissions is, again, about apparently closing off one of the ways the observers might think the trick is done. But in this case, it's another double-bluff. The Faraday cage is a Trojan Horse. It was brought in, you were told, to make electrical transmissions to Lafayette impossible, but its true purpose was to facilitate them.'

'How?' I asked. 'Rudi Klein built the cage.'

'At Mather's request. And then what adjustment was Klein required to make before the tests began? The installation of a video camera, thus running a cable feed directly into this supposedly isolated environment. And if a cable is carrying information out of the cage, then it can also be carrying information in.'

I recalled our discussions over monitoring Lafayette while he was in the cage, the decision to install a camera rather than a window.

'But the camera was my suggestion,' I told her.

'It's another aspect of the deceiver's talent to make important parts of his plan seem like someone else's idea. In this case, he just had to keep his mouth shut and wait: someone would have suggested the camera, and in the unlikely event that they didn't, as a last resort he'd have suggested it himself.'

I thought of Mather's relief when Rudi said it could be done without compromising the cage; it hadn't struck me or Rudi that Mather, from his own professed scientific knowledge, ought to have known for himself that it wouldn't affect the integrity. So perhaps his relief was part of the bluff, but more likely it showed his genuine pleasure that I had been successfully manipulated and another piece of the plan had fallen into place. However, it still left the enduringly baffling question of how the fuck Lafayette knew what was on those drawings.

'There was no monitor in the cage,' I pointed out, 'just a camera, and we'd have noticed if he was staring at anything, surely.'

Moira reached into the lever-arch file and lifted two sheets of paper that she'd moved to the top. She placed them on the table, either side of a plate of artichokes. 'This was what told me how it was done,' she said. 'See if you can work it out now that you know the answer is right in front of you.'

On the left was one of my own drawings, my Bunteresque tubby schoolboy reaching for an ice-cream cone. On the right was Lafayette's reproduction, indubitably the same subject, but slightly different in its emphasis. While mine had shown the whole body, Lafayette's depicted a head and shoulders, allowing a more detailed face in profile. His Bunter's mouth was, like mine, greedily agape, but featured the slightly whimsical added detail of buck teeth, unsuccessfully restrained by a dental brace.

The three of us stood up, Michael and Laura coming around to flank me as we pored over the pictures.

It was Laura who got it.

'He could hear you,' she said, eliciting an approving nod from Moira.

'The pictures were described aloud as part of the protocol,' Moira reminded us. 'As demanded by Mather, to rule out ambiguity. But it was so that Lafayette could hear what he was supposed to draw.'

'I still don't get it,' I confessed.

Laura pointed at my own drawing, her finger indicating my tubby schoolboy's torso, his exaggerated girth stretching a pair of . . .

'Bollocks,' I said.

'No, braces,' corrected Laura.

'"A fat schoolboy with braces reaching greedily for an ice-cream cone",' Moira read from a photocopy. 'That's the precise description that was said aloud in the target room and heard in the Faraday cage.'

'Lafayette's American,' Laura reminded me. 'They call braces suspenders. He heard braces and a focus on eating, hence . . .'

'There's lots more, if you care to flick through them,' Moira said. 'Albeit finer details, but easy to spot once you know what you're looking for: tell-tale signs that someone is drawing from description rather than from sight.'

'So how did he hear it?' Michael asked, beating me to the punch.

Moira walked across to the laptop and hit the space bar, causing the machine to whir its way out of hibernation. She had a video player maximised to fill the screen, the paused image showing Lafayette in the receiving room next to Rudi, both of them approaching the Faraday cage.

'Watch this,' she said, and pressed Play. Rudi reached for the door to the cage, and as he did so, Lafayette ran a hand through his hair before venturing inside. She wound it back and played it again, then switched to a different file open in another window, showing the same approach on a separate occasion. As Rudi reached for the door, Lafayette's hand went to his hair; more specifically, to the left side of his head, perhaps even scratching his ear as it passed.

'I've not watched all the files, but in all the ones I *have* watched, he does this same movement at this same point, while Dr Kline is one pace ahead of him and reaching for the door. It's subtle, as any conjuror's actions are subtle, but he's putting something in his ear: some kind of receiver I'd guess, picking up a sound feed from the target room. My assumption is that Mather has doctored the video camera and there's a transmitter inside it, relaying the signal from the cable to the earpiece.'

'So much for the strip-search,' I muttered.

'Pure theatre,' Moira said. 'Though I've no doubt it was thoroughly conducted.'

'Lafayette made a crack about drawing the line at cavity searches. You're not saying . . . ?'

'No need. After Mr Playfair's shenanigans, it was stipulated that Lafayette be permitted a toilet trip before the tests commenced, so that he'd have no excuse to go wandering around unsupervised. Again, the security measure was actually built in to circumvent the protocol. Lafayette gets strip-searched, and having satisfied everybody that he's got "nothing up his sleeve", he goes off to the privacy of a toilet cubicle where he or Mather has stashed the earpiece. Then he sticks it in one of his conveniently baggy jacket's many pockets until showtime, at which point he palms it and sticks it in his lughole.'

So there you have it: the answer to how it was done, and with it, the answer to my wee teaser from before.

The words: 'Mr Watson, come here, I want you'; an image of a ventriloquist's dummy; a drawing of a castle. What do they have in common?

The answer is that all three were communications carried out using electrical devices. Told you it was a stinker.

I sat in a daze for a moment.

'Professor Niall Blake initially suggested a conjuror be brought in as an observer,' I reflected. 'Lafayette said this was an attempt to ridicule and hamstring the project before it had even begun, said they might as well carry out the research in a big top. But I guess we all know now why that was so unacceptable to him. I was the suggested compromise. Mather must have been kicking his height. I would hate to speculate just how little time it took you to see through this, Mrs Loftus.'

'It's another old story, I'm afraid,' she replied. 'Psychics object to conjurors being present, usually coming out with the "negative vibrations" malarkey. And scientists are too often unconsciously complicit, objecting to the idea of a conjuror for their own arrogant reasons: they think it sounds vulgar and unscientific; plus they never believe that someone who does mere tricks can possibly be smarter than them. It sounds like Professor Blake was an exception, but he ought not to have backed down.'

'He was somewhat out-flanked,' I told her. 'Long story. I feared I'd let him down, but I'm relieved I got there in the end.'

'You haven't got anywhere yet,' Moira stated bluntly. 'You have no proof of any of this, only speculation. Believe me, Mather will have removed the incriminating gadgets the second the tests were finished.'

'I've still got the right to submit my findings to the *Journal of Nature*. That should put a spoke in their wheels.'

'Not getting their paper published will be a minor setback. The press won't splash it like they splashed the Project Lamda story.'

'I can guarantee the paper I work for will go pretty big on it. This is about credibility.'

'No it's not,' she insisted. 'This is science versus woo. You need proof, and even then you'll be struggling. All you've got is a hypothesis. I would strongly warn you to keep your powder dry, Mr Parlabane, and choose very carefully when to play your hand. These people always plan several moves ahead; and this is their game you're playing, not yours. If you don't tread finely, you'll find your ingenious ploy is precisely what they were relying on, and just when you think you've got them in your crosshairs is the moment you feel the trapdoor open beneath you.'

## C:\Documents and Settings\Jillian\ My Documents\journal_dec_4-11.doc

There are two things of which it is said you ought never to see how they're made: laws and sausages. Having been behind the scenes at Holyrood a few times, I'm damn sure I won't be visiting a sausage factory any time soon.

I love Dominic and I'm immensely proud of what he's achieved, but there are times when I feel like the wife of a gangster or perhaps a boxer: I know he's very good at what he does, but I'm not comfortable with the attacks he's exposed to, and nor do I like to think about some of the things he must get up to in order to produce results.

This is not sour grapes; I can say that because ultimately I believe the Spiritual Science Chair will get what it is after and that Dominic will be instrumental in that, but it is one in the eye for anyone who thinks I've got undue influence over my husband, or those idiots who talk about 'womanly wiles'. Yes, we discuss politics, and I know where a few bodies are buried, but nobody could describe any conversation that goes on in our house as 'lobbying'.

I'm a journalist; I'm at my best when I'm on the outside looking in. I hate it when I come directly into Dominic's sphere, and this time was no exception.

Even the way the meeting was set up reeked of the politics game, leaving me feeling used and a little dirty. I was, perhaps understandably, the conduit, but the very fact that it was done through what is in politics termed 'back channels' was the first indicator that all was not going to run smoothly. Dominic – and perhaps more significantly, his bosses – knew that it was the Spiritual Science Chair as an entity that had requested a meeting, something they did not wish to be seen to accede to. Instead, it was proposed that Dominic would meet informally with Lemuel and his people, and that the meeting would be strictly off the record. If Lemuel announced that it was taking place, or made any public pronouncements about his Spiritual Science Chair being granted access to the education minister, then it wouldn't happen and the department would deny any such meeting had ever been planned.

Under such circumstances, it was difficult to believe Lemuel was about to be taken seriously when the meeting *did* take place.

'It's just spite that they're making us come in through the back door,' he told me. 'Still smarting from the bloody nose we gave them over that sex education bill. I don't blame your husband, you understand,' he assured me, 'but the people he works for never forget.'

Lemuel did insist that the meeting take place at Holyrood, and not some hotel or restaurant. This was agreed, with the proviso that there should be no hacks or photographers show up 'coincidentally' to report that he, Lafayette and Jonathan Galt were on their way into the Parliament building. An exception was made for me, it being (no doubt grudgingly) accepted by party bosses that I could be trusted not to stitch up my husband.

I met Lafayette and Mather off a train at Waverley Station and we grabbed a coffee before getting a cab together from there. I needed to talk to Lafayette about some ideas for the second book. He told me we were 'living the second book right now' and said the Spiritual Science Chair's work was the most exciting chapter in his life story by far. However, I was keen to explore some areas less widely discussed by the public, such as his work with the police. He had mentioned this in passing a few times, but was very hard to pin down on the subject. I thought this was because of confidentiality agreements that he was wary of breaching. It turned out I was on the right track, but the truth was something a lot more bitter.

'I'd love to be able to talk about it,' he said. 'I'd love to be able to set the record straight. But those sons-of-bitches are holding all the cards. If they come crawling, I don't know . . . I think if a kid was in danger, I'd have to do the right thing, but murder cases, after the fact, when you can't change anything, nah. It ain't worth it. They ask for your help, then they claim they never heard of you. It's because they don't want you getting the credit for doing their job. I could kind of understand it, if it was purely a matter of confidentiality, but they're pretty under-hand about it. There was this case in New Orleans, shit, same thing in Atlanta . . . No. You tell anybody you were involved and man, they don't mess around when it comes to laundering their own image. They'll set you up, make you out to be an attention-seeking freak, deny all knowledge they ever contacted you. But somewhere in their files, it's all down in black and white.'

So that looks on the surface like a dead end, though it might turn out to be the biggest story in the book. Typical Lafayette. Always hiding his light under a bushel. And people say he's a self-publicist. If they only knew the truth. Need to see if I can cultivate some friendly contacts Stateside. I'll look into it after Christmas, winter's probably a good time for a trip. Swap Scottish winter for Louisiana? Yes please. Must talk to the publishers. Meantime, I'm writing this little episode out in full, as it's bound to end up in book two or maybe another project. The area is really opening up.

Dominic normally comes down to the lobby to meet me when I visit Holyrood, but not this time. I think I'd have got more hospitality extended if I'd brought his in-laws. Lafayette, Mather and I were ushered upstairs by a plooky-faced gofer, and found Lemuel and Galt already in a meeting room. (Naturally, we weren't convening in Dominic's office.)

When Dominic arrived, he was in the company of his deputy minister, Brenda McGhee. I noted Lemuel and Galt trade a look of pleasant surprise that despite the other conditions, they were being given access to both of the department's senior-ranking officials. I was less encouraged, knowing the game: wheel out the big guns and Lemuel couldn't complain that he wasn't being taken seriously. Hear him out, nod sincerely, say very little, then send him away with a pat on the head and a late-dawning sensation that he's had his pockets picked.

That, however, was not quite how it panned out.

Lemuel began by inviting Mather to talk a little about the paper awaiting publication by *Journal of Nature*, in order to demonstrate how the Spiritual Science Chair was already being taken seriously by the wider scientific community. Lemuel then sketched out the broad-brush version of the Chair's position, which was that the school science curriculum should be amended to recognise the wider implications of this new field of study.

'We're only at the beginning of our explorations, I must stress,' he said. 'But what we think we're starting to see is hard evidence of things that schools currently teach are impossible or don't exist. This has huge ramifications for the veracity of the material being put before our children.'

'I would agree it is certainly very much a nascent area of science, Mr Lemuel,' Dominic said, which I knew was a preface to refusal. 'And with respect, it strikes me that you're getting very far ahead of yourself. I'm no scientist, so I don't know what Mr Mather's recent project does or doesn't prove, but I do know that your chair is barely up and running. Even granting that it has got off to a flying start, I would find it very hard to go to science educationalists and say that this is an area that merits inclusion in—'

'We're not talking about incorporating anything that's going to clog up the works,' Lemuel interrupted hastily. 'We've only just begun our journey, as we've already acknowledged.'

'Though I'd have to ask whether,' Galt added, 'after the discovery of X-rays or the invention of radio, anyone suggested we wait a few years before teaching our children about it.'

'I think we probably waited for some degree of scientific verification,' Dominic replied. 'And we perhaps reckoned we could hold off a fortnight, at least. This project is barely concluded and the ink isn't dry on your reports. What's your big hurry?'

'If our children are being taught something that's wrong, I don't think there's such a time as too soon to correct it,' Lemuel countered.

'And is there a specific scientific fact you believe our teachers are—'

'Mr Reilly, let's not be disingenuous,' Galt said, cutting Dominic off. 'We both know there's a major curriculum review under way, likely to be finalised in a matter of months, and that if we miss the boat, it could be years before there's the chance to change it again. In five years' time, the Spiritual Science Chair will be a thriving academic institution with some extremely exciting work to its credit, and I'd agree that *then* would be the time to propose specific areas of study for schools. But if those intervening years are spent keeping children's minds closed, then that would be a real waste. All we are asking in the mean time is that children are taught that there *are* these new areas of science, and that there *are* competing scientific theories explaining major aspects of the world, the universe around us.'

'Including Intelligent Design?' Dominic asked. 'Because I can guarantee this: if those words end up on any policy document, I'll have a queue of angry scientists from my door to the top of Salisbury Crag.'

'Oh, I've seen a few angry scientists myself in my time,' said Lafayette, chuckling. 'But I always have to ask myself: what are they so angry about? And if they're truly men of science, what are they so scared of? If there are two possible explanations, children deserve to know that, so that they can look into them both and make up their own minds. Isn't that the philosophy any education department would espouse?'

'Mr Lafayette, with respect, you're new to this country, so believe me when I say that we have enough trouble in Scotland over the issue of religion in schools without doing anything that would suggest we were bringing it into science classrooms.'

'But we would argue, Minister,' said Lemuel, 'that it's this very distinction, this mutually exclusive distinction between religion and science that in itself needs to be addressed. The reason scientists rightly recoil from the prospect of religion entering their turf is that they fear belief being substituted for evidence, but in fact we are interested only in getting children to look at the scientific evidence that lies *behind* beliefs.'

'They're already teaching about Intelligent Design in England,' Galt pointed out. 'A curriculum revision instigated by *your* party. We're finding cross-party consensus that children should be taught about it if there are competing scientific explanations for something. Meanwhile, polling we commissioned in Scotland shows a majority of voters to be of the opinion—'

'Oh dear God,' interrupted Dominic. 'Please don't tell me you're going to start calling for a referendum again.' He spoke with a smile, as though making light of past enmities, putting a civil face on a strong point: Lemuel had caused a lot of grief for this administration, and in particular Dominic's predecessor. It was Dominic's way of saying that he acknowledged the power Lemuel had to make life difficult, but at the same time reminding him he had made few friends in the Executive with his previous campaign.

'No, no, please,' Lemuel responded, a look of sincerity conveying he wasn't on the war path here today. (Astute too. Dominic is a stubborn sod and if you make him dig his heels in, you've blown it.) 'This is not about opinion polls, Mr Reilly, this is about a sea-change in attitudes. The polling only shows that the public's way of thinking about these matters has advanced and the hardliners are lagging behind. I say hardliners rather than scientists because it's not all scientists who think that way. The hardliners say it's pitting science against belief, but an awful lot of people in this country *hold* those beliefs, and they've held them for centuries in spite of scientific developments that we were frequently assured would dispel them. Maybe these beliefs have endured because they're built on something fundamental, something primal: things we simply *know* but don't yet understand *how* we know.'

I noticed Brenda nodding in approving agreement, but Dominic's face showed a strain. He was being pulled in different directions, which ought to have been an encouraging sign, but in my experience, when strained, Dominic tends to snap back pretty hard to where he felt the ground was most solid before. This usually means the strongest pulls are coming from his party and his church. Dominic has been a devout Catholic only slightly longer than he's been a member of the Labour Party. Both have seen plenty of radical changes in his lifetime, but they're still his foundations: his tribes and his touchstones. He's not one of what my fellow scribe Allan Massie once called the Glasgow Irish, but he's fiercely loyal to his roots. As I had warned Lemuel, if he could appeal to those roots, he'd be in the door; and if he challenged either of Dom's twin pillars, his arse would be oot the windae, as my father used to say.

'I'd agree that there are ways in which religion and science are finding themselves less at loggerheads,' Dominic replied. 'But unfortunately, the first one I can think of is the issue of

Darwinian evolution. The Catholic church recognises evolution and has been signatory to a multi-faith pronouncement rejecting Intelligent Design.'

Lemuel smiled in a way that told me Dominic had said exactly what he was waiting to hear.

'A case in point indeed,' Lemuel said. 'The point being that times are changing. Pope Benedict recently fired Father George Coyne from his post as director of the Vatican Observatory because Coyne has publicly disagreed with the Holy See's new position on this matter. The Pope doesn't deny Darwin's theory, but believes the process is directed by a higher intelligence: God.'

'Cosmologists are speculating that our entire universe could have been designed by higher intelligence,' Lafayette interjected, speaking with the charisma and authority he brought to his commentaries on *Borders of the Known*. 'In fact, that there could be billions of such universes in a greater metaverse. Physicists have known for more than a decade how the birth of a new universe is triggered. I'm not saying they know how to set one off like a firecracker, but they know the principle: they know that universes can theoretically be created by higher intelligence.'

'You see?' asked Lemuel. 'Science and religion are not so far apart as the hardliners on *both* sides would have us believe. The work we are doing will explore areas that may ultimately lead to the reconciliation of science and religion, driven apart for centuries but once upon a time one and the same thing: a search for truth. We want our children not to be told that we already have the answers, but that there may be greater truths waiting to be found. You're a religious man, Mr Reilly: wouldn't you like to see that happen? Scotland has a great tradition of faith and a great tradition of science. Wouldn't it be fitting if it showed the way forward for the rest of the world, as it has done in so many ways before?'

'I'll let you know,' was the gist of Dominic's response, if not his exact words. The meeting was wrapped up with the usual politeness and platitudes, but everyone knew there'd been no lightning flash on the road to Damascus.

Dominic had to go off to another meeting, but Brenda walked down to the main lobby with us. Nobody said very much, though I noticed Lafayette drop back and talk softly to her as we passed beneath the arcs and shafts of dark-grey concrete. She looked a little shaken, almost on the edge of tearful, but nonetheless very sincere as we said our goodbyes.

'What was that about?' I enquired.

'I had to ask her,' Lafayette told me. 'All the time we were in there, I just kept getting this sense, this signal. It was like fear and pain, intense fear of loss, and the name Elizabeth. Then this powerful wave of relief, euphoria, and beneath it a strength, but the strength was coming from somewhere else, someone else. Someone called Julia.'

'Brenda's daughter Beth was knocked down by a car a couple of years ago,' I said. 'She was in a coma for a few days.'

'Yeah, she told me. She pulled through. She told me Julia was Beth's late grandmother, on her father's side. So much love. Powerful.'

We waited until we were out of doors and out of earshot before beginning our post-mortem. We stood on the wide concourse before the building, pale winter sunshine beginning to dip behind the Parliament, but picking out Holyrood Park and Salisbury Crag in a lush green beneath a cold, cloudless sky. I felt as frustrated as anybody because I could read Dominic, and knew he was sympathetic to the ideas but hamstrung by politics. Even when he's trying to play it cute, Dominic usually tells you exactly what his thinking is very early in any given discussion. On this occasion it had been that he couldn't afford the controversy. Didn't want a media storm, didn't want grief from further up the command chain.

'Dominic is open to the thinking, but he's not passionate about this, not enough to risk any rough rides,' I told them.

'I agree,' said Lemuel. 'The only reason we got this meeting was a fire-fighting exercise because of the furore over the sexual health bill. Truth is, we're kidding ourselves if we think we got it because of Project Lamda, or because we've done anything that's impressed anybody in there. They were just hearing us out so we don't make a fuss.'

'Believe me,' I told them, 'Dominic is not the kind of man who will shrink from a fight or a controversy if it's something he really believes in. It wouldn't matter whether he was up against the press, the scientists or his bosses. He fights for what inspires him. You need to show him something that will make him realise how exciting and amazing this field really is.'

There was a silence. I became uncomfortably aware that several expectant eyes were now upon Lemuel.

Dominic doesn't share my new-found enthusiasm for the study of the paranormal (and to be honest, a couple of years back I was pretty ambivalent myself), but the one thing that truly intrigued him, despite himself, was the incident at Glassford Hall. I say intrigued, but it is more like an appalled, fearful mistrust, a box he doesn't want to look inside but can't help thinking about. He knows me and respects my judgement enough to believe I didn't make anything up about that night, but has always been reluctant and uncomfortable whenever I've attempted to discuss it.

Most tellingly, he has consistently refused to listen to the tape, and is not afraid to admit that this is because he fears what he may hear. 'It would be like those terrorist beheading videos that are on the internet: it's something I don't want inside my head. Once I've heard it, I won't be able to *un*hear it.'

Dominic is, as is well documented, a religious man, and I strongly suspect that his beliefs in God and an afterlife are so strong that he genuinely fears the implications of what is on that tape. Consequently, for all it scares him, it is also the thing most likely to make him see the importance of the Spiritual Science Chair's aims.

Lafayette knew this too. I'd talked to him often enough about that night, and Dominic's take on it had occasionally cropped up. He and Galt had subsequently tried to get me to prevail upon Lemuel, but I had always refused. This was enormously, painfully personal for Bryant, his most private affair and thus solely his decision. It must have been hard enough allowing me to write about it, knowing it was potentially opening him up to ridicule over the subject of his dearest love and greatest vulnerability.

Lemuel sighed, casting an eye back upon the Parliament building, site of so many past battles, glories and pains for him, mostly in otherwise happier times.

'We all have to make sacrifices, I suppose,' he said. 'Needs must when the devil drives, eh?'

# V

The aide said that guys like me were 'in what we call the reality-based community', which he defined as people who 'believe that solutions emerge from your judicious study of discernible reality'. I nodded and murmured something about enlightenment principles and empiricism. He cut me off. 'That's not the way the world really works any more,' he continued. 'We're an empire now, and when we act, we create our own reality. And while you're studying that reality – judiciously, as you will – we'll act again, creating other new realities, which you can study too, and that's how things will sort out. We're history's actors . . . and you, all of you, will be left to study what we do.'

Unnamed senior Bush administration adviser, to journalist Ron Suskind, summer 2002, as quoted by Al Franken in *The Truth . . . With Jokes*

# Fall of man

We're getting close now: ever closer to the end that is not the end, and with it the revelation that alters all perception and inverts the safest of assumptions. I'll admit I'm as guilty as anyone. I thought I knew the truth; thought I had seen through the deception and had the measure of the deceivers. Aye, gaun yerself, Jack. Instead I was to discover a shattering *absence* of deception: an all-changing truth of terrifying consequences.

The essence of that truth was preserved in iron oxide like a fossil in the rock. Only when it was unlocked by magnet, signals turned into sound, sound turned into numbers, and the numbers analysed, compared, re-analysed, checked, re-compared and double-checked, did we understand truly what we were dealing with. Only then did we realise how completely wrong we had all been, and learn how a human voice really can speak beyond the grave.

They say your whole life flashes through your mind in those last moments as you face death. I can't say that was my experience, but what I recall most vividly is a powerful instance of *déjà vu*. It was Sarah's voice in my head, saying: 'For Christ's sake, be careful.'

I've read a lot of explanations for that most unnerving of sensations, that feeling that you've lived the same moment once before; and sometimes it feels as though you remember living it again and again, a repeating loop of time like an image caught between two mirrors. The woo tendency would claim these are memories of past lives or glimpses of future ones. Neurologists proffer that the sensation is caused by small irregular electrical discharges in the temporal lobe which result in the experience of recall when there is no content to be recalled: thus we think we are *remembering* what we are actually immediately perceiving. Some psychologists maintain that we absorb vast amounts of sensory data that we are not conscious of taking in: the feel of a certain weave of carpet underfoot, for example, or a smell we can't identify and are anyway not paying much conscious heed. They suggest that this weird, inexplicable feeling of familiarity may be caused by precisely that: encounters with things we do not realise we are already familiar with.

My money is on the neurologists having it right, but I'll admit that's not an informed scientific opinion, merely my own gut instinct. However, in the case of the *déjà vu* I'm specifically talking about – Sarah's voice saying 'For Christ's sake be careful' – the explanation is more simple and prosaic than even theirs.

I'd heard her say it a thousand fucking times, usually when I was imminently and irrevocably about to do something dangerous, reckless or just plain daft. In this case, it was at least two of the above; arguably all three, but with my track record, something that is merely reckless as opposed to *knowingly* reckless almost counts as a responsible undertaking.

You don't declare war on somebody until you're absolutely ready for the battle, especially when you know you'll be fighting it on their ground. That's what Moira had been endeavouring to teach me up in Inverness.

*I would strongly warn you to keep your powder dry, Mr Parlabane, and choose very carefully when to play your hand.*

So that's why I went blundering in, all piss and vinegar, smugly goading Lafayette and Mather that I had them sussed, like some RKO movie villain vaingloriously boasting about the genius of his plan when the final act has still to be played out. What can I say, they'd pissed me off. My behaviour was only to be expected, and like I said, I wasn't being *knowingly* reckless.

When I pitched up near the end of Project Lamda with Michael in tow, I had no idea what signals I was sending. I was unaware the guy's mother had written one of the best-known mainstream works on psychic fraud, but it was safe to assume Mather and Lafayette had instantly registered the significance of his surname. I was unknowingly throwing down a gauntlet, identifying myself as no longer a neutral (if sceptical) observer, but a hostile witness.

If Michael hadn't been so bloody reticent about that whole area of his life, then I'd like to think I'd have played it more canny. Aye, I'd like to think so, but I fear that would merely be a conceit: my enduring difficulty throughout this whole business was that I didn't know *how* to play it canny with these people. They kept running rings around me. Thus it was in keeping with my track record regarding these guys that I should be impatient to ram it up them as soon as I finally had something to hit them with. Once again, however, there were crucial things I didn't know, and in this instance, I can say for sure that forewarning quite definitely *would* have caused me to change my approach.

I had heard through one of my Holyrood sources that the Spiritual Science Chair did, as predicted, get their meeting with not only the education minister but his deputy too, albeit under semi-clandestine circumstances. The word was that Brenda McGhee, despite being sent along purely for face value, had been quite taken aback by what she heard and was privately expressing warm support for the chair's position. Dom Reilly was said to be sympathetic but, despite the shag points it would doubtless earn him at home, didn't consider it worth a fight with party bosses. That, however, was working on the assumption that his party bosses would be agin it, a conclusion perhaps based more on the involvement of Bryant Lemuel than on an accurate reading of the straws in the wind.

Holyrood had recently endured the DSH farrago as well as, since the Parliament's inception, the constant sabre-rattling of the ever-volatile Cardinal Doolan, undeterred if not entirely untainted by lingering questions over the extent of his involvement in the Moundgate scandal. What scared me was the possibility that senior New Labour figures might come to see the Spiritual Science Chair's proposals as a cheap and painless sop to the religious lobby. Informal cross-party polling had recorded worryingly high levels of support for what they saw as a harmless and open-minded idea. One MSP even made a comparison with Section 28. 'The argument back then was that it was okay to teach kids *about* homosexuality as long as we weren't promoting it. Doesn't the same thing apply to Intelligent Design?' And there was unlikely to be much outcry from on high down south: Tony and Cherie were, after all, documented woo enthusiasts, the missus especially, and anything that smuggled

281

God into the classroom was unlikely to meet much opposition from the outgoing Reverend Blair.

However, my guess was that the Spiritual Science Chair didn't have sources as good as mine, and given that I'd heard Dom Reilly didn't exactly send them away dancing, I figured they'd be open to offers of support from any quarter. Thus the opportunity I needed seemed to open up at just the right time.

I called Easy Mather and told him that, having had some time to reflect upon what I'd seen, I was now almost ready, if it wasn't too late, to submit a concluding piece that would endorse the other contributors' findings. Without coming over too apologetic, I explained how I'd been fairly spooked by the whole thing and therefore felt a little railroaded when he'd asked for my submission at such short notice, so soon after the end of the tests. My subsequent comments to the press had been largely coloured by this sense that things were being driven forward too hastily, but now that I'd had sufficient pause for thought, I was able to produce a judgement based on rational analysis rather than gut instinct and reflex.

I'm a bastard of a good liar when I need to be.

He bought it. He sounded delighted, though that of itself didn't necessarily mean anything. The beauty of this was that even if he didn't believe me, I knew he had to act like he did: he needed to maintain the impression that there was no question of mistrust between us, because anything else would be a tacit admission that we both knew he was a fraud. However, the proof that he didn't suspect I had got any wiser lay in his agreeing to set up one last test. If his alarm bells had been ringing, I was sure his and Lafayette's schedules would have just been too full to accommodate me. As it was, they found a spare evening within a fortnight to carry out one final demonstration, as I suggested, 'in lieu of the day's testing that got dropped due to Gabriel being ill'.

Moira had opined that the rigged video camera would have long since been spirited away, and possibly even the Faraday cage dismantled. However, I knew for a fact that the entire Project Lamda set-up had been mothballed for possible inspection by the *Journal of Nature*, and guessed the secret gizmos could be quickly redeployed and the routine repeated if it was required to impress somebody else.

Mather's only suggested obstacle was the availability of Klein and Ganea, Rudi now being committed to another research project in the evenings and Heidi overseas until the end of term. I assured him that the full conditions didn't need to be met as I didn't mean to include it in my account as a formal test. 'We could just get some students to fill in,' I said. 'I only need to see Gabriel do this one more time to satisfy myself about a couple of things.'

'Like what?' he asked.

'Well, it sounds embarrassing,' I said with a bashful laugh, 'but mainly I need to know I wasn't dreaming, wasn't seeing things and caught up in some mass delusion. Coming in fresh and clean, I can satisfy myself that I saw and heard what I thought I saw and heard.'

'That sounds like solid scientific thinking to me,' he said.

You've no idea, I thought.

I took the circumspect decision to show up accompanied by Laura rather than Michael; like I said, I wasn't being knowingly reckless. It had been over a year since Lafayette's event in the KUU debating chamber, but folk in his line of work rely on a strong memory for names and faces. I guessed despite the numbers of punters he pulled his stunts on, there was a good chance he'd remember her, and if he did it would give off the right signals that I had turned up with an apparent believer.

Mather had managed to procure both of our protocol-versed student volunteers, Catherine and Juliet, which was just as well, because my own volunteer helper got a phone call shortly after we had all convened in the base and announced that she had to leave.

'My flatmate's locked herself out,' Laura told everyone. 'I'm really sorry, Jack, I'll be back as quickly as I can.'

So sadly she wasn't there to witness my big smug moment of glory; though she did return, as promised, in time to soak up a bit of the satisfyingly poisonous atmosphere that lingered in the aftermath.

I felt like Lafayette must have done, knowing I had aces up my sleeve and that my marks were credulously playing into my hands. And just like Mather, I had every intention of writing a paper on it too.

We tried to follow the procedure as closely as our limited personnel allowed. It was tempting to suggest we skip aspects of it, but I didn't want to seem too accommodating lest it arouse suspicion. There being only two female students to supplement us, supervising the strip-search had to be done by Mather or myself. The 'resentment' and 'mistrust' over this between him and Lafayette having long since dispelled, I thought it safe to suggest Mather do the honours. This served also to imply that I remained ignorant of their complicity, but even more advantageously, it gave me a few revelatory (for them) and highly entertaining (for me) minutes alone with Catherine and Juliet.

Once we were all reconvened in the base, I requested that I be the target subject once again, something both Mather and Lafayette seemed happy enough with. Every step we took through this familiar rigmarole was a step nearer my unequivocal endorsement of the paper, so if I was the one generating the drawings again, there could surely be no doubt in my mind over anyone else's complicity. Lafayette even passed on the contact phase, saying the signals were strong the second I walked into the room; though not strong enough to warn him I was about to do the bastard like a kipper.

Catherine was chosen by Mather to accompany Lafayette to the receiving room, leaving Juliet with me in the target room. Ideally I'd have liked Mather downstairs with his pal, but I didn't risk suggesting it: trying to position him away from the control area might have triggered his alarms. Besides, he'd never have gone for it. Mather hadn't always been in the target room during the tests, but he had always had a means of seeing the drawings, just in case. Predictably, therefore, he opted for a seat in the monitor room.

It was Moira's deduction that the audio feeds from the target room were being piped directly to the relay transmitter in the Faraday cage, but I assumed Mather would have a personal back-up, some form of transmitter secreted about himself so that he could get messages to Lafayette from wherever he was in the building. I waited until he was en route to the monitor room to smear some lip-balm over the lenses of the target room's two video cameras. I didn't overdo it: I didn't want the view totally obscured, just blurry enough to make the drawings indecipherable.

We got the signal from Catherine that Lafayette was ready, and though it wasn't in the protocol, I got a signal telling me Mather was in position too, in that I could hear the video cameras buzz and whir as he tried in vain to get them to focus.

'I'm having trouble with video,' Mather said over the intercom. 'Can't get a clear picture.'

I got up and made some play of looking into one of them. 'Are they dead? The light's on. Can you see me?'

'I can see you, just not fully focused.'

'That's okay,' I said. 'It's not an official test, so I'm not going to make a big deal of it if there's a minor bug. It would be more of an issue if the camera in the Faraday cage wasn't functioning,' I added, as guilelessly as I could muster.

I began work on my drawing, which took me less time than normal as I had not only decided on my subject, but practised it in advance. Once it was done, I gestured to Juliet, who neglected to verbally appraise my masterpiece, instead simply writing down her description.

'Is everything okay?' Mather asked through a speaker, wondering why nothing was being said and no doubt starting to worry.

'Yeah, I'm just reading Juliet's description to make sure I agree it's accurate.'

'Can you read it to me?' he said. 'I couldn't see the drawing because of the camera problem.'

'Oh shit, sorry,' I said. 'I forgot to say. Minor alteration to the protocol; we came up with it while you were doing the strip-search. Written descriptions only. Nothing verbal. Just to see how it goes.'

I placed the description and the drawing inside the lead-lined box, then gave Catherine the green light while a silence grew on the intercom. Mather was asking himself some very testing questions, wondering how to play it no doubt, just in case my protocol suggestion was a shot in the dark and they weren't truly rumbled.

'Yeah, that's a pretty good idea,' he said eventually, regrouping. 'But I could have done with a heads-up. I think we'd better call this test a void, but we'll adopt your new protocol for the next shot.'

'Nah, let's see how Lafayette gets on,' I suggested. 'We pulled a switch on him before, remember? And he still aced it. This isn't a trick to catch him out.'

'Yeah, but . . . look, I'm sorry, but I gotta call this one a dud. I've got problems here with the cameras, a change to the protocol, it's just sloppy, Jack. I'm telling Catherine to bring Gabe out.'

Lafayette emerged shortly after, clutching a blank sheet of paper, shaking his head and telling her: 'Everything seems, I dunno, like blurred, chaotic. Is there trouble up there?'

'A few technical glitches,' Mather informed him. 'But we should be good to go again in a minute.'

I have to admit, I was impressed that he didn't mention the change in protocol to Lafayette. Very slick. Okay, he knew Lafayette would have heard at least one and probably both sides of our exchange, but Mather was still ballsy enough to make out he was going along with my alteration *without* telling our test subject.

We were indeed good to go in a minute: the minute it took for Mather to 'decide' he should join us in the target room, what with the camera problems and everything.

He sat nearby, getting himself a good view of the paper as I recommenced my artwork.

'I'm going for the same image as before,' I said quietly. 'Give him two bites at this cherry.'

I drew a man in a standing position, holding a stick in front of his face, then drew a vertical line to represent a wall, and a horizontal one to represent the floor. Below it, I drew a second man, sitting at a table, a pen in his hand.

'All right, a man at a desk drawing a picture, that's funny,' said Mather, who only *thought* he was getting the joke. He was speaking for the benefit of Lafayette. I thought about insisting on total silence in compliance with the altered protocol, but decided it would be more fun to hear him come up with flimsy reasons for giving a running commentary. Plus, I wanted Lafayette to be hearing this. The camera in the Faraday cage would even record the look on his face as the truth dawned, but I had a feeling they wouldn't be letting me review the footage later.

'Not finished,' was all I said to Mather, though I gave him a knowing smile, like I appreciated him being on my wavelength in drawing the test subject as his own target.

I added a video camera pointing at the seated man.

Mather nodded, smiling. 'I get it, I get it. A video camera. It's Gabe in the cage.'

I drew a small appendage on the bottom of the camera, giving it a corona of arcing lines to suggest radio transmission. I added more and more lines, showing the waves making their way across towards the man's head, then reduced the width of the arcs as the line of transmission headed directly into his ear.

I could hear Mather breathe in.

Finally, I drew an oval on top of the standing man's stick, changing it into a microphone. And just in case there was any doubt, I wrote the words 'Cheating Cunt #1' above the standing man and 'Cheating Cunt #2' above the seated one downstairs.

'Right, Juliet, I'm finished,' I said. 'You can write your description now.' I turned towards Mather. 'Do you maybe want to leave the room for a minute so you can, oh, I don't know . . . help me out with a pretext here: eh, scratch your arse in private? Go for a pee? Tell your china what he's supposed to be drawing? Don't forget to mention the captions: they're really important.'

He just stared at me, saying nothing. In my time I've felt a lot of hate coming my way at such moments. This was well up there.

'Hey, Gabe, you getting this?' I said loudly. 'Easy'll be out in a minute with your description, but I was just telling him not to forget the captions about cheating cunts.'

As I believe I said before, there was a bit of an atmosphere when Laura returned from her mission with the door keys.

'What did I miss?' she asked.

Aye, dead funny. Here's another belter. Grave humour, you might say, definitely aiming for the 'last laugh' category. Without doubt, one hell of a comeback:

He knew when the flat would be empty. He made it his business to know an awful lot about people who were usually oblivious of his deeper interest. Daytime. Broad daylight. Nobody's

287

suspicious of a guy creeping around at eleven o'clock in the morning, are they? Same as nobody thinks twice if they pass an unfamiliar face in a shared close with nine doors in it, especially in student-land where they can be four or five to a billet.

Aye, it's still me talking. I'm not going all omniscient on you. All I'll say is, it's amazing what information and insight you can become party to once you 'cross over'.

I'm saying eleven o'clock, but that's just for talking's sake. I don't know what time he came. He: Easy Mather, murdering bastard.

Want to know how he got into our flat? He had keys cut. How ironic is that? In fact, he had keys cut for the homes of everybody in any way involved with Project Lamda, and probably had a wee poke around all of them at some point.

Fucking knicker-sniffer.

Okay, I can't substantiate that last claim, but I do know that he and his ilk are creepy wee shites. On the train to Sneck, Laura told me about Mabel Wragg, and Michael filled in any blanks she left. Mediums and their confederates are sticky-fingered bastards if you give them the chance, and house keys literally open up a host more possibilities than they'd find in just your handbag. Thon wifie who found her missing engagement ring in an ice cube in her own freezer, the punter whose missing document showed up on a shelf in a bookshop. These items – and others that would later 'apport' themselves from the ether in the immediate vicinity of the medium – would have been carefully selected and removed from their owners' homes.

In my case, this particular medium's confederate wanted to remove more than some petty object for an apport. He wanted to remove my ability to pose a threat, as well as my ability to respirate or indeed take up space above ground.

What he did could as easily have killed Sarah instead. He didn't care, probably reckoned same difference: a devastated widower wouldn't be in much shape or inclination to worry about this silly old nonsense.

The slimiest thing is the thought that he had almost certainly let himself into the flat before, looking for little clues about my life, Sarah's life, stuff Lafayette could use for his amazing feats of clairvoyance. And while he was at it, he perhaps noted a few things that might be worth bearing in mind were I to become a problem. It was easy enough to come and go: not only did he have keys, but unlike our place back in Edinburgh, there was no burglar alarm, never mind the other wee adjustments I had made over the years to detect and deter unwanted visitors. It was, as I've mentioned, a rented flat, and we didn't know how long we were likely to be in it. Plus I hadn't had anybody try to kill me since McKinley Hall.

It was an old traditional Glasgow tenement built to house the middle orders: large rooms, high ceilings and huge bay windows. These would have been classic sash-and-case affairs prior to the place being recently renovated to tempt the rental market, but were now double-glazed with an inoffensive but utterly unconvincing 'wood effect' uPVC. Used to be that you swung your biggest windows inside on metal hinges in order to clean them, but modern building regulations had declared this verboten for safety reasons. I didn't recall any mass instances of folk plummeting out of tenements with a chamois in their hands, but the HSE had spoken and your double-glazed units were compliantly constructed to flip over almost completely in order to let you clean them 'outside in'. It was done with a very nifty counterbalancing system: release a couple of switches and the unit pivoted with an ease that belied the considerable weight of its two huge vacuum-separated panes plus the uPVC and aluminium housing them. It didn't take much physical effort, but crucially, you did have to lean forward and push outwards against the frame.

Mather was clearly a practical-minded and versatile bugger. He knew just what adjustments to make, what minor components to remove. You'd almost think he'd done this before, but who am I to speculate. He rigged it so that the window sat innocently in place; you could even have slid it up slightly if you wanted to let in some air. But if you clicked those safety switches and tried to flip the thing, as I was about to discover . . .

I had no clue the frame had been sabotaged, no hint that the place had been disturbed, and no bloody sixth-sense warning that my number was up. The somewhat woo-credulous philosopher Colin Wilson speculates that as humans we have primal instincts, inherited from our animal past but dormant through millennia of civilisation, that nonetheless can awaken in times of peril to warn us that something is amiss. His example is an account of a hunter suddenly deciding to change paths through the forest and consequently avoiding a hungry tiger. He attributes sudden, apparently irrational and otherwise inexplicable decisions which result in us avoiding danger to this dormant instinct subconsciously noticing and interpreting details about our environment. My alternative theory is that it comes down to skewed and self-selecting data. If you got a scary wee feeling and crossed the road, but fuck-all happened, you wouldn't tell anyone about it. Also, and even more importantly in this context, it's only the ones who suddenly took action and survived who are around to tell the tale. If you *don't* get a scary wee feeling and consequently *don't* take some intuitive evasive action, you get eaten by the tiger.

Or fall four storeys out of a fucking window.

It was the day after my wee Project Lamda reprisal. Mather didn't waste any time, perhaps reckoning I might not have got around to writing up my supplementary report for the *Journal of Nature*. I had been in the flat all afternoon but hadn't been into the living room. It was Sarah who called my attention to it.

'Jack, have you seen this?'

There was purple paint smeared over the central and largest pane of the room's triple-wide bay windows. Paint from a paint-*ball*, I was able to recognise.

'Somebody's taking the piss,' I said.

Sarah gave me a concerned look, the one she reserves for when she thinks I'm making light of something that she suspects may be ominous. She was thinking the same thing I immediately asked myself: was this something to do with McKinley Hall? But I didn't think so, other than as covered by my initial response: somebody taking the piss with a wee allusion to well-documented events. It could have been Rory Glen, overgrown wean that he was, or it could just have been some prick who knew this was my window and thought he was being hilarious. No point worrying about it. At least it made a change from allusions to the cannibalism.

It was a hell of a mess, though.

'Will it come off?' Sarah asked as I filled a bucket in the kitchen.

'Aye. It's water-based stuff. If somebody really wanted to ruin our day, they'd have fired up some gloss.'

I took the bucket into the living room and moved a low table out the way to let me in closer.

'For Christ's sake, be careful,' she said, like she always did when I was washing the old sash-and-case windows back in Edinburgh. She had shared the HSE's concerns about my swinging the whole pane inside, largely because she could picture it swinging back and bouncing me right through the gap.

'Don't worry,' I said. 'These things tilt right over. Wait and I'll show you . . .'

Q: What's the last thing that goes through a fly's mind as it hits a windscreen at seventy miles per hour?

A: Its arsehole.

That used to be one of my favourite jokes. It's not so funny now, when I think about what happens to a human being after falling four storeys on to a concrete pavement.

As I said before, my life didn't flash before me. I can tell you what did go through my mind as I grasped that window-handle, but before I do, there's something you ought to understand in my defence. It is that while I admit I have been reckless, I'm not fucking stupid; or at least not as stupid as I may have made out. My own fault, of course: I haven't told you everything. Must be a symptom of hanging around Lafayette and Mather too long: you get a taste for the juvenile pleasure of gratuitously misleading people. I didn't lie, but it's amazing what a small change of perspective can do. Try this one on again:

You don't declare war on somebody until you're absolutely ready for the battle, especially when you know you'll be fighting it on their ground. That's what Moira had been endeavouring to teach me up in Inverness.

*I would strongly warn you to keep your powder dry, Mr Parlabane, and choose very carefully when to play your hand.*

So that's why I went blundering in, all piss and vinegar . . .

Okay, let me take you back a few days.

The Spiritual Science Chair had announced, with all the

fanfare that a woo-hungry media could be guaranteed to deliver, its next, 'potentially earth-shattering' project. The now legendary and hitherto fiercely protected recording made by Jillian Noble's humble wee Dictaphone during what the press release called 'a psychic disturbance' was going to be handed over for independent analysis. The tape, purportedly featuring the late Hilda Lemuel's voice as heard during some soirée at Glassford Hall three years back, was going to be entrusted to two voice-analysis experts, both of whom could boast unquestionable pedigree. One, Henry Liekowski, had more than two decades' experience with the FBI and was still retained by the Bureau on a consultative basis. The second, Marcel Voderoux, had provided consultant services to police forces throughout Europe. Bryant Lemuel had given permission for Jillian Noble to release the recording to these experts, but just as crucially, he was also supplying them with videotapes featuring his wife's voice in order to provide samples for comparison.

In short, they were playing their ace. But there were those of us who were waiting for this, and had made it our mission to trump it.

I called Moira to ask her what she thought had really happened at Glassford Hall, and found her not at home but considerably closer than Inversneck. A reconciliation – or at least a truce – having been effected, she was down to visit Michael for a few days.

I took a drive round to his place.

Moira laughed as soon as I mentioned my question, and told me, to my considerable surprise, that all the answers were in Jillian Noble's book.

'It's a sincere and faithful account,' she said. 'You just need to take it at face value, but read from the perspective of knowing Lafayette is in cahoots with Easy Mather, and that the boy Mather is a dab hand with his wee electronic gadgets. Then it all becomes clear.'

Michael and Laura were dispatched to Byres Road to buy a copy of *Encounters in the Borderland* and returned inside half an hour. Obviously it didn't take two people, but this pair were joined at the hip. Moira took us through the relevant chapter. I felt considerably less dumb than when she had explained Project

292

Lamda, but it was still a bit of a beamer. Talk about staring you in the face.

'One of the first things she says about Lafayette that night is that he was tired and a bit under the weather, suffering from jet-lag. This is standard practice for the charlatan about to impress a captive audience. Read enough accounts of Hoffman at work and you'd think the bastard had ME: every report will mention how he said he was ill or tired. It's to make you think they're off the boil, not operating at full capacity and therefore not sharp enough to be up to anything deceitful.

'In this case it was also a pretext for lots of comings and goings, in and out of the room. Lafayette has to go out for some air after dinner, which he is apparently too ill to eat much of. Mather goes with him but returns alone. Lafayette returns for a while, but feels faint again. Now Mather has to go out to "fetch Lafayette's pills". Note that Lafayette actually gets more pale and ill *after* taking them, so it's likely this was their true purpose, to make him look more genuinely wracked and distressed. Noble also notes that the pair have already been staying at Glassford Hall a few days. A few days. Think about *that*.'

'A few days with the run of the house,' I said, recalling Mather's unmonitored access to the Randall Building. 'Plenty of time to set the stage for his boy's big show. The electrics, the heating, the chimney. Not to mention secreting a speaker system.'

'A load of those wee Bose numbers,' Michael suggested. 'They're small enough to be hidden about the place, and no wires. That would do the trick.'

'Lights flicker and dim,' Moira resumed, skimming the text with her finger. 'The fire suddenly blows out. All dramatic but easily engineered theatrical effects. The temperature spookily drops: give Noble credit, she does at least acknowledge a correlation between these last two developments. It's my assumption that Mather tampered with the thermostat while he was out the room and it had been getting colder ever since, but the fire blowing out was an intended cue for everyone to suddenly notice.'

Moira giggled as she read ahead.

'Get this,' she said. 'It's absolute textbook standard seance practice. Lafayette gets them all to form a circle and join hands,

293

plus the room is practically in darkness by this point. Next he rebuffs Mather, tells him to stay out of the circle. "*Just* her friends," he says. Nice touch. Now they're all circled around and concentrating on Lafayette, leaving Mather free and unwitnessed to do what mediums' accomplices have been doing for over a hundred years, which is orchestrate the whole show. Used to be a matter of playing musical instruments or making a few objects float past. But in the modern age, Mather merely had to press some buttons on the wee remote control in his pocket.'

'But what about the voice itself?' asked Laura. 'How could they fake that?'

'Again, the clues are in the book. She talks about white noise, a whooshing sound like the wind, with this voice barely audible in the midst of it. All they would need is someone doing a half-decent impersonation, even just the right accent, and their imaginations would do the rest.'

'But how could Lafayette and Mather find out what Hilda Lemuel sounded like? And how could they discover that stuff about the honeymoon? La Castillo wasn't the name of the place, it was a private joke between the newly-weds.'

'There's *no way* they could have known that,' Moira gushed with exaggerated wonder: the words people always said when a psychic had impressed them.

Laura nodded. 'There's always a way,' she conceded. 'But I don't see why they're going public about getting the recording analysed. I'd have thought Lemuel's reluctance to pick at that particularly painful scab must have suited them down to the ground.'

'It's just their next big play to keep themselves in the public eye. The results won't matter,' I said, getting it wrong as usual. 'They know the media won't pick up on the story if the findings are negative. If they're asked at all, they'll just claim the results were inconclusive.'

'But the results won't be inconclusive,' Moira corrected. 'And they won't be negative either. They're bringing in experts: not stooges, I mean real, *bona fide* experts, giving massive gravitas to the whole thing, and those experts will conclude that the voice on the tape belongs to Hilda Lemuel.'

'How?'

'More basic conjuring: a variation on Find the Lady, in fact. The Spiritual Science Chair will control all the materials, like the conjuror controls the cards or the three cups and the ball beneath. They'll need comparison recordings, which Lemuel will supply: most probably home videos. He will submit these, officially to the chair, but in reality to our two chancers. Lemuel will verify that the comparison recordings contain his late wife's voice, but you can bet it won't be his late wife's voice that's on whatever gets submitted to the audio analysts. All they need is to dub the same actress over Hilda Lemuel's voice and the experts will correctly verify that it is the *same* voice on both sources. They might not even give them the videos: they could hand them the audio track alone and say it's been lifted from the authenticated tape.'

'But surely they'll notice the recording's been adulterated?' I said. 'Even if Mather does a bang-up job. You said these guys will be real experts.'

'Experts in voice analysis, Mr Parlabane, not audio forensics. They'll have been carefully picked for what they're *not* expert in as much as what they are, believe me. And regardless of whether they detect any anomalies on the tapes, the question they will be charged with answering is simply this: is it the same voice on both sources? To which the answer will be an unequivocal yes.'

What we needed, therefore, was our own analysis, and that meant our own samples for comparison. We would also require someone with the hardware and the knowledge to perform the tests. Luckily I knew a guy who owned a recording studio and who was something of an adept when it came to matters of electronic engineering. I say 'adept' where people generally tend to use the word 'whizz', because this was not an individual to whom the word 'whizz' was ever likely to be realistically applied, unless somebody taught a three-toed sloth how to use adjectives.

I phoned a contact of mine at the BBC, Jacqui Young, a news editor with whom I'd worked when she was still in print journalism. I remembered that Hilda Lemuel had been involved in fundraising for a charity called Scottish Aid to Africa, and guessed there was a chance the Beeb's news archives had her on some B-roll. Jacqui ran searches for me using both Hilda's name and the name of the charity as triggers. By the end of the next day she had located a piece of unbroadcast footage, featuring Hilda giving a brief speech introducing the celebrity guest who had been the real subject of the news story. She spoke for less than a minute, but it was a crystal-clear professional recording, and it would be more than enough.

Locating a copy of Jillian Noble's 'Voice of the Dead' recording was a wee bit trickier. I confess it did occur to me to just ask her for a copy, in the interests of science, purely to see the look on her face, but I didn't want her tipping the wink to her paranormal pals so I desisted. I was playing it canny, keeping my powder dry, remember? We all were.

Ah, the art of misdirection. Just because you live by it doesn't mean you can't be utterly suckered by it. Especially when it's being practised by someone you've already written off as a mug. Aye, time for the truth: that brash wee interlude, Return to Project Lamda, was not just me declaring war; it was me engaging the enemy on a diversionary front while a raiding party did the real damage elsewhere.

You may remember I was accompanied by Laura rather than Michael, so as not to put Mather and Lafayette on their guard. Her time, however, ended up being largely consumed by an errand involving helping a friend gain access to a locked property. The first thing I did upon arriving at the Randall Building was dip Mather's jacket pocket and remove his keys, which I passed to Laura. She then surreptitiously texted Michael, which was his signal to phone her and provide the 'flatmate in distress' call that necessitated her departure. Having excused herself, she headed out of the Randall Building and across to the courtyards, where the Spiritual Science Chair had its office.

We had reasoned that a piece of 'evidence' as crucial as the Glassford Hall recording would be far too valuable to them for it not to be backed up, and more than likely several times. It therefore took Michael all of about ten minutes to locate the file on one of the office's two PCs and copy it to a flash drive. Laura then returned to the Randall Building and slipped me the keys, which I popped back into the pocket of Mather's jacket, still hanging over the same chair as when I'd lifted them.

Michael and I took the flash drive and the BBC footage directly that same evening to my, ahem, techno adept at the studio he owned in Paisley. The place was down a wee cul-de-sac just off Love Street, its neighbours mostly spray shops, scrap dealers and joineries. He had chosen the premises despite the incongruity of its light-industrial location for two principal reasons. One was that it was hardly the priciest real-estate footprint in the area, but just as crucially, he'd reasoned that there would be very few passing neds, and of those even fewer were likely to suspect that the building housed a state-of-the-art recording studio well worth the burgling.

I almost had to double-check we were at the right address when I arrived at the door and failed to smell hash. It had been a couple of years since I'd been there, but he'd surely have mentioned a change of premises when we spoke on the phone, I reasoned. I rang the bell and waited. And waited. After six or seven minutes, as I explained to Michael, I would ordinarily have started giving greater credence to my change-of-address theory, if it wasn't that previous experience had taught me ten minutes was well within the parameters of what the proprietor considered acceptable response time. And that was when he *was* expecting you and *did* actually hear you ring the doorbell.

After about eight minutes, the door began to shake with the reverberations of several bolts being withdrawn, and a minute or so after that, it finally swung open.

'Mon in,' he said, already retreating back into the red-bulb dimness of the interior. 'Oh, and check thaim by the way,' he added, indicating a pile of glossy and embossed blue cards sitting on a low table just inside the door. I heard him laugh, a deep, snottery rumble, familiarly full of phlegm and juvenile amusement. Business cards. He actually had business cards these days. Must have been a part-ex deal, or just his latest self-amusement exercise in emphasising his unique unmarketability as a businessman or even a human being.

The name on his business card was Cameron Scott, but as far as I was aware, even the guy's mother called him Spammy.

'I hope you're on exes, man,' he said. 'I couldnae get warez versions of the gear you need for this cairry-oan, so I've had tae cross a bit ay a personal Rubicon and actually spring for some licences.'

'You'll be fully reimbursed, Spammy.'

'It's the cost tae ma self-respect I'm worried aboot. Cannae put that on an invoice. Or a fuckin' VAT return.'

I handed him two discs: one a DVD of the news footage and the other a burn from the file Michael pinched.

'Do you know what you're doing with this stuff?' I asked. It pays to be blunt with Spammy. Tiptoeing around his feelings can be done on a pogo stick and he won't necessarily notice you're having a go at him; or won't acknowledge it anyway.

'Ach, fuck, aye,' he said confidently, with a brightness to his face, and in particular his eyes, that ought to have been reassuring but was instead a bit unnerving. I wondered if he'd had his hair cut, was that it? It seemed shaggy and billowingly voluminous as ever, but these things can be comparative. Maybe he'd had a trim and the weird effect I was experiencing was because I could actually see his face properly. 'Demonstrating differences in the voice patterns shouldnae be too big a struggle. Would be mair of an ask if you were lookin' for conclusive proof of similarity.'

'We're guessing it won't be hard playing spot-the-difference once the samples are isolated,' Michael said.

'Ye mean cleanin' up aw this white noise shite aff the Glassford Hall hingmy so's we can hear the wummin properly. Aye, that's gaunny take a wee while.'

I looked at him with some concern. A 'wee while' in Spammy Time . . .

'Don't panic,' he told me. 'Just processor time, and a lot of wee niggly operations. I'll get straight on it. I've nothin' else lined up the night and, tae be perfectly honest, I'm jist oot ma bed.'

He laughed as he caught me looking at my watch. It was after nine. At night.

'You do seem pretty bright-eyed and bushy-tailed,' I remarked. 'Something's different about you, but I cannae pin it doon.'

He looked quizzically at me for a moment and then rolled his eyes.

298

'Aw, aye. Nae hash.'

*That's* what it was.

'You've given up?'

'Have I fuck. But I cannae have any roon the studio, ye know?'

'Yeah,' I said, though as I spoke I realised I didn't. 'Eh, no. Polis, is it? Fire risk?'

'Naw. Fuckin' smokin' ban, man. This is a place of work.' His eyes bulged briefly as if some pertinent moment of realisation was resonating inside his mind. 'Fuckin' amazin' whit ye can get done when you're no fucked oot yer heid,' he added. 'Cannae believe it. I'm actually startin' tae like bein' busy.'

Now *that* was much stranger and infinitely more far-fetched than any phenomenon Lafayette ever discussed on *Borders of the Known*.

And while Spammy got busy analysing the recordings, I got busy too: busy doing what I should have been doing all along, which was sniffing out the dirt on Lafayette. Never mind 'assume cheating'; 'assume scumbag' was more my enduring philosophy, and it was testament to Lafayette and Mather's arts of misdirection that they had diverted me from it for this long. In fact, 'assume nothing' was the real lesson Moira Loftus had made me relearn.

Taking Moira's cue, I gave Jillian Noble's book a second read. The sensation of feeling like a tit quite palpably returned; but not as much of a tit as I suspected Jillian was going to feel.

The thing that struck me hardest was her description of discovering that, despite his efforts to conceal it, Gabriel Lafayette was the seventh son of a seventh son. The first time I had read this, I didn't ascribe any great significance to it. I rationalised that, despite what superstition dictated, this was not such a coincidence for someone in his eventual line of work, as it may even have been the awareness and discussion of this distinction that led him into the psychic game in the first place. I also reasoned that, in a country as populous as the USA, it was a statistical inevitability that there *would* be a few males born the seventh son of a seventh son. It didn't prove anything, I had decided. Now, however, with the scales fallen from my eyes, my response to reading this revelation was instead pertaining to Lafayette's provenance on the distaff side.

*Gabriel Lafayette was the seventh son of a seventh son.*

'Yer maw,' I said aloud.

Noble had arrived at this amazing discovery after receiving an abusive email casting doubt on Lafayette's background, causing her to approach Mather for assistance in probing deeper into this murky area. A wee while later, Mather facilitates a phone call to one of Lafayette's brothers, and the startling story – along with Lafayette's self-sacrificing and honourable efforts not to trade off it – comes to light.

So hands up who *doesn't* think Mather sent that email?

This brother, Tobin Davenport, now lived in Los Angeles, the book said. Well of course he did: Mather and Lafayette had to supply Noble with the number of a confederate Stateside. Ideally he'd have been living in the Big Easy, but there was an outside chance that even Silly Jilly would get suspicious if they supplied her with a 310 area code and told her it was New Orleans. Clearly they didn't have anybody they could rely on back in Louisiana. Los Angeles, however, was a different story. Los Angeles was where Easy Mather was from, home to Reed University, where he 'discovered' Lafayette. It had been home also to my prying wee self for a time, and somewhere I still held a few useful contacts and favours (not to mention the odd outstanding assassination contract).

I made some phone calls, starting with my old friend Larry Freeman of the LAPD, as he had the wherewithal to look in a lot deeper and darker places than my other associates enjoyed.

'You know, Jack, despite our president's best efforts, there are still some civil liberties in operation over here,' he warned me. 'Unless I got probable cause, then I could be in contraventions up the ass if I disclose certain information about private citizens.'

'Don't sweat it, Larry,' I told him. 'I'm guessing you're mostly going to confirm what I suspect by finding certain *absences* of information. And I'm guessing probable cause will make itself apparent soon enough too.'

'It usually does when you're involved.'

He got back to me a few hours later.

'I can't tell you anything about Tobin Davenport,' he said. 'For the reasons we discussed.'

'Rights of privacy?' I asked, drily feigning concern.

'No, the other reason we discussed.'

'He doesn't exist.'

'Well, if he does, he ain't payin' taxes. There were two *Toby* Davenports, but one of them is nine years old and the other doesn't have his own private number at the nursing home.'

'What about the esteemed psychic himself?' I prompted.

'*Nada.* Or should I say, *rien.* According to Louisiana state records, there was nobody born of that name or even "Gabriel Davenport" to a Marie Lafayette or Marie Davenport within twenty years of the given age. I didn't ask them to check beyond that. Ditto the names given for the supposed brothers. No, wait, there was a Philippe born to a Marie Davenport and there was a Jean-Jacques born to a Marie Lafayette, but they're not related to each other. Gabriel Lafayette is quite definitely not your boy's real name.'

I could actually hear the grin across his face as he said this.

'And would you perhaps be in a position to tell me what is?'

'All in good time,' he said. 'But first we gotta deal with your other request. The one possibly pertaining to probable cause.'

'So Easy Mather *does* have a jacket,' I said.

'No. No police records dealing with that name. But there is a file on one Edward M Charles, middle name Mather. Known to his associates by a nickname deriving from his first and last initials.'

'EC. In for fraud, perchance?'

'Oh, lots and lots of it, yeah. The one part of his story that is true is he served in Desert Storm. According to his lawyer's mitigation, he joined the army to sort himself out after a string of juvenile offences. He had a pretty glowing service record. He was an army engineer. Very useful with electronics, apparently. Plus thirteen CKs.'

'CKs?'

'Confirmed kills. However, what his lawyer left out of the mitigation was that he was dishonourably discharged over an attempted embezzlement. Old habits die hard. Seems that detail kinda stunk up his CV, so he had some trouble finding gainful employment after the war. A familiar and tragic tale. He did just under two years at Las Almeitos Pen. Found work at Reed

University under a halfway-house outreach programme they ran in conjunction with the jail. He worked there as a lab technician.'

'Where he meets our mystery guest.'

'No, our mystery guest has already stepped into the picture by then. I ran a check on known associates, only came up with one, a Jake Salter, but he died before Mather went to jail.'

'Mather offed him?' I suggested.

'No. I sourced the file on that too. Guy died at home. No suspicious circumstances. So having struck out there, I asked a guy at Las Almeitos who Easy's buddies were on the yard. Turns out he shared a cell for three months with a con doing time for, among other charges, impersonating a police officer.'

'That gets you jail time?'

'Oh yeah.'

'So how did *you* beat the rap?'

'Yeah, you're still a laugh riot, Jack. Anyway, we had this real squalid little serial case here a few years back. The Chaperone, he got named. Sex killer, preyed on schoolgirls. Story got out after the first victim was found that she had lied to Momma about going to her girlfriend's house after school to study. Turned out to be tabloid bullshit, but as usual it stuck. Anyway, this asshole was busted pretending to be a badge, close to the crime scene of corpse number four. He ended up getting grilled as a suspect, but the explanation was a lot more pathetic. He was trying to get some inside skinny on the case so he'd sound more convincing to reporters when he told them he had been brought in as a psychic consultant. Dunno why he tried so hard: turns out reporters all over the US had already swallowed his claims to have worked on several previous cases across the country.

'I pulled his file. Turns out another of his convictions was for trespass, housebreaking and conspiracy to defraud. He broke into the home of a recently deceased widow in Marin County. He wasn't caught in the act: fingerprints tied him to it later. And he wasn't there to steal anything, just take some notes and move a few items around. The real target was her younger sister, another widow. The trick was to convince her the old girl was communicating through him. He divined where important missing documents and heirlooms were, that kind of thing.'

302

'And he wasn't looking for a fee.'

'Of course not. Though the late older sister was strongly suggesting from beyond the grave that this charming medium ought to get a taste of her legacy. He was shit outta luck, though. The younger sister had a son who was hip to the scam. He called the cops and our man got busted.'

'Boo! So, spit it out. What was the name of this honourable and enterprising citizen?'

Larry paused only a moment to savour that inimitable feeling, shared by cops and hacks alike, of delivering the goods.

'His name was Grady Lappin. Born New Orleans, Louisiana, May fifth 1955. Father, Bobby, a three-time loser, mostly short-con work. Mother, Marcia, occasional hooker when palm-reading and crystal-ball-gazing weren't making the rent. What you might call a natural-born liar. He got it in his mommy's milk and learned the rest at his daddy's knee.'

So Lafayette, or Lappin, had been in the psychic scamming game all his days, but strictly small-time until fate paired him up with Mather. His father had been an ill-starred short-con artist, but with Mather's assistance he shook off his daddy's loser legacy and started thinking bigger. Long con: longer than any other, because it was open-ended, no sting, just pay-off after pay-off after pay-off.

He came up with a new name, and hid his association with Mather, so that Mather could 'discover' him and his powers while undertaking some research work at a reputable university. Mather fudged, exaggerated and outright faked his own credentials in order to play the authenticating scientist in the pitch Moira said had been used since Vaudeville. Consequently Lafayette developed – if you believe Noble's book – a growing reputation in US psi circles and beyond. This eventually brought him to the attention of Bryant Lemuel, and shortly after, he and Mather set fair for Blighty, where Lemuel's patronage and influence opened up to them a virgin paradise of opportunities. They earned themselves a devoted following, an acclaimed TV series, a burgeoning respectability for their field, a prestigious foothold in academia, and with it the beginnings of influence in a nation's politics. Not bad for two crooks and the Fox girls' big fib.

And for their next trick, they were about to kill me.

I phoned Reed University after I finished talking to Larry. I asked some questions and confirmed a couple of things, but the guy I really needed to speak to was unavailable. I hung up, then shortly afterwards heard Sarah's key in the lock. She called me into the living room, showed me the paint on the glass. I filled my bucket, moved the low table out of the way, approached the window.

'For Christ's sake, be careful,' Sarah said.

Not a sentiment I was exactly renowned for heeding.

Weren't the truly ironic famous last words meant to be your own?

# Dark truth by Dictaphone

So now, at last, is revealed to me the stark, inescapable reality
that it truly was Hilda Lemuel's voice we heard on that merely
terrifying night at Glassford Hall. Merely terrifying because
then, we were afraid of what we did not understand, scared by
daunting possibilities. But now that I have seen the possibilities eliminated, leaving only the truth, I also know what it truly
is to be afraid.

The memory of the incident never faded, never became any
less vivid. Even if it had, I retained in my possession the most
powerful mnemonic for restoring my recall, but it wasn't needed;
nor was I often drawn to put myself through the upset of
listening to it. On the odd occasion I began to, I usually switched
it off before even a minute had elapsed. I'm not absolutely sure,
but I think I may have listened to its entirety only once.
Nonetheless, even I have had my doubts these past years: times
when I could not help but simply ask myself what I *really* heard.
I knew I hadn't imagined it or misremembered it, because I had
the recording. But as I racked my brain and contemplated the
implications, the possibility that it would one day be revealed
to be an elaborate hoax always seemed a temptingly easy way
out. If it turned out to be a fake, then, yes, we'd all feel a little
bit silly, but it meant the whole mystery and the imponderables
it implied could be put away.

But now the door to the easy way out has forever been closed
and locked, as surely as the one I'm staring at right now is
closed and locked. Now the fact that the voice was real, and
really Hilda's, has been demonstrated to me in the most incon-
trovertible and empirically irrefutable way.

I know this is being recorded. They want me to speak. Then
let them hear this. Please God, let everyone hear this.

I'm losing track of the time. How long has it been? Was it
yesterday? Was it really just yesterday morning I learned that

Jack Parlabane had been killed? It already seems so long ago. It must be. I can't be sure. I don't think it matters.

I found out first thing, when I saw it in the newspaper, and it struck me that there was something rather tragically appropriate about that. Lord forgive me, but the phrase 'it's what he would have wanted' popped unworthily into my head. Well, I suppose at least I didn't dwell upon the irony of someone known to have sought advantage through the practice of cat burglary meeting his end by falling out of his own front window.

The police hadn't officially released much in the way of detail, but 'sources' (ie a cop informally tipping a favoured reporter the wink) said the accident was believed to have been caused by a malfunctioning double-glazing unit. If so, the company who installed it were going to need one hell of a lawyer.

It wasn't front-page – a sad final indictment for any hack – but did make the page-three lead, which was more than an accidental-death story would have ordinarily merited. I suppose the fact that, loathe him or really loathe him, Parlabane was one of our own was the reason the news editors gave it decent play. I couldn't begrudge him that.

I won't be hypocritical about this just because he's dead. I didn't like the man one bit. I had often thought that we'd all be a lot better off without him, and though I couldn't say I was happy to have got my wish, I didn't come over all sentimental about him either. It was really only when I read mention of the fact that he was leaving a wife that the personal element struck me. When I read her name, her age, how long they'd been together, I remembered the two of them at that dinner, remembered that I'd once caught a glimpse of him as a human being with a normal life. It was easy to imagine him hiding in some underground lair during daylight and manifesting himself only in pubs and newspaper offices once dusk had fallen. The idea of him having once walked somebody up the aisle was genuinely jarring.

Other than that night at the university, I had only ever met him once before, at some press reception in Edinburgh, for what I can't remember. Emboldened, I must confess, by a glass of wine too many, I walked over and took him to task over something he'd written in his column that I was convinced – and remain so – was a deliberate dig at something I had published a few days previously. His rant was arrogantly disparaging the idea that religion was concerned with pondering the mysteries of the universe. 'Dark matter,' he wrote. 'Only thirteen per cent of the mass of the universe is accounted for. Nearly nine tenths is made up of something that we not only can't see, but can't detect at all because it might even be made of a different species of matter from the kind we comprehend. *That's* a mystery of the universe that truly intelligent people are pondering, and it's a bit more involved than doing the Alpha Course.'

My own column, needless to say, had espoused the merits of this highly commendable Christian philosophical initiative.

'Billions of people around this planet believe in God,' I told him, trying to wipe the smirk off his face. 'A great many of them far more intelligent than you. Brilliant minds, some of the greatest of our age, and of ages before, share this belief. Isn't it incredibly arrogant to say they are *all* just wrong and you're right?'

It was at this point that the limitations of alcohol in emboldening one for debate revealed themselves; viz, the drink convinces you that your say will, in one sally, silence your opponent. I now know only a faulty double-glazing unit could silence Jack Parlabane.

'First,' he said, 'billions of people have probably not even *thought* about it, but they're counted as believers by default. You have to opt out of belief in God, when instead it should be a conscious opt-in. But to answer your question, millions of people once believed in Zeus, Cronus, Poseidon, and yet you don't. Why not? Minds as great as Aristotle and Socrates believed in these gods. Isn't it incredibly arrogant to say that they were wrong and you were right? See, you're an atheist too, Jillian – there's loads of gods you don't believe in. I just happen to believe in one fewer than you. If you ever stop and ask yourself why you don't believe in all the others, then you might start to understand why I don't believe in *any*.'

As I said, I didn't like the man one bit.

But while reading about his widow may have jarred me into thinking of him as a person, that was nothing compared to the jolt I received when I went into the office and found that he had sent me an email only hours before his death.

Einstein once said, 'God doesn't play with dice.' I don't believe in coincidence, even less so when someone like Jack Parlabane is involved. Thus there was more than mere morbid curiosity at play as I read what must have been among his final words.

The email had no greeting, formal or informal. It listed three names, all female, next to mobile telephone numbers. The names were Melanie Alderton, Catherine Selby and Juliet McLair.

'From one hack to another,' it said, 'your sources are unreliable. Here's some new ones. Ask Melanie why she was fired from Project Lamda. Then ask Catherine and Juliet about Project Lamda Revisited.'

I'm pretty sure that if Parlabane hadn't just died, I'd have ignored and instantly deleted it, but the circumstances imbued his message with portent. I didn't feel I owed him anything, but I somehow felt obliged to honour what could well have been his last request. If nothing else, there was bound to be a story in it of some kind.

My sense of honour and decency notwithstanding, even as I reached for the phone I knew I was going to regret doing this. I just couldn't possibly have envisaged how much.

I spoke first to Melanie, as suggested. She wasn't expecting my call and evidently hadn't been primed. She didn't mention Parlabane and therefore gave no indication of knowing he was dead. I wasn't sure it was my place to break it to her, so left her to find out through other channels. She told me she had been fired from Project Lamda, as I already knew, for leaving a cupboard unlocked and thus potentially compromising the security of the project protocol.

'I understood why I was fired,' she said. 'Even though the security wasn't actually breached. But what I didn't understand was why I wasn't warned. I had left the store cupboard open before, and Mr Mather had seen me leave it unlocked. I had even seen him go back and forth from it without locking it himself. Then all of a sudden, one day, he goes nuts and kicks me off the project.'

It did seem puzzlingly inconsistent, but I didn't follow the significance it was supposed by Parlabane to hold. Not until I spoke to Catherine and Juliet.

I had to leave the building and take a walk around the block before I could gather myself sufficiently to call Gabriel. Upon first hearing it, it was a shocking notion, but as I took the air and calmed my thinking, I began to see more clearly. There was no proof of Parlabane's theory about Gabriel and Mather being partners or using hidden transmitters: only a half-baked and ultimately abandoned stunt, by the sound of it. Neither Catherine nor Juliet said they saw this hidden microphone or earpiece or whatever; they merely witnessed Parlabane grandstanding with some typically profane illustrations.

However, they had both sounded very convinced and not a little angry about having been 'used', as they each put it, and in that I caught a glimpse of where I'd be left if it turned out Parlabane was right. I was extremely keen to hear what Gabriel had to say about it, and surprised he hadn't been on the phone yet to let off steam. I grabbed a very large latte on my walk, found a quiet corner of the coffee shop and called him up.

'Jillian,' he said, sounding uncharacteristically downbeat. 'Howya. I take it you've heard?'

'About Parlabane?' I said.

'Yeah. Goddamn shame. I mean, safe to say we didn't see eye-to-eye . . .'

'Me neither.'

'But the poor son-of-a-bitch, seriously. With his wife looking on, too. It's just . . . horrible. And the worst thing is, I think I saw this but I couldn't warn him.'

'You saw this?'

'Yeah, I mean, one time when we were talking, I saw it. There's this line, this membrane between the world of the living and the world of the dead, and sometimes I can see where people are in relation to it. I'd seldom seen anybody who seemed so close to it. I thought it was because of something else, something dark in his past: killers appear real close to the line, but then so do doctors.'

'His wife is a doctor.'

'Yeah, I know. That probably clouded it too, and I guess I misinterpreted it. What I was seeing was that he was actually close to dying.'

'Well, the reason I'm calling is that it seems in this case you're not the only one receiving messages from the dead.'

'Excuse me?'

'I got an email from Parlabane this morning, sent yesterday. He gave me the numbers of three students who had been assisting on Project Lamda. Melanie, Catherine and Juliet. I called them. And on the late Mr Parlabane's valedictory suggestion, I asked the latter pair about what the email called Project Lamda Revisited.'

There was a very long silence on the other end of the phone. I heard him sigh, heard the muffling crackle of a hand covering the mouthpiece.

'Gabriel?' I said.

'Yeah, shit, sorry,' he resumed. 'Well, it's a crock, believe me. Parlabane's got them all dancing on his strings. I hate to speak ill of the dead when he ain't even buried yet, but the guy just couldn't accept what happened at Project Lamda, couldn't accept that his prejudices were proven wrong. He cooked up this lame theory, something that would explain it all in a way he could deal with. It says it all that it took him so long to come up with something, really.'

'What about this girl, Melanie? She says—'

'She's lying. She was shit-canned from the project, so she was the obvious and easiest person for Parlabane to recruit. The other two I'm more disappointed with. I thought they were smarter than that. Thought they had more integrity, you know?'

His words hung unanswered, echoing through my head. Gabriel's point about Melanie was a strong one, except she hadn't mentioned Parlabane, let alone the idea that Mather had fired her to create a *façade* of integrity. I'm not claiming to have a sixth sense about these things – just a couple of decades of a journalist's experience – but I didn't get the feeling she was lying to me. And for the first time, I was starting to fear Gabriel might be.

'Were they right, Gabriel?' I asked, attempting to keep a slight tremble from my voice, trying not to think of what I might be flushing away here. 'Are you and Easy in this together?'

He sighed, his breath crackling on the line.

'Jesus, Jillian, *no*. Of course not. Look, can I call you back? This ain't a good time. I'm kind of in the middle of something here. Something real big.'

'Okay,' I said.

He promised once again that he'd call me back, then hung up.

I finished my coffee slowly, then walked back to the office in a bit of a daze. I kept glimpsing snapshot visions of what this could all mean for the Chair and for Lemuel, not to mention my career and reputation, but some psychological censor kept shutting them down before I could really examine them. Part of me imagined that not only would Gabriel not call back, but that we might well never talk again.

I leapt to answer each time my phone rang, but each time it was other people discussing matters that I was aware I was barely taking in.

I didn't get a lot done, but it seemed nonetheless a very long day. Then, just as I was getting ready to go home, my mobile chimed and my heart quickened as I saw Gabriel's name appear on the display.

'Look, I'm sorry I had to cut you off before. Something real big has happened, something massive.'

'What is it?'

'I can't talk about it over the phone, specially not a cellular. But it's huge, and I want you to be in on it before anybody else. Can you meet me first thing tomorrow?'

'Can I . . . yes, sure,' I stumbled.

'I can't reiterate how confidential this is at this stage, okay? You can't tell anybody where you're going or who you're meeting.'

'Sounds very Woodward and Bernstein,' I mused, excited.

'Believe me, those two never got an exclusive like this.'

Two of the most disturbing phone calls I was ever party to – outside of my dad's death and Keith on the wind-up when he was pissed – occurred within a matter of hours on the same day. They happened in reverse order, the slightly less disturbing first. My mobile rang while I was sitting in Mum's car, stuck in the permanent jam that is Great Western Road. She was down to stay the weekend again, the second time in as many weeks. We were kind of making up for lost time. Things were defrosting between us, but you couldn't go as far as to say we had settled

311

our differences. We were simply avoiding the issue, something accomplished more easily amid the distraction of having a common enemy to worry about. I was still refusing to accept her cheques, but had bowed to her demands that I let her buy some new bed linen for the flat on the inarguable grounds that she wasn't sleeping another night on the manky and frayed efforts the place boasted at present. Boasted? Grovellingly apologised for, more like. We were on our way back from John Lewis in the town when the call came in. I didn't recognise the number, or the voice when I answered.

'Hullo. Izzat . . . eh . . . Michael?'

'Yeah.'

'Aye. Eh . . . listen. It's Spammy here. We met yesterday. Reason I'm callin', I couldnae get Jack and I need somebody tae take a wee look at this. It's fair freakin' me oot, man. I dunno whit's the score wi' Parlabane. Landline's permanently engaged and there's just voicemail on his mobile. It's no' like him at all. Anyway, can ye get ower tae Paisley? I need confirmation that ma heid's not on upside doon.'

I decided that petrol expenses would not count as accepting my mum's ill-gotten gains and asked if she could hit the Clyde Tunnel.

On the way over, I rang Jack. Spammy was right. Landline engaged, no reply on the mobile.

Spammy answered the door in what, going by what Jack told me, must have been record time. I'd been informed that him expecting you didn't necessarily mean he was particularly primed to respond to you actually showing up, but in this case it seemed he was genuinely anxious to see us. I realise it would be redundant to mention that he looked pale; I got the impression Spammy wasn't someone who ever caught a lot of UVs if he could possibly help it. However, even allowing for that, he looked notably colourless, and seemed restlessly animated in vast contrast to our brief meeting yesterday and in utter contradiction of all Parlabane's descriptions.

He led us anxiously to the studio's control room, where several computer monitors were haphazardly perched above banks upon banks of switches, dials, slides, junctions and a veritable vermicelli of wire and cable. My natural inclination to geek out over the cornucopia of technology was on this occasion tempered by an intimidating impression of chaos and a configuration – like some advanced theory of mathematics – that only made sense inside one gifted but slightly insane individual's mind. It was tempered further by the unmistakable awareness that Spammy was extremely spooked.

'Noo, just tae confirm, so I'm no' just confusin' masel: this wummin on the BBC tape, she's deid? Definitely deid?'

'Yes,' I told him.

'At the time the other recording was made?'

'It was six months after her death, yes.'

Spammy sighed. 'Fuck, man. Scary biscuits. Check this oot.'

He indicated one of the monitors, which showed two multi-coloured patterns of lines, each a visualisation of a digitised sound pattern.

'The one on the left is the BBC one, by the way, and the one on the right the Glassford Hall recording, all cleaned up. I've been comparing them all night, havenae been tae ma bed. I've isolated different frequencies, modulations, put them through all kinds of filters, blown stuff up, compressed samples doon. Problem is, this isnae really my game, you know? I thought spot-the-difference would be nae tosh, but I was strugglin'. Started tae think I must be missin' somethin'. Even double-checked I hadnae been a daft tool and fed in two samples fae the wan source, but naw.

'So, cut a long story short, I got on tae a mate oot in Singapore that works in security. He fired me this piece of software doon the line: state-of-the-art voice authentication, slightly amended tae turn aff the anti-spoofing.'

'Anti-spoofing?' Mum asked.

'Aye, it tests for liveness, tae defend against folk using a recording of somebody's voice. Obviously that's nae good because these are baith recorded sources. Anyway, I programmed it tae require the BBC voice, but turned aff specific phrasing, so it's no' lookin' for a particular sentence. Watch that monitor on the right.'

We looked. It showed a 3D padlock animation above the words: 'Awaiting authentication'. Spammy picked up a mouse and clicked on a triangular Play icon on the first monitor. Hilda

Lemuel's voice boomed from what seemed to be all directions, coming from a plethora of speakers. 'And as together we demand justice for Africa, we're very honoured to be able to welcome . . .' she said, before Spammy cut her off.

The padlock opened. Spammy reset it.

'Awaiting authentication', it stated again.

Spammy clicked on the Play icon beneath the other source. The speakers boomed once more.

'I'm not cold . . . I'm not lost.'

I felt a shiver run through me like nothing I'd felt before.

Up on its screen, the padlock opened.

I looked at my mum. Her eyes were wide. I could tell she was trembling.

There was one of those DVD layer-transition moments, everything on hold for a few secs.

'It's the same voice,' Spammy said.

Gabriel gave me the address for the rendezvous and some directions. I'd expected it to be somewhere in town, or maybe even across in Edinburgh, but instead he'd asked me to drive out to a hotel in the Trossachs, near to Port of Menteith. It took me a little over an hour. When I got there, I assumed he'd made a mistake or I'd misheard his directions. The hotel in question, down a single-track lane through some dense and, today, rain-sodden woods, turned out to be closed, and not just for the season. It looked fairly dilapidated, the windows grey and lightless, though not boarded up, as presumably there wasn't much in the way of casual vandalism out in the middle of nowhere.

I approached slowly, not trusting my car's axles with the depths that might be hidden beneath some of the vast puddles on the narrow track. I was planning to park and call Gabriel on his mobile to ask for new directions when I saw that there was another car sitting outside the hotel, tucked away almost out of sight of the approach road. It was a black Mercedes, which further confused me, as Gabriel has a Bentley. It flashed its headlights by way of acknowledgement, then I saw Gabriel get out of the driver's seat and beckon me across, indicating the passenger side.

I parked in the nearest space not overgrown with bushes, and ran the short distance to the Mercedes, pulling my jacket over my head and trying not to think about what was happening to my shoes. I pulled open the door and climbed inside. We both laughed at the intensity of the downpour and how wet I'd got inside just a few paces.

'You okay?' he asked. 'Sorry about the cloak-and-dagger stuff. It's just that—'

Which was when I sensed movement behind me and felt the needle pierce the side of my neck. I turned around, glimpsing Mather where he had materialised in the back seat, a hypodermic syringe in his fingers, then Gabriel leaned across and pinned me to the seat, facing forward, until I lost consciousness.

When I came round – the second time, that is – the pain was a constant dull throb. I told myself it was dull, tried not to concentrate on it, tried not to look down, but I was aware of the damp touch of cold blood beneath my bare foot on the concrete floor. With that came snatches of the real pain, the pain I'd felt when he did it and the pain still coursing through me but which some merciful mechanism of my brain was striving to mute.

If only it could do something about the fear.

I'm so scared of dying; dying here, in this dank and desolate wreck with its smell of damp and rodents, never seeing Dominic again, never going home again. I want to go home. I don't want to die.

But that's only half the fear.

There's a chance, a tiny chance; maybe only a chance to *give* myself a chance. The longer I live, the longer I hold out, the greater the possibility – though perhaps not much greater than zero – that someone will find me. And therein lies the other part of the fear. I don't want to die, but nor am I sure I can pay the price it will cost to keep myself alive.

I was still tied to the chair, hands behind my back and my bare ankles lashed to the front legs.

That's how I found myself the first time I came round. I was actually quite calm, initially, but that was just the after-effects of the drug. I was too woozy at first to understand the situation; I remember thinking I must have been restrained to stop me falling off this chair, like it had been a considerate thing for someone to have done. Then my faculties began to restore themselves. What really brought me to was the feel of the cold concrete underfoot. What had happened to my shoes? I wondered. I didn't remember taking them off. Did they fall off while I was drugged?

Then I saw the bolt-cutter lying a few feet away on the floor.

The throb has a sharpness through it every few pulses. I couldn't afford to think about that. I looked up at the ceiling, cracked and bubbled, lit by one bare dangling bulb. I didn't want to catch a glimpse of the blood on the floor, see how far it may have spread. But from the corner of my eye I could see the blue shape that I knew was my jacket, lying only feet away. I'd watched him remove my mobile from inside and drop the garment carelessly on the floor beside me. I turned my head and noticed that my Dictaphone had slid most of the way out of the side pocket. It was just resting on the cloth, having been jolted free when the jacket hit the ground.

I hadn't heard any sounds for some time. I didn't know if he was still in the building or not. He was leaving me to stew in my own sweat, fear and urine, that much I was sure of. But how far away was he? Would he hear me if I tried this? The last thing I wanted was to bring him back into the room. I tried to recall whether I had heard a car driving off. No, I'd have remembered that. But I had been passed out from the shock and pain: how long I didn't know.

I couldn't hear anything, just the occasional call of birds and the constant sound of rain. I had screamed as loud as ever in my life tonight, but it had been swallowed up by the peeling walls, the rain, the trees and the night. Nobody could hear me, nobody but him if he was near. I wasn't going to be rescued. That didn't mean I would just give him what he wanted when he came back, because to do that would be the end. But deep down I understood the end was inevitable. Nobody knew I was here, or who I was with. I'd done as I was told, fool that I am. Biggest fool in the world that I am.

There was only one thing I could still do. It wouldn't save me, but I needed to feel I was fighting back, needed to give myself something else to hold on to now that hope was dying.

This was going to hurt, I knew, but all pain is relative, and I had just had my scale brutally recalibrated.

I shook the chair, shifting my balance, pushing against the floor with my good foot and applying as much pressure as I could tolerate with the other. Every inch was agony, coupled with the jolt of fear I felt as every movement of the chair reverberated around the bare walls. If he was next door, he'd be in to investigate immediately, especially when he heard . . . *this*.

I saw a flash of white and felt a wave of pain pass through me from my shoulder, right down my side and then, like the tail of a whip, in my injured foot. I had tipped the chair sideways and was now lying on the hard floor next to the jacket. Contorting myself as far as my bonds and my muscles would allow, my fingers reached the cloth and pulled it between them like a sewing machine until they touched the cold metal of the Dictaphone.

It took a few fumbling attempts, but I managed to start it recording, then nudged it back out of sight into the pocket. I started speaking, telling my story to the bare walls and the tiny device. Let everyone hear this. Please God, let *someone* hear this.

'She sounds so scared,' Spammy said.

Undisguised and undistorted by the sound of wind and background noises from the room at Glassford Hall, the voice on the recording did not sound mysterious or ethereal. It simply sounded like a terrified woman, drawing upon whatever courage she had left to hold herself together and get her words out without choking.

'It's horrible,' Mum said. She stood staring at the digitised pattern as Spammy played back more samples. When you're only listening to a sound, it's hard to know where to look.

Her mobile rang, its melodic tone a welcome, incongruous jolt out of our disquieting contemplations. Or so I thought until she answered it.

She didn't speak at first, other than a couple of muttered 'yes' acknowledgments. Then, as she listened, I could see in her eyes that it was something dreadful.

'Oh my God,' she said. 'Oh my God.'

I saw her physically shake, eyes filling. Her fingers whitened as their grip grew harder and harder, threatening to break the mobile at its clamshell hinge. She swallowed and held the phone to her chest as she met my anxiously impatient gaze.

'Parlabane,' she said, a tremble in her voice.

'What's happened?' I asked.

She sat down on the room's only seat, a stool tucked just under the mixing desk.

'It's bad,' she told us. 'It's very, very bad.'

# Dead man talking

The big questions remain.

Is there an afterlife?

A heaven?

A hell?

An eternity of walking the earth as a formless vapour with nobody to talk to except Gordon Smith 'the psychic barber' and Derek fucking Acorah? Sub-questions: While walking the earth, can you hang out in cute lassies' bedrooms? Can you turn up at mediumship demonstrations and communicate: 'Derek, you're a wanker' or 'Gordon, you're a lying fud'?

Well, this just in: the answer to all but the sub-questions is no, according to all reliable data. (Though do feel free to have a go at the Derek and Gordon bits; you don't even need to be dead.)

That's what all the evidence says: no.

Sorry.

Contradictory evidence may yet come to light some day, but for now, the verdict is, I say again, no.

Just accept it.

However, that being the case, a smaller question remains: where did *I* end up after the window fall?

Allow me to describe. I'm somewhere bright, somewhere high. When I look down, I can see people obliviously going about their business. It's fragrant here, rather small, but comfortable and cheery, if a little on the girly-girly side for my tastes. Sarah might have liked it, if she was about fifteen or twenty years younger. It's not heaven, and it's certainly not hell, but I am dead. I know that for sure: I've read it in the paper.

I said the answer to all but the sub-questions was no. You *can* hang out in cute lassies' bedrooms, and like the Derek and Gordon bits, you don't have to be dead. I'm in Laura Bailey's bedroom. However, she's not about to breeze in and start blithely undressing with no heed to my presence, which is just as well, because if Sarah walked in on a scene like that, I really would end up dead.

I did warn you.

*Yes, it's amusing just how wrong a person can be, and just as funny how gullible. But as you will learn,* anybody *can be fooled, especially if they place too much trust in a single human source rather than objectively evaluating the data.*

Remember that?

Now, don't get huffy. I never lied. I may have misled, but I never outright lied. You can check. Just bear in mind what a little change of perspective does to the same information, the same story, same words.

A body did fall from that window, plunging four storeys behind a sabotaged double-glazing unit. It just wasn't mine. Or even animate.


'For Christ's sake, be careful,' Sarah said.

'Don't worry,' I said. 'These things tilt right over. Wait and I'll show you . . .'

I had my hands on the switches that released the safety catch and was just about to flip them when the phone rang. I was going to proceed anyway and let Sarah answer it, but she said, 'That'll be for you,' with a weariness, borne of many years a journalist's wife, that told me she had no intention of playing the receptionist yet again.

I let go of the window and walked to the hall to pick up the nearest handset. Sarah was right. It was for me. It was Dr Melissa Argenta from the Psychology department at Reed University, CA. She had been teaching a class when I phoned, but rang back immediately she got the message, such was her intrigue at learning Mather was passing himself off as a university-accredited scientist.

'Easy came to us through the Las Almeitos outreach programme,' she told me. 'A lot of these guys don't hang around long past parole, but he did. He was good, highly gifted around a circuit board, I can tell you that. But he held no position higher than lab tech, and he most certainly doesn't have a degree from here. I'm sure he could have had, as he was smart enough, but no.'

'He's also claiming to have carried out parapsychology research work,' I informed her, walking into the living room. 'Through which he discovered the abilities of one Gabriel Lafayette, a psychic from New Orleans.'

'Hmm,' she said. 'Also not true, but not entirely false. I believe you were trying to get in touch with a former colleague of mine, Karl Creedy. That's who you would have been best to talk to about this. It was Karl who had an interest in parapsychology. He'd kinda sidelined in it here at Reed for years. An evenings-and-weekends thing, mostly, as opposed to something he was going to get away with spending department funding on.' She said this last with a small chuckle.

'I got you,' I said.

'I mean, he published one or two papers, but not the sort of thing to make a splash for the simple reason that they were largely about protocols.'

'I've read extracts.'

'Then you'll know nothing ever "happened". No psychic feats were performed. Nobody slipped anything past Karl. Easy was interested in the field too, and helped out on quite a few experiments. From what Karl said, Easy was pretty adept at anticipating how cheating could occur. Not entirely surprising, I guess, given that he was a convicted fraudster. Good guy to have on the team.'

'But he wasn't leading the team?'

'Goodness, no. I imagine he was allowed a little more autonomy as time went on, but it would always have been Karl's show. As far as I'm aware, this Lafayette was never tested in any way that came under the official auspices of the university. Easy may have carried out some work on campus premises, and might even have used Karl Creedy's protocols, but it wasn't supervised by Karl, I know that for a fact. It would be down in black and white if it had been.'

'Do you have a number for Karl Creedy? Where is he working now?'

Sarah was staring quizzically at the window, trying to work out how this flip-rotation mechanism worked.

'Oh no,' Dr Argenta said. 'I'm sorry. Karl's dead. Must be five years now. God, is it that long already? Sorely missed, too.'

'I'm sorry. Five years, you say?'

Sarah slid the window up a few inches, exposing the safety catches again.

'That's how I know for sure he never worked with Lafayette. The department's official parapsychology interests effectively ended with Karl's death. Anything Easy might have done after that would have been just amateur dabbling.'

I thought of Niall Blake, another man who had stood in the way of Mather having free rein to play the scientist on a university campus. 'How did he die, if you don't mind me asking?'

'Oh, it was an accident, a stupid, tragic accident. He fell out of his apartment window. Or rather, the report said the *window* fell right out while he was cleaning it. There was some paint . . .'

I didn't hear the rest, as I dropped the phone and hauled Sarah back from the pane.

'Stay away from the window, please, honey,' I said, as calmly as I could manage.

I thought of Mather, his relaxed, seemingly resigned expression at dinner when it seemed Blake would prove intractable. He had already taken the matter in hand with a little joinery work. It might not happen for a day or a week or a month, but he knew it would happen. Lafayette's machinations were merely aimed at getting the chair established; its uninhibited and unscrutinised autonomy would require Blake being removed permanently.

I told Dr Argenta I'd phone her back, and that the LAPD might be calling too. Then I called Larry again.

'This known associate of Mather's,' I asked him, 'the guy who died at home. What did he die of?'

'Jake Salter. Gimme a minute,' Larry said. I heard him put the receiver down on the desk and the rustle of papers, then a couple of booms as drawers were opened and closed.

'Carbon monoxide poisoning,' Larry read. 'Guy's water-heater malfunctioned.'

'Dislodged bird's nest in the flue blocked the vents,' I said.

'Shit, Jack,' Larry spluttered. 'How the hell did you know that?'

'I've been hanging out with psychics.'

I picked up my mobile again from the spare room I was using as a makeshift office. I needed to let Michael know.

I had switched the phone to voicemail while I was on to Larry the first time because I didn't want any interruptions. It looked like Spammy had been trying to get me. I'd call him in a minute, but I had to talk to Michael first. No. Moira. I should tell her instead. Learning that your two dead friends were actually murdered and that the intended target was really yourself was something that might best be broken by your mammy rather than some shifty hack.

I called her, gave her it as concisely as I could. I heard the tremble in her voice as the facts hit home, anger no doubt mixing with a revisitation of all the fear, relief, guilt and confusion she must have felt before. She sounded muffled as she spoke to someone else.

'Parlabane,' I heard her relay. 'It's bad. It's very, very bad.'

Then she spoke into the mobile again: 'You'd better get over here. We're at the studio with Spammy. We've got some rather disturbing news for you ourselves.'

'There are two possible explanations for why Hilda Lemuel's voice is on that recording,' Mum said.

My anger was not *yet* uncontainable. I felt like a collapsing star, this super-compression taking place inside me as Mum told me what Parlabane had discovered. I knew that the tightening, the inward motion, had to be finite, and after that my rage would go supernova. The real anger was yet to explode, and I was afraid of what it would do to me and anything in my path.

'I'll rephrase that: there are two *alternative* explanations for why Hilda Lemuel's voice is on that recording, but only one of them is possible. And that is that she was still alive when the original recording was made. Mather and Lafayette abducted her, interrogated her to procure details known only to herself and her husband, then recorded her saying the phrases they needed. After that they murdered her, almost certainly by drowning, before dumping her body in the river. Then, six months later, they put on one hell of a show at Glassford Hall.'

'Now that's what I call a long con,' said Parlabane.

'Not to mention high-yield,' Mum resumed. 'Lemuel was known to be supportive of paranormal practice and research, and doled out plenty of money accordingly, but through this they snagged him almost exclusively as a kind of super-patron. Lemuel was always credulous of this stuff, so he must have thought Lafayette was a colossus in the field. Lafayette and Mather knew the Glassford Hall story itself would be a powerful springboard for launching Lafayette in the UK, but having the money and clout of Lemuel behind them has allowed them to scale unprecedented heights.'

'How did they know about him?' Parlabane asked. 'I didn't think Lemuel had much of a profile outside the UK.'

'If he's into woo and he gives out money, his name will be well known in woo circles. Just like they trade details on regular sitters. In the Noble book, Lemuel himself talks about being inundated by charlatans, especially after his wife died. But fortunately he had by this time met the nice Mr Lafayette, who was able to warn him off and win his trust by telling him how his competitors worked their scams.'

'And the beauty of it is that Lemuel had no idea their paths had crossed until well after Hilda's death,' Parlabane suggested. 'Though I'd be sure if the cops contacted their colleagues at Immigration, they'd find some interesting dates of entry into the UK for one Grady Lappin and one Edward Charles.'

'Unfortunately, that's about as much as the cops *would* find all this time later,' Mum said. 'This recording, of itself, proves little. We've no way of proving that it was in their possession, let alone what means we believe they used to play it at Glassford Hall.'

'We've nothing but motives and conjecture to tie them to any of these domestic "accidents", either.'

I felt the anger surge again as Parlabane alluded to the night my friends had died instead of me. I'd been distressed enough by the thought that only chance had put Grant in the flat in my stead, but knowing it had been murder and I was the target brought it all back tenfold. And the worst of it, the thing that was really creating my own internal neutron star was the fact that the fuckers had got away clean.

I recalled Lafayette's phoney reading of me at the Randall

Building. He knew all about it, even the dead bird. I'll admit that part had me spooked and reeling, but once I had composed myself again I simply assumed he had somehow found out about the gas engineer's findings. It could have been in the local press or even circulating around campus for all I knew. Guys like Lafayette thrive on finding out details you assume they couldn't know, but thinking back now, maybe the bastard just got cocky.

My mum taught me psychics can't resist showing off if they've got a particularly juicy piece of information to put to use. Stanislav Hoffman one night learned from an assistant on stage that Bruce Lee had just died. He knew the audience couldn't have heard this, so he came over all faint and told the audience he'd received a terrible feeling that something had happened to Bruce Lee. Next morning he was a prophet as well as a psychic. However, the same stunt backfired on him years later in London when he heard something on the radio about a plane crash near Paris. He was meeting with two French journalists who were imminently returning to that very city. He told them not to travel by plane because he'd had a premonition of a crash. Unfortunately for him, it was yesterday's news, even appearing in that morning's papers.

Had Lafayette dropped a bollock and I just didn't spot it? I recalled Mather's response. He'd looked rattled; I had assumed this was because he was in awe of the psychic's powers. Was this merely part of the act, or was he genuinely dismayed that his partner had thrown in such a detail?

I'd never know, because it didn't matter. Lafayette might have surprised and annoyed Mather by using it, but he wasn't taking a risk. The fact about the bird was in the engineer's report, and there was no way of proving Lafayette hadn't seen it. As I just mentioned, sourcing supposedly controlled information is the psychic's stock-in-trade.

'We've got nothing,' I said bitterly. I knew my mum sensed the extent of my fury because she put a hand round my waist the way she had when I was losing it as a kid. Her own anger was just as great, but she had always been better at channelling it towards constructive use. I could tell that that was what she was doing right then, in fact. Her eyes narrowed in concentration but weren't focused on anything or anyone. In a moment, she'd either sigh with frustration or nod to herself.

Her eyes twinkled just a little and alighted on Parlabane.

'Your window was definitely rigged?' she asked.

'Aye. I attached some climbing cord to support it and had a wee look. There's incredible weight on the thing. The way it pivots, the bottom would have come up and chopped me around the thighs, flipped me right out.'

'But it's still in place, so as far as they could see if they passed by to check, it hasn't been touched.'

'No. They think either I've not noticed the mess or I'm a manky bastard who cannae be arsed cleaning it. Why?'

Mum nodded to herself.

'One thing that's consistent about mediums,' she said, 'is that they don't share their poor dupes' daft beliefs. They're the ones putting on the show, so they above all know it's not real. But in this world, anybody can be fooled, and I think I know how we could make Gabriel Lafayette a true believer.'

'I'm listening,' said Parlabane, intrigued.

'The man has spent half his life pretending to talk to dead people. I'm betting he'd shit blood if he thought it was happening for real.'

Parlabane grinned with the darkest relish. It was genuinely disturbing.

'I'll need to call in a few favours,' he said, 'But your wish will be my command: I'll make sure the bastard shits himself.'

'And I'll make sure he bleeds,' I added.

So that's us up to speed: why I found myself hanging out in Laura Bailey's bedroom. I had to stay out of sight all day, what with everybody thinking I'd snuffed it thanks to the papers running the story. Ursula Lomas was the police source: the cops were in on it entirely. I called in a favour from my old mate Fraz, who's now at the *Evening Times* in Glasgow. He was informed the story was shite but got promised an exclusive if this came off. So far it had worked a charm. All it had taken was the last edition of the evening paper to run it for the morning dailies to pick it up. Shamelessly egotistical I know, but I couldn't resist asking Laura to get me copies of all of them. If nothing else, it served as a quick-reference guide to which news editors I was on good or bad terms with merely from which photo they'd chosen to illustrate the piece.

I felt a bit like the star in his dressing room before a command performance: everybody else has been running about making preparations for the show, but I can't emerge until the curtain rises and the audience is ready for me. Michael was dressing the set; Spammy was soldering circuits and preparing some of the visual effects; Moira was polishing the script; and Laura was dealing with the rider, which for this show included a jar of hydrofluoric acid.

The hardest thing was being away from Sarah at a time like this. She was already playing her own part, that of the shocked and grieving widow. I was aware of how that must feel very creepy for her, not to mention the irrational fear she might have of tempting fate, so I estimated she could probably use a hug. The last I saw of her was just before I released the ropes and let the window and the dummy fall. After that, with the police and an ambulance on stand-by round the corner, I knew there would be a wee circus at the front door, allowing me to smuggle myself out through the back close and into Moira's waiting woo-funded BMW.

'For Christ's sake, be careful,' Sarah said, before I let the rigged apparatus drop and swiftly made my exit. Remember I mentioned a more simple and prosaic explanation for that particular feeling of *déjà vu*? There you go: I really *had* experienced the whole thing before.

It was only three o'clock, but it was almost dark already. It had rained so hard all day, it was only by comparison that you could talk about light. My mobile rang: Moira. We were set.

The cops had been watching Lafayette since last night, after I spoke to Ursula. Checks with Immigration found that passports bearing the names Grady Lappin and Edward Charles entered the UK a fortnight before Hilda Lemuel's death, and departed again the same day as her body was found. The polis would be on the look-out for Mather too, but he hadn't been at his flat overnight.

The work had started as soon as Lafayette left home. He was

327

renting an undeservedly well-appointed main-door flat in Dowanhill, probably paid for by the Spiritual Science Chair. Woo merchants never put their hands in their pockets if they could possibly avoid it. The polis had got on to the landlord and obtained a set of keys, allowing Moira and her charges to get busy. The cops were less proficient with regard to tailing the bastard. He drove his car – one of those hideous new Bentley 'sport' pound-sign-with-wheels vulgarities – into an underground car park, but wasn't picked up on foot leaving the place. It was speculated that he had switched cars, though Moira was sure it wasn't because the tail had been sussed. She guessed it was something he often did, as well as probably disguising himself too: he had to be unrecognisable if he was out divining information for future amazing feats.

There was a plain-clothes cop at the underground car park under orders to give us a bell if he saw the Bentley leave again.

Ursula drove me to Dowanhill, briefing me on the dos and don'ts. Jenny had diplomatically neglected to tell her enough about me for her to realise this was futile; either that or Ursula was merely covering her own liability with a 'don't come running to me' admonition.

I walked inside and did a technical once-over with Michael and Spammy. We did well to get through it without laughing. It was all extremely silly, but thus came into the category of fighting fire with fire. They'd started it, after all.

Ursula phoned my mobile. She had been up to high doh over the whole thing, anxious that we should get a result and nervous about ever having to explain to her superiors just what the hell we thought we were doing in the event that we failed. Nonetheless, she saw the ridiculous side too.

'Bentley's just left the car park,' she said. 'This is your Act One beginners' call.'

The silence, the waiting, is a torture in itself. This eternity he's granted me to contemplate this most hideous of dilemmas: accept my death or prolong my life through pain. *Such* pain, dispensed so dispassionately that I am under no illusions that mercy, disgust or even boredom would rein in its duration. Such pain.

It was when I saw the bolt-cutters that I understood everything, too late.

I didn't need his explanation. I was way ahead of his words by that time.

Port of Menteith. The Trossachs. Less than an hour from Glasgow. Less than an hour from Glassford Hall. This was where they'd taken her.

*I have absolute faith that I will be waiting for a 'rational' explanation of what happened next until the day I die.* My own words, my own book.

'I need you to tell me some secrets, Jillian,' Mather said. 'Things that only you and Dominic would know. Little nicknames, perhaps.'

I broke down at that point. It was when he said Dominic's name, and I remembered Bryant's helpless, naked grief exposed by Hilda's voice as she mentioned that shared private nickname for their honeymoon suite.

I shook my head. My throat was constricted, but I managed to spit out the word: 'No.'

He just shrugged, like he didn't expect it to be straightforward.

'This part was easier with Mrs Lemuel because she thought it was a kidnap,' he told me. 'She thought we needed the details for verification and thought that cooperating would help get her out. From your response, I can tell you have grasped otherwise. I knew you would: you're a smart lady, Jillian. That's why you don't have any shoes.'

He lifted the bolt-cutters from the floor and walked closer to where I sat, lashed to the chair.

'We decided it would be most plausible if Hilda drowned. This meant she couldn't be otherwise damaged without raising suspicion, but as I said, she thought she had reason to cooperate. You don't. Not yet.'

He pulled open the bolt-cutters. I felt metal brush my skin and instinctively tried to leap away, but all I could do was squirm, trying to curl my toes under themselves.

'You're going to have an automobile accident. There are a lot of plausible random injuries that searing metal could inflict in the course of a car crash. And afterwards there'll be fire, to cover up whatever you make it necessary for me to do to you.'

He slid the pincers sideways between my big toe and the one next to it, the ends reaching almost halfway along my foot.

'I don't have to do this. We can do it the easy way.' He smiled at the pun, like we were talking over coffee. 'And look on the bright side. You'll get your wish that your husband should become more open-minded to these matters. You'll convince him far better dead than your living efforts have achieved, and play your part in opening the minds of a whole generation of Scottish kids. So, let's take the civilised route. You tell us what we need to know, and you give us the performance we need for the microphone, and I'll make sure it's quick and painless. A lethal injection. Exactly like in the car, you'll just slip away.'

I closed my eyes and cried.

'What do you say?'

I clamped my lips together and shook my head.

The first thing Lafayette did upon returning home to his flat was have a long, hot shower. This was a course of action we had both anticipated and were counting on, but unlike our subject, we hadn't based this prediction of his behaviour on any prior observation or clandestine research. Rather, it was a guaranteed response to his being pelted with eggs by Laura the moment he got out of his car. She had been waiting in ambush, and lobbed several at him with maximum ferocity while screaming: 'You're a creep, Lafayette. You're a lying, cheating, fucking creep.' This done, she feigned bursting into tears and ran off, leaving him dripping, gooey and not a little on edge outside his front door.

He entered, muttering and sounding rather shaky with the shock of the sudden, unprovoked assault. I'd imagine his pulse had been given a bit of an adrenalin boost, which was precisely how we wanted him. He stood in the wide hallway, just inside the front door, where he hauled off his jacket and let it drop to the hardwood floor. No point in hanging it up when it was bound for the dry-cleaners or possibly the bin. I should mention that I was in another room at this juncture, an apparently little-used spare bedroom, which was our centre of operations.

However, there were several unseen cameras trained on him, not to mention microphones. He didn't notice any of these, though this was unsurprising as they had been carefully concealed. Less carefully concealed was the large dry-ice machine that had been tucked behind the sofa in his living room, but we correctly reckoned that wouldn't be his first port of call.

He took off his egg-stained shirt and jeans too, tutting as he mounted a little pile of washing on the polished wood. Then, with a slightly shivery sigh, he stomped into the bathroom, where he caught a brief look at his thoroughly egg-spattered hair in the half-length and apparently perfectly normal mirror before climbing into the shower and closing the door with a petulant slam.

While he was under the spray, the world outside his safe little cabinet was changing to become an altogether more disturbing place. It was his big Lewis Carroll moment: Arsehole Through the Shower Glass.

I could hear the gasp live as well as through my earpiece.

Lafayette stepped out of the shower to be confronted by the mirror again, but it was not his reflection that met or elicited his hanging-jawed stare. For one thing, it was too steamed up to reflect anything, but more startlingly, there was now a message on it. It read:

Grady Lappin
5.5.55
Murderer
J'accuse

And underneath the words there was a small drawing of a window.

Not that Lafayette was in a position to distinguish, but the handwriting was Moira's. She had etched the mirror earlier in the day using hydrofluoric acid, which causes water vapour to condense quicker on the treated area. Minus the steam, you'd need a microscope to detect any changes to the surface of the glass. Lafayette didn't have a microscope handy, only a towel. He wiped away the writing, no doubt now very concerned that there might be an intruder in his home, only to discover, as more steam condensed and the writing promptly reappeared, that he was being visited by something much more frightening.

The lights flickered and dimmed to almost but not quite nothing. He tried turning the bathroom light switch off and on, to no avail. Tightening a towel around his waist, he opened the door slowly and reached a hand along the wall outside, seeking the switch for the hall. He flicked it up and down, but no light came forth. The only light source, other than the now dimmed bulbs in the bathroom, was a tiny spill from around the door-frame of the spare bedroom, but he wasn't well positioned to detect this: geographically or psychologically. I reckon it was about then he noticed that the hall was not just dark, but hazy too: impossibly, inexplicably misty. And suddenly very, very cold.

Sounds began echoing around the hall, like the breath of a female whisper without the words. They came from all different directions, randomly criss-crossing in a way that was as disorientating as it was unsettling. Then the whispers finally coalesced, forming a single word: 'Grady'.

With that, Lafayette abandoned all heed of the facts that he could barely see and that he was dressed only in a towel, and dashed desperately for the front door. He found it locked, the keys he had left in it no longer there. He turned around and stood with his back to the door, breathing hard.

The first voice had been Moira's, recorded earlier the same day. The second was Hilda Lemuel's, recorded by the BBC and rendered infinitely more spooky by Spammy Scott's audio trickery.

'Justice,' it breathed. 'We . . . demand . . . justice.'

'Holy shit,' Lafayette spluttered, in an almost involuntary emission.

Then with a WD40-begging creak that we could not have scripted, the living-room door swung inwards, revealing only further mist and darkness. Lafayette stared towards it but did not move one inch nearer. In the extraordinarily unlikely event that he had gone into the living room to investigate, he'd have found only one burly polisman and one slightly less burly but of late simmeringly violent Michael Loftus.

Now came the principal reason for the dry ice. It was time

for me to make my appearance; if not, strictly speaking, my entrance.

My image materialised in the hall, fifteen or twenty feet from Lafayette, my arm extending slowly to point an accusatory finger straight at him. I was actually only a few feet away, being scanned from several different angles by cameras linked to Spammy's laptop. A holographic laser-projector in the living room was trained on the hall, turning the millions of dancing motes into a nebulous three-dimensional screen. The sampling rate for the cameras was fairly low as was necessary to generate a live holo-gram, but that in itself added to the effect, making the image less solidly formed, more ethereal, more wispy, more, what was the word? Aye: ghostly.

I'll admit that if you actually see the footage, the whole shebang looks a wee bit eighties-rock-video. Mostly it's the dry ice, though I'd concede that thon leather jacket of mine is maybe not as mode as I'd liked to imagine. But the crucial thing is, this was not about what was going on before Lafayette's eyes and ears: it was about what was going on inside his head. Inside there, he was projecting more vividly than anything connected to Spammy's laptop, and it was my task to nourish his febrile imagination with the food of nightmares.

'Grady Lappin,' I said, speaking quietly, breathily (and maybe just a little hammily), my words electronically amplified out in the hall. 'Born May fifth, 1955. Murderer. Murrrrderer.'

Okay, more than a little hammily.

'Holy shit,' he said, his voice dry, unable to rise much beyond a whisper. 'Holy shit. Holy shit. Holy shit.'

Hammy or not, I was as good as my word. I had him *holy* shitting himself.

'I feel your fear,' I said. 'Like you feel my anger. But it's not my anger you have to fear. I'm just the messenger. There's much worse than me coming for you, Grady.' (Did I lie?)

At this moment, Spammy racked up the spookomatic by adding two figures to the hologram, dawning into vision at my back, giving a sense that they were approaching, distant, but far larger than me. They were both fully rendered 3D anima-tions of authentically stygian demons from one of Spammy's computer games. One was called, he told us all with obvious

333

pride in their appropriateness, a hell-knight and the other an imp. They made no sound, simply marched menacingly forward before fading out again.

They did the job. Lafayette audibly whimpered.

'Oh Jesus,' he said, appealing to entirely the wrong court.

'We . . . demand . . . justice,' re-echoed Hilda's voice.

'You need to make your peace in this world. That's the only way to ward them off. I've been sent because I'm the closest point of contact to you in the dark world beyond, because I was the last to die at your hands. Or at your bidding, for is that not the truth?'

'The last . . . ? My . . . ? Yes. Not my hands, not my hands.'

'At. Your. Bidding.'

'Yes,' he admitted, his voice choked with fear if not regret. And not a little pleading. 'But it wasn't me, it was Mather. Easy killed you. Blake too.'

'And the students?'

'Mather killed them as well. And the Lemuel lady.'

'She's close, Grady. Hilda's close. She needs to hear you *admit* what you did to her.'

'It was Mather, I swear,' he said, now weeping. I'd like to say it was remorse, but who would I be kidding; it was self-pity all the way. 'I just distracted the dogs. I never laid a finger on her.'

'No, Grady. You need to make your peace. You can't blame Mather for everything. He'll be meeting all of us too, in time, but we're here for you first because we know you're in this together. *I* found that out – that's why I had to die. You couldn't hide the truth from me then and you certainly can't hide it from me now. Nor can you hide it from *them*,' I added, cueing Spammy to give him another glimpse of my supporting guest stars from *Doom 3*. 'This was all your idea. Don't lie to me. Recording Hilda's voice and then killing her was your idea.'

'No. I mean, the concept, okay . . . but the Lemuel lady wasn't my idea. That was Galt.'

I got lucky at this point, as Lafayette interpreted my expression of gaping astonishment as otherworldly anger and dismay. He slumped down almost into a crouch, cowering against the door.

'Oh Jesus, I swear it was Galt. I'm just a po' boy from New Orleans. I never had money, not real money. Galt offered us the big time.'

'Lies,' I improvised. 'Why would Galt want to so beneficently help you on to the gravy train?'

'It's the ID thing. He's tight with these neo-cons back home. We're helping him get it into the schools. That's gotta cut some ice, hasn't it, you know . . . upstairs? I mean, we're working to help God.'

I could have broken cover and booted him in the haw-maws then and there when he said that. But I had to stay calm.

'By killing people?' I demanded. 'You're working for what you always did: a wedge. What's he paying you? Hilda wants to know what her death was worth. What was it worth?'

He was trembling, his voice shaky with stuttering breaths.

'W-w-we get a million dollars clear. If it goes through, in Parliament. That's why we had to pull the same thing with Noble, convince her husband like we convinced Lemuel. But . . .'

'You killed Jillian Noble?' I asked with genuine disbelief. I knew nothing about this. I'd emailed the daft cow just the other day.

Some glimmer of hope played across his expression, only a straw to clutch, but clutch it he did.

'No. We . . . I . . . She must still be alive. You said you were the last one, so that must mean she ain't dead yet.'

This was the end of the show, I knew. The game had changed utterly, in a way no-one could have foreseen, the stakes urgently higher. Ursula was listening in from a car downstairs. She'd be giving the order to her man next door to move in. I beat her to it.

From Lafayette's point of view, I walked forward and disappeared into the swirling mist. Then the spare-room door along the hall swung open, spilling light and dispersing some of the dry ice. I walked towards him, now a fully realised, solid form, but to him no less a horrifying or inexplicable apparition.

'Where has he got her, bunny boy?' I demanded. 'Where is Jillian Noble?'

Lafayette clambered upright again in a panic, staring right at me.

'You're not real,' he said. 'This is a dream. An illusion. A hallucination.'

'Oh, we're shit-full of empiricism and rationality now, aren't we? But I am real. And so's he,' I added, indicating the figure of Michael, who had emerged at my rear. Michael smacked him in the face with everything he had, a real stoater. Lafayette reeled back against the door, where I pinned him as the big polisman restrained Michael.

'I told you there was worse than me coming for you. Now you tell us where Mather's got Noble or the demons really get unleashed.'

'I'll tell you, I'll tell you,' he blubbed, trying to pull a hand free of my grasp so that he could put it to his bleeding nose. He babbled out a location, near Port of Menteith.

There was a hammering at the front door. Michael unlocked it to let Ursula in.

'We have to move fast,' I said. 'And I'd recommend bringing this prick along in case he's lying.'

'I'm telling the truth, I swear. And I want some credit for it if she lives. I want a deal. Cut me a deal and I'll give up everything.'

'You already did,' I told him, pointing out one of the hidden mikes on a coat rack.

'You motherfucker,' he growled, anger rising through his craven snivelling.

'Get it up ye,' I retorted, while he was huckled outside towards a police car, still only towel-clad. 'See, you might have done your homework on Kelvin Uni when you first came here, but you never studied up on Glasgow, pal. This place has a nasty history of razor gangs, and you just got fucked by the newest one.'

'The Occam's Razor gang,' said Michael.

The senses, I now know, are so easily fooled. The mind, imprisoned in solitary by the subjectivity of its own perception, is at its most lost when it cannot call for a corroborative witness. The pain, the fear, the cold, the thirst and, most of all, the isolation, leave me unable to determine and, for any length of time, resolve what is real.

336

Slowly, though, I reach a cold, dawning, despairingly inevitable understanding. It is not that I am going to die.

It is that I already have. That I am in hell.

Something has blanked out what was too traumatic to register. He came back, with the bolt-cutters and with his syringe, and somewhere between the ministrations of these two instruments, I died.

But for my sins, I remained in this place.

For what could be more like hell? Being in permanent, despairing fear, between bouts of torture, all the time knowing there is no hope. Knowing only agony for yourself and anguish for your loved ones over what they will suffer too. The loved ones you have failed.

I hear sounds again, movement in the building. I try but cannot prevent myself sobbing as I hear footsteps approach beyond the door.

Then it opens, and I see the figure framed in the aperture, and I *know* that I am dead; I know that this must be the realm of the damned. For he is dead also, and surely to God, Jack Parlabane *must* have gone to hell.

# Here after

To my wife Sarah's tectonically earth-shuddering rage, Galt
walked. It was infuriating but sadly not surprising: eluding every
last tendril of the law was second nature to a creature like him.
The testimonies of Lafayette and Mather – in Galt's words to
the press 'the desperate lies of two murderous conspirators with
a vested interest in spreading the blame around' – were
supported by no physical evidence whatsoever. But as far as I
was concerned, his implication of Galt was one of the few things
ever to emerge from Lafayette's mouth that actually rang true.

'He's tight with these neo-cons back home,' Lafayette had
said, and indeed my own wife had already been tangled in the
web of Galt's American religious connections.

It didn't take much digging to uncover his links with several
American right-wing Christian groups, but most significant was
a long-term involvement with the Creation Science Forum, an
umbrella organisation of vast and growing influence, not to
mention quite enormous financial resources. The Creation
Science Forum was, in a number of guises and through just
as many chequebooks, leading the battle to get equal-time
legislation passed in American states in its aim to supplant
evolution theory with Intelligent Design. But their war was not
only being fought on the home front. My research uncovered
that the CSF had links with conservative Christian groups in
just about every country in the Western world.

One academic I spoke to said he was 'having to fight the
battles of the Enlightenment all over again. Medieval ideas that
were killed stone dead by the rise of science three to four hundred
years ago are not merely twitching; they are alive and well in
schools, colleges and universities.'

The weirdest and most disturbing thing about the neo-cons
is that they believe their own bullshit: they dream up lies for
political ends and then forget that they made them up. Decades

before anyone had coined the term neo-con, these same people cooked up the 'Domino Principle' theory as a justification for aggressive anti-communist foreign policies. The argument, which they knew to be preposterous but politically expedient, was that if one country turned communist, then pretty soon so would its neighbours, and before we knew it the world would have turned red without the Soviets having to lift a finger.

Now it emerged that they had forgotten they made it up, and believed the Domino Principle would work *for* them. Get one country to adopt Intelligent Design in its schools, and the next one would be easier to convert. Scotland must have been represented to them by Galt as a vulnerable and strategically important domino, with its fledgling semi-autonomous parliament and constituent role within the greater UK. Get a foothold there, to bolster efforts already in progress south of the border, then with the UK embracing ID, the next stop was Europe. Yeah, I know it's absurd. What can I say, they're fucking nuts.

But while I was looking into Galt's links to the CSF, Moira uncovered a far more macabre connection between all of our principals. One of her contacts in the US was able to tell her about a woman named Meredith Platt, who had been Gabriel Lafayette's most vocal cheerleader in US woo circles. She died three years back, leaving Lafayette almost $100,000. Meredith, who was suffering from cancer, had not expected to outlive her husband Bobby, but he died a few months before she did. He never returned from a fishing trip on the local lake, though his body washed up, drowned, a few days later. Meredith had never disclosed the details, but passionately told anybody who would listen that Lafayette had a gift like nobody she'd ever encountered.

Meredith didn't only have cash to spare for rewarding self-less and strictly non-payment-seeking psychics. She was a generous contributor to a pressure group that formed part of the Creation Research Forum, and regularly attended the CRF's annual national convention. Even in her failing health and her state of bereavement, she made it along to her final shindig when it was hosted in South Dakota four years ago. So did Gabriel Lafayette and Easy Mather, who were often in solicitous orbit around her, particularly at such woo-credulous gatherings. And so did, according to the CRF's books, corroborated by Sioux Falls hotel records, one Jonathan Galt.

We passed this information on to the police, but perhaps understandably, it wasn't good enough for the Procurator Fiscal, and the smug bastard walked away clean. However, it *was* good enough for some. Bryant Lemuel, a man long renowned for his bluntness and direct approach to getting things done, walked into Galt's office one morning with a double-barrelled shotgun and blew his fucking head off.

And there was much rejoicing.

Lemuel handed himself over to the police immediately and has lodged a plea of temporary insanity. If you can define several decades as 'temporary', he might well get off. After some of the mince he's believed in down the years, proving he went genuinely bonkers over the revelation that his wife was actually murdered should be a piece of piss. I mean, psychic surgeons, for fuck's sake.

The tough part might be finding a new lawyer, given how things worked out with his last one . . .

Somewhere and somehow, in between the ferment of the aftermath and its reprise in the trials, I finished my degree and graduated, though in the end I didn't leave Kelvin Uni. I'm doing a PhD, studying the molecular outflow of . . . never mind, it's pretty technical. Laura's taught me all kinds of social skills as regards interacting with the wider non-geek strain of the species. My work involves the Boomerang Nebula, that's all I'll say. It's the coldest place in the known universe if you don't count Aberdeen.

Laura didn't graduate. She wrote a book instead, published as soon as the verdicts were in, and boasting a foreword by none other than my mum, whose own work, *Beautiful Deceivers*, has now been republished. I really didn't think we'd last as a couple, given the rocky ground of mutual upset and confusion our relationship was founded on, but so far, so good. We've even been on holiday together and that didn't end it, not even when she realised the awkward and bulky extra item of luggage I brought with us to Tunisia was actually a Schmidt-Cassegrain telescope. She confessed to relief. She thought I'd simply never told her I was a golfer.

Parlabane wrote a book about the affair too, as did the chastened but no less brass-necked Jillian Noble. All four are trailing in the bestseller lists behind *Second Seeing is Believing*, the autobiography of Aurora Goodwin, 'psychic sensation' in her native Australia and the new presenter of *Borders of the Known*.

There is much work to be done.

My mum and I reached an agreement regarding our late impasse.

'People should always have the freedom to believe what they want, Michael,' she argued. 'No matter how silly, groundless or absurd. It's a basic human right.'

'Granted,' I said. 'But in every society, freedom must always be balanced with responsibility. People often *know* that their beliefs are based on nothing; some see it as a harmless self-indulgence and others are actually proud of it. It's not harmless and it's nothing to be proud of. Yes, you have freedom to believe what you like, but you should be responsible enough to acquaint yourself with the facts and adjust your beliefs accordingly. Otherwise you're clogging up our cognitive evolution.'

'It's a good point,' she conceded. 'A very good point. One I'm proud of you for formulating. So I'll do you a deal, Michael, okay?'

'I'm listening. What are the terms?'

'I'll give up the fortune-telling if you give up that dreadful brown coat.'

# Acknowledgements and further reading

This book was inspired by and is indebted to the works listed below; some exploring humanity's unfortunate credophile tendencies, and others demonstrating that religion and superstition cannot compete with science when it comes to the truly bizarre and awe-inspiring.

*Flim-Flam! Psychics, ESP, Unicorns and Other Delusions* by James Randi

*The Supernatural A to Z* by James Randi

*The Truth About Uri Geller* by James Randi

*Why People Believe Weird Things* by Michael Shermer

*The Psychic Mafia* by M Lamar Keene

*Deception and Self-Deception: Investigating Psychics* by Richard Wiseman

*The War For Children's Minds* by Stephen Law

*The Universe Next Door* by Marcus Chown

*Bad Astronomy* by Phil Plait

*Hiding the Elephant* by Jim Steinmeyer

Using the licence of fiction, only one genuinely impossible phenomenon is depicted in this book. It takes place on page 124. If you can't work out what it is, go to www.brookmyre.co.uk for the answer. But be warned: it's geeky and self-indulgent, just like the author.